Secrets Unveiled

by

Richard Albion

This is a work of fiction. Names, characters, places, and incidents are either the product of the author's imagination or are used fictitiously, and any resemblance to actual persons living or dead, business establishments, events, or locales, is entirely coincidental.

Secrets Unveiled

Cover Art by *Diana Carlile*

The Wild Rose Press, Inc.
PO Box 708
Adams Basin, NY 14410-0708
Visit us at www.thewildrosepress.com

Publishing History
First Edition, 2021
Trade Paperback ISBN 978-1-5092-3618-3
Digital ISBN 978-1-5092-3619-0

Published in the United States of America

This was like something out of a spy novel. I spent the next hour relating everything that Otto had told me to George—from my visit to his apartment and finding his daughter there, to telling him what I'd discovered in the French notebook.

George sat, listened, and thought pensively before speaking. "I am sorry to hear about Otto, but these events are not necessarily connected—probably are—but not necessarily. From what you've told me, it could be the nefarious people he and his father had dealings with in post war Paris. They tried to exit a business that is hard to leave. Otto may just be a loose end they wanted wrapped up. All this stuff you are dealing with pre dates that—back to the war and the German occupation of France."

"Why now? I'm not sure I believe in coincidences."

"Maybe Otto knew he was short on time and needed to get the stuff to you. He must have known his past would catch up with him sometime. He wasn't stupid. He couldn't protect himself forever. He chose the time well, and if I may say, the right person to ask."

Dedication

To the Mistress of all, she knows who she is.

Frances Sevilla, editor extraordinaire, who is making me a better writer.

Diana Carlile got the "feel" just right for the cover, and got it in one.

Chapter One

The sound of the heavily studded prison door thudding shut, sent a chill down my spine. It had been some years since I'd last heard it. That sound leaves a scar you learn to live with. I really had been one of those who'd been framed. Not a high-risk prisoner. I was actually innocent of the charge, though no one believed me. Most of my so called "friends" disappeared at the time of my arrest, and a few more after sentencing. Only one remained by the time of my release.

My new friends don't particularly care what I have or haven't done. The reason, and the only reason, I'm back here is at the request of an old inmate, one with whom I became friends. We met in the prison library. He was older than I was…old enough to be my father. The two of us felt drawn together by our individual histories in the art world, and our need for an intellectual escape. Otto's crime had been making forgeries, and he was guilty of his crime. Me? I was convicted for selling a forgery. My story was enough common ground for us to begin talking. From there we developed a friendship, and I learned a lot from him.

My reverie was rudely interrupted by a voice I'd come to hate. Chief Warden Warren.

"Harper, and to what do we owe this dubious pleasure of your presence?"

"You mean Mr. Harper. I am no longer one of your whipping boys."

"Well, Mr. Harper." Sarcasm dripped like poison from his lips. "Why are you here?"

"I came to see Otto." I wasn't going to say anything more than absolutely necessary.

"Ah yes, your forging friend. It seems he had an accident, and at his age... Well, I need say no more. Guard, please escort Mr. Harper to the infirmary."

As I turned to follow the guard, Warren barked a laugh. "Don't stay too long, you might get to like it here."

Thinking a silent, *fuck you*, I followed the guard down familiar corridors. Even though I was beyond his jurisdiction, it still felt uncomfortable. At least I was free while the Chief Warden remained locked up in his own prison.

We reached the infirmary, where I met another guard who checked my bag of already well-inspected prison currency...cigarettes and chocolate.

Seeing Otto propped up on starched pillows, was a shock. His face was gaunt, his cheeks sunken. He looked thinner, much thinner than I remembered. He opened his eyes as I approached his bed and smiled, then he raised a hand in feeble greeting. The guard returned the bag of goodies and warned me not to give him anything else. I put the bag on Otto's bedside locker and sat on the steel chair.

Otto beckoned me closer, his voice quiet but still with a determined edge. Moving closer, I figured Otto was putting on an act for the male nurse who was keeping a very close eye on us, no doubt at the Warden's instigation. Or maybe I was being paranoid.

Otto started talking with an urgency I hadn't expected. "Peter I am pleased you came. I need to tell you something, but first you must promise not to repeat it to anyone at all. If you agree to do what I ask, you will have no regrets I promise you."

Puzzled and intrigued I consented to Otto's request. "I promise. I'll tell no one unless you give the okay, all right?" Otto smiled and nodded, satisfied at my agreement.

He looked more relaxed gathering his thoughts, then he started. "Peter, as you know, I have a German ancestry, even though I was born in France. My father, Ekkehard was a young man at the end of the Great War, an artist struggling to survive. People were trying to fill their bellies not worrying about what was on their walls. It was a hard time for everyone, yet he somehow kept his head above water, working at whatever paid a wage. He met and married my mother, Frieda who was a talented seamstress. She helped support my father. He was teaching as well as painting by that time. Times were still tough, and then politics, as always started to creep into all levels of society. National Socialism reared its ugly head."

The pain in his voice was so real, a deaf man could hear it.

"My father and mother didn't want to join the Nazi party, although they supported the general ideas of unity in Germany, etc. They regretfully told me they had been fooled, along with many Germans, about the Nazi Party. They did not believe all that rubbish about the Jews, Gypsies, and the other minorities."

Otto paused. I was not sure if he was lost in memories, or tired of talking. After a short while he continued.

"Anyway, by the time they realized what was going on, it was too late. Co-workers had noticed my father's artwork, many were in the Nazi party, and they passed on his information. They thought he was a loyal dedicated German, and drafted him into the propaganda department, and trapped him in the party machine. He learned all sorts of techniques, and along with creating propaganda materials, he learned extensively about copying and forging. Part of his new job, when not creating propaganda, was to authenticate the identity papers of people scooped up in Gestapo raids. Many people tried to leave Germany at that time, and he confirmed or denied their papers as genuine or fake. For those trying to escape, his act of defiance was to accept some fake papers as real, allowing an individual or family to escape. However, he had to be very careful.

"In some ways, it was a wonderful time for Germans. Everything was going well, and life was good. Really, it was just the calm before the storm."

He paused again collecting his thoughts.

"Peter, I had siblings I never knew. My parents had four children, and my mother had been awarded a Reich medal for having Aryan children. They supported the Reich with future Nazis. Then the war came. At first, as history tells it, all went well, and the Reich went right up to the coast of France. Very easy. It left my father with very little to do. Someone that he never identified, if he knew, had the bright idea of moving artists to the capitals of the conquered territory and copying the masterpieces of the world. That idea reached Goering, who supported the idea. Goering had already started to amass a huge collection of "borrowed" paintings from museums all across Europe.

"The task was to copy as many of the old masters as possible. Artists were told it was to protect the originals in case the Allies decided to bomb cities like Paris. It made sense in a perverse way. The Reich sent my father's group to Paris to work in the Louvre. They were well supervised by the SS. The artists, prisoners themselves, weren't going to argue with the SS. They had all seen enough people disappear.

"The work was easy but laborious, and my father became frustrated when instructed about which paintings to copy. He was never allowed to choose. Time passed, then rumors began about the allied invasion and how Hitler planned to destroy Paris. The artists never knew what happened to the original paintings. They assumed the originals went to Berlin. The artists switched out some of the original paintings, putting copies in their places. Security became more lax, as the military organized a withdrawal from Paris.

"Before anyone knew what was happening, the allies arrived, and Paris survived. My father and most of his group were in the hands of the British Army. That group had it fairly easy since they were not strictly military. The artists had also forged their own papers, making themselves look like conscripted workers. My father had not heard from Frieda or any of the children. He worried of course and waited for the war to end. On his release, he still had not heard from his family…any of his family…so he decided to remain in Paris, a city he had grown to love.

"In his time he met people who were useful, shall we say, in less than legal matters, like identity papers, ration books, etc. Starving again after another war was not for him. He made good money forging documents, not really caring who or what, as long as the client could pay. He had nothing to live for other than money. No family. Nothing.

"Then one day, Frieda showed up in Paris. Alone. She had been out scavenging for food when an air raid hit, killing all their children. She blamed herself, and it took four years of grieving and resolve to find my father. She planned to tell him the tragic news if he was still alive, face-to-face, about what had happened. Then she intended to end her own life. When she found my father, he cried for the first time in many years, hugged her, kissed her, and told her they were starting over in Paris. She couldn't believe he didn't turn her away. How could he blame her? It was a war. They settled in Paris, and I was born a year later.

"We had a good life in Paris, keeping a low profile. My mother used her sewing skills to find work in the couture houses of Paris. My father had consistent work forging, running a print shop as a cover and front. It was all very idyllic for me. I grew up listening to the story of our family. My father made the forging business sound like an adventure, secret and romantic. Later it turned out I had a brother still living who showed up a couple of years later. Hans had survived the bombing, but lost his memory.

"Of course, I followed my father's example. He mentored me well at his side, while I attended college, and studied art. I had the advantage of having a very talented tutor from a very young age. After graduating, I tried to earn a living as an artist, but was always more interested in the less legal side, and assisted my father. He did not age well after my mother died. The war killed her. It was just not quick.

"As my father became an invalid, he told me a tale, making me promise not to tell anyone. If I ever needed it, it would be my retirement. I never opened the things he left me. Now it's my turn to pass it on. I want you to have the legacy.

Shocked, I listened and agreed to whatever he asked. I had already promised to keep quiet. In for a penny, in for a pound. "Talk about keeping secrets."

He looked at me with sad eyes and a wan smile. He continued his story. "Let me finish, you can admonish me later. Because we were very good and, more importantly, very careful. We survived. We made good money. But the people we were involved with became greedy and moved into the drug business, then on to all sorts of other nasty businesses. I suppose we shouldn't have been so high and mighty. We certainly weren't innocent, but we had our limits to what we would do. After my father died, I moved to London using the contacts we made over the years. Finally, I met and married a very nice English girl, and we had a daughter, Felicity. My wife died in childbirth. Sometimes I think there is a curse on my family. Felicity and I grew apart. I haven't seen her in years. You are the closest to family I have now, and one of the few people I trust. Obviously, I was not as careful as I should have been, or I would not be in my present predicament.

Otto leaned forward and his voice dropped even lower as he told me, "You will pick up the things my father gave me from my apartment. My solicitor will give you the key. There are documents hidden in the backing of the copy of a small Seurat study and in the family Bible. It's hollow. Break the lock if you have to.

Be sure you take all the items. There will be six—the Bible and painting are initially of most use to you. Two others will be of use to you later if you work out the information from the Bible and painting. Two are red herrings as you say in England."

"What are the other items? Please Otto just in case."

"A small Dresden porcelain music box, a Durer print, an eighteenth-century tea caddy, and an Egon Schiele sketch. That is everything. Please be careful, Peter."

Otto collapsed back against the pillows. This time he was not acting. He was exhausted, his face was sallow, and eyes watered from his efforts. He whispered, "Peter, will you do this favor?"

"Yes, but I make no promises, other than I will look and try. You helped me in here. It's the least I can do to thank you."

"I do not think you will regret it."

"Why are you so sure if you did not look at the contents of the packet? Is there something you're not telling me?" He bridled at that comment.

"Of course, I am not telling you everything. I want you to find out for yourself. That way it is safer for everyone," he said, making me wonder what I had gotten myself into.

Maybe it was just Otto's way of arousing my curiosity. He gave me the name, address, and phone number of his solicitor, making me repeat it back several times, to ensure I had it right.

I was about to ask him some more questions when the guard called time. He stood too close to us for any further confidential conversation. So I said, "I'll visit as soon as possible." That brought a smile to Otto's face. He must have understood that I meant to visit his apartment, but the guard assumed I meant to visit Otto.

I left, Otto looked even more fragile.

Talk about surprises. Wow, a daughter. Otto certainly played his cards close to his chest. We had been close…or I thought we had. The whole time I was inside, he never mentioned any family. It made sense with his family history.

I chuckled, which brought a sharp look from the guard escorting me back to the visitor's entrance. Screw the screw. I was getting out. Free again, and I fully intended to keep my promise to Otto.

When I collected my belongings from the locker, where I left them, I noticed someone had been through the locker. My wallet and cell phone were not exactly in the same place where I left them. That bastard Warren, I bet. I had no idea what he was up to, but I sure as hell didn't trust him. He could have cloned my phone. Now I would need a new one. Shit, I liked that phone. Not enough to risk having my movements tracked or my conversation being listened in on.

While trying to absorb all Otto had told me, I sat in my car, mulling over all the information. It would take time to process everything. Otto's apartment would be the first stop. His tale certainly had gotten my curiosity going. Curiosity had me eager to find out what was in the mysterious package. At worst it would be interesting. My decision had been made as I'd promised Otto. I made my way from Wormwood Scrubs prison, and headed east back toward central London. Traffic was heavy but moving.

Chapter Two

One of my pleasures after I'd been released from prison was just driving around. Being free to go anywhere I wanted when I wanted. Loving London, I'd gotten to know it very well.

Samuel Pepys once said, "When one is tired of London, one is tired of life."

Not sure, I would go that far, I can't imagine living anywhere else.

Then traffic snarled up at Edgeware Road, so I took the back roads until I reached Wellington Road, where the solicitor's office was located. Without an appointment, I didn't expect much from my visit.

Happily, the office manager told me that Otto's representative, Mr. Gerard Fortesque was in and free, if I wouldn't mind waiting.

Mind? I was thrilled.

She took my name and left me to examine the offices. They were old school—dark wood and lots of legal looking tomes lining the walls. Minutes passed, and I was lost in thought when the office manager returned.

"Mr. Fortesque will see you now."

Brought out of my reverie, I thanked her, and followed her into a large office. Mr. Fortesque was ancient but spritely, with clear sharp eyes.

He stood and held out his hand in welcome.

"Pleased to meet you Mr. Harper. I understand you know Mr. Schmidt?"

"Yes, he asked me to check a few things for him at his apartment, and told me I should ask you for the key."

"Yes, indeed. I do need to be careful. May I see some identification?"

"Of course," I replied, pulling out my driver's license and handing it to him.

He studied it carefully, and returned it. "Thank you, Mr. Harper. All seems to be in order. Mr. Schmidt has always been a very organized client, leaving clear instructions. He recently updated them, instructing us to give you a key to this property. Please excuse me while I retrieve it for you."

Fortesque left, and I pondered when Otto had updated the instructions. He must have been sure I would do what he asked. The solicitor returned with a small envelope and handed it to me along with a neatly written note displaying an address. I noted the address and thanked him."

"No trouble at all, Mr. Harper. I'm always happy to oblige Mr. Schmidt. Good day."

Leaving the office, I had the impression he was glad to see the back of me, probably assumed, correctly, I was a jailbird. Otto's apartment was not far from the solicitors office.

Continuing up Wellington Road until it changed into Finchley, I found Otto's address. A nice neighborhood…a nineteen-thirties art deco block, looking well cared for. Otto must have done well in his past and invested his ill-gotten gains wisely.

Next stop was the mobile phone shop, same

provider as I had now. My old phone? I would keep it, and use it just for business, too involved to change everything over, and my partner would not like the churn. The telecom shop was not busy, and I soon had a new phone, new number, and a feeling of satisfaction. If I were being monitored, the listeners would be very bored with the mundanity of a small antique business. I laughed at the thought of someone listening to hours of talk about antiquities.

Heading home, I stopped at the shop in Camden Town, to say hi to my partner, George. We caught up on everything that transpired while I was out. Nothing much of importance going on, so I headed to my apartment in Stoke Newington. The traffic by now was horrible, and there was no point getting mad at it. I used the time to ponder why Otto had waited so long. Thinking back to the meeting with him, he'd made it sound as if time weren't important. I missed the underlying urgency—feeling it more than it being anything definitive.

Damn it, I was probably going to regret my next move, but well, that's life. I pulled back into the traffic and made my way back to Otto's apartment. Eventually, I found a parking spot. The art deco edifice was impressive and beautiful. Using one key to enter the building, I pocketed the key ring and took the stairs—a decision I regretted by the fourth floor.

Regaining my breath and composure, I found the apartment number and used the second and third keys to unlock the door. As I did, I saw a shadow cross the peephole and heard the sound of the door chain fastening. What the hell? I checked the apartment number. The door opened and a woman's voice asked,

"Yes? May I help you?" She remained out of view. The voice was calm and even, just questioning.

"The owner of the apartment asked me to check on something." The door opened to the fullest extent of the chain. A tall slim woman appeared looking a little taken aback. She looked me over then nodded, as if she had come to a decision. "And you are?"

"A friend of the owner. And you are?"

She ignored the question and asked, "Have you seen Otto recently?"

"Yes, today."

Before I could add anything, the door shut, the chain rattled off, and the door opened wider. She stood aside allowing me to enter. I walked passed her and stood awkwardly, not really knowing what to do next. The door shut and I heard the sound of the chain being replaced.

"Your name please?" she asked.

"Peter Harper." I saw a flash of recognition cross her face. Smart and careful, she recognized my name. Interesting. But she had definitely known my name.

"Sorry, I am Otto's daughter, Felicity. She held out her hand. It was firm and dry. Long fingers curled around my hand. They felt good.

As we broke the handshake, she said, "Please sit down. I have not seen Otto for some time, years in fact. Not seeing him bothers me more than where he is." Not exactly, the story Otto had told. She waved me to a large comfortable armchair and offered me a drink.

"Whatever you are having is fine."

"I was about to open a bottle of chardonnay. Is that good?"

"Perfect."

Then she asked, "How long were you in with him?"

I thought I'd covered myself pretty well, losing the habits I'd gained inside. "A while. Does it show that much?"

"No, not that much. It was just an assumption. Otto's circle of has been somewhat limited for the past few years."

I would have to be on top of my game with her. I followed up with, "Otto kept me from being *very* bitter, as opposed to *just* bitter. Sorry to be so cloak and dagger. I'm following up on a request from him."

She looked up sharply, staring at me as if deciding what was going to happen next. "Let me get the wine. Then, we can chat."

I nodded in assent as she left the room. I watched her. She was stylishly dressed, without the clothes wearing her, and she moved easily. She obviously kept in shape—a runner, I would say from the way she moved. Her jewelry was simple and elegant—earrings and a gold chain, a wide, gold-colored cuff on each wrist, and no rings on her long fingers.

Felicity returned with two glasses, a plate of crackers, and a wedge of ripe brie. We sipped the wine. I didn't want to be the first to break the silence. I just wanted to observe her, lost in thought. She was a very attractive woman.

"I am sure you are wondering why I let you in so easily," Felicity said.

I nodded in the affirmative.

"First, I can take care of myself, and second, we are being CCTV'd. It's set up as a precaution against burglars. So why don't you begin?"

"First, I didn't expect anyone to be here. Otto led me to believe his apartment would be unoccupied." I let the unasked question hang.

Felicity looked at me directly. "I come here sometimes. Otto is the only family I have. It's comforting to sit and imagine what could have been, or still could be. What are you doing here?"

"Otto asked me to do him a favor. So I am."

"How did you get the keys?"

"From his solicitor. Where did you get yours?"

"Had them forever. What was the favor Otto asked of you?"

"He asked me to check out some items he left here, make sure they were still in good condition, and he wondered if I would get current values on them."

"Items?"

"Yes, six items."

"Well then, I won't keep you. You don't mind if I accompany you?"

I bridled at that. "Don't you trust me? Scared I may lift something?"

"No. Sorry, that was not my intention. I am just curious."

"Sorry, I'm a bit thin-skinned sometimes."

"That's understandable, I suppose. Can't be easy when you get out."

Looking at her, I found her expression was unreadable. God, she was disarmingly attractive. "Let's get on."

The Seurat was a beautiful copy. If Otto's father had been the one to paint it, he certainly had talent. It was a damned good copy.

My specialty before my incarceration was late

nineteenth and early twentieth century paintings up to World War II. This Seurat, even as a fake, was a very good painting. The brush strokes and the way the artist applied the paint reflected a deep knowledge and understanding, of how Seurat himself worked. Wrapped up in my work, studying the painting in my hands, I had become oblivious to what Felicity was saying to me.

She brought me back to the *now* when she asked if I would like to wrap up everything and put them in bags.

"Sorry, I've been distracted. This is a really good painting even if it is a fake. Do you know who did it?"

She shook her head. "Not for sure. It was probably Otto's father. Apparently, he was a very talented artist. Please be careful with everything. These things connect me directly to Otto and family. Even if I never met them, it's important to me."

"No problem. I promise to be meticulous in their care. Look, here is my card. It's our shop. You can stop by anytime to make sure I am treating them properly."

She accepted the card with a smile, then deserted me to get the wrapping materials.

When she returned, Felicity glanced over my shoulder as I worked. "You work quickly, and neatly for a man. Why do you think he wanted you to check on these six?"

"Thank you. I think there was a compliment in there somewhere. And…I have no idea why he chose these. Otto just asked me to look at them."

"Really? Isn't that an odd request?

"Odd or not, he asked." Without thinking, I asked, "What do you do? …Sorry that was nosey. You don't have to tell me anything."

"That's all right. I am an assistant curator at the Victoria and Albert museum. Rare documents and manuscripts."

I bit my tongue and stopped myself from asking more questions. However attractive she was, and she was, I didn't need to know her, just follow up on Otto's request and get it sorted.

"Will you stay in touch?"

"Yes, and I will tell you when I am done with the valuations." It dawned on me that she'd called Otto by name, not dad or father. That got me wondering.

"Thank you. I'd appreciate that." She gave me her business card.

The Victoria and Albert museum. A place I knew by heart. I tucked the card away in my pocket, and thanked her for the two bags that concealed all the items. The painting although small, took up most of one bag, the Bible most of the other, and the rest of the items fit divided between the two.

We said our goodbyes, and I left, taking the elevator down. The Bible and the painting were heavy, but not as heavy as the responsibility I felt. Reflecting on the man who Felicity called Otto, I began to believe that perhaps the distance between them was as wide as Otto said. The feeling that I'd stepped into an ominous situation haunted me as if someone just walked on my grave. I shivered, and returned to my car, making sure to carefully store away the bags.

I'd just made promises to two members of the same family. I must be slipping. After getting my release, I promised myself I was number one, and George my business partner was number two. Everyone else had to get in line. Sitting, memories took me back to the events that got me to the here and now.

Chapter Three

I was accused of selling a forgery. My signature was on the authentication documents yes, but I never authenticated that particular painting. Case closed, especially when the prosecution found out the title of my college thesis was "How to Identify Fake Works of Art." Everyone assumed my guilt. It seemed obvious to all that I had to be on the take. I was a scapegoat par excellence. All very neat.

I spent three years at Her Majesty's pleasure. Luckily, I received a light sentence for a first offence and no violence. And yet to me there is a score I must settle with Mr. Charles Fentiman, the gallery owner. At some point, I will collect in full.

George was the one friend who'd been waiting for me outside the prison on my release. He was the only friend who'd stuck by me. After a very stiff formal British handshake and brief hug, I found I was working for and with him. By the time we reached his car, I also discovered I had an apartment. George had paid the first month's rent. It was one of his brother's, yet still a gesture I appreciated. Suspicious to say the least, and going on past experience, my friends had disappeared. George was a true friend. He had always believed me innocent.

George explained why he needed me. His older brother Sir Stephen had inherited the family title, estate, and farms. George after a stint in the British Army had bought an antique shop. He was superb with artifacts, silver, furniture, and porcelain. Not so good with paintings and prints. In fact, he was a disaster and found them a mystery. He needed help, especially since tourists bought many prints. Even though it was not my specialty, I knew more than he did, and what I didn't know, I had quickly learned. It was the best thing that could have happened to me. Something to interest me, keep me occupied, and mostly gaining someone's trust. There was no way I would have been able to get a job in any reputable gallery, or even teach. I was luckier than most who get out of jail.

Now I needed to get back to my apartment. A man, standing in the entrance of Otto's building had been studying me. Before I got a good look at him, he turned away. The fellow seemed familiar, but I was sure I didn't know him. I have an excellent visual memory.

My mood was pensive, and I took my time getting home, frequently checking my rearview mirror. Not that I would have known if anyone was tailing me or not.

Chapter Four

Before I risked taking the shopping bags into my home, I parked a few doors down from my apartment and looked about. Then I headed directly up to my apartment, thankfully avoiding my nosey neighbor. Blinking at the brightness of the room, I drew the curtains and let out a deep sigh of relief without quite knowing why.

Not having eaten anything since lunch, my stomach complained. I ordered a delivery take-out from my local Indian restaurant. Easy enough since I knew the menu by heart. I sat, looking at the bags on my table, wondering where all this would lead me. I pulled out the Seurat painting first and laid it aside. Next, I took out the good size Bible with a substantial cover and lock. That would be the second item to examine. The other items, I checked—each piece beautiful in its own right.

Carefully prying the backing off the Seurat painting, I removed the wedges that held a sealed packet in place. Whatever the contents, they were well wrapped in waxed cotton cloth, sealed on both ends and down the long seam. I laid it aside. Picking up the Bible and fiddling with the lock, I became frustrated when the lock refused to open. I took a deep breath and tried again. Whatever I did worked this time. The lock popped open. I flipped back the cover, and rifled the pages. A cut out revealed a neat packet, wrapped, and neatly fitted into the space. Rifling the pages a bit more to loosen them, I pulled the packet out, put it next to the other one, and wondered what secrets they would unveil.

I covered the table with newspaper, placed the two packets on top, and examined the exterior closely. Both were wrapped in waxed cloth, and the cloth had weathered time well—good quality materials that protected against light and moisture. All the seams sealed with sealing wax, which had become brittle with time, broke easily under my fingers.

Choosing the one hidden in the Seurat, for no reason other than it was first, I carefully scraped off the remaining wax revealing a stitched seam in the cloth. Using my scalpel to pick at the stitches, they parted easily under the sharp blade. The contents inside? Two small notebooks, one had a German legend on the front, the other plain.

I opened the German motif notebook, first—a ledger, neatly written in German. The language was foreign to me. Closing it, I put that one aside for George to examine if I felt I had no other choice. The second notebook was in French. That I could translate. My French was fluent. A little rusty, but nothing practice wouldn't cure. The handwriting was old fashioned, yet still clear, it looked like a copy of the German notebook.

The doorbell rang, shocking me back to reality. Food. I quickly covered the table with more newspaper and answered the door. Amir was standing there with a big smile and my dinner. Quickly, I took the food from him, and handed him a tip, then shut the door abruptly.

I took the food to the kitchen. Not bothering with a plate, I pulled the lid off the two containers, and sat with the fork in one hand and the notebook in the other. Struggling to get my brain thinking in French between mouthfuls of aromatic food, I managed to start translating the notes.

As I read, the contents resolved to be valuation notes on paintings—no titles only the artists and what seemed like a catalogue number—page after page of old masters. If what Otto had said about his father was true, these could have been the paintings he and his peers copied from the museums of Paris. The contents were in French and the currency in Francs. I assumed it had been written by collaborators, or under duress. Either way, the amounts were staggering for copies unless they put the value of the original on the copy. It was still a mystery. Why would Goering have agreed to and organized such an elaborate scheme. Maybe the German notebook or the other packet would have more information. Slowing my eating, I considered any possible reason for copying so many paintings. The story of protecting the originals…that just didn't ring true. There had to be more.

Enough pondering. I moved on to the second packet. Similarly sealed, it didn't look so old. Perhaps Otto's father had opened and resealed it. Repeating the process, scraping off the sealing materials, the stitches parted easily. This packet also had two notebooks. One again in German. I put it with the other for George's translation. The second was in French and looked like the biography of Otto's family. Otto had said he'd left out some of the story. Maybe, this would fill in some gaps.

Beginning to read, I became so absorbed that I forgot to eat. Otto hadn't lied except by omission. He'd told me the truth as far as it went, but he had omitted a good part of the history. I read on with fascination. Skipping over the parts that confirmed what Otto had told me in person, and I concentrated on the stuff he hadn't. I assumed this was his father's writing.

Filling in a lot of gaps, Otto's father explained how he stayed in Paris after the war—how he'd made contacts in the Paris underworld, and had a successful career in forgery. He confirmed the story of Frieda and the rest about how they started a new family with Otto and the story of how Hans reunited with the family.

Their printing company was a success, covering for all the forgery work they did. Hans's talent centered on sales and eventually he branched out into an exclusive art gallery. After their father's death, Otto moved to England for a fresh start and a new life. Hans stayed in Paris. I wondered if Hans was still alive. Otto's career in England remained a mystery. The main information still missing from the story was confirmation about the artists' wartime activities in the Louvre, and what happened to the paintings.

It was a lot to take in from someone who I thought I knew. Perhaps he was just being careful—hiding as much as he had. He'd been in a precarious position all his life—what with the forging and fake work he and his father were doing. Especially after being involved with such unsavory people in the later years. The biography gave me much to consider. I went to bed with a mind full of questions. Including Felicity. There was something about her that didn't quite fit. An issue for a fresh day.

Chapter Five

The sun streamed through a crack in my bedroom curtains, spotlighting the particles of dust dancing like demented diamonds. Damn, I had forgotten to set my alarm. Staggering to the phone, I called George and told him I was running late. After a quick shower, I swallowed a cup of tea, ate a slice of toast, all while trying to call the prison. Crumbs covered the table and I'd smeared marmalade over my phone. My connection was put through directly to the chief Warden.

"We were about to call you, Harper. Any reason you wanted to see Otto so soon?'

"Yes, none of your business. But seeing as you asked so nicely, Otto asked a favor of me, and he needs to confirm something for me to do it. Satisfied?"

"No, but it'll do for now. As I said, we were about to call you. It seems Otto had an accident last night and is not doing well. Get here as soon as possible. You are the closest thing to a relative we could find."

How did he have an *accident* in the prison infirmary? "I am on my way."

"You will be met at the gate."

Bullshit. Accidents don't happen in prison infirmaries. Deliberate assaults do.

There was rush hour traffic, so making my way to the prison was torture. I was expected, and therefore escorted directly to the infirmary where there were more warders than usual. The Warden was hollering at someone, and he turned to have another go at a guard who looked like medical staff. He was mad as hell, and it showed.

When he saw me, he clamped his mouth shut and waved me over. Before he could start on me, I jumped in and said, "Otto has a daughter. I can call her and get her here if you will allow her in."

"We couldn't contact her. How did you, when we couldn't?"

"Otto told me about her when I saw him yesterday. That was the first time he said anything to me about a family."

"She can visit. Call her. I doubt he will last long. I would also like a few words with you, Harper."

"Still Mr. Harper to you," I retorted, as I dialed Felicity's work number. Giving my name, I said the call was urgent regarding her father. The call ended abruptly.

"Make it quick, Warren." He looked pissed at my lack of formality. Touché. No longer an inmate, this place still made me very uncomfortable—mad shadows. He ushered me into his utilitarian office and shut the door behind us.

Turning to me he smiled. "Mr. Harper," with sarcastic emphasis on the Mr., "I don't blame you for not liking me. I don't care if you are innocent or guilty. That is not my problem. My job is to run this prison with the least trouble, and yes, protect all the inmates so they do their time and get out of here. Someone knew what he was doing assaulting Otto, mostly inflicting pain with minimal damage. He was after something. The beating was not serious enough to kill...usually.

However, Otto is older and not in good health—probably from years of inhaling all those nasty chemicals he used. I think you know something about this incident."

Looking at him, I played the innocent bystander. "Why should I know about anything that goes on in here? I have been out for years, and only exchanged a few letters with Otto. The contents I'm sure you know as well as I do."

"Assault in a prison infirmary is not some minor matter. That means it was someone in authority, or on the nursing staff. Trust me I will find out who it was. So why did Otto ask you to visit him now? He hasn't had any visitors before. None.

"I don't know. Ask him. Can I see him?" I was not going to make this easy on Warren, partly as defense for Otto, and partly payback.

Reaching the infirmary, Otto weakly beckoned me over to him. I had to lean into him, to hear him.

"Peter, I am sorry I got you involved, I haven't told you everything. If you are still willing, there is more information you will need. They are in two of the smaller pieces. You will have to figure it out yourself." With labored breathing, he held me with surprising strength, saying in whispered tones with emphasis. "Find my daughter, and tell her I am sorry."

"Otto, Felicity is on her way now."

His eyes flashed open wide. "Do not trust anyone." Otto fell back against the pillow, his eyes shut and a thin smile formed on his lips.

Leaving his side, I returned to the Warden's office. My cell went off. It was Felicity, saying, "Get to the prison, quickly."

"Harper, Mr. Harper. I'm trying to help Otto, and now you. Because if this can happen inside Her Majesty's prison, it sure as hell can happen outside. You are Otto's known friend. That could be dangerous to you."

We sat in silence for some minutes. I tried to figure out if Warren was truly pissed off because of what had happened in "his" prison, or if he was trying to find out what Otto had told me, or both. Deciding silence was the best course of action, we sat without speaking.

He looked tired. His intercom buzzed and a voice announced Felicity Schmidt was asking for a Mr. Harper. The warden said to bring her to his office.

Waiting in silence, the atmosphere felt heavy. A knock and the door opened. Felicity came in looking uncomfortable and questioning. The chief Warden rose from behind his desk, greeting her formally, saying he was sorry to meet under such circumstances.

Warren's behavior toward Felicity seemed different. With inmates he was heavy handed, a thuggish brute. With her, he was solicitous and gentle. We all moved to the infirmary, and he spoke quietly, preparing her for a changed Otto. Even so, when she did see Otto, she was obviously shocked.

She said she hadn't seen him forever and walked to his bedside so she could sit close to him. She reached for his hand and pulled in close. Otto remained un-responsive, just lying there unconscious. He looked worse than when I had seen him a few minutes earlier. I didn't expect him to make it.

Fuck, I should have kept in touch with him.

Looking over to Warren, Felicity was visibly upset, and Warden was talking to her. He moved his head in the direction of the exit, I nodded back, and we returned to his office. He asked Felicity if she needed a drink. Composed, she declined his offer. Looking at me, she asked what Otto had said to me. After what he had said, I was not going to tell anyone everything, so I gave her my version.

"He asked me to look after you, make sure you were all right. That was it."

Warren chimed in, "And why would he ask an ex-con to look after his daughter."

"Perhaps he was concerned about her? Maybe he wanted to make up for his failings as a father. He asked, and I said yes."

Felicity said she wanted to leave and stood. Ready to go, I followed her. She was prepared to leave before me.

I could feel Warren's eyes drilling a hole in my back as we were escorted out. I didn't turn around.

When I caught up to Felicity, she was staring out of the small, barred window. I asked, "Can I give you a lift?"

She jumped at my voice and nodded in acceptance. I helped her through the small door and out into the parking lot. When we settled in my car, she asked again about what Otto had said. "Was that all Otto said? Look after me."

"No, but I wasn't going to tell Warren anything more than I had to. Otto asked me to find you, make sure you were all right. He also told me there was information in the family heirlooms. He told yesterday that there was a family secret, and it would take care of you. That's it."

Feeling badly about bending the truth, Otto had

said not to trust anyone, and I took that to heart. What Felicity didn't know couldn't hurt her.

We rode in silence for a while before she asked, "Can you tell me what's going on?"

I looked over to her. She looked worried. Not surprising under the circumstances. "I don't know myself. Not yet. When I can, I will."

Catching what looked like a slight smile on her lips, I stopped to drop her off at the museum, and she waved.

As I pulled into the traffic, I waved back. Knowing George wouldn't be upset when I told him why I was late, I called him anyway.

On the ride to the shop, I thought of what Warren said about Felicity and me being in danger because of what was going on with Otto. Possible, but we didn't know anything...yet. Otto's documents needed a safe place, as well as all the other items.

Idiot! Where better to hide antique items than in an antique shop. Not the documents, they were mine to hide.

Stopping off at my apartment, I looked about before I entered my building. Cautiously I opened the door to my apartment. No problem. Retrieving the packets of notebooks, I pried open the covering on the door of my bedroom, bedroom side. Previously, I thought it was a crime to cover the Victorian molded doors as a fire precaution. Now I was thankful. If anyone searched my apartment, no one would ever think to look there.

Carefully collecting the six items Otto said I needed, I loaded them into two shopping bags, and stashed them in my car. Then I went to work. George was miffed about my being late until I told him what had happened. He expressed his concern and noticed the two bags I brought in with me. Then his curiosity took over.

While I unloaded Otto's treasures in our office, one by one, George expressed his delight with each unveiling—particularly the music box and the tea caddy. He was delighted at what he thought were finds for the shop, asking, "Where did you obtain these? They are great."

"They belong to Otto, in trust for his daughter. He asked me to look after them."

George picked up on that. "Why is he in trouble? Or is it his daughter?"

I had to trust someone, regardless of what Otto said. George's assistance was critical in deciphering the German text. "Hold on. I'll make some tea, and tell you all I know."

George knew about Otto, so while the kettle was heating, I updated him about what happened and the hidden note books.

"I called the prison this morning to see if I could get another visit. It was too easy. They let me in because Otto had been attacked last night, and he isn't doing well. Warren was surprised I'd contacted Otto's daughter when he couldn't find her. He let her in to see her father. It was an odd meeting. Her and Otto? Something about their interaction felt off. Maybe because she hadn't seen him for so long. Anyway, it felt strange. Otto told me not to trust anyone, and there was information hidden in the other pieces that would help me figure out his family secret."

George was silent while I told him the tale that

Otto had told me the day before. He was a good listener, storing up questions for me when I had finished. Surmising it was part of his military training, George always said if you listen closely, you might get the answer to your question without asking it. My tea had grown cold, and on the way to reheat it in the microwave, George started his commentary.

"Nicely told Peter, logical and no frills. I do have some questions though. Have you secured the notebooks? You were smart to bring the rest here, a good hiding place. Especially, if you don't know what you are looking for. It will give us a reason to examine all the pieces without causing suspicion. Does Otto's daughter know what you are doing?"

"No, I haven't told her much, yet. I did say if she wanted to check up on me, she could visit."

"Good, keep the notebooks at your place. You said one, or more are in German?"

"Yes, the French one looked like a copy of the German note book. You will have to confirm that. The other two, one in French, one in German, look different. How is your German?"

"Rusty, I haven't really used it much since leaving Germany. It'll come back, bit like riding a bike I presume. You never forget. You just get a bit wobbly."

I laughed at that, feeling better I'd confided in George. The day became busier, and we did not have a chance to inspect the objects until the late afternoon.

Closing the shop, we started with the objects I didn't think had much to offer, according to Otto. Starting with the Durer print, I put on cotton gloves to handle the print. I didn't want any acids from my hands damaging a work that had survived hundreds of years.

The piece looked to be an authentic print, good quality paper and in great condition considering its age. On inspection, it revealed nothing—not that we actually knew what we were looking for. Same with the Egon Schiele sketch, nude women, in an erotic pose, almost pornographic, and Schiele was prosecuted for pornography in Austria. Carefully handling the paper, finding nothing, that would make me doubt, it wasn't an authentic piece. It revealed nothing, other than being a great piece of art.

George said, "Otto or whomever had a really good eye. What do you want to examine next, music box or tea caddy?"

"Tea caddy. We will leave the music box till last." I looked over the tea caddy. The silver fittings were hallmarked. George would identify those. If he didn't know them from memory, he would find out. The wood was in great condition, the interior was complete, and all original. The only thing missing was the key to lock it.

George noted, "Not surprising the key is missing. I would have been surprised if it had been with it. Rare to have the key after all these years. Wait up, let me see that."

I handed the caddy over to George. He handled it easily and confidently. He chuckled as he pressed and pushed. Click a small flap opened at the back, and a key fell out, along with a scrap of folded paper. George exclaimed, "Bingo. Some of these caddies had secret spaces built in. Thought it was worth a shot, especially with the quality of the piece."

I grabbed the paper. The key was a nice surprise, but the paper was totally unexpected. Maybe something useful that even Otto had not known was there. Carefully, I unfolded the old paper, a note hand written in German. I shrugged and handed it to George. With a flourish he put on his glasses and looked at the note. A frown creased his forehead. He was mouthing words, trying to understand the note.

I needed to know now. "Come on George, what does it say?"

"Hold your horses, Peter. This handwriting is faded. I can read most of the words. Just trying to get a feel for the whole thing so it makes some sort of sense in translation. Like I said, my German is rusty."

As George wrestled with the note, my regular cell went off, not a number I recognized. Not wanting to answer, then a thought quickly flashed through my mind. I answered, it was Warren. His tone was cold.

"Mr. Harper?"

"Yes, what do you want?"

"I am very sorry to inform you that Mr. Otto Schmidt passed away late this afternoon from his injuries. Of course, I will be leading a full investigation. I am sorry, and you have my condolences."

"Have you told Felicity?"

"I called her first. I will be in touch with her about arrangements. Goodnight Mr. Harper."

George looked up, saw my face, and asked if everything was all right.

"Not even close." I told him Otto was dead.

All bets were off now, and I felt free to tell George what Otto had asked of me. This was like something out of a spy novel. I spent the next hour relating everything Otto had told me to George—from my visit to his apartment and finding his daughter there, to telling him what I'd discovered in the French notebook.

George sat, listened, and thought pensively before speaking. "I am sorry to hear about Otto, but these events are not necessarily connected…probably are…but not necessarily. From what you've told me, it could be the nefarious people he and his father had dealings with in post war Paris. They tried to exit a business that is hard to leave. Otto may just be a loose end they wanted wrapped up. All this stuff you are dealing with pre dates that—back to the war and the German occupation of France."

"Why now? I'm not sure I believe in coincidences."

"Maybe Otto knew he was short on time and needed to get the stuff to you. He must have known his past would catch up with him sometime. He wasn't stupid. He couldn't protect himself forever. He chose the time well, and if I may say, the right person to ask."

"Thanks, George. It doesn't feel so good right now."

"You are going on with this aren't you? You know I am in whatever you need."

"What if it gets dangerous? I am out of my depth, and I can't ask you to just jump in."

"Dear Peter, I just volunteered. Besides, two heads are better than one, even better if one of them is mine."

Laughing at his comment, I said, "Thank you. The last thing Otto said to me was *"Do not trust anyone."* He was warning me.

"You've had a nasty surprise. We can worry who said what later. Let's go get something to eat, go back to your place, and take a gander at the note books, deal?"

"Deal" I was not sure what I had done to deserve a friend like George, but I was glad he was a friend.

Chapter Six

Making sure the shop was secure and setting the alarm system. We took the Dresden music box with us. Being early evening, the restaurant near my apartment was not busy. The food brought me back to earth. George and I conversed intermittently. Telling him why I got a second phone. He thought that was a good counter measure. He asked for the number, and memorized it, rather than load it into his phone. Each of us were caught up in our own thoughts.

George picked up the tab, and we made our way to my apartment.

On entering, the feeling someone had been there hit me, nothing I could put my finger on. Things were not exactly in the right place, nothing you generally would notice. Was I becoming paranoid? Looking out my window and seeing nothing suspicious, I closed the curtains and retrieved the notebooks. As I was doing that, George put on a pot of coffee, and asked if I had a note pad he could use to work on, I supplied pad and pens, and let him get at it.

Thinking that if someone had been in my apartment and nothing was taken, maybe they left something. I wrote a note and shoved it under George's nose. *Don't say anything. Could the apt. be bugged?*

He nodded in understanding saying, "How about pouring the coffee, while I value these items?"

I smiled. "Coffee, coming up. Take your time with the valuation." I puttered about with the mugs, and rattled spoons. All the while thinking where I would put a bug. No landline, I only used a cell phone, make that pleural. Checking the lamp bases, my laptop looked undisturbed. Would I recognize a bug if I saw one…nope, I needed professional help.

Miming to George, I was going outside to make a call. One of the few good times in prison, if any prison time is good, was giving lectures, on art and art history to the other inmates. Otto and I put together a series of lectures—we tag teamed. The lectures were a break for the inmates, and it kept us busy. We included as much gossip and salaciousness as we could, and many artists had that lifestyle in spades. Several of the inmates attended every lecture we gave, and we kinda became friends. The variety of inmates who attended surprised me, as did their reasons for being in prison and their range of talents. One in particular who I connected with was Tel, an electronic expert extraordinaire, and all-around fixer, with a London accent so thick you could cut it with a knife. I made the call to him on my new phone.

"Tel? Peter Harper, I need your services."

"Is it legit? I'm go-in straight.

"Not sure, I want my place checked for bugs, is that legit?"

"You not in there now are ya?"

"No outside, down the street, on my cell."

"Good, don't say anyfin you don't want errd. See ya at 7:00 a.m. Gi'me your address."

"That's it?"

"Yup. See ya.

He hung up. That was easy. Hoping I was wrong about the bugs, but sure I wasn't, all we had to do was wait. Waiting is a form of torture. I've learned patience, but that doesn't mean I like it. Returning to my apartment, I found George smiling holding up a written note saying that he'd translated the piece of paper from the tea caddy. It was note to the owner's wife, reminding her to get supplies, from the newest merchant in town, and to make sure she got a good price. The merchant was a father and sons venture, Pierre Duffy and Sons.

So much for mystery and intrigue. Back to the present. George tucked into the first of the German notebooks, what I assumed was a catalogue of valuations on the copied paintings.

The Dresden porcelain music box kept calling to me. I examined the outside carefully, taking in the beauty of the painted floral decorations. The lid was an ornate floral bouquet, the colors as bright and vivid as the day the artist made it. Not being into porcelain the way George was, I still couldn't deny the beauty and quality of the piece. Whoever made this piece was at the top of their game. Once I opened the lid, the center rose, and the box began to play a tinkling piece of classical music. George looked up and smiled. I continued to examine the inside looking for clues and allowed the music to play on.

After finding nothing, I worried that I'd have to take the piece apart—not something I wanted to do. But reaching no results on the outside, I had little choice.

I retrieved my workbox from the spare bedroom and opened the watchmaker's kit. The small screwdrivers were ideal to extract the music mechanism and get into the guts of the music box. Wearing magnifying glasses, I further examined the box and found a few, very small scratches around the retaining screws. Invisible to the naked eye, the scratches didn't look new. I imagined someone, at some point, already had been inside. The screws turned easily. I picked them up with tweezers and put them in a small dish for safety. Checking that I had removed all the screws, I gently twisted the mechanism, and the whole thing lifted out smoothly in one piece. After a brief look, I put it aside and inspected the inside of the box. Again there was nothing, no pieces of paper or instructions, nothing on the inside of the box itself.

Otto must have had a reason for telling me about the box. If it wasn't the box then it had to be the mechanism. I lifted it with renewed interest and inspected every detail. German manufacturer. Good quality. In great condition. I was puzzled.

Suddenly, it hit me. Why did a German manufactured mechanism in a German porcelain case have a Paris address engraved on the opposite side of the manufacturer's name and address. Items were often manufactured in one country and sold in another, but usually by a retailer, and then their information was on the outside not hidden away on the inside.

Writing out the address, I double checked to make sure I had it right. The address location was in an area of Paris known for its antique shops and galleries. Interesting though, there was nothing else—no name— which you'd expect to find there if it were a retailer. This was the information Otto wanted me to have. Along with the notebooks, I should have enough to go on. I hoped. Depending on *anyone* is never good, but I desperately needed someone I trusted to translate the German notebooks. That meant I needed George's language skills.

Returning the music box to its original pristine condition, I checked to make certain it still worked perfectly. It did. Then to make sure, I had gleaned everything I could from these items, Felicity would have to wait sometime for me to return them. In addition, I was curious to see, if she would ask about what I'd found. How hard would she push to get answers?

After a couple of hours George looked tired, and I said, "Valuation time is over. We can complete the rest tomorrow."

He started to say something, then changed his mind. "Good idea. There is no rush. The original pieces are good, and the fake painting is a nice copy. We can complete the values later, and then the owner can decide what to do with them."

He left with a nod and a smile.

I switched off the coffee machine, leaving the used mugs in the sink, and went to bed. I had a hard time falling asleep and harder time staying asleep. It was a restless night. So when my phone alarm went off at six, I dragged myself out of bed and had a shower.

Finally feeling better, I cleaned up from the previous night and made breakfast. Time slowed while I waited for Tel to show up. I eagerly hoped he'd be on time when my doorbell rang right on the dot of seven. I looked out my front window and saw an electrician's van parked across the street, then checked the door's peephole.

Opening the door, Tel put his finger on his lips. I

got the message and said nothing. Tel carried a bag over his shoulder and a short wand like stick in his left hand. Standing a side, Tel walked past me adjusted something in the bag. He put on a set of headphones and started walking around my apartment. Moving slowly, he moved the wand in every direction, often going over the same area more than once, from different directions. He stopped to make notes after leaving each room. After a complete circuit of the apartment, Tel went back into the living room, then my bedroom and the kitchen. Standing near my front door, I waited. He came out of the kitchen and motioned me to follow him. We went outside and across the road to his van.

"Right then. Yore bugged. They's an older type like, but they works. I marked where each of them's lowkate-ed. Question is, jue wanna get rid of em, or leave em and play silly buggers wiv oose listenin.

"What do you suggest?"

"Leave em an jus be real careful on what you says in the ouse. If you takes em out, they can jus put more in, or set sumfin up outside the house thas harder to find like."

"Okay, leave them, and I really appreciate this. What do I owe you?"

"Nuffin. On the ouse, and if you needs anyfin else, give us a bell. You was alwis awright inside…didn't treat us like rubbish."

"Thanks Tel, I appreciate this."

"Cheers mate."

Going back inside, I looked at where Tel had marked the listening devices—not the obvious places I would have looked. Not a surprise. I texted George on my new phone a short message. Told him to be circumspect about what we said in my place and on my work phone. Even if he didn't recognize the number, he would recognize the content.

He replied promptly, "Okay." Good enough, I packed up the music box, and took it back to the shop. Ready for what a new day would bring.

Chapter Seven

The day was normal, not busy, not quiet. It gave me the chance to Earthmap the Paris address. What I found looked like a residence not a business. I would have to visit Paris at some point, and then I'd look it up in person. There was still so much we didn't know.

George tucked himself away in the office, working on the German notebooks. He read the one in English giving him the background on Otto and his family. I asked him if he thought I had missed anything. He said no. By lunchtime, the effort of translating had exhausted him, and he needed a break. George went to get us lunch. I stayed at the shop, our usual routine. We'd discussed what we should do and decided that normal was the best policy.

Minutes after George left, the door chime rang, and Felicity entered. "I hope I am not disturbing you?" She seemed hesitant.

"No, not at all. My partner has gone to get us something to eat. I can call him if you would like something and add it to our order."

She smiled and declined the offer saying, "I took some time off. I have Otto's funeral to arrange. Not really hungry right now, thanks."

There was an awkward silence. She looked tired, from grief? I wanted to hug her and comfort her. What the hell was I thinking? I didn't know her, but I wanted to be near her. Again, *Otto*. Not father or dad. I almost missed her comment.

She continued, "To be honest, I didn't feel like working today, and I was curious to see where you worked."

"Welcome, to our humble cave."

Her smile lit up the room. Damn, she was attractive. There was still something shielded, a wall around her, something I couldn't quite put my finger on.

"How do you keep track of your inventory? At the museum, it's all carefully identified, catalogued, labeled, and stored. We only rotate items on display, and rarely sell or transfer anything."

"Simple. We buy and log in the item, price it, and then hopefully sell it quickly. In that case, we log it out with the price. Have to keep the taxman happy. Everything is computerized. We recently started to photograph and scan items to improve our record keeping."

She was digging, so I deflected. "I've been examining the items Otto wanted to have valued. They are all very good quality, even the fake Seurat. The original pieces are great examples of their work. I will have them back to you as soon as we are done examining them. It's taking longer than I expected."

A frown crossed her face. She was composed. "No problem as long as I get them back in good shape of course."

"I thought you were very trusting to let me take them. I'll give you a receipt for them. That way we are all covered. Would that be okay?"

"Sure, if Otto trusted you, I will."

"Thank you. I suggest that I return them all to you in one delivery, if that is acceptable?"

Good, she nodded in agreement. That way it would give me an excuse to see her. Just then, George came in with our lunch. He assumed Felicity was a customer, nodded, and I stopped him before he went into our office. "George this is Felicity, Otto's daughter."

"Pleased to meet you, Felicity." He stepped up and shook hands formally. "Please accept my condolences on your loss."

I watched her carefully, and that odd expression crossed her face again. It was brief, but it was there.

"Thank you. Peter was explaining how careful you are with your inventory."

George laughed and said, "Part the taxman, part military discipline, part neurosis. Not sure which is the dominant factor."

Felicity laughed and asked George if he was involved in the valuation of the pieces.

"We have split it. I do the 3-D stuff. Peter does all the flat stuff. The tea caddy and the music box are really nice pieces. If you ever want to part with them, I would be pleased to assist in getting you the best price and no commission on our part." George played the *don't know anything game* very well.

Felicity responded, "George, that is very kind, but I couldn't part with any of them. I appreciate the offer. Anyway, I had better be going. Sorry to disturb you."

She turned to leave, and as she reached the door asked, "Peter, you will tell me what's going on when you can, won't you?"

"Of course, and please let me know about Otto's arrangements. Yes?"

"Yes, I will as soon as I know."

After she left, I went to get my sandwich from the office. The rest of the day went as usual with people trying to sell us their heirloom junk, some time-wasters, and few good sales. All in all an average day. As we locked the front door, I turned to say good night to the jeweler next door and saw the man I had seen in front of Otto's building. He turned away quickly and looked into the shop window in front of him. Too much of a coincidence I thought before I said good night to Kevin the jeweler.

I asked George to bring his car around front. "Keep the engine running and make sure the doors are unlocked."

He didn't question me.

Moving to the curb as if waiting, I sauntered easily along the edge of the pavement. When I was directly behind the man, I put my hand in my pocket, pointing my finger through the fabric as if I had a gun. It worked in movies, so why not try it? When George pulled up, I told the man to get in the back seat of the car and to slide over. He complied with remarkable ease.

George pulled out into the rush hour traffic, and the man turned to me and smiled. "Hello Mr. Harper, allow me to introduce myself. I am Allen Warren. I believe you know my father, Chief Warden."

"What are you doing snooping around me? I don't like your father, and I certainly don't like people who snoop. So tell us where we can drop you off and not see you again."

The man continued with a knowing smile. "You labor, I believe, under a misunderstanding. I am not snooping. I am protecting. My father hired me off the books to make sure nothing happened to you or Felicity."

George, who was driving in circles, asked, "Peter, what are you involved in? The warden and private eyes?"

Allen responded with a quick reply, "We prefer detective."

I was pissed and let him know it. "All the same to me. Snooping private eyes. I don't need or want protecting."

Allen continued, "A pity. My father would like to discuss an issue with you regarding Otto and a legacy."

George started to speak, "We had a visit—"

I jumped in, "George, don't say anything. Just let me think." Decision made. "All right, we'll see your father."

He started to explain everything, as if we were just going to listen, when I interrupted. "Where is he? At the prison?"

"No, at home waiting for us."

"You're very sure of yourself. What made you think I would agree to see your father?"

"Curiosity. You obviously cared for Otto and would want to find out what my father knows."

I bridled at that. "Am I that transparent?"

"No, committed. I am going to call and tell him we are on our way." He made the call, speaking briefly, and gave a timeline.

We lapsed into an uneasy silence. The only break was Allen giving George directions. Did I really hate Warren, or was it what he stood for, the injustice? The directions were toward north London, passing through Kilburn, onto Neasden. George followed Allen's directions and pulled the vehicle into a vacant spot in front of a modest semi-detached house.

As soon as we all exited the car, the front door opened. Chief Warren looked around and ushered us into the house. It was a very male domain—clean, cluttered with books and papers, and obviously lacked a woman's touch.

Allen introduced George to his father, and then we all sat in well-used, comfortable chairs. I remained silent, waiting for Warren to start talking.

A frown creased Chief Warren's forehead as he composed his thoughts and politely asked, "Would you like a drink?"

I declined with a shake of my head. George said he would take a whisky and soda.

"Allen, would you see to it?"

Allen left the room and returned quickly. He handed George his drink and the other to his father. Nothing for himself.

I asked, "Warren, did you bring us here to waste time?"

He stared at me. "No, not at all. Just collecting my thoughts and deciding where to begin. I may be a bastard—" I snorted at that comment, but let it go. "— but I am an honest and ethical bastard. I have seen a lot of inmates in my time, and Otto was the most secretive and quietly dangerous inmate I ever met."

I had to interrupt. "Dangerous? How? He was an old man."

"There are a lot of ways to be dangerous. That's why I think he was killed. Otto had a lot of secrets. He knew a great deal about both the UK and French underworlds, the London and Paris crime world in particular, plus all the contacts he inherited from his father. The European Union has made commerce so much easier including crime, smuggling, inter-country transport, etcetera. There were rumors circulating that Otto was in the process of making a deal to get an early release. The rumor implied he was willing to give up everything he knew for it. As you noted, he was not aging well. I checked and double-checked. They were rumors, nothing more. He'd made no requests to any official department. His legal team also denied it, but they would anyway. When I explained what I had heard, they confirmed they had not received any instructions from Otto concerning a deal. I did find out, however, that Otto had put you in his will."

"I have not heard that. Are you sure? When did this happen? You're lying."

"The solicitors would not divulge much. Getting that tidbit about you was from a contact who knows people. And no, I won't tell you who it was. You may want to check with Otto's legal representation. Anyway, I became interested in you, and this is why I believe both you and his daughter could be in danger."

"You told me you didn't know about his daughter until I told you. Another lie?"

"Suspecting he had some family, I checked the birth registry. I hadn't been able to locate her. She seemed to have disappeared."

I couldn't let that one go without comment. "So much for honest and ethical, bastard!"

Warren looked uncomfortable, not something I had ever seen on his face. "It was for your protection, and I was not going to take a chance."

"So what now? I don't know anything about what

happened to Otto. I hope you get the son of a bitch who did it, but I don't know how I can help."

"I am not sure, either. I have a question. Why did you visit Otto's apartment after you had seen him? The same day, no less."

"Otto asked me to do him a favor." I wasn't going to make this easy for Warren, and I hoped George played along.

Warren followed up with another question, "So what favor did he ask?"

"Nothing much."

"Stop playing silly buggers, Harper."

"Ah, we're back to bullying now, are we? George, time to go."

"Harper, stop. I know you removed some items from Otto's apartment. I want to know what the connection is."

"George, let's go." We stood up and stopped dead. Allen was standing in the doorway holding a shotgun pointed directly at me. That shut me up. I know very little about guns. Staring down the barrels into two enormous black holes didn't make me want to know more.

Allen politely said, "Please sit down. My father is not finished, yet."

I looked at George. When he shrugged and sat down, I followed his lead.

"That's better," Warren said. "I don't think you are involved in his death. If I did, you wouldn't be here. I want to know everything about everything so I can concentrate on getting the perpetrator nailed solid. Getting back to the point, what did Otto ask you to do for him?"

"He asked me to collect a few items from his apartment, check them over, and get them valued. He knew I would get an honest valuation, and be fair if he ever wanted to sell them. We are working on that now. We haven't finished doing the research or provenance of the pieces. Happy now?"

Warren looked at me, and I stared back straight faced. No way in hell, was I ever going to reveal what Otto asked of me. Felicity didn't seem to know, and I wasn't going to tell her, either—not until I was satisfied Warren had no connection to her.

"Not really. I don't think you're telling me the entire story."

"Why don't you ask Felicity? She'll tell you exactly the same story I have." That one caught him by surprise. *Ha got ya.* He obviously had already asked her, and she'd told him more or less what I'd just told him.

Warren asked another question I expected. "What do you think the items are worth? Rough estimate?"

"Like I said, we haven't finished our research. The fake Seurat? A couple of hundred quid. It's a good copy and a nice painting for a copy, not really valuable though. The frame is probably worth more. The rest of the stuff will take some time. They're all original, good quality, and in great condition."

"Uh huh. If I need you further, I will contact you through Allen."

George chimed in, "Actually, you will need to contact us through our solicitor. This is bullshit, and you know it. Held at gunpoint? Illegal questioning? You are the one in trouble if you bother Peter again. You are not the police. You're a jailer. Peter has paid his unjust debt, so please stay away from him and us. We will be leaving now."

"Thank you, George." I agreed about leaving.

Warren seemed to sag and suddenly looked old. I still didn't feel sorry for him. He took his parting shot. "Time waits for no man, Harper, not even me. Retirement is looming, and I will not leave with this hanging over me. Otto's death happened in my prison, and I will have satisfaction in settling that score. I have my suspicions. Trust me, I will not let this go until justice is done."

I barked out a laugh at that comment. Justice? The word left a sour taste in my mouth.

Allen stood aside still holding the shotgun, but let us pass.

.

Chapter Eight

We got in George's car and drove off in silence, each with our own thoughts. George finally broke the silence. "I think I will break out my side arm, just in case."

"You have a gun? I thought it was almost impossible to get a license for a handgun in England? You do have a license, don't you?"

"I do, yes it is difficult to obtain one, and yes I do have a license being a former officer in her Majesty's Army and a business owner with a lot of expensive inventory. Oh, and it doesn't hurt to have a brother who is a Justice of the Peace. Things can be made to move along."

Another surprise. I knew George's family had followed British tradition—the oldest male child inheriting the title, estate, real and otherwise. I guess having a family history and the right connections works wonders. Knowing George had my back gave me some comfort.

We lapsed back into silence.

The interaction with Warren had been unnerving like nothing I'd ever experienced before. In a way, he was right. We could be in danger. This was a warning. Best we be careful and hope the situation related to Otto's criminal past, not his father's distant past. The first step would be George completing the translation of the notebooks.

We made our way to my place, parked, and then entered my building. I immediately saw the carnage as my apartment door swung open. Whoever did this knew their business. The apartment was thoroughly and systematically turned over. I couldn't say it was professional, but they were thorough. From the way it looked, they'd started at the far end of the apartment and worked toward the front door.

The mess was an unpleasant shock, since I usually kept my apartment pretty tidy. Not knowing where to start, I gaped until George broke my stasis.

He tugged on my arm, and we left down the back stairs before speaking. "Do you know what they were after? And did they get it? Next, do we call the police or Warren?" George's question rattled me.

"What? Oh. I assume whoever did this had something to do with Otto. They were obviously looking for something specific, and I don't think they got what they were looking for. You hid the German notebooks at the shop, right?"

"Yes. And they're well hidden. I doubt anyone would try to break in there. That security system is one of the best."

"I don't think they want what Otto left me. I think they were looking for a list of contacts and/or customers from his criminal days. That makes more sense from what Warren told us about the *deal* rumors. Someone set him up and finished the job. They searched here in case Otto had given me something incriminating. From that mess in my apartment, the only thing I could tell that is missing is my laptop. We call the police not Warren. He could be behind the break in. He knew exactly where we would be—with him. Allen called and gave him our arrival timeline."

"Peter, I don't think so. Even with that timeline, he would have had to have a team ready to move. I am more inclined to believe he got his son to bug the apartment. This search is more of a crime of opportunity. Whoever is responsible was watching you, and when you left for work, they took their opportunity. This looks more like a way to cover all the bases to me. The missing laptop confirms it. Warren didn't need to ransack the place if he was bugging you. You didn't give him a reason to go that far. I am beginning to think these are two separate but parallel issues. Will you be okay here waiting for the police? I am going to the shop to check, just in case, and to get back to work on the notebooks."

"Yes, I'll be fine. You go, but call me when you get there. I'll call you later when the police finish here. Which I'm sure will take forever. Thanks for your support."

"No problem, Peter. Besides, this is getting interesting." He left with a laugh.

I called the police and reported the break-in, then went back into the apartment. Leaving everything in the apartment as I found it, I sat and waited for the boys in blue to show up. To confirm the notebooks were safe I had to check. I found my screwdriver in the kitchen mess and pushed the debris aside on the way to my bedroom. I pried off the covering of my door and discovered the notebooks were still safely hidden, then replaced the panel and waited.

The police showed up...eventually. Knowing no one was hurt, they took their time. George called me from the shop. All was well there.

A continuous stream of uniformed and forensic officers moved in and out. Fingerprint compound covered everything. A cleaning service would be needed to get that crap off all the surfaces. At least they were being thorough.

After making my statements to different detectives, I added they would find my fingerprints on file because I was sure they would be comparing notes. I also noted nothing other than my laptop had been taken, and I assured them I would report anything else I discovered missing, later.

Finally, they picked up all their equipment and cleared out, leaving me with the impossible chore of trying to tidy up. My downstairs neighbor called and asked if everything was okay. I said it was nothing and not to worry. I hoped I was right, and followed up with George, letting him know, all was well.

Making a dent in the mess took me the rest of the evening, and by ten o'clock I'd done enough to live with. I was beat and worried. Whatever was happening was happening too quickly for my taste. I downed the last of my beer and went to bed. Tomorrow was another day—hopefully a better one.

****

The phone rang like a fire alarm, waking me in a second. What the hell? My eyes focused on the phone, my new phone. It was George. Before I could say anything, excitedly he said, "I am sending you a text. We need to get together."

"Do you know what the time is?"

"Oh, shit. Sorry, didn't realize it was that late. I was caught up. Check for a text." He hung up.

I fell back against the pillow trying to summon the energy to get out of bed. I threw on some clothes and blearily headed to my car, until I realized I had not read his text.

—Translated, awesome stuff…unbelievable…meet me at the shop ASAP—

That brought me fully awake. A second one followed.

—PS sorry 'bout the hour—

Sitting in my car with the engine running and lights on, I waited to see if anything moved. I glanced about the quiet street, but I didn't see anything. Nothing moved. No other lights. Nothing. Deciding to do some evasive actions, just in case, I drove around the block. I took a roundabout way to the shop and kept an eye on my rear mirror. No one appeared to be following me.

With little traffic, I made it to the shop in good time, even with the detours. I parked in the rear and knocked on the door, letting George know I had arrived.

He sat bleary eyed until he saw me, then he jumped up excitedly. "Peter, if half of this is true, it's an amazing find." His words tumbled out over each other. He was never like this, not even after a record day at the shop, or even about getting a great find at a bargain price.

"Slow down. Start over so I can understand."

He stopped, then taking in a deep breath said, "Peter, you were right. One of the notebooks is a valuation of the art works…a more detailed version than the French one you read. I am still puzzled by no identification of the artists in either notebook. Makes our life more difficult. Anyway, that can come later. If this list of prices is anywhere near accurate, I assume the total is millions of millions at today's prices, based on the value of the originals. This is exciting. The question is are the paintings we're looking for the originals or the fakes? The other notebook is actually the exciting one. Directions to where the storehouse vault is located in the basement of the Louvre. The Nazis dug it out and made a vault. However, it doesn't say if it was for the originals or the fakes…or what the hell it was for. But the directions were precise."

"Wouldn't that have been found by now if it was so big and obvious?"

"Not if it was bricked up. The SS covered up the construction by saying it was a mining operation meant to be blown up on Hitler's orders, along with all the other major buildings and bridges, before they retreated out of Paris. Done in secret, one of the artists risked his life to stay behind and watch what they were doing. He made notes, figuring out that amount of construction was not for demolition purposes. That is what the notebook details. He also says the artists made a pact saying they would not let the Louvre be destroyed. This is awesome stuff. These guys were heroes. If caught it meant certain death. We don't know which paintings ended up there, if any, and are they still there?

"Back up a minute. What I got from Otto was that towards the end of the war some of the artists, including Otto's father, switched out originals scheduled for shipment to Germany for copies, and they hid the originals in Paris. I assumed they recovered the originals, and those are the paintings in the Louvre. But are you saying some originals could still be buried in a vault in the Louvre?"

"I guess I am."

"Do you think they could have been stashed in the storeroom all this time without being discovered?" I had to think this through. It was a lot of new information, and so much didn't make sense yet.

George asked, "Do you think Otto knew?"

"No idea. Otto didn't say. He may not have known. All he said was that the notebooks and the information in the music box would get me where I needed to be."

"Peter, it doesn't make sense. These weren't some second-rate hack jobs. These were old masters. Don't you think the French authorities wouldn't have checked and examined every inch of every painting before putting them back on view?"

"Maybe, I need to think on this some more."

George thought for a moment before saying in a gleeful voice, "So, I'm thinking that a *buying* trip to Paris is in order. We need to check out this story. Everything we have discovered so far leads to Paris."

"Otto's death was in an English prison," I countered. "Besides, I don't feel like walking into the Louvre of all places and asking if I can examine some of their treasures, using the excuse that I think they may be fakes. Or worse, breaking into the place looking for a vault that may or may not still be there."

"Shit. Sorry, Peter. Otto was your friend." George paused. "Agreed, approaching the Louvre may not be the best idea, especially with respect to your record."

I grunted at that. "If Warren can sort out Otto's murder, prove it was about the recent past not the distant past, and get the ones responsible, then we may be clear to continue with his request. If it's all connected, then we are in jeopardy because this will be worth a fortune to a lot of people."

"True. So what do we do?"

"For now, nothing. We just continue our daily lives. No trips, other than ones already planned. Nothing out of the ordinary. We become as boring as possible."

George snorted. "That shouldn't be hard for you. You never seem to get out and about, not even coming down to the family shack in the country."

Oh sure, the country shack, my ass. George's family had a Georgian mansion on an estate. His elder brother, Sir Stephen ran the family estate, including all the farms. George always invited me, and I had always been made welcome by George's family, but I rarely went.

Tired, and tired of thinking, I needed to go back to bed and get some sleep. "Good night, George. Thanks for the translation. I need to get this sorted out in my own mind. Make sure you keep the books really safe."

I picked up Otto's Bible. Perhaps because it was Otto's, I needed it now, or maybe I just wanted it near me. Passing George on my way out, he gave me a withering look. I just smiled.

After locking the back door, I got in my car, and went directly home. If anyone was following me, I was too tired to care. Besides, they probably should have figured out where I was going.

Cautiously I opened my apartment door to nothing suspicious. I walked to my bedroom undressing as I went and let my clothes fall where I dropped them. I was asleep before my head hit the pillow.

****

Shattering morning sounds hit me, startling me.

This was too bloody early. I hadn't reset the alarm from the previous night. Hitting snooze didn't work. Too late. The damage was done. I was fully awake.

The coffee machine dripped away, and I decided to shower as my wake-up juice brewed. Under the stinging jets, I thought about what to share with Felicity, finally I decided to tell her only what I had to. How to deal with her personally was an entirely different issue. I wasn't sure how to respond to my feelings for her, not yet anyway. I didn't completely trust her, and I wanted to keep her curious enough to see how patient she was. As I dried off, I wondered why I'd experienced the odd feeling of needing to take the Bible home with me.

After I dressing, I put the big Bible on the kitchen table. It was not very valuable for anything other than sentimental value. The age? I would put it at probably late 19th century, printed in French. So not an heirloom. Something Otto's father had picked up in Paris for the sole purpose of hiding the notebooks. Perhaps it wasn't the most secure place to hide something valuable. Inspecting the front cover binding, it looked intact with no indication of tampering. Rifling the pages where the notebooks had been hidden, nothing, just pages, flimsy from having the center cut out. Working my way down the pages, I stopped and turned the Bible over. Opening the back cover, I checked it for tampering or remedial work. Nothing new there. Flicking the pages, I noted they did not act as they should. I pulled on a chunk of pages.

What an idiot! Cursing myself for not being more thorough, I discovered there was another packet hidden in the back of the Bible, same as the front packets, wrapped in cloth, and sealed. This one felt like a single thin book.

Before I did anything further, I texted George, telling him I would be in late and would explain later. Going over the Bible, I examined every inch, checking page by page. This time I was not going to miss anything. Re-examining everything I already examined—outside covers, inside flysheets, the spine binding—I got out my scalpel. I started to deconstruct the entire book. Taking care. Although the book was not a valuable one, I had to respect the maker's care and craft.

Lifting the edges of the interior paper, I peeled them back to reveal the stitched binding. I carefully cut away the binding stitches. As soon as I lifted the block of pages away from the cover, I saw a small piece of paper hidden midway down the spine. Removing it, I unfolded the paper. It contained a key and a handwritten note in German. More for George. Putting it aside, I continued to dismantle the Bible, making sure I had not missed anything else.

By the time I finished, I was convinced I had all that the Bible had to offer. Not that I knew exactly what that was. The key looked like a safe-deposit box key. I wondered if the location was still in existence, and if so, who'd paid for it all this time? Maybe the box had been defaulted and the contents sold off. Somehow, I didn't think so. Too much thoughtful planning had gone into this puzzle so far for that.

The next question? Where was the box? With the apparent age of the key, I suspected Paris. George had been right. We would need to make a trip to the City of Light. However, we had to wait and see if Warren would resolve Otto's killing.

Next came the packet. Same process—scraping off the sealing wax, picking open the stitches with my trusty scalpel, and then I revealed a note book that was a little larger than the others, but slimmer. Opening it, I immediately became frustrated. German. *Damn it*. Why couldn't they have done everything in French.

I didn't bother going any further.

After cleaning up, I put everything away tidily, packed the key, the note, and the notebook in my bag, and went to work. We must have enough information now. All we needed to do was collate, organize, and understand it.

Once at the shop, I felt lighter than I had in days, but George looked tired like he had been on an all-night bender. Which in a way he had—just without alcohol.

He waved to me. "I'm too old for this shit, even if it's worth it."

I commiserated and put the kettle on for a pot of tea. When all was in progress, I showed George my discovery. "I'm not sure why I took the Bible home with me last night." I paused. "There was something tickling the back of my mind. I couldn't put a finger on it. Anyway, I re-examined the book and found something interesting."

George brightened up at my words. "What did you find?"

"Another bloody notebook in German, and a key wrapped in a note also in German. Please do your thing?" I handed him the book, the key, and the note.

The tea finished brewing, so I put a large mug in front of him, and he grunted his thanks as he took the key and note first. Within minutes he was smiling and asked me to get him the tea caddy. Popping open the secret compartment, he took out the note with a triumphant exclamation.

I asked, "What's the connection?"

"Otto's father was a sneaky bugger. The note we thought was about ordering some tea from a new merchant is written in the same hand as the note with the key. That's not kosher considering the date of the caddy itself. I think they are linked. Any idea on the key?"

"Safe-deposit box."

"Yeah, my thought exactly. Paris or Germany?"

"My guess? Paris. That's where all this happened. The age of the key fits the timeline."

"Damn it, Peter. I missed that. Too busy with the note. I think it's a clue, or code to bring the two together, or maybe give the bank name. You're the French expert. What do you think?"

"Art works, not codes or riddles. Anything you can tell me about the tea caddy?"

"Well, it's English-Georgian, really nice piece, and expensive." He stopped and thought. "Otto's father probably hid the information. I don't see this as being the original hiding place, at least not for the note. The Bible probably would have been the original place. The French and Germans, unlike us English, are not known for their love of tea. We assumed it was tea because the note was in a tea caddy. The note was generic, saying to go to the new merchant. It didn't mention anything specific."

I finished my tea and asked, "The merchant is the name of the bank? Not one I've heard of. It must be a private one, not one of your big commercial ones. The bank would need to be old, established, stable, and very discreet. How would the box be paid for after all these years?"

We were silent for a while before George postulated, "How about an account at the bank which bears interest and the fees for the box are automatically debited? Otto's father, Ekkehard right?"

I nodded in agreement. "He opens the account and dumps in a chunk of change, which he figures will keep the thing going for a few decades. He, Hans, Otto, or someone can then retrieve what's in it, and by that time everything will have quieted down, they will be in the clear."

"Great story," I said. "We don't know what's in the box, the size or anything. From what we do have, we know the Nazis built a secret storage space in the Louvre. We don't know if the paintings are, or were ever, in that location. If they are, however exciting this is, we have a problem. I, for one, am not breaking into the world's biggest museum, because I sure as hell do not want to see the inside of a French prison. Hell, this caper is going sideways."

"Hey, Peter, have faith. We have a lot to go on, and like you said, we can't do anything until Otto's death is resolved."

Mollified, I started to think about how sneaky they had been. They must have figured out a way to get the paintings, eventually. They couldn't rely on the Nazi built room remaining undiscovered. No, there was definitely something we were missing, but we had made progress that was for sure.

George continued, "I think Otto knew he was on borrowed time. He was in a dangerous environment, and you really can't walk away from that life. He was safe as long as he was working for the underworld. They knew he had too much to lose. Being in prison, he had a lot to gain by getting out, especially at his age. Maybe the rumors, about him spilling what he knew, were true."

"I don't think so. He would never put Felicity in danger. Dealing with the authorities would put her and everyone he knew in danger. Nah, I don't see it like that."

"Think about it. It makes sense. He was getting on and not in great health. By doing that, he could spend his last years with his daughter."

"Except they were estranged. The result of the rumor is he's dead. We don't know who was behind it. He knew he was signing his own death warrant."

"Good point. The authorities could have promised to protect him."

"If so, that didn't work out too well, did it?"

"All right, I'll give you that one. I wanted to make sure that you were convinced Otto wouldn't have done a deal."

"I was always convinced. I don't believe it was in his or anyone's best interests for him to turn on his previous contacts. Are we done with this?"

"Yes, we move forward when you think it's appropriate. I have two sales to visit this afternoon. I'll get to the book today if possible—tonight will be the soonest. All right?"

"Yeah, no problem. I'll look into the bank and see what I can find online."

With the division of labor sorted, we went our separate ways. George out for the afternoon, I remained at the shop. One of our regular customers popped in to see what new pieces we had. Nothing caught his fancy. Some American tourists bought a selection of prints of "Olde London Towne". Not exactly collector quality, but a nice set of four landmark buildings, and a set of six scenes of the eighteenth-century Thames. We were getting an increasing number of print sales, and I would have to start looking for more print inventory. To maximize our print sales, we needed to stock a good selection—a nice problem to have.

Lunch came and went. In between customers, I pondered on Otto's life and his request. Something was still bothering me like one of those thoughts that flits around in your head but you can't pin *it* down. Reviewing all the info we had, everything seemed to jibe. Whatever *it* was would percolate into my consciousness when it was ready, no use forcing it.

I looked up the French bank. It was easy to find the name of the exclusive private bank, but not much else. George came back from the sales, successful at one and not at the other. He complained the prices at the second sale were not worth the effort, and he would probably not be going back to that auction room. I asked how bad it was.

"Bloody silly prices. Nice items, but the bidding was out of order. They had to be dilatants or foreigners with more money than sense. Never mind. I got some nice pieces at the first sale, at reasonable prices, so we'll make some money on them. I will show you later when I've unpacked them."

I asked, "Will you be able to get to the last book tonight?"

"Peter, you damned slave driver. Let me bring in

the goods, get a cuppa tea, and I will start on it now. Good enough?"

"Yes, thank you. I'll bring in the stuff from your car to save time and put the kettle on, and I'll even bring you biscuits with your tea. How's that?" I said it with a smile.

He flipped me off and grumbled as he went into the office. As my gaze followed him, I noticed a man looking in the window. I was sure he'd been hanging around before. I'd become more aware of my surroundings since the Allen Warren incident, and now that I'd had a good look at him, he would be easier to spot the next time. Either that, or I was becoming completely paranoid—not necessarily a bad thing under the current circumstances.

When I took George his tea and biscuits, he'd already buried himself in the notebook. He had an English-German dictionary, a note pad, and several colored pens by his side. He grunted a thank you, as I put the refreshments down and quietly retreated. I didn't want to disturb him any further, hoping he would get the translation done swiftly. Closing time came around and still nothing from the George. As I closed up, I kept an eye out for the suspicious man. Nothing. All secure, I went back and disturbed George.

He looked up as I entered. His eyes were red and tired looking, but he smiled and said, "Motherlode. This book details which paintings were copied, with notes regarding when they went to Berlin, dates and everything. I have read most of it and am now translating it so you can read it. You will make more of it than I can. I recognized most of the names of the artists, and a few of the paintings. There is also a subset of works that I am not sure about."

"Great, thank you, George. I know I'm not very patient, but you have done a great job putting up with me and doing this."

He chuckled and mentioned his German was improving quickly. I couldn't resist... "Does that include your accent?"

George laughed outright at that. "Always had a crappy accent, good grammar and colloquialisms, but I was always an Englishman speaking German. Never in a million years would I be taken for a native." We both laughed, knowing my French accent was very good.

Chapter Nine

We closed up the shop, set the alarms, and decided to have dinner at the local pub. Before I could tell George about the man I'd seen, he told me he thought someone was following him when he visited the sales today. Describing the man I saw, George shook his head and described a different man.

This was a new development, and I for one was not comfortable with it. We ordered our food, taking our drinks to a quiet table in the corner where we would not be overheard. I asked George, "Are you sure you were followed?"

"No, it could have been someone attending both sales. I knew people who were at both. It was just a feeling that he was more interested in me than the items on sale. Maybe I am getting as paranoid as you."

"Nothing wrong with that. Let's just keep an eye out. Possibly Warren and his cronies. We will just be careful. If it happens again, let me know. Then we will do something about it."

"What do you have in mind?" George asked.

"Nothing concrete, but I did make some useful contacts inside."

"You aren't going to do something stupid that could get us all in trouble, are you?"

"No idea at the moment, but nothing that could hurt us…I hope."

George gave me a curious stare and left it at that. We chatted about the items he did buy and the general state of the business. We were doing fine, and the prospects for the upcoming tourist season looked even better. After a leisurely dinner, we both felt more relaxed and at ease. He also promised to have a complete translation of the new book tomorrow by close of business.

We parted ways, and I went home. Looking around as I traveled home, I saw nothing to raise my suspicion. Still I entered my apartment cautiously, not sure what to expect, if anything.

I settled down to a quiet evening looking over some sales catalogues where we couldn't afford to buy anything. Still nice to dream. My cell went off as I finished pouring a beer. I didn't recognize the number, so taking a chance I answered it, remembering I had to be circumspect about what I said in the apartment, as the bugs were still in place.

"Hello."

"Hello, Peter." The voice I recognized was Felicity's. That was a surprise."

"It's Felicity. I hope I am not disturbing you?"

"No, not at all. I was just going over some work stuff. Nothing important. What can I do for you?"

"I wanted to let you know about the funeral. It's this Friday at Highgate Cemetery. Otto had everything arranged. All I had to do was push the *go* button. Will you be able to make it? It will be a very quiet affair."

"Of course I will be there. What time?"

"I managed to get an early time. 9:00 a.m. Is that all right?"

"Yes, it won't be a problem. I'll be there."

"Good. After the internment, I have to see Otto's solicitor about his affairs. Do you think we can meet for lunch or something?"

"Sure, I would like that. Would you like me to be with you for the reading of the will?"

"No." She answered quickly. "No, I mean, thank you. I'll be fine. I am sure it's all very dull and ordinary."

"Okay. Then I'll see you at Highgate on Friday 9:00 a.m. sharp. Night."

"Thank you, Peter, I appreciate it. Oh, one thing. I don't suppose you have made any progress on that issue my father asked you about?"

The conversation felt stilted while I waited for that question. I'd hoped she wouldn't ask. Never mind. I had to answer.

"No, not much really. We have been busy at the shop, and George was off on a buying trip. Hopefully, I will have something to tell you on Friday. No promises."

After I put down my phone, I rubbed out the frown creasing my forehead. I put aside the buyer's guides I was going to peruse so I could do some thinking about this woman. I instinctively liked her, and I certainly found her attractive, though guarded. It was as if she had an invisible wall around her.

George had suggested I should take home the shop laptop until I got my own replaced. I plugged it in and powered up, then impatiently waited for the wireless internet connection. Sitting with my feet up, I played around entering different names and changed parameters in the search engines. An hour later, I quit after finding some of the information I wanted, not as much as I needed, but enough to set me on a course of action. Closing up, I went to bed after thoroughly checking all the windows and doors, and putting a chair under the front door handle, just in case.

At the first jangling sound of my phone alarm, I woe and jumped out of bed. I had things to look into today and they wouldn't wait. Breakfast was take-out from the greasy spoon near the shop, and I was just finishing it when George arrived, surprised to find me in before him.

I announced, "Have things to do, and people to see. I will be in and out all day. Any problem?"

"No, a quiet day for me. Anything I can do to assist?"

"Nope, just do the translation, as promised. That will be perfect."

He smirked and added a bit of sarcasm to his words, "I will get right on it."

"Thank you," I said, straight faced. I grabbed my jacket and went out the back. To me, public transport made more sense. It would be quicker and efficient for my purpose. I was certain, or at least I thought it would be easier to spot someone following me.

As I made my way to the Camden Town Tube station, I called Tel to thank him again for the infestation issue, and to ask his advice regarding surveillance, but I had to leave a message.

Aware of my surroundings, I headed down to the southbound platform of the Northern Line. I was not in a rush, letting the first train come and go. I hopped on the next train at the last minute. I didn't see anyone doing anything suspicious. Changing trains at Leicester Square to the Piccadilly line would take me to

Knightsbridge, which was only a short walk to the Victoria and Albert Museum. Felicity deserved a return a visit after taking the time to come to the shop, and I had an ulterior motive if it worked out. If not, there was plan B.

Brompton Road was busy as usual, and Harrods was swamped with locals and tourists. As I made my way through the throng, I thought I saw a man who had been on the first train…maybe. As I moved away from Harrods, the pedestrian crowd thinned, and I made better time. Packed with students and visitors, the Victoria and Albert Museum buzzed with activity. Making my way to the information desk, I asked if Felicity Schmidt was available.

"Do you know which department she works in?"

"Rare books and manuscripts."

"Thank you. Please wait."

The information clerk picked up a phone and spoke quietly, asking if Felicity Schmidt was available. She nodded several times before she hung up and addressed me. "I am sorry, but she is not available today, may I take a message."

"No thanks, I just popped in on the off chance."

"May I say who called?"

"It's all right. I'll call her later. Thanks again. Goodbye."

That was useful even if I didn't see her. In fact more useful. It fit with the theory I was beginning to formulate. While walking back to the Knightsbridge tube station, Tel called back.

"Ullo mate, evrefin okay?"

"Hey Tel, thanks for getting back to me. Got a question for you."

"Fire away."

"My partner and I think we are being followed. We are not sure, but we want to know one way or the other. Do you know anyone who would like a job following me and my partner?"

"I might know a geezer or two who would take that on. Payin' in cash?"

I chuckled. I was sure Tel could get anything organized if the price was right. "Of course, it will be cash in hand, yours or his?"

"I got nuffin to do wiv this transaction. Cheers. I'll get im ta give ya a bell. Same cell numba?"

"Yes and thanks, Tel. Appreciate it."

"No worries. Pleasure doin' business wiv ya. Cheers mate."

He hung up. I continued to the tube station, and yes, I saw the same man who I'd seen on the way to the museum. That was just too much of a coincidence. He looked bland, a generic Londoner, if there is such a thing. No outstanding features, clean-shaven, glasses, a pale colored light-weight coat, and dark trousers. A leather shoulder bag—that was always in fashion in London, especially with the Country set. He did not turn or make any sudden moves when I looked directly toward him. He ignored me and continued walking in the same direction he was going, toward the same Tube station. Glad I'd made the call to Tel, now I just had to wait and see who called back.

George was with a customer when I arrived back at the shop. Slipping into the office, to see how far he had progressed with the notes, it looked good. The day was going well so far.

I called Felicity's cell, because I wanted to ask her

to visit the shop, an excuse to show her a couple of her father's pieces in their best light.

Felicity answered on the first ring. Not surprised, I had expected the museum to contact her, telling her someone had been asking after her.

"Sorry, Peter, I am off site today. You should have called me first. I could have saved you a trip." She sounded sincere.

"Oh, I was in the area…had other stuff to do. I thought I'd drop in on the off chance. Anyway, I thought you would like to take a closer look at two of your father's pieces—the engraving and the sketch. Although the sketch is probably too new for your liking, as it's only a hundred years old."

She laughed at that. "I would not classify myself as an expert on that era, but I would enjoy seeing the print up close."

"Then come on down. I will be at the shop late tonight. Come around the back. It's easier to open up after we have closed for the day."

"I should be back by six. Would that be okay?"

"Sure, I am not dragging you away from anything important?"

"No, a quick trip to authenticate a few pieces in private hands, or at least take a look to see if any need restoring…if they are authentic. I'll come straight to your shop when I'm finished."

"Excellent, look forward to seeing you, and if you haven't had dinner, there are lots of reasonable restaurants nearby."

The call ended, and I needed to prep the items I wanted to show Felicity. The Durer engraving of *Knight, Death, and the Devil* and the Egon Schiele sketch *Two reclining nude women.* Before I started to remove them from their respective frames, I inspected them again. Again nothing.

Wearing gloves to protect the print that had survived since 1513, I took my time removing the engraving from its frame. I removed the print from the matt. Examining the matt, I confirmed it was museum quality, acid-free, and not a recent job—probably fifteen to twenty years old—and in need of replacement. The engraving itself was in great condition for being five-hundred years old. I was getting a thrill just thinking that Durer had drawn this image, and perhaps he had even done the engraving himself. Touching something so beautiful, the skill it took, the time, patience, and attention to detail—this is what I lived for. Feeling my eyes tear up, I put the piece down before a tear slid down my cheek. I carefully placed the print between two heavy sheets of acid free paper, taped the edges closed, and put it in our safe.

The Schiele sketch was larger, but this made just as deep an impact on me as the Durer had, yet in a different way. This engraving was an exercise in draftsmanship and technical execution done to perfection. The reaction to the Schiele sketch was immediate, emotional, and definitely erotic. It was very different, yet it demonstrated the same sure hand at draftsmanship. The two nude women reclining, were reclining after what? Sex? With each other or a third party? Schiele left that to the viewer to decide. These two women were real. Artists sketched from life. Now a hundred years later, I wondered how they lived. Both were long dead, and Schiele had immortalized them.

Following the same process, I sandwiched the

sketch between two sheets of acid free paper and taped the edges, then I put this one on the next shelf, below the Durer, in the safe. Done. Now all I had to do was wait. Pulling off the gloves, I left them in the office and went out into the shop. George was smiling about something—a sale for sure.

He said he'd just closed a sale for six pieces of Georgian silver to a Japanese executive. That made our day, financially.

Mentioning that Felicity would be coming by after we closed, George raised an eyebrow and winked at me.

I shook my head. Must have given away my feelings, because I was attracted to her more than anyone I had met in some time, but she seemed cold…not the right word…guarded was a better description. She appeared to be the sort who would not allow anyone to get close. Perhaps it was her father's death. Anyway, romance was not my motive for tonight.

The rest of the day was relegated to dealing with customers, waiting for Tel's contact to call me, and finishing the prep of the two items for Felicity's perusal that evening.

As I clock watched in anticipation of seeing Felicity again, customers came and went. Some bought. Most didn't. Ah, the way of the antique world. As the hands on the clock slowly moved towards evening, I became as nervous as a teenager on a first date. What was wrong with me?

Chapter Ten

We closed up satisfied with the day's sales, I said goodnight to George, and waited for Felicity. A few minutes later, my non-business cell went off, it was George.

"Hey what's going on, you forget something?"

"No, but I am sure I am being followed. The same car has been behind me ever since I left the shop. One or two cars back, never directly behind me. Checking my mirror often, and as cars turn, it's always there. I am going to take some evasive action."

"George don't do anything crazy. This isn't the movies."

"No, I am going to do some around the block moves, and odd turns to see if they bite, if not, I will keep an eye out for the car when I get home. They may assume I'm going home and beat me to it. Be careful yourself."

"Got it, text me when you get home."

"Will do…cheers."

Being occupied all day, I had pushed the thought of the man I'd seen in the morning to the back of my mind. On my way home later, I'd be sure to look for him. I began to wonder if I should have asked Felicity to visit. I didn't want to put her in danger. Then again, as Otto's daughter she was already involved. At least she didn't really know anything about what George and

I had unearthed. Thinking of that reminded me he left the completed translation on my desk.

George's neat handwriting sprang from the page. He had translated verbatim, and it read a little awkwardly. Some things just do not translate well. The contents were clear regardless of the translation. Reading the text, I was struck by how the feeling of stress, almost fear, came off the page. The paintings were the treasure of the Louvre, there were a few, notable ones missing from the master list. The most obvious was the *Mona Lisa.* No one in their right mind would try to copy that one, not even Goering, the damned thief.

Reading the text beginning to end while I waited, the part that caught my attention was the subset of paintings. The list was an interesting mix of Renaissance through the Romantics. I needed to figure out why they were a subset. That would have to wait until tomorrow.

Retrieving the two pieces from the safe, I placed them, on the large, covered worktable, I placed the cotton gloves on the table in between them. Re-reading the translation, an odd thought popped into my head just as a knock broke my concentration.

Felicity had arrived. I opened the back door. "Welcome, I hope this isn't inconvenient?"

She seemed very aware and a little on edge. "No not at all. Just a long day. I wanted to see the pieces up close. Did you find anything in regards to Otto on them?"

"No, not a thing. We do have some leads from other sources, though. If anything comes of them, I'll let you know." I watched her expression as I spoke.

A flicker of annoyance, gone in a flash, crossed her face. "Fair enough. Let's see the pieces."

I led her through to the workroom and asked if she would like anything to drink.

"Not at the moment," she said.

"Well here they are. I prepared them earlier to save time." Quickly, I sliced through the small pieces of tape holding the sheets of paper together on three sides. I peeled back the top sheet exposing the Durer print. Her face was emotionless.

I said, "Go ahead it won't bite, I am sure you have handled items much older than this one."

She smiled and agreed, cautiously picking up the print by the edges. She laid it flat on her left palm and moved under a stronger light source, lifting one edge at a time and glanced across the surface, obliquely looking for something. She held the print in her left hand up against the light source and shielded her eyes with her right. When she was done, Felicity placed the print back in the center of the paper.

"Thank you, I have always seen it in the apartment, but I never really looked at it. I guess I see enough at work. At home, I try to relax. Working at the museum is more stressful and tiring than people realize. Like today, my trip was interesting. One of the gentleman's items was an obvious fake. I was surprised it got by him. The others were authentic. The travel was tiring, that's all. The history in what we handle is unique and irreplaceable."

That was an interesting comment. I said, "I understand. Trust me, we have long days here too."

She smiled and asked if we could look at the other piece.

"Of course, forgive me." I covered up the print and re-taped the edges I had cut. Slicing through the three sides of the Schiele sketch cover, I pulled back the top sheet revealing the erotic subject.

Felicity took a sharp breath, and almost blushed, commenting, "It looks so much more alive out of the frame. This is the first time I have seen it as it really is. Everything pops. The drawing is so fluid. The women are so natural and very erotic." She was staring at the work. The subject and nudity obviously didn't bother her. She was engrossed.

"This one won't bite either."

She took me at my word and lifted the sketch, looking at it closely. She examined every inch, looking through the paper. Which I'd also done.

I had seen and checked out the watermark. It was one more indication, the sketch was original. I said as much. "I did check out the watermark. It definitely dates to the right period. We could do a definitive check on that. The company is still in business today, and being Austrian, I discovered they kept impeccable records."

"Really? You are thorough."

"Just part of the service, ma'am." That raised a smile.

Finishing her examination, she returned the piece to the center of the paper, and I again re-taped the edges.

"Are you hungry? I asked. "There is a good Thai restaurant just down the street. If you don't mind being seen in public with me?"

She looked at me questioningly. "Well the only times I have seen you have been inside Otto's apartment, the prison, and twice here at the shop." She gave a throaty laugh saying, "I don't mind being seen in public with you, and yes, Thai sounds good. We go Dutch."

"If you insist."

I returned the items, carefully to the safe, and after doing a final tour of the shop I escorted her out the back door before I set the alarm, killed the lights, and locked up. We were good to go. We made the short walk to the restaurant in an uncomfortable silence. Being a regular, the owner came over to say hello. We ordered drinks— white wine for her and a beer for me. Already knowing what I was going to order, I concentrated on watching Felicity over the top of my menu. A text disturbed my thought's. It was George arriving home with nothing to report.

Felicity and I decided to share and ordered. The relaxed atmosphere of the restaurant was welcome, and the drinks helped.

She opened the conversation. "I need to apologize. I have been a bit off lately with all that has been going on. Thank you for being such a good friend to Otto. I'm sure he treasured your friendship. It's all been a bit much really, and to be honest, I think only you and I will be at the internment. I don't know anyone else to contact, do you?"

I thought about that. It was a leading question.

Answering honestly, I replied sadly, without judgment, "I don't know anyone. Otto kept a lot private. I didn't know about you until a few days ago, and I was supposed to be his close friend."

"If you think of anyone, please let them know of the arrangements."

"Sure." That seemed to break the ice. The food arrived, and the aromas wafted around us. We tucked into the steaming dishes and chatted inconsequentially about our pasts—how life was strange, what it threw at us, the twists and turns it made us take. This was a different Felicity, more relaxed and open, perhaps not as guarded. It seemed neither of us wanted the meal to end, but it did. We split the bill as agreed.

Once outside the restaurant, I held out my hand, saying goodnight. Felicity took it and pulled me into, a light brief hug, thanking me for a nice dinner. Our eyes met, and we both leaned in and kissed, our lips brushed gently, tentatively…almost not touching.

We briefly parted, but then our arms wrapped around each other, and we pulled together. This time when our lips met, they firmly joined.. This was not a friend's kiss. This was a *beginning of something* kiss. Separating, we both started to say something.

I said, "You go first."

"I was just going to say, thank you for a nice night. See you Friday."

"Yes, it was, and yes, you will. Good night."

Our hands lingered in each other's, and we went our separate ways. Her perfume was a fresh clean scent I would remember the way it lingered long after she was gone. The evening had been one of revelations, intriguing and disconcerting.

During the trip home, I was thinking about Felicity, but I was aware of the people around me. I would feel better having a tail that worked for me, and not for someone unknown. I wished Tel's contact would call me.

Felicity was becoming an issue for me. She had

again asked about Otto's request, and I wouldn't be able to brush off her questions much longer. If I tried it might be obvious, or it would look as if George and, by extension, I were incompetent. I didn't want her to have a bad opinion of me, or make it look as if we were hiding something. Each was equally bad. Friday, after Otto's burial, I would tell her the broad outlines of what we had discovered.

Decision made, I went to bed and slept the sleep of the innocent, which I most certainly was not.

Chapter Eleven

The next morning when George arrived, I was already in the shop with the coffee ready. This was getting to be a bad habit. I hoped he didn't begin to expect it. Surprised, he offered to spring for breakfast. I immediately accepted, and we walked to the local greasy spoon.

When I mentioned my plan to include Felicity in some of the information, George was dubious about telling her some of what we'd discovered. "Are you sure? We really don't know how big this thing is or if any of it is real. It's been what, almost seventy years? A lot could have happened in that time."

"True, but if we don't try, we look incompetent or devious. I will only tell her the broad outline of what we found and say there's more work to do. That's no lie."

"Agreed. But I am still concerned we are being followed. Have you heard anything back from your friend?"

"No, if I haven't heard back by lunchtime, I'll call him and see what's going on. By the way, nice job on the translation. I'm going to study it again today, and I may have questions for you on words or phrasing."

"Be my pleasure. Doing it was kinda fun, in a sick sort of way."

We picked up our order and returned to the shop,

keeping things as normal as possible. We did what we usually did—opened on time and went about our daily routine. We hoped to drive anyone observing us to boredom. Mid-morning my new cell chimed to life, and although it wasn't a number I recognized, I answered, "Hello, Peter Harper."

"Ullo Pete, a moochal friend askt me ta give you a bell. Good time?"

"Yes, no problem."

"E says you mite ave some work for me."

"Possibly. My partner and I think we have a tail when we leave our shop. Also…my place was turned over. The police think it was a random event. Both my partner and I think otherwise. We have seen the same people too many times for it to be a coincidence."

"Wot x-actly you lookin for?"

"Someone to follow us and check if we are actually being followed. Does that make sense?"

"Yeah-kinda. If you is bein follad, do you want me ta do anyfin abat it?"

"What can you do?"

He chuckled at what he perceived was my naive question. "You jus leaves that ta me. I am available now like. Gimme the address where ya is then we can set up a trap ta mak it eezy onall of us."

I gave him the address of the shop, and he said he would call me when he was set. I asked how much he would need in payment.

"Depends dunit, if yer not bein follard, a ton ul do. If you is bein follard, and I takes care of it, make it free n haf ton, in cash mind. Thas a discount, cos of Tel. Usual, it would be a pony ta take care of sumpthin like this."

His accent was so thick, you'd think it was a different language. So a hundred pounds for nothing, and three hundred and fifty to take care of it. I was glad of the discount, from five hundred, although I would happily pay it. Hoping it would be a hundred, it wasn't the cost that bothered me.

"Deal. How will I get the cash to you?"

"Drop it orf in'a onvelope at the Kings Ead pub, wiv Taxi Wun on it. Oil text ya the ad'ress. Tel says yore awright."

He hung up, and I explained to George about the deal I made. He seemed at ease with it, shrugged his shoulders, and carried on with what he was doing. I went back to reading the translation for a second time, studying every word and checking for contradictions or errors, not with the translation, rather with the contents.

As I read it over again, it occurred to me we were looking at this the wrong way. What if the subset of paintings hadn't left Paris? What if the copies were sent to Berlin and the originals had been stashed in Paris? Only the artists would be able to identify which were which. The paintings were not going to be inspected in Berlin, and certainly not by anyone with the expertise to detect fakes? This was the Third Reich after all. They worked on the assumption that everyone would do their job without question, quietly and efficiently, no bucking the system.

This was a wild thought—the works listed in the subset could be originals. I thought more about it, trying to poke a hole in this scenario. After the war ended, the French curators would have examined all the stolen pieces as they returned them to the Louvre and other museums. That would have been a monumental task. Maybe they did a cursory inspection, seeing only what they expected to see. If the paintings were in the original frames, that would have been a good way of diverting attention away from the painting itself. Perhaps the French discovered they were fakes, put them back on the walls of the Louvre anyway, and were secretly hunting for the originals.

One thing was for sure, I had to go to Paris. Everything pointed to Paris, and I was intrigued about the address revealed in the music box. On further investigation, the private bank seemed more like an expensive storehouse for securing high-priced items for very rich people. We still needed to find out if the secret storeroom the Nazis built had ever been discovered. If so, what if anything was in it?

Reading the transcript for the third time that day, I was interrupted by my secure cell ringing. It was the same number as earlier. Tel's contact. I answered.

"Hi, it's Peter."

"Ullo mate, ready for some fun?"

"Hi, not sure I would call this fun."

"Dan't be so serious. Oil andle anyfin that comes up, if it do, that is. I needs you two, ta take a ride. Drive round to the front of the shop, going sowf toward the Wes End, you won't see me but oil be follerin ya and check'n out if any ones after ya. Got it?"

"Yes, give us a few minutes, and we will be around front. You know our car?"

"Yeah, oh and one of ya keep this numba on and open. Oil give ya instructions on the route. That way we can chat, an no one ull know abat me. Oil aw-ways be a few motors back from yors. Cheers mate."

Tucking the transcript away safely, I found George

to tell him what we were doing. He nodded in agreement. We locked up the shop securely —same procedure as if closing for the night. We jumped into George's SUV, and he drove. My phone was out and in the holder on the dash.

After calling back the last number, a voice immediately said, "Nice careful drivin. Don't want anyone gettin suspicious, do we? Got ya. Just follow me directshuns, and wi'l sort this out, awe right?"

The voice on the other end of the phone gave us directions, taking us on a less traveled circuitous route into the center of London. Whoever it was, sure knew his way around London. After about twenty minutes of following directions, the voice broke in with a different tone.

"Yup, you got a tail fur sure…an a goodish one. Took me long enough to spot 'em. So far, it looks loike one car, wiv two geezers. Keep going till I tells ya uver-wise."

We kept going, following the directions from over the phone. He was taking us into narrow side streets and told us to slow down, go through the intersection, and take the first left. Then we could go for a long drive, before returning to the shop.

George and I looked at each other, shrugged, and said fine. Slowing down, we went through the intersection, and before the next left, George looked in his rear-view mirror and smiled.

I asked why.

"We just lost our tail. Whoever they were are jammed into a builder's dumpster. Very neat. They were three cars back. Your friend was in front of them, he signaled to make a right. As they pulled up, he swerved into them, ramming them into the dumpster, and trapping them in their car. A motor bike came up, our friend jumped out of the car, onto the back of the bike, and was gone. Very neat indeed, worth every penny, just for the entertainment value."

"You find this entertaining? We were being followed, and we still don't know by who or why."

The phone came alive again.

"Well then, takes care that, dunnit. They was the *filth*." Slang for the police. "Got ta recognize the car they was usin'. Thanks for the fun. Any time I can be of fur-ver ussistance, giv us a shout fru Tel. Cheers mate."

The line went dead, and I was sure the phone was tossed into the nearest safe place, where it would never be found. The bigger question was why the police were following us. Two lines of thought—they thought I was involved with what happened to Otto, or they were on the trail of the *quest*, for want of a better word, that Otto had set. My logic and gut both said it was the former. Thinking I had a way of pushing that one. George agreed with me.

We decided to take the day off for a change and not worry about any missed sales. We'd just enjoy London. We parked the car at the nearest tube station and rode the tube into the West End. Public transport is so much better and cheaper than driving in central London. After a leisurely lunch in Soho, we wandered through Green Park, walked up Piccadilly, and then perused the exclusive shops in Burlington Arcade. I stopped at Prestat, insisting I needed to pick up some chocolate truffles. Because we were early, we managed to get a table for afternoon tea at Fortnum and Mason.

This was an indulgence for both of us. We rarely

took time off and treated ourselves. As close together as we worked, we didn't spend that much leisure time together. Which was a shame because we clicked as friends. We chatted, reminisced, and mainly talked about where we were going with Otto's puzzle.

Otto's tale had grabbed both of us, and we were determined to follow it wherever it took us. With tea over, we made our way back to the SUV. As usual, there were no parking spots near my apartment, so George double-parked to drop me off. As he drove off, I walked back toward my place thinking it had been *quite a day*, and reminded myself, I had to get the cash for Tel's mysterious friend.

Approaching my front gate, I noticed a man leaning against the railing. As I got closer, he stood up. Anxiously I looked around for help. No one, not a soul was near.

I kept walking, and he moved in front of me as I reached my gate. He introduced himself, "Mr. Harper, I am Detective Inspector Blake. I would like a few words with you if you would be so kind."

A police officer. I felt a wave of calm come over me and said, "Sure, come on in."

We entered the building and went directly up to my apartment. He looked around with a curious eye, taking in everything.

"My apartment was broken into, a couple of days ago. Is this a follow up?"

"Not quite, Mr. Harper, but it may be connected." He paused to let that sink in.

"So, what is it?"

He looked confident. Remembering my apartment was still bugged. Perhaps the cops bugged me. No, that would require a warrant. Anyway, they could record what they wanted. I would still be careful.

"You visited a friend in Wormwood Scrubs, correct?

"You already know I did, at his request."

"Well, we are looking into his demise. It reflects badly on the prison service when someone gets killed in their care. We would like to know why he asked you to visit him."

"Don't you ever coordinate with other departments? I already told Warren. You do know Chief Warden Warren? Otto asked me to value some of his artifacts and look out for his daughter. That's it. That's all. End of story."

"And how were you to do that?"

"How the hell do I know? Just be there for her, I guess. She seems to be doing all right for herself."

"Are you sure there is nothing else?"

"Like what?" I said, deliberately letting him get under my skin. I was giving him the idea he was in charge.

"If I knew that, I wouldn't be asking, now would I?"

"Never know with you lot. You must have checked me out, so no I am not fond of you or your justice system that puts the innocent behind bars."

"Well, you do seem to have kept your nose clean since your release."

"Otto was one of the few friends I have…had, and you are asking *me* about his death. Why not try to find out who *is* responsible. Look inside your precious system—warders and medical staff for starters."

"We are investigating all avenues of interest."

I let out a barking laugh at that. "Cop talk for we haven't got a fucking clue. Priceless. My taxes at work. If there is nothing else, I would like you to leave."

"Out of curiosity, where were you today. Your shop was closed?"

"We took the day off."

"A little unusual isn't it? Middle of the week, you close up without notice and take off?"

"One of the few perks of being your own boss."

"Did anything unusual happen on your 'Day off'?"

"Such as?"

"Traffic accident maybe." Sarcastically I responded.

"No officer, if we had been in an accident, we would have reported it, like we are supposed to."

He laughed at my response, saying, "I am sure you would. However, would you have stopped if you witnessed an accident?"

"Of course, if we had anything to offer, or we could help. Why?"

"Nothing major really. There was an incident, where a vehicle matching your partner's was observed leaving the site of an accident."

"I can assure you, we didn't see anything, other than the usual sights of London."

"Good to hear, although that statement is pretty vague." He changed subject back to Otto. "For what it's worth, I don't think you are involved, and I agree, it is probably an inside job. You needn't repeat that to anyone. Like I said, we are following up on all leads. You must admit it's suspicious that you show up and the next day he's dead."

"Check the phone records for when Otto called

me."

"Oh, we have. Another reason I don't think you are involved in his death. And you seemed to be one of his few friends."

Bitterly I responded, "Inside or out, yes. Please leave."

He said goodnight and left. His visit had been disconcerting. However, it did reassure me that Otto's death was under investigation, and not the puzzle Otto had set me to solve.

Texting George, I told him he would probably get a visit from the police. I hoped, he'd read it before he got home so he'd be prepared.

A text popped back.

—Got it, thanks.—

My good deed for the day. The pieces needed to fit together. Without much progress, I started organizing the details of what we had so far, in my head. In spite of going to bed early, sleep did not come easily. My mind churned over the events of the past few days, and I decided to contact another person I'd met in prison, who'd been released and was back in business.

Chapter Twelve

Feeling groggy, I woke to the alarm as if I were hung over. Coffee would remove most of the cobwebs. I set up the coffee, then ran the water for my shower and called George.

He answered on the first ring and said, "Thanks for the warning, yesterday. I had a detective sergeant waiting for me with some questions. I wasn't sure what you would have said to some of them, so I was vague and non-responsive. When it was factual, I gave details. We should be okay when they compare notes. Anything at your end?"

"I must be special. I had a detective inspector. Other than that, not really. He asked about Otto, etcetera. He did mention he didn't think I was involved in Otto's death. They are either trying to allay my suspicions or are convinced I had nothing to do with it. Either way, I am in the clear. See you soon."

Laughing to myself about the bugs that were still up and running, I hoped the person listening was bored out of their skulls.

George was already in the shop when I got in, and we had a few minutes before we opened. We compared notes as best we could remember about the questions the police had asked. Our answers were consistent but not identical—so unrehearsed. That would be in our favor.

I checked the time and unlocked the door. Time to open up. No sooner had I turned the door sign from closed to open, the door jingled and in walked Detective Inspector Blake, followed by a younger man he introduced as DS Anderson.

Surprised by the visit, I said so. "To what do we owe the pleasure of this early morning visit?"

Blake said, "Oh, a few follow up questions just to clear up some loose ends. Not a problem is it?"

"Not at all," George and I answered together.

Blake continued to speak while Anderson watched us. "First, I don't suppose either of you know anything about a car that was in an accident yesterday?"

We answered in the negative. I said, "I thought I answered that question already.

Blake continued, "Funny that, because it happened on the route you took into the West End."

Mistake.

Neither George nor I had mentioned the route we took. The only way they would have known is if they were the ones following us.

I smiled, which set off Anderson. "Think it's funny—a car accident?"

"Not at all," I responded, calmly. "What I think is it is funny that you think we're stupid. Neither of us mentioned what route we took. The only way you'd know that is if you were following us. So were you following us? And if so, why?"

That shut up Anderson, and Blake realized he'd made two mistakes—one was letting that piece of information slip and the second was treating us like idiots.

"It was for your own protection. We were watching

everyone associated with Otto. We weren't sure who was involved. From the start we assumed it wasn't you, but you could have become collateral damage."

George chipped in, "Not kosher Inspector. We should have been told if you thought we were in jeopardy."

"Like I said, we weren't sure what role anyone was playing. Better safe than sorry. Getting back to the accident, are you sure you don't know anything about it?"

We asked where the accident happened. Blake told us. George said he was driving, keeping his eye on the road, and that he didn't see anything.

I told them I was the passenger and people-watching out the side window.

"Just the same, it does seem suspicious to us, that the car following you, was in a planned accident."

"What do you mean by *planned*?" I asked.

He gave us some details but left out a lot. Especially, the part about the driver leaping on the back of a motorbike and escaping.

"I hope no one was hurt," I said, and that actually brought a laugh from Blake.

"No one was hurt. Only their pride. That's all for now, gentlemen. Well, one more thing. Mr. Harper, I don't suppose, you have been in contact with Charles Fentiman have you?"

That question caught me off guard.

"I want nothing to do with that bastard. He set me up—framed me. You know all of this, or you wouldn't have asked. Is he involved in Otto's death?"

"We don't know, yet. As I said, we are following up on all leads. His name came up as being in contact with Mr. Schmidt in the past. You wouldn't know about that I suppose?"

Something else Otto had conveniently forgotten to mention to me. He knew about my issue with Fentiman. Only now was I finding out they knew each other. What else was I missing.

Thoughtfully, I responded, "No. Otto never mentioned him. He knew how I felt about him."

"If you do happen to make contact, please let me know. I am sure we'll be seeing more of you."

My parting shot…"Not if I see you first."

The door closed behind them, and George and I let out a collective sigh. Just hearing the name Charles Fentiman disturbed me. He was at the root of all my legal troubles. His name coming up surprised me and not in a good way. But we had other fish to fry right now, so I pushed Fentiman to the back of my mind.

Instead, George and I questioned one another about what we should do. Finally, we decided to carry on as usual and continue digging into the information and clues Otto left us. I'd put off Paris until we were sure it was safe.

I visited the bank to pick up cash, then stopped by the pub to drop off our mystery drivers' payment in non-traceable twenty-pound notes, as requested.

George reviewed his work on the translation just to make sure it was accurate. He also came up with questions about Otto's father. "There would be records of him somewhere. If nothing else, the Germans were excellent record keepers."

"All the war stuff is now open and available. If we had a starting point, we could probably get some information on Otto's family, and maybe more on some of the others who were in Paris at the same time."

"Good idea, George...although it means you'll have to go to Berlin for sure. Possibly other places in Germany as well, depending on where the information leads you."

"We'll put that trip off for now, too."

****

Friday morning I pulled out the darkest of my three suits, not that I wore suits much these days, making sure I was on time to meet Felicity at the cemetery. Otto never mentioned religion, and I doubted he had been religious. I was proven right. The funeral director and his staff were the only others there, apart from Felicity and me.

It was a sad day but a beautiful, sunny, cloudless one. A slight breeze ruffled the trees and bushes as if they were saying goodbye to Otto in place of family. Anger rose within me. Otto was or had been a friend, even if we hadn't seen each other since my release. I actually had been looking forward to meeting with him again on his release, but instead of *hello*, it was goodbye forever. All I had left of Otto was a favor to complete.

Felicity was stoic, shielded, and distant as I expected. The internment was over in a blink. I noticed only a few people in the cemetery—one couple quite close to us who looked like a grandfather and his granddaughter.

"I need a drink," I said. "How about you?"

Felicity agreed.

Knowing I could park at the cemetery, I had driven when Felicity told me that due to illness the solicitor's office had put her off until the following week.

As we drove back to her apartment, she was quiet. It was still early when we arrived. She said, "There's a good restaurant with a bar around the corner."

"Let's get that drink," I suggested, and she nodded.

The restaurant was as advertised, quaint and cute. The barman told us to wait a few minutes, as he set up for the lunchtime rush. We weren't in a hurry.

"How are you doing?" I asked Felicity.

"Better than expected. It makes me feel guilty seeing someone off. It makes me really want to give up everything and make the most of my time here. There's so much to see, do, and experience. I haven't scratched the surface of what is out there."

That was a surprise, and it sounded sincere—the most truthful thing she'd said to me so far. I wasn't sure how to answer, so I went with my feelings. "Circumstances can certainly change your perspective about what's important."

She looked at me. A puzzled look crossed her face, and then a light bulb went off. She mouthed a *sorry*.

I shrugged. "Hey, I am doing all right. Better than expected. It's exactly those circumstances when you find out who your real friends are. I'm surprised no one else showed up. Your father must have known other people."

"He was old—probably out-lived a lot of his contemporaries. It's not a life style that promotes longevity."

The bar man took our order for drinks and gave us the lunch menus. While we looked, neither of us spoke. I settled for a steak and kidney pudding, with mashed potatoes, and glazed carrots. I wanted good English comfort food. Felicity went with a smoked salmon and rocket salad. The drinks arrived, and we placed our food order. I raised my glass to toast Otto after the waiter left, and we clinked glasses.

"To Otto," we said in unison. Then we both went silent again.

She spoke first. "Are you busy this afternoon?"

"Not really. Why?"

"I don't feel like being alone today, and work is not really an option either."

"What would you like to do?'

"Could we go to the National Gallery? I don't want to impose…but would you mind?"

"That would be fine. One of my favorite places."

That was a surprise, and a pleasant one. Before my incarceration, the National and Tate galleries were second homes to me. The history and the amazing talent of the artists on display never failed to awe me.

A cloud between us lifted, and we chatted easily over our food. Felicity told me a little about her childhood, and I told her mine. This was the most relaxed I had seen her. She seemed to be more at ease and willing to talk. Although, whenever I tried to talk about her job, she steered the conversation back to personal things, or me and mine. I didn't really mind, I liked her and the air of mystery about her. Already, I had figured somethings out about her, but I would be patient and wait until she told me her secrets.

We split the bill again. She insisted.

Chapter Thirteen

Making our way to Trafalgar Square, Felicity was easy company, as she linked her arm through mine. It felt good in a way that I'd missed. Since my release, I'd had my share of dates and girlfriends, but none stuck. There was always something missing with them or me. With Felicity, it was easy, maybe too easy. I was falling for her, and I didn't want to stop it.

The impressive façade of the National Gallery invited us in. We strolled the galleries and I felt right at home as I regaled Felicity with stories of the artists and the subjects. I couldn't resist telling her the juicy and scandalous stories woven into their history. She laughed in all the right places and asked smart questions which I answered. Some were a stretch and I had to dredge my memory for answers. Time had passed quickly— quicker than I wanted.

As our visit came to an end, we retraced our steps back to my parked car. Standing close, I asked her if she would like me to see her home, but she said it was nearby and she'd make her own way.

It was an awkward parting until she asked, "Could we do this again?"

"I would be delighted. May I call you?" I smiled.

"Yes, I'd like that." She reached up, putting a soft hand against my cheek, and kissed me. I experienced the same jolt I had the other night. Then she was gone as I stood rooted to the spot longer than I realized, lost in thought. Finally, I got in my car.

Felicity had not asked about Otto. His burial would release me from my promise not to tell anyone—a promise I had already broken by involving George. Though only by necessity. All the way home, the problem to tell or not went round and round in my head. Decision made. I would tell her some of what was going on. Not all of it. Not yet.

I wanted to, but there was something about her I needed to resolve.

It felt good to make a decision that fit in with the other pieces I was juggling.

****

Days turned into several weeks of seeing Felicity. Each time it felt better. I told her enough of Otto's request to pique her curiosity, and I fed her little pieces as I began to know her. Her fascination grew. To her, this was an unknown part of Otto's history, and she was cautious about getting involved. By the fourth time I saw her, she claimed she wanted to help me solve Otto's puzzling request—if I wanted her help. I did.

Toward the end of the fourth week, George and I were checking our inventory for a print and watercolor sale coming up. I wanted to attend since the sale looked to have some undervalued collections going under the hammer.

As the doorbell rang on opening, we both glanced up. Detectives Blake and Anderson walked in. A surprise—an unpleasant one. I put on my best sales face and welcomed them. "Good day Inspector." Nodding to his sergeant. "What can we do for you today?"

Blake answered, "Tying up loose ends and

delivering some good news. We have arrested a suspect in the death of Otto Schmidt."

"That is a surprise, and a good one." I asked, "Who is he?"

"We are not at liberty to divulge that yet. I just wanted to let you know we have someone."

"Thank you for that. Will it make the papers? I want to know about the trial and when it goes public."

"I doubt it. We will be keeping this one as quiet as possible. Avoid embarrassment. You get the idea?"

"Cover up, you mean? Never mind. I really don't care as long as he goes away for a very long time."

Both police officers laughed at that, Blake continued, "Rest easy on that one. They are going to bury him. What I can say is that you are definitely in the clear of any involvement in this situation. Otto's past really caught up with him."

"Does Felicity know about this?"

"Yes, we informed her first. You were a courtesy."

"Thanks, I appreciate that."

"Our pleasure. Before we leave…a warning. Don't ever take things into your own hands again. We know you arranged the accident to the car following you. We can't prove it, but we know it. We are not pleased, and if anything ever comes up, we will be on you like toffee on a blanket."

I looked as astonished as I could and replied innocently, "How could I do that? I am just a shop keeper."

"Our friend the Warden said you got to know some other villain's when you were locked up. That's how relationships work, isn't it? We are sure you got one of those reprobates to assist. It wouldn't surprise me if you were fencing stolen property through here. Take the warning. Goodbye."

"Inspector Blake, with all due respect, fuck off." George jumped in and took offence at that comment, "You ever try pulling that crap with us or harass us, you will not be pleased with the result. I also have some friends in high places, higher than the Warden or your superintendent. Some in not so high places, most of whom served in Her Majesty's Armed Forces. You may go…and don't bother coming back."

I smiled at them both as they turned to leave. "Don't forget to tell Warren that his son can remove the illegal bugs he planted in my apartment." I had to have my last say.

Blake looked as if he were about to say something but thought better of it, and the two detectives left. The bell over the door made a tinkling sound, a sound that was music to my ears.

"Wow, George." I was surprised how vehemently he went off on Inspector Blake. Learning the hard way, I was wary of police. "Thank you!"

Before I could say anything more, George said, "I hate when someone, anyone, tries to use their position to bully people. We embarrassed the boys in blue, and they didn't like it. Still, it's no reason to take it out on you, or us. I believe it's called a teachable moment."

"Thank you anyway. I needed that. The justice system needs work. I got burned, and it still bothers me. Don't trust it."

"Understandable really. I'm surprised you are as well-adjusted as you are. Either that, or I'm in worse shape than I thought."

That comment made us both laugh, and we didn't

stop for several minutes. It was a tonic, and I believe we both felt much better. The stress of Otto's case eased. I hadn't realized it had been so intense. The rest of the day passed without incident.

Re-reading George's reviewed and revamped translation, without Otto's death hovering over us, I thought it was time to put ourselves to work on the puzzle he had given me. I processed a plan in my head, only because I was not going to put anything down on paper or computer that I didn't absolutely have to. The plans looked good in my head. Now I had to run them by George. He would be doing the legwork in Germany.

He was all in. He thought getting any background we could on Otto's father and the artists' group that had worked in Paris would be helpful. If not helpful, it would be confirming, and at worst do no harm.

****

Otto's solicitor finally recovered his health, much later than expected. A clerk officially requested me to attend the reading of Otto's will, as I was a beneficiary. On the day of the reading, Felicity and I were the only ones present. She had been surprised when I told her the solicitor had requested my attendance.

The solicitor, Gerard Fortesque, looked even older than when I had picked up the key to Otto's apartment. He was mostly bald with a ring of thin white hair surrounding his pate. The light behind him made it almost look like a halo. He spoke in low tones as if this were a religious experience, which to him it probably was. When he spoke of Otto, it was in glowing phrases about how thorough he was in organizing his affairs so there would be no issues on his passing, and how the good order of life would remain undisturbed. Step by step, he followed the process he had been following forever, and he would not be hurried.

Felicity sat straight and stiffly in one of the uncomfortable high-backed chairs as Gerard droned on in legalese. Then the surprises started. Otto left four apartments to Felicity, the one he had occupied and three others on the same block. All were rented out and looked after by a management company. The balance of his investment accounts totaled just over four-hundred and eighty-thousand pounds.

Felicity's face cracked in surprise. The amount sure as hell surprised me. Obviously, Otto had been smart and careful. Maybe a life of crime could pay off with more than a crappy ending.

Finally, Gerard told us there had been a new codicil to the will that named me, Peter M. Harper. I was to receive fifty-thousand pounds in cash and investments, the deed to his workshop, the contents in storage, and the property currently let to a business on a long-term lease. Gob smacked is what I was. I stared at Felicity who stared back with a completely blank expression. I'd had no idea. Then it hit me. He was funding me to complete the favor he'd requested of me. The man was certainly thorough and organized.

Yet, there was one more surprise in store. Otto explained everything through his legal man.

Gerard read on. "If Felicity, my daughter cannot be found within a year of my demise, or predeceases me, having no children other than Felicity, I leave everything to Peter M. Harper with the understanding he uses fifty percent of the assets to set up a trust to help and provide for young artists in need of financial assistance. Peter M. Harper will solely choose the recipients of the trust."

What the hell was going on? Not expecting or wanting this, I was shocked. Felicity's expression had not changed. We were both as surprised. If that was what Otto intended, that was what he got.

Gerard wrapped up by putting his hands together as if in prayer and asked, "Do either of you have any questions?"

Felicity said nothing, just shook her head in the negative.

Otto had a limited circle of friends, and I was floored that he had put me in his will. I asked, "When did this change in Otto's will happen?"

Gerard pretended to think, and referred to his documents before answering. "Some months ago. I assume, post your release."

Why would I be surprised at that comment. That was my only question.

Gerard followed up by giving us details regarding how the transfers of deeds, investments, and cash would take place, and the timeline for it all to happen. When he was done, he put his sales pitch in. "Of course, if either of you needs legal representation, myself, and my colleagues would be delighted to represent and assist you in any way."

We declined the offer. Although we did follow up by adding *for now*.

As we left the stuffy office and exited the old building, I said, "I don't know about you, but I need a drink. Would you like to join me?"

Felicity accepted with alacrity, and fortunately the nearest pub was only a few doors down the street. We popped in and sat in silence for some time with our drinks. Both of us had a lot to think about. Finally, I asked, "Were you surprised at Otto's estate?"

"Yes, completely. I didn't realize how careful he was with his assets. To the point, I didn't even realize he owned four apartments."

We both smiled, and I asked, "Aren't you a little put out about Otto having me in the will?"

"No, it's his will, his wishes, and as I said, we weren't that close."

I retreated into silence again, thinking through what I needed to do, and how to say it. "Felicity, I think, with what we have discovered about Otto's father, we need to visit Paris. All the clues lead there. It's where it all started. Are you up for a road trip?"

She looked surprised, then grinned and agreed that it was probably the next move.

I relaxed. She could have pushed back at my suggestion. What she didn't know was that before we went to Paris, George was going to Germany. He was going root around the archives for any info on the original project at the source, and see if anything still existed.

"When do you plan on going to Paris?"

"Not sure. I have a few things to clear up and a couple of sales to visit. I would guess in a week or so. Can you put in for the time at work?"

"Sure. That won't be a problem. I have plenty of holiday time, and I am giving good notice."

"I'm excited," I said.

"Me too." She looked anticipatory.

Feeling the same, I said so. "It'll be good to finally get going on this project."

We agreed to meet in a couple of days to finalize our plans for Paris, then we finished our drinks and went our separate ways. Having some ideas about Paris, I needed to make some calls to folks from my student days. I could pick up a take-out meal on my way home from work to tide me over while I found the numbers I needed for the calls. Hopefully, the memories would not be too painful.

Chapter Fourteen

The numbers I needed were in my pre-incarceration boxes. I would have to trawl through the stored stuff. I'd reclaimed all my belongings from a relative's attic, where they'd been stored until I got out. Since retrieving them, I hadn't touched most of them. My *stuff* fit in a few large boxes. The clothes still kinda fit but were looser than they had been. My books filled the shelves. The rest was nothing more than a box of flotsam and jetsam from my previous life, stashed in the back of a closet.

Finding what I was looking for, I held my old phone and a ratty, well-worn address book tentatively. I flipped through the address book pages, ugly memories returning, and wondered if anyone of these so-called friends would take my call.

Time enough to worry about that when I called. Nothing ventured nothing gained.

I plugged in and powered up my old phone. I hoped it still worked and had the numbers I needed. When the screen came to life I pressed contacts and the screen flickered then changed to a list. The names blurred as my eyes teared up.

Apparently, I had not moved on as far as I thought. Clearing my vision, I quickly scrolled through all the names, stopping only to note the few I wanted to contact.

When I finished, I had a short list of the names and numbers. The calls, actually the thought of the calls, made me anxious, but I couldn't put them off. Starting with Paris, an hour ahead of London time, I started calling. Beginning immediately wouldn't give me time to prepare what I was going to say, but it prevented me from bailing on my chore. If they still had the same number and if anyone took my call, I'd have to wing it. If, if, if. A lot of ifs.

The first call was to a small hotel in Paris. Reception answered. I gave my name then asked to speak with the owner. I was put on hold. Awhile later, still holding, I was about to hang up when a voice came on the line. Yvette, dropping all her h's, spoke in almost, but not quite unaccented English.

"Peter, 'ow are you, I was so sorry to 'ear of your troubles. I did not believe it for one moment. Are you in Paris? You must come and see us."

Surprised at the warmth of the greeting, I felt a smile return to my lips. I had to interrupt her, or I would never get a word in. "Yvette, no, no. I am in London, but planning a trip to Paris, and I was hoping to stay with you. If you have room for two guests, separate rooms."

"Of course, I will make sure we 'ave room for you and your lady friend."

"How did you know it was a lady friend?"

"Oh, you English are so stuffy when it comes to the affairs of the 'art. You cannot keep secrets like that from me. It was in your voice. When are you coming?"

I glanced at the calendar and gave her the dates and Felicity's name. Yvette put me on hold, then came back after a short silent pause. "There. You are booked in."

She carried on as she had so often done. "I am looking forward to seeing you again and meeting your "friend". Oh-oh. Madeline will be overjoyed to see you, too!"

I had forgotten Yvette had a daughter. She must have grown since my last visit. Yvette's welcome relieved me, and because this call had gone so well I was encouraged to make the others. Seeing Paris again would be good.

Not all the calls went as well as the one to Yvette. Two did not answer. I left messages wondering if I would hear back. There was one disconnect with no further information. The only number left on my list was also in Paris. I called but got a busy signal. I'd wait ten minutes and try that one again.

Time up, I called again. It went through. The answering voice spoke fluent French with an English accent. I asked in English, "Alistair? Alistair Brown?"

"Who's asking?"

"Peter Harper."

A silence hung like a lead weight, making me think this call was not going to go well.

"You stupid son of a bitch. Why didn't you call me when you were in trouble? And why the hell haven't you called before now. How long have you been out?"

Not really having a good answer to any of his points, I said, "Going by what happened to most of my so-called friends, I guess I didn't want another disappointment."

"Fuck them. I am not one of those idiots who ever thought you were guilty. Peter, you should have called me. Anyway, it's good to hear from you, finally. Are you doing okay?"

"Yes, better than okay. Actually, I am fine. Are you still making a living teaching and painting?"

"Nope, even better. I am painting and teaching. I actually don't have to teach anymore. I do it 'cause I love it." He laughed a full-throated laugh. The joyous sound hit my ear, and I smiled at the image I had of him from years ago. The man lived life in a big way.

"Why the call now? In trouble again?" He chuckled at his own bad taste joke.

"No, but I am coming to Paris in a few weeks. You up to meet for a drink?"

"Is the Pope Catholic? You name the time. As a resident, I will name the place and pick up the tab. Deal?"

"Yes, it's a deal, and thanks for taking the call."

"You must have had a shitty time. We all have our crosses to bear. Call me when you get here. Looking forward to seeing you. Cheers."

That one call made all the worry over the others worthwhile. After making a few notes on my phone, I went to bed.

****

George was on board with my plan and timeline, though we didn't like closing up the shop. Not open meant no business, but this time we thought the risk was worth it. The way we planned the time was the most efficient for both our needs. We would only close for two working days—Friday and Saturday—though, that was bad enough.

George made his arrangements for Berlin. The ferry and train to Paris, as I had always done before, was the least expensive way and the obvious choice for me. But something about the comfort of a non-stop trip intrigued me. I wanted to do the Chunnel. The imaginative side of me thought it would be romantic to arrive at the Gare Du Nord Station around six in the morning just as the aromas of French tobacco mixed with rich brewed coffee and fresh baked breads scenting the Parisian dawn. My decision was made.

Felicity sounded pleased when I called, and we made a date to go over our itinerary. Getting used to seeing her made me more comfortable in her presence, and I'd started to miss her when we weren't together. Our date proved to be both relaxing and efficient. She went along with the planned itinerary, and after I explained more details about what Otto had left us, I noted her reaction. The new details were a complete surprise—all very new to her. I still kept some details from her, though I was not completely sure why.

****

Early, on the day of our departure, I attended two sales looking to buy prints for the business. The events were excellent, and I spent all I'd allotted on some excellent buys and at better prices than I'd expected. Knowing we would turn a nice profit on those purchases made me feel easier about taking this time off.

I checked the time, surprised and excited to see it was nearly time to meet Felicity. I gathered my things and gave her a quick call. "Ready for Paris?"

"Who is *not* ready for Paris?" she teased.

To prove it, she was ready and waiting downstairs when I arrived at her apartment. I helped her into the cab, and we made our way to the station. On the way, the awareness that I was falling for Felicity in a big way hit me. I smiled to myself, unruffled by the realization.

Whatever happened, I wouldn't regret it.

The idea of taking the Chunnel train to Paris thrilled me, and my excitement must have been contagious because the usually quiet Felicity agreed there was no other way to travel. She made me wonder if she enjoyed a little speed and living on the edge.

We breezed through security, made it onboard without a hitch, and the train left on time. We passed through the various shades of green of the English countryside, until everything went black. Then just as suddenly, the lights blazed on when we entered the Chunnel. It didn't feel like a tunnel, more like a surrealistic, dark night where you can't see anything beyond the windows.

We dined and had more to drink than we should have. Having to repeatedly remind myself this was business and not a romantic get-away was more difficult because of my feelings for Felicity. Well, if something happened, I would consider it a bonus.

Chapter Fifteen

Arriving in Paris was always a pleasure. Only a hundred miles from London, as the crow flies, it's an entirely different world when you arrive. We travelled light and quickly found a cab. Giving the address of Yvette's hotel, the driver shot off like the devil was on his tail. He wove in and out of the Parisian traffic as only cab drivers can, and soon we had crossed the city.

We came to a stop outside the hotel, and the driver opened the hatch from his seat, not bothering to get out and assist us with our bags. For a second, I thought about leaving it open, and forcing him get out to close it. Then thinking better of it, I slammed it shut. He was just being a Parisian taxi driver.

We entered the small hotel reception area where the young woman at the desk pushed the tourist form in front of us. Before I had a chance to put pen to paper, I heard a loud *mon Dieu*. And looked up. Yvette was standing there.

"Peter! It is good to see you after so long. You look pale. Introduce me to your friend?" After multiple kisses on each cheek, I introduced Felicity.

"Felicity, Madame Yvette put up with a lot of rowdy art students, and treated us better than we deserved."

She puffed up at that, saying, "Pouff, it was nuzing. They were all so serious and drank so much. Ha! But zey all grew up, and some still come back to see me. Peter, you know Alistair? E is living in Paris now. E is famous and E still visits. 'Ere are your keys. Please come and go as if zis was your own home. I will see you later. *Oui*?"

We escaped up the stairs, as there was no elevator in this small hotel. The rooms were as small, clean, and tidy as I remembered. We did have adjoining rooms. No connecting doors.

After Yvette's husband had been killed in a car accident, she had used the insurance money to pay off the mortgage and update the hotel. A risk, but it paid off. She did a lot of business with college student trips—offering special rates and providing the information only locals know about. From the brief glance I had at the register, it looked as if she was still on top of her game. The hotel was busy.

Felicity and I dropped our bags, then decided to take a stroll around the neighborhood to get our bearings and some air. We walked off the travel stiffness, and of course, we had a glass or two of wine. The weather cooperated—sunny without being hot, a slight breeze, without being chill. We sat outside the restaurant-bar, taking in the passing traffic, and people watched. Even being busy, Paris did not seem to have the same frenetic pace of London. It was a nice change. We relaxed in the sun, sipped our wine, and listened to the chatter of life as people walked by. London was my city, and that would never change. Paris was a close second.

Eventually, we meandered back to the hotel. Felicity went up to shower and change for an early dinner. Making sure she had gone, I asked the receptionist if there was any way to get a phone listing for the Paris address I gave her—the one I'd found in the Dresden music box. She said she would find out. After thanking her, I went up to shower and change.

A quick shower, a change of clothes, and I was ready. Before I went down to meet Felicity, I tried to call Alistair. When he didn't answer, I left a message.

I'd arranged to meet Felicity in the small hotel bar. Yvette and I were chatting when she came in. Her tight sweater showed off her figure, and the skinny jeans accentuated her long legs. She wore a *chic*, silk scarf tied around her neck and carried a jacket over her shoulder. She had changed. There was something different about her, not just the clothes. She was the same but different.

The new look was fresh and glamorous, and the completed picture had me agreeing with Yvette when she exclaimed, "*Magnifique!*" She gave Felicity a warm greeting of cheek kisses, while just stared.

Felicity was already under my skin, and *this* whatever it was, was something I didn't need but couldn't resist. I was hooked. "You look fabulous."

She laughed. "Don't act so surprised. Besides, you clean up pretty well yourself."

Even Yvette agreed and chimed in, "*Oui,* so *chic* you could pass for a Parisian, and zat is a compliment."

I thanked them both, and we said our good-byes, and outside we picked up a Lyft. As a surprise, thinking this would be a treat especially for someone who claimed not to have been there before, I'd booked a table at Le Vieux, a traditional French bistro on the *Ile de Cite,* with a view of Notre Dame Cathedral.

The ride was short and easy. When we were shown

directly to our table and seated, I asked, "Felicity, will you trust me to order for both of us?"

"Yes, but no frogs legs."

"Okay."

The waiter was surprisingly friendly. He and I discussed the menu then I placed our order. While Felicity and I toasted each other with a nice red wine and snacked on a fresh crusty baguette, we discussed the view. The food arrived in short order, and we tucked into a feast.

We conversed and ate as if we had known each other for years. After, we decided to take a stroll around Notre Dame, arm in arm. We absorbed the atmosphere, and when we had walked enough, we headed over the bridge to Hotel de Ville, picking up a cab along the way. We walked up to our floor, slowly, as if trying to extend our time together.

I said good night to Felicity, who seemed as reluctant as I was to end the evening. We didn't even kiss. Instead, I entered my room and quickly shut the door, not wanting to start something, we may not be prepared for. Thinking of the calls and visits we had to make the following day, I began to get ready for bed when a knock on my door broke my train of thought. I opened the door absentmindedly and a set of lips attached to mine.

Felicity pushed me back against the door, and we slid into my room, locked lip to lip. She clamped herself against me, and I hugged her back, responding equally to her kisses. I kicked the door closed, not wasting any time.

The warmth of her body passed through the thin robe she wore. She was soft, and inviting, and we were lost in our passionate embrace. For a moment, we broke apart, breathless. Staring at her, I was certain she wanted me, but did she want me as much as I wanted her? Because I wanted her more than anything or anyone I'd wanted in a very long time.

She breathed rapidly, and seemed ready to say something, but didn't.

I asked, "Are you sure?"

She nodded in ascent, reaching behind my head, pulling me to her. We kissed again with a hunger that needed satisfying before we separated. After a long look at each other, we smiled, knowing what was going to happen.

Bare chested, I wore loose pajama bottoms. She was a vision with her throat flushed and her silk robe pulled tight against her hard tipped breasts. The vision of one leg bared to the hip as the robe slipped aside made my cock harden in response. A large bow at her left side called to me. I reached out and slowly pulled the trailing ends. The bow dissolved. I eased the robe completely open exposing her tan lines. The silk robe was tantalizing the way it was draped over her shoulders. I used my fingers to slide it the rest of the way off, and she allowed it to fall into a limpid pool at her feet. Naked, she made no attempt to cover herself.

She hooked her fingers into the waistband of my pajama pants and sank to her knees, pulling them down with her. My erect cock sprang free and stood jutting out in front of me like an invitation. I heard her groan as she took me in her mouth and the heat sent shock waves of pleasure through my entire being. My legs felt like rubber when Felicity released me. I pulled her up, until her breasts grazed my chest.

We kissed frantically. Moving toward the bed, we stumbled, staggered along the way, until we fell onto the bed, all arms and legs, with our bodies tangled in the throes of our hunger.

She lay on her back as we stroked each other. Rising up, I sucked on one pebble-hard nipple while teasing the other with my finger. She squeezed my nipple and reached for my hardened shaft.

I released her breasts, and moved down her body, marveling at her smooth, toned condition. The feeling of her muscles moving beneath her skin as I explored her turned me on.

She giggled when I licked her belly button, and then she shuddered in anticipation of where I was heading. Her mound, covered in tight trimmed blond curls, was neat and inviting—an invitation I gladly accepted. I moved between her legs as she spread them wider for me, and her feminine fragrance enveloped me. I was on my way to paradise, enjoying the way she responded to every touch. Once in position, I teased her with my tongue.

Lapping at the insides of her thighs and her mound, never quite touching where she wanted to be touched the most. I maneuvered my way closer and closer until I teased that magic spot. Her back arched, then she pushed herself against my face. I smiled and my tongue worked on her, in her. I was lost in the sensuality of pleasing her.

Felicity was not a passive partner. She writhed and groaned, grinding against me with her movements and guiding me with her enthusiasm. "Yes, that's it. Yes, more."

Losing her to her rising desire, she pulled away

from me. Staring deep into my eyes she said, "I want you in me. I want you to fill me. Please. I want you."

How could I refuse? Lifting up, I leaned forward, bracing my arms at either side of her head. She grabbed my rigid cock and guided me inside her. There was no resistance.

Moving slowly, I slid into her until she moaned, and then her thighs spread wider, welcoming all of me.

I savored every sensation between us and began pumping in and out. Rocking slowly at first, building a rhythm, and increasing my thrust. My world was fixed on the sounds she made while I pleasured her, and my own hunger—wanting her and the promise of satisfaction at our joining. She gripped me and released me, well-timed with my thrusts. The heat and pressure felt exquisite.

Knowing I would not be able to hold out much longer, and wanting to come inside her, all I could hope was that I'd bring her to climax first. We were one, each focused on the other.

Her breathing became uneven, staggered, and broken, coming in gasps like someone drowning in pleasure. Her hips bucked under me, once, twice, then she went rigid, freezing for a second before her body released its orgasm. Shuddering and moaning aloud, the ecstasy of her release pushed me to thrust deeper, pump faster toward my own. My balls tightened with my increasing arousal, and she released a long, drawn-out moan of rapture when my thrust went deep and held. I climaxed hard and long until I was fully spent. The only sound was that of my own breath exploding.

As I was coming down, Felicity brought me back to earth. "Stay inside me."

Reality set in when my arms began to ache. I lowered myself onto her, and still inside, rolled us to our sides. We were silent for some time. I stroked her warm, smooth skin, and listened to the rise and fall of her breathing.

Felicity broke the silence. "I hope you won't regret this." When I chuckled softly, she asked, "What's so funny?"

"I regret things I haven't done. I don't regret anything I have. Prison reinforced that in me."

"Not even selling that fake painting?"

That comment took me by surprise. I answered vehemently, "Not me. That was not me. I was framed by my boss, Charles Fentiman. I just couldn't prove it. If you don't believe me, why are you here? You obviously knew about my past before we came to Paris."

"I'm sorry. I didn't mean to accuse you. It came out wrong. Sorry. I am here because I want to be. Will you tell me your side of the events?"

"Placating, or do you really want to know?"

"Peter, I want to know. I want to hear it from you."

The mood was broken, so I moved away from her. She started to move closer to me but stopped when I rolled onto my back. My mind drifted to the day of my arrest. In a monotone voice, I regaled her with the events in all their horrific details.

"The frame fit so nicely only an idiot would have believed me. My legal representation was hopeless, and I couldn't afford any better. A sympathetic judge gave me a *lightish* sentence. Mostly due to it being a first offence without violence." Holding nothing back, I told her everything, including my hatred of Fentiman.

At the end, there was silence. I was still back there—in my past. Finally, Felicity said, "Thank you. I understand now."

"You probably don't, and that's okay. I think you need go back to your room. I need to do some thinking."

She reached over and kissed me lightly on the forehead, then eased herself off the bed. She slipped her robe on. "Sorry I spoiled the night. I hope you rest easy."

Not likely.

After she left, my thoughts led me in a direction I didn't expect, and the result was encouraging. Sleeping better than I expected, I woke the next morning needing coffee and a shower. I wondered how Felicity would respond after last night's interlude of sex and accusations. I'd take that as it came. There was research and investigating to do.

On the way to breakfast, I passed the reception desk and the receptionist said, "I was unable to find a telephone number for the address you asked about. I am sorry."

I told her I appreciated her efforts and thanked her.

The dining room, which doubled as a breakfast room, was almost empty. My stomach grumbled when I smelled the coffee, and Felicity was already there.

She smiled a shy smile as I entered. At least, she was still smiling. That was a good thing.

"Hey, look…I'm sorry," I said. "You hit a raw nerve last night. I apologize for my reaction."

She stared up at me and visibly relaxed. "No, no…it was stupid of me. I wasn't thinking straight. I apologize. I shouldn't have brought it up, and certainly not then…or in that way." She colored a little.

I laughed, and then she smiled and joined in. The tension disappeared, and all I could think was how good the coffee smelled.

Yvette came in, greeted us both, and brought me a big cup of café au lait and a plate with a chunk of yesterday's baguette, toasted, and a croissant, butter, and preserves. Forgetting how good such a simple breakfast could be, I tucked in. She also announced that she had a surprise for me. Wondering what that could be, Martine her daughter walked in. I stood when she ran up and hugged me. We kissed on each cheek.

"Peter, it is sooooo good to see you again. Maman told me about your troubles. I know you didn't do that terrible thing. It's not in you. You have too much love for art. How long will you be staying? I must show you what I have been doing."

Yvette shushed her exuberant daughter. "Out, now. You will be late for class." Martine blew me a kiss and rushed off, shouting she would see me later. "Hasn't she grown up? She is studying to be a painter. Her work is very good, even if it's her mother saying so."

Looking at Felicity, she said, "Peter was always her favorite. He did not tease her or make fun of her. Many of the others did when she said she wanted to be an artist. He always listened to her seriously. At the moment, she is working at the Louvre."

Felicity and I quickly looked at each other. "We will be there today and tomorrow. Maybe we could meet up with her? Would you text her?"

"Better yet, Peter, I give you 'er number, and you a can contact 'er. I am sure she will be delighted to see you."

Yvette shared her contact information with me, and I told her we'd text when we had a better idea of our schedule. We finished breakfast and headed into the Parisian sunshine. Still wary after the previous night, I kept a bit of a distance between us while we walked to the Metro. Felicity caught up and put her arm through mine as if it was the most natural thing. It did feel good.

We took our time to the Chemin Vert metro station, then changed lines, and exited at the Louvre Rivoli station. Back in the warming sunshine, Felicity asked, "What's our plan?"

"First, we will do an outside review, walking the exterior of the Louvre. There's no rush. After a good stroll, we can break for a coffee and pastry. I will text Martine and arrange to meet her wherever she is working."

Felicity looked puzzled. I explained, "Part of her curriculum will be copying the old masters. The practice improves their skills and gives them an understanding of technique and process. It is much harder than people imagine. That's another reason I am so interested in Otto's story. The painters who copied the old masters during the war had to have been excellent artists in their own right." I added quickly, "Not that I approve of palming them off as originals."

Felicity smiled at that. "I know."

We strolled arm in arm around the exterior of the amazing Louvre, and took lots of selfies and pictures of each other. Each picture had a purpose—a specific point of interest to me, or what I needed based on Otto's information, to renew my previous knowledge of the area. Others disguised my purpose from Felicity. The rest? Gut instinct.

By the time we finished our circuit, we stopped and sat outside a café to rest and people watch, enjoying the moment with our coffee and pastries.

I wasn't sure Felicity understood why we were examining the outside of the Louvre, so I asked her, "Any idea why we are looking at the outside of the Louvre?"

"You are going to break in."

I almost choked on my coffee. "Are you nuts? No thanks. I have done enough time in prison, and I sure as hell don't fancy a French prison. A breakout, maybe, depending on circumstances, and that will be a last resort."

"Are *you* nuts? Isn't that as bad as breaking in?"

"Only if you're caught, and no one expects a break *out*, only *in*. Besides, I am still missing some information—a missing link. When I get it, I hope all this will be past tense."

"I hope you're right. I am really starting to like you, and I don't fancy visiting you in prison, any prison."

That sounded like a warning, another interesting comment to put in the thought box called Felicity. "I like the sound of the first part."

We finished our break and holding hands, walked to the main entrance.

Martine, whom I had texted on our break, met us there and greeted us warmly. We skipped the line as she hung guest badges around our necks, then she asked us what we wanted to see first.

"Your work," I said. That pleased her. It showed in her smile.

We sauntered through the huge galleries, past

Gericault, Fragonard, and Delacroix. They still moved me in their grandiosity, but they did not speak to me as did some of the smaller, more intense canvases.

We stopped at an easel draped in a stained drop cloth, and Martine asked if we were ready. We chorused "yes" and with a flourish, she unveiled the canvas. Martine revealed her work, a nearly finished copy of Thomas Gainsborough's, *Portrait of Lady Alston*. The quality of her work was superb. She had talent, at least in copying.

"Why did you choose this painting?" I asked.

"I didn't, my professor chose it for me. To test me. Flesh I can paint, portraits and nudes, they come to me easily. For some reason, I have trouble with fabric. It always looks stiff and hard, so, I have to learn how to make it look soft and fluid."

"You have learned well. I'm impressed. He certainly gave you a hard task." I glanced over to Felicity and found her staring at me with a blank expression on her face.

She jerked back to the present. "It is wonderful." She nodded and complimented Martine a bit more.

We all chatted for a little while longer, and then I made our excuses, saying we had a lot to look at. As we moved away, Martine called us back. "Wait, since the last time you were here, we have had some excitement. You must promise not to tell anyone."

She looked at us for confirmation, we both nodded in agreement. "When I was here the very first time to copy, the basement was being renovated and they found something." She stopped for dramatic effect. We all leaned in, and she whispered, "They found some Nazi construction."

The shock must have registered on my face.

Martine continued, "Yes, no one knew about it."

Sounding surprised, I asked, "What did they find?"

She answered with a smile. "Nothing. Here is the story. The Nazis dug out and made a large storage room, very well constructed with racks to hang paintings on. They were all empty. The only things found in there were bits and pieces—some coins, a German uniform button, and of course swastikas all over the place. The security forces were called in just in case it was booby-trapped as part of Hitler's plan to blow up Paris at the end of the war. They examined the whole area and found nothing."

She continued, "They collected all the old curators and anyone who worked here during the war—those who were still alive. They were asked about any construction at that time. All they remembered was a lot of comings and goings. They assumed the Nazis were mining the basement to blow it up along with all the other monuments and bridges in Paris when the order came."

This was an unpleasant surprise. I had to think. Otto had been so sure his father had carried out a switch and stored the paintings. Well, they weren't in there now.

Was I on a fool's errand? Still I was missing something. I was sure the paintings existed. It was a matter of finding them. Maybe the safe deposit box would yield some answers, or the address from the music box. Which to follow up on first? Walking into a private bank and not knowing their procedures, not even knowing what name it would be under, didn't seem like a good idea. No, the address was a safer bet, and I would need to lose Felicity to do that.

Martine continued to talk about the discovery and brought me back to reality with her excitement. She recalled how it had been kept *very quiet*. How no one really knew about the space, and now it was going to be renovated and used for the original purpose, storage." She added with a chuckle, "Without the Nazi emblems."

Again, we thanked her and wandered through the Louvre, but my mind was not there.

Felicity said, "You are a Jekyll and Hyde."

"What do you mean?"

"I watched you when you were discussing the painting Martine was copying. Your face literally lit up. You were almost glowing. Your body language confirmed you were totally focused on that moment. It was joyful. The happiest I've seen you, and now, at the flick of a switch, you are back to being closed."

I didn't know how to take that. Sure, she was sincere in her comments, but I was not so sure she was correct in her observations.

"Really? I'm preoccupied with all this crap. Why couldn't Otto have just said…go to such and such a place and you will find all the paintings? All this cloak and dagger over some fakes is frustrating me."

As we wandered on, soaking in the endless display of amazing paintings, a thought struck me. What if the Otto's paintings were the originals and the fakes were hanging in the Louvre? No, that was too preposterous to be true. We assumed they were valuing the fakes as if they were original, not the originals themselves. I had to lose Felicity and get to the address in the music box. How could I do that without seeming to dump her?

This was Paris, the "City of Light" and all the shops you could ever want—from the old school Haute Couture of Chanel through the funky punk of Jean Paul Gaultier, down to cheap *chic*, retro, and flea markets. Tomorrow would be Saturday, the first day of the Marche aux Puces St-Ouen de Clignancourt, a mouth full for a title, but it was Paris's largest and most famous flea market. With the nice weather, it would be busy and thriving—a perfect day to experience the atmosphere and maybe pick up a bargain.

Pleading business, I would persuade Felicity to take the time to visit the flea market while I investigated the print shops for future options to stock our shop. A few hours would give me enough time to find and visit the mystery address.

Exhausted, we stopped and found the Louvre Café for lunch. Although it was the best museum food ever, it was overpriced. They had to make the money to maintain the place. It was both mentally and physically draining, wandering museums as large as this one. We ate mainly in silence, reflecting on what we had observed until I broke the silence. "Well, what do you think?"

"I'm exhausted! This is more tiring than any museum I've ever visited. It makes the V&A seem tiny, or maybe I'm just used to it. By the way, I want to thank you for asking me to come. You didn't have to."

"No, I didn't. I wanted to. It was only fair since we are here because of your father. Besides, we seem to be having some fun." I smiled and she returned my smile.

"Tomorrow I need to visit some print shops for our business, and I expect you will be bored out of your mind. I have an idea—why not take the opportunity to visit the famous flea market at Clignancourt?"

"Are you trying to dump me already? Just kidding, but I haven't heard of the famous flea market. Where is it?"

"It's on the northern outskirts of Paris. Don't worry. It's on the Metro. Last stop on the line. All you have to do is follow the crowd. They will take you right there."

"Even on my own, it sounds like fun," she said with a fake pout.

"More fun than shopping for paper in print shops, I can assure you."

We both laughed. I had my time, but Felicity consenting to separate so quickly raised a specter I would consider later. Agreeing on the next day's plans, we continued to walk the galleries of the Louvre until we admitted we were on overload.

"Felicity, I have one warning about the Marché. Don't buy anything at the first stalls. Go further into the market and keep an eye out for the really good stuff which is usually deeper in the market."

"Ah, good shopping advice. I appreciate the tip." She squeezed my arm affectionately.

When we returned to the hotel, we each planned to take a quick shower. Someone other than maid service had been in my room. Just a feeling. Nothing missing. I hadn't really brought anything of value, and what I did have, I kept on me. Perhaps it was paranoia, but I was going to be careful.

Feeling refreshed, I waited for Felicity in the small reception area. She came down not long after me. We kissed and left for an early dinner which is almost unheard of in Paris. Yvette had checked for me and discovered that a restaurant I'd liked from my college days was still open. A Normandy country place, Le Coq Rouge. They served good plain country fare with lots of game and sauces. I remembered long tables where everyone sat together. I was looking forward to seeing it again and sharing it with Felicity. It was only a few streets away on the Rue de Braque.

We walked hand in hand. I was getting used to this and liked it. The restaurant was busy and the sounds of people relaxing and enjoying life enveloped us. We sat next to a big family enjoying the food and conversation. Luckily, they spoke English, so Felicity was included in the dinner conversation. My French was quickly getting the rust knocked off, and I almost forgot the reason we were in Paris. The respite, while we drank Normandy cider and finished off the meal with *calvados* digestifs, the pear and apple brandy of Normandy, with toasts to our new friends was wonderfully enjoyable.

We made the walk back a slow and leisurely stroll. Once back at the hotel, we walked up the stairs, and tonight it was my turn to lead. At my door, I held Felicity's hand a little firmer and entered my room, drawing her inside. Turning, I pulled her gently to me and kissed her—not with the passion of the previous night, but with a calmness of something that was meant to be.

We undressed each other slowly, without hurry or expectations, and this night we climbed into bed, cuddled, and snuggled. Tired, we didn't need sex, just the comfort of knowing we were together, and we fell asleep tangled up in each other.

Chapter Sixteen

The sun streamed through a crack in the curtains, announcing we had overslept. Still tangled up in each other, my hand had fallen asleep, and actually it had been the pins and needles that woke me. Carefully, I extracted myself from Felicity—still sleeping, her hair spread over the pillow—looking like a pre-Raphaelite dream. As I studied her, a frown briefly crossed her brow, and she wriggled deeper into the bed.

In the middle of my shower, a hand on my back made me jump. She giggled. I hadn't heard her wake up and come into the bathroom. She joined me in the shower, and again she covered me in soap, and I returned the favor. Her firm body felt wonderful to touch. She was beautiful, and I was fascinated with her curves. We spent time on each other and then, with all the soap gone and tan lines standing out against the wet flesh, we dried each other off. Felicity returned to her room for a change of clothes, and something suitable for her adventure to the flea market. I dressed, tidy but casual, as I would for a buying mission.

Breakfast was almost at an end when we finally descended. Yvette looked at us with a knowing smile as only a Frenchwoman could, and I smiled back as only an embarrassed Englishman would. Felicity and I ate quickly and left for our separate adventures. I assured her that getting to the flea market would be easy with only one Metro change at Strasbourg St. Denis. We kissed briefly and parted, going in opposite directions. And as I made my way to the Left Bank, I called Alistair, leaving a message.

I took a taxi to the Rue Serpente. It ran parallel to Boulevard St-Germain and ended at Boulevard St-Michel. I had the driver drop me off at the corner, where I stood observing the quiet street. A few people carried shopping bags.

I had memorized the address, so I slowly strolled down the opposite side of the street looking at the building located between the boulevard and the cross street of Rue Hautefeuille. It was a typical Parisian building, a business at street level, and apartments on the floors above. The business looked closed, so I crossed the street and walked directly to the address. A notice on the door translated to: *By appointment only.* There was an intercom. I pressed the button, and almost immediately a man's questioning voice answered in accented French asking if I had an appointment. I responded in French.

"I do not. Otto Schmidt has referred me to you. My name is Peter Harper of London."

Silence, a long pause, then the disembodied voice asked, "Your name again, please?"

"Peter Harper."

"One moment please."

The intercom went dead. As I stood waiting, I finally heard the locks move. The door opened on two security chains. Through the small opening, I saw an elegant older man with a full head of silver hair, a narrow moustache, and neat goatee beard. I couldn't see much else. His sharp eyes, behind distinctive glasses, looked me up and down, assessing me. He asked, "If I may ask, how were you referred to this address?"

I couldn't blame him for being careful.

"Via a musical reference from Dresden."

Perhaps that was both cryptic and clear enough for him to know I had the music box and had discovered the clue. The door closed, and I heard the chains sliding open. The door opened, the man stood back, and waved me in. He was above average height, slim, and very elegantly dressed. His suit was reserved and obviously tailor made. He wore a brocade waistcoat and a silk Windsor knotted tie on a striped shirt. The polish on his shoes was mirror like. He moved with a fluidity that belied his obvious age.

He ushered me into a temperature-controlled gallery hung with modern paintings. I shivered after the warmth outside. He indicated we would go through to the back, and he securely locked up behind me.

That made me wonder how safe I was. *Shit*. I was so naive about all this mystery stuff. No one knew I was here. Having to trust only Otto, who was dead, I was not reassured.

We entered his well-appointed office. Everything reeked of quality. He indicated a chair. I made myself comfortable, sat, and waited. He sat opposite, steepled with his finely boned hands, and looked at me as if he were making a decision. When he spoke again, he switched to accented English I couldn't place, not French or German, a hybrid accent. He spoke English fluently.

"Mr. Harper, if you will indulge me, I have some questions for you?"

"Of course, ask away."

"You mentioned, I believe the name Otto Schmidt, correct, yes?"

"Correct."

"How did you come to know Mr. Schmidt?"

I knew that complete honesty was the only course to follow. So I jumped in. "We were in the same prison."

He barked out a harsh laugh. "An honest man, a rarity. I had assumed that, and I have you at a disadvantage. I have heard of you although you do not know me. I will introduce myself later if appropriate."

I took a leap of logic and said, "You are Hans, Otto's older brother. The one who came back from the dead."

The look on his face was one of surprise. He responded, "You are correct. You obviously have the documents hidden by our father, along with all the other information, which led you to me. Otto has communicated with me only briefly since he was sentenced, and that was about two years ago. He mentioned you as one he trusted, and that at some point you would probably be contacting me, if you were as smart as he thought you were. He was right, yes?"

"I hope so. I am sorry to say he is deceased. You have my condolences."

"I appreciate your courtesy. I already knew he had passed. That is not why you are here though is it? Otto sent you on a mission. He was careful, though not careful enough, it seems. Yes?"

"No, not careful enough. The person who actually killed him was French. The authorities believe a criminal association from his past activities."

Hans waved his hand in dismissal. "Pouf, rubbish.

Otto could not hurt nor do that group any damage now. I would suggest that it is his associates of the more recent past in the UK. How far are you willing to go to resolve this?"

"You don't believe the person who killed Otto is the one responsible?"

"For actually killing him? Yes, but he is not the one behind the killing. That would be someone higher up the food chain. Yes?"

"If you say so. There is much I don't know...yet. I don't even know if I can trust you."

Hans barked out another short laugh. "That is the smartest thing you have said so far. Trust takes time and has to be earned. We will talk, or I should say you will be talking. I need to know exactly how much Otto told you, and how much you have found out by yourself, plus whom you have told. Are you willing to divulge that to me, here and now? Yes?"

"Yes, but I would like to ask you something in return."

"And that would be?"

"I will leave it for later, if I may?"

"I can refuse your request, yes?"

"Yes, but I don't think you will."

"Perhaps."

I started from the beginning, detailing how I met Otto and how our relationship had developed. Then years inside and outside. How Otto had called me and given me the information about his request. That I had collected his items, and I included George for his German expertise. I went over what we had done, and how the police had watched me to find out if I had anything to do with Otto's death, how we had put the picture together, and why I was now in Paris.

Hans listened in silence his expression never changing, absorbing everything I was telling him. When I had finished, he asked one question. "You obviously liked my brother very much. You would like to find out who was actually responsible for his demise?"

"Yes. If you are sure that the killer was under orders."

"I am sure. I was hoping you would be amenable to the task. I have no other living relatives, and I am too old to undertake this alone."

No other relatives? What about Felicity, didn't he know about his niece? Was Otto that secretive, or was that a lie or something else? Another comment to file away. This was quite a collection of pieces which I needed to fit into the puzzle.

Hans offered to make coffee. I accepted, and we talked on. Doing most of the talking, I filled Hans in with more details about George and my business relationship with him. That caught his interest. Then I told him about Otto's financial bequest to me. I left Felicity out of it. After all, it was Hans who brought up the thing about trust. I also left out most of the information I had gleaned from the packets Otto left me.

If Hans was who he said he was, he should know all of what I knew and more. I watched him as intently as he watched me, looking for reactions to what I was telling him. Hans was almost expressionless. I would not want to play poker with him. He did let little tells slip, and even then, I wasn't completely sure of what I saw. He was looking for hesitations and perhaps outright lies.

I stopped, tired of talking. We were both silent. Hans broke the silence.

"That is all very interesting, and I believe you have told me the truth. I am sure you have left out matters and details, as you should. I would expect no less. You said you have a question for me?"

"Yes."

"Then please ask. I will answer truthfully if I decide to answer at all…yes?"

"Do the paintings really exist?"

Hans chuckled, and shook his head before saying, "Peter, you have a refreshing bluntness about you. I like that. You do not want to waste anymore of your time if it's a fairy tale…yes?"

"Correct, even if they don't exist, I will find out who ordered Otto's murder, for me and you."

We relapsed back into silence. He disappeared into his thoughts, and suddenly he looked older. I waited, watching, looking for anything. He was like a statue. The only move he made were his eyelids, blinking infrequently. He took a deep breath and was back with me.

He said, "I do apologize. I had a difficult decision to make. In answer to your question, yes, the paintings do exist. In all, sixteen masterpieces. There were going to be more, but they ran out of time. That is all I am prepared to tell you at this juncture in our relationship."

"We have a relationship?"

"Yes, Peter. We do. And one that will become better as time progresses. I see you have patience, as well as bluntness."

"How so?"

"You haven't asked to see the paintings."

"Would you have shown them to me if I'd asked?"

"No."

"As expected, so why would I ask?"

Hans laughed at that. The laughter made him look younger. "I really do believe we are going to get on famously, yes? They are secured away safely."

"Not, I hope at the private bank?"

He looked up sharply. "You have done your research very well. No, they are no longer stored there. That was always a temporary location. They absconded with them before the planned move into the Louvre's secret storeroom, which has recently been un-secreted. There never was anything in that storeroom, or so I am told."

"So Hans, where do we go from here?"

"We will proceed cautiously, and I am sure you will want to check out my background, or at least as much as you can find. I will be coming to London shortly, and we will connect, I will bring proof of their existence with me. I think it best if we do not speak again until I visit you. Do you have a secure cell phone?"

"Yes, I have a new one, and only two people have that number, I will share contacts with you."

Hans said "no" sharply. "We will memorize each other's number. Nothing is to be written down, and the phones not to be used unless it is significant, yes?"

Shrugging I agreed. We went over each other's number several times until we were both satisfied the numbers were in our respective memories. Standing, we shook hands formally. Hans walked around his desk and hugged me. "To resolving Otto's death."

Then without another word, Hans showed me out of the gallery. Standing for a few moments, letting the warm sun wash over me, the sunlight felt reviving after spending just a short time in the temperature-controlled gallery. Even with all the talking I had done, the time had passed quickly.

Now I had to visit the print shops before meeting up with Felicity. Making my way to the first store, I meandered looking for bargains.

Chapter Seventeen

Keeping an eye on the time, I made two purchases in the print shop. The assistant packed and wrapped them perfectly for travel. As I made my way to rendezvous with Felicity, I used the time to think. Hans confirmed the paintings existed, and I had needed to know that. Now I did. Next. I had to get him to trust me, and importantly I had to figure out if I trusted him, or anyone other than George.

We had decided to meet near the Pompidou Centre, take in the modern art, and then eat a late lunch which would leave the afternoon open. Felicity was waiting for me at our arranged spot when I arrived. The way her hair caught in the sunlight took my breath away. She obviously had had some fun as she was carrying a couple of small shopping bags.

We kissed and held hands as we crossed to the café. "I'm starving," I said, deciding we needed lunch. That also meant a glass of wine, or two.

When seated, and while waiting for our drinks, she went off on how wonderful the flea market was. She'd picked up a couple of Hermes scarves at a silly price compared to new ones. She'd also found a small, enameled jewelry box. All her purchases were very personal and showed, to my way of thinking, exceptionally good taste. But then again, I was prejudiced. She finally noticed my package and asked to see what I'd purchased. I declined, saying they were already pack for travel, but I'd be glad to show her when we returned to London.

Felicity asked, "So your visit to the shop was worth it then?"

"Yes, I think so. I made some connections, and that never hurts."

Something in her voice, maybe the way the question was phrased, tickled the back of my mind, so I said, "I also found an interesting gallery on the Left Bank. The owner was in and not busy, so I had a chat with him. The price point's way out of my league, but it was fascinating."

There, I told the truth, though not quite telling everything. Felicity relaxed into her delightful self again. We downed our drinks then found the main entrance to the Pompidou and dropped off our packages at the coat check. The next couple of hours perusing the galleries so different from those at the Louvre, finished us on sensory overload. But before leaving, I excused myself and picked up a few post cards from the museum shop for future use. All were of paintings Felicity had liked.

My phone had been on silent in the museum. When I checked, there was a message from George. He discovered some interesting stuff in Germany and found a helpful official who on his return would send copies to his e-mail for translation.

Another positive step. I couldn't wait to see what George had found.

Felicity asked, "Anything important?"

"No, just George checking in."

We sat and enjoyed the afternoon heat, watching

people as they hustled by living their lives. I wondered what it would be like to live in another city. You often take what you have all around you for granted. I did—until I lost it. When I got released, I did all the touristy things. The Tower of London. Yes, another prison. St. Paul's Cathedral, Westminster Abbey, and all the other stuff. I don't take them for granted anymore.

Felicity must have sensed something. She asked me if I was all right.

"Yes, I was just thinking how much we take for granted until we can't. I appreciate all the things I can do now—like enjoy Paris with a beautiful companion."

She smiled and almost blushed. "You are too kind, sir. I am just a poor English girl."

We laughed, paid the tab, and left a good tip before slowly walking back to the hotel.

The receptionist called out to me that I had a message, and she handed me a folded note. It was written in English, but I didn't recognize the sloppy handwriting. Looking at the name, Alistair Brown, it must have been Yvette's writing.

"Do you mind making the call for me on the house phone?" She smiled and dialed the number Alistair left.

A voice answered in French on the second ring.

"Alistair? It's Peter, Peter Harper."

"Yes, Yvette told me you were in Paris visiting and thought I would like to know. Like I said when we spoke, dinner is on me. I did call your cell but no answer."

"We have been doing museums all day. My phone has been on silent. Sorry, I should have checked sooner. We don't have any particular plans for tonight if that works for you."

"I'd love to catch up."

Something in his voice triggered a warning. This felt like more than catching up.

I said, "I will okay it with my companion." I put my hand over the phone and asked Felicity. "Any objection to having dinner with an old friend from my college days?"

"No, objections." She shrugged.

"Sure, Alistair. We're up for that. When and where?"

"As I said, this is my town. You pick the time, and I'll handle the place and the tab." He said, the last with a chuckle. We agreed on a time, and Alistair said he would call with the hotel details.

After, Felicity asked, "Who is he? You said most of your friends left you."

"They did. Alistair was already here in Paris. He dropped out of college to follow his dream of being an artist. He definitely had the talent, but that isn't always enough."

"Talent sometimes needs luck as well," she added.

"I assumed he was like all the rest. I didn't contact him until recently, and he was extremely welcoming. According to Yvette, he is doing pretty well."

"Good for him. Maybe some people's dreams do come true. Well, perhaps this is a good opportunity to catch up, or whatever."

"You don't mind?"

"No, I don't mind. We can always get together back home. Besides, you don't know how it will go tonight, could be an early one." She winked at me—a knowing wink.

"I'm sure it will be an early one."

We went up to our rooms to get ready for dinner, and while I was showering, I had time to think about the day. Hans was interesting. He'd made it clear that trust was a big issue. Only time would cure that one. I would do what was necessary to convince him trusting me was a good idea.

Felicity was a different matter. I'd fallen in love with her, though I still didn't want to admit it. The heart has a way of doing what it wants despite our best intentions. Certainly, I was not immune to her charms, physical and otherwise, but she was keeping secrets from me—fighting with something. All I could do was let her sort it out. Patience. I hoped it worked out for both of us.

Alistair Brown, a name from my past pre prison life. I'd always liked him. We'd actually been close at one time. That was long before he escaped to Paris to find fame and fortune, and he seemed to have found it. I was curious what in his voice had triggered a warning in me. Thinking done. There was nothing I could do until he told me.

All in all, the shower felt good. I dried off and dressed for the night.

I tapped on Felicity's door. "Almost ready," she called before she opened the door.

As she tied and retied her recent Hermes acquisition, she studied her handiwork. Nice shirt, great jeans, all set off with the scarf, she looked satisfied that she represented Parisian chic adequately. Then she kissed me.

Wow.

We went down to reception and collected the address of the restaurant that Alistair had chosen. The receptionist handed me a folded piece of paper with a smile, saying, "Your friend has good, if expensive taste. Bon appetite."

We took a Lyft to the chosen restaurant. Goumard. As a student, I had gazed in the window sniffing the fragrant food scents with no way to afforded them then. We were early and sat at the bar waiting for Alistair. He rushed in, just on time while apologizing. "Time got away from me."

He was effusive as he told us, "I was in two minds about where we should dine. A toss-up. It was between Le Grand Vefour and here. Having a vague memory of you saying you wanted to eat here when you made it...here we are. Beats fish and chips in newspaper huh?"

His laugh was infectious, and yet still I felt the undertow of something unsaid.

We took our drinks to our table, enjoyed the conversation. It flowed with the wine, and the glorious food, and Alistair was charming. We included Felicity in the reminiscences, making her laugh. Mostly at my expense, but I had no problem with that. The food was exceptional, and toward the end of the meal, Felicity excused herself.

As soon as she left, Alistair became serious and said, "Peter I need to talk to you in private. Can we meet tomorrow?"

"No. We are leaving for home tomorrow morning. Why the urgency?"

"Can I call you next week? Or would you mind if I visited you in London? I would rather do this face to face."

"What's this all about, and why can't you tell me

now?"

"It's complicated, and it involves Fentiman."

I exhaled sharply. That came out of left field. Fentiman was one person I didn't want anything to do with. "I don't want anything to do with that son of a bitch. He's already screwed up my life enough," I said coldly.

"I know. That's why I need to talk to you. Felicity is coming back. Can I call you? Please."

"Call me next week at the shop."

Giving him my card, we put smiles on our faces to welcome Felicity back. The rest of the meal went smoothly, as if nothing had occurred. Alistair, as promised picked up the tab. We parted with promises of talking the following week. Felicity questioned that. Palming her off, I said it was just us reconnecting, and that Alistair was thinking of getting a place in London. He asked me if he could crash at my place while he looked about for a place of his own. The lie slipped off my tongue easily, and was believable. She took the lie.

We walked back to the closest Metro station. She slipped her arm through mine, and we snuggled as we walked. Pushing Alistair to the back of my mind, tonight I had other things more to the fore, and they were all Felicity.

Going up to our rooms, I stopped in front of mine, and held Felicity's hand. Face to face, I smiled, and she nodded. We entered my room and kissed, slowly and longingly. Without rush or fuss, we undressed each other, taking turns to remove our clothes. Caressing each other as we did, exploring each other's body.

When we were naked, I stared down at her then kissed her neck. She shuddered. Moving slowly downward, I took turns kissing her hardened nipples puckering her pebbled aureole. I heard a sharp intake of breath, and the slow hiss as she exhaled and relaxed into the moment. Kneeling in front of her, my mouth found her belly button which I explored with my tongue. This brought another low moan from her.

Erect at the sight and feel of her body, the sounds coming from her had me ready. I was not going to rush the pleasure. I nuzzled her mound, teasing her curly trimmed hair, inhaling her fragrance, and exhaling a moan of my own.

She grabbed my head for balance and locked her fingers in my hair. Pushing her hips forward, she pulled my face deeper against her. Felicity began to rub herself all over me, as I lapped her with my tongue. Her legs began to tremble, then she quickly pushed me away and sank to her knees.

Kissing with more ardor, she encouraged me to stand.

When I did, she gripped my rigid cock with one hand and took my balls with the other. Felicity took me deeper and deeper into her mouth. Her lips and tongue worked magic on my cock. Slathering me with saliva, she slid her hand up and down, and her mouth made soft sucking noises.

Hard as I could ever remember being, I couldn't wait. I wanted to be inside her. As the thought struck me, Felicity said, "I want you to fill me."

Helping her off the floor, we supported each other, staggering unsteadily to the bed. We ripped back the covers and fell onto the fresh sheets. I landed with my back on the bed, and Felicity climbed on top of me.

Sliding down until she straddled me. Situated

above my erection, she settled back down until I filled her. The tight, warm sheath felt perfect surrounding me.

With her eyes clamped shut, she started to ride me. Clearly focused on the rhythm and pleasure, I watched her move up and down with her breasts bouncing in rhythm. Even in the dim light of the room, she bewitched me. Remaining as still as a rock, I enjoyed every moment of every sensation.

She squealed and stopped, rigid, collapsing on my chest. When she tried to roll to one side, I spread her legs wider, and sank back into her warm channel. Pushing in and out of her, I kept pace with her chanting. "Yes, yes deeper."

Picking up the pace, I thrust more forcefully against her, and she began to groan—low, deep moans. Her tightness gripped my length, but the blunt head of my dick was in her so deep, I didn't know where one of us began and the other stopped. Feeling the tension in my balls, the ultimate contraction, I rose up to finish—unloading inside her as deep as I could, again and again.

Felicity let out a long low, heart-rending sigh. Then as her rapid breathing subsided, we collapsed, physically spent. We rolled to one side, and I managed to stay in her as she pushed back against me. Cuddling, we fell asleep.

I awoke alone in the bed. Coming to, I heard the water running. I got out of bed and joined Felicity in the shower. The hot water brought me fully awake, and I appreciated her body. Touching her all over, as the water ran off in rivulets, we washed our lovemaking off each other, sensually taking our time. For all my foreboding, I felt at ease with this woman in a way I'd never felt with anyone before.

Felicity returned to her room to pack, and I dried off and did the same. Later we had breakfast with Yvette and Martine. In the course of the conversation, when I thanked Yvette for contacting Alistair on my behalf, she looked a little abashed.

"I was not sure you would want to speak to im. You two were such good friends, I ad to try." She gave a Gallic shrug, as if it were the only logical thing to do.

The fact he had brought up Fentiman's name bothered me. I'd have to wait and see what Alistair wanted. I was not in a rush to find out.

The breakfast was easy and the conversation the same. Martine said she was going out sketching. There were too many tourists in the galleries on Sunday to concentrate. She said she hoped we would visit Paris again soon, looking pointedly at both Felicity and me.

****

Packed and ready, we left Yvette with hugs and promises we would stay in touch, and I meant it. The trip home was an easy one. Felicity was quiet, napping for some time, and our conversation in-between was sporadic and comfortable.

Once we reached London, I asked if she wanted me to see her home, but she declined saying the next day would be a busy day. Parting at the station would be easier than at her apartment. I did not want to leave her.

My apartment seemed emptier than usual when I arrived home. I already missed Felicity's presence. After unpacking, I called George for a short conversation. Briefly we agreed to meet at the shop first thing.

Chapter Eighteen

Monday crept around like a shroud. The weather, after the sunny days in Paris, was typical, bloody awful English weather. Overcast and gray, it was miserable without being truly horrible. Feeling hung over, cranky, and miserable for no good reason, breakfast and coffee was going to be picked up on the way in.

George was already involved when I arrived. His greeting was much too bright and happy for my mood as he busied himself eating, drinking tea, and translating the papers he had collected in Berlin. Continuously referring to his notes, he ignored my mood and, I must admit, his demeanor eventually cheered me up. His enthusiasm about what he'd discovered tugged my frown into a smile, even going into the story of how he had charmed the assistant into giving him the copies he requested at no charge.

Oh no wonder the good mood...he'd got laid. Although it had cost him dinner, he said it was worth it, with a wink. Go you, George!

Unveiling the two prints I purchased in Paris, he was impressed. Especially, when I told him how much I paid for them. The day was getting better.

Leaving George to carry on with his translations, I dealt with all the customers. Business was busier than usual for a Monday, but I wasn't complaining, and by lunchtime, George had done enough for us to sit, eat, and go over our individual adventures.

Starting, I relayed the shocking news about the Louvre. "When Martine revealed the storeroom was empty, I began to think we were on a fool's errand. That led me to think the paintings could be at the bank."

Going through the trip in chronological order, I told him about how I had persuaded Felicity to go to the flea market solo, and then how I used that time to visit the address in the music box. Pausing for effect, I revealed it was Hans, Otto's older brother. I went into details of that conversation, ending with news that Hans would be visiting us soon.

George was excited about that development and related what he'd found. "Thank God for German efficiency. They had a stack of documents relating to the occupation of France and Paris in particular. As I wasn't looking for dirt, or military stuff, they were very forthcoming with the records. The archivist was very helpful. Everything Otto told you about his father's work and the events is true. The group fell under the Ministry of Propaganda, where they all originally worked. They were farmed out when the need for propaganda decreased. They copied a huge number of paintings, all listed and documented as to where the original went and where the copy was, and who had painted it. Everything was documented down to the last detail."

He paused for breath before continuing. "There were some interesting details. The French government was obviously very happy to get the originals repatriated after the war. Each and every painting was returned to its place of origin and, due to the vast number, only superficially examined. However, there were a number of missing paintings in the documentation, meaning the originals never left Paris. That fits in with the info from Otto. The artists substituted the fakes before shipping. Official docs and sources confirm everything Otto told you. My question is what do we do now if the paintings are the copies? Where does that leave us?"

I'd been thinking about that issue a lot. "George, let me finish before you say anything. If you were the post war government of France, after having your national treasures looted and taken in the thousands, and you discovered you were getting them back by the railcar load, would you be looking at the ones that never left the walls of the Louvre or the ones that were taken and were being returned?"

"The ones coming back of course—to make sure everything was kosher and to check for damage, etcetera. What are you getting at?"

"I may be nuts…but hear me out. Consider this option. No one ever examined the paintings that never left the Louvre. What if Otto's father and crew switched the originals for the copies? They had the originals and left the copies hanging in the Louvre. Why would anyone check? Once Paris was liberated, Otto's father and crew became prisoners. Those paintings would be in limbo, neither in the Louvre nor in Germany."

"Come on, Peter, the Louvre curators must have examined the paintings since their return, if only for cleaning," George said.

"But if no one expected a fake, why would they look for it? The artists who copied the paintings were very talented—at the top of their game. They would have used the same types of paint used by the original artists. Most of the paintings on that list are on panel. Easy enough to get the correct wood from old houses and religious buildings of the time period. Even with today's forensics, the wood would match the period perfectly, and why would anyone do that unless suspicions were aroused. The curators would have had such a workload checking everything, the last thing they needed on their plate was to check works that were left in place. The Louvre is so massive it would have been an immense task, impossible to undertake."

We were silent. Having said it out-loud, it sounded implausible—ridiculous even to me.

A frown crossed Georges face. "Yes, it sounds nuts, but if it's true…" he said, then paused again. "We are in over our heads. If you are right, we will be sitting on sixteen priceless treasures. We need to think this through."

"I agree, and that is what I will do when I chat with Hans."

"When is he coming?"

"Don't know, he was kinda vague, and I didn't push him on it. I think with Hans, patience will be rewarded. Oh, by the way, I almost forgot, I contacted an old friend in Paris."

"Who was that?"

"Alistair Brown. Before your time, I think. He dropped out of college and moved to Paris before he graduated."

"The name rings a bell. Can't say I ever met him. What happened? Did you meet?"

"Yes, he took us to dinner. Looking back, it was kind of over the top." I paused, and thought back on what he'd said when Felicity left us. "He mentioned he wanted to talk to me, privately, and mentioned Fentiman's name. He is supposed to call me this week."

George looked up sharply. "Fentiman, why did he want to talk to you about Fentiman?"

"He didn't or couldn't say. I'll wait for him to contact me. I am not going out of my way to talk about that bastard."

We returned to shop business and dealt with our customers. In between, we did the usual chores of book keeping, inventory, and keeping the place clean and tidy. The mystery Otto had set me on was never far from my thoughts. One valuable thing that prison taught me was patience. Hans would show up when he decided to show up. Alistair would call when he would call. Running various scenarios through my mind, all came out to the same-dead end. There was something telling me this was a big one—so big I could not fail to resolve it.

We settled back into working and I, my usual boring life style. Still, I kept an eye out for anyone playing silly buggers following us.

Tel came back weekly to check on my apartment. It had been debugged. We assumed it had been Allen Warren working off the books. Tel also thanked me on behalf of the "driver" and said if I ever needed a driver, or "anyfin else ta giv-im a bell."

Thanking him, I said I would.

The days passed and there was no call from Alistair. In a way, I was relieved. No contact from Hans, either. Figuring he was testing me to see how long I would last before calling him. I was up for that challenge. I wouldn't blink first.

Felicity and I met when we could. She stayed over

at my place. Me staying at hers was a rarer occurrence. It seemed odd at first. Hers was a much nicer apartment. But she said she just preferred seeing me in my own space. We were spending time together. I wasn't going to argue the point.

I used the post cards I bought in Paris to send her quick notes, saying things like…*your perfume reminds me of Paris*, or *I miss your smile*, and *you are always in my thoughts*.

She thought they were romantic. Maybe it was. I just needed to do it.

We had been back three weeks, and we were opening the shop on Monday when my phone, my second phone, went off. *Hans. Finally.*

"Good morning, I was beginning to think you had forgotten me," I said it with a laugh of relief.

"Certainly not. I had some business matters come up, which I had to be deal with promptly. One I would like to discuss with you when I come to London. That is the reason for my call. Would you be available? Say Wednesday?"

"Wednesday would be fine, nothing going on that I can't rearrange. Do you want to meet at the shop or where you are staying?"

"I will advise on my hotel when I am checked in. Dinner will be my treat."

"I will look forward to hearing from you. Safe travels."

"Thank you. I appreciate your good wishes."

That had to be one of the strangest and most innocuous calls I had ever had. No names, no locations, no times. Anyone listening would have nothing, except a day and not even sure if it was this week, next week, or next month. Hans was certainly careful.

Almost as soon as my call with Hans ended, my other phone went off. A Paris number I didn't recognize. I answered. It was Alistair, and he jumped in before I could say anything.

"Sorry about the delay. Got caught up in something, then work, a right fucking mess. Can I come and see you? I am going to be in London later this week, probably Thursday, latest Friday. I'll be staying in the West end or maybe Bloomsbury. I am not sure yet. Anyway, can we meet? I really do need to talk to you."

He stopped for a breath. He sounded like he needed it. The way he went on caught my attention. This was not like him at all. He sounded frantic, and that was the opposite of the Alistair I had known.

Maybe I would regret it, but I said, "Sure, Friday would be better for me. After we close up the shop. Let me know where you are staying, and we'll meet. Call or text this number."

"Thank you. I really appreciate this. Cheers mate. See you Friday." The difference in his voice was remarkable, all I had done was agree to meet and have a chat.

Little did I know, my life was about to get more complicated in ways I couldn't imagine. Sometimes karma works in mysterious ways.

Tuesday dragged by like a holiday with unpleasant relatives. Wednesday arrived with a sense of anticipation. Up and in the shop early, I felt antsy, not sure what time Hans would be in London, just that it would be today. I found it hard to concentrate. I puttered about pointlessly, sorting things that didn't need sorting and polishing things that were spotless.

George told me to calm down. "It's Hans playing silly buggers again." George was probably right. That didn't make it any better.

I was thinking about lunch when Hans's call came in. "I apologize. My flight was delayed. I am staying at Claridge's on Brook Street. You know it?"

Yeah sure, I knew it, a five-star hotel way out of my price range. I probably couldn't afford to eat there, never mind stay there. Had to be five hundred pounds a night and up.

"Yes, I know where it is."

"Good, shall we say six tonight in the bar? We can go from there to dine. I will book somewhere appropriate."

"Six is fine. See you then.

Hans hung up, and I swore under my breath. Framed, did prison time, and it seemed all the people I knew who were involved with the art world were making scads of money. Legal or otherwise and staying in fancy hotels. Alistair was doing well living in Paris. Well, whatever restaurant Hans had reserved for dinner, I was ordering the most expensive thing on the menu.

Chapter Nineteen

The short call with Hans calmed me down. We were moving forward. The rest of the day passed uneventfully. I said goodnight to George, and left to meet Hans at his hotel. Using the tube, I got off at Oxford Street and walked the rest of the way. I made good time and arrived early.

I waited at the bar, sipping my overpriced gin and tonic, and positioned myself so I could see who came and went. About halfway through my drink, Hans walked in, looking like he owned the place. The man was dapperly dressed in a three-piece suit, a shirt and tie that would definitely attract attention, cufflinks that were obviously expensive but subtly so, and shoes buffed to a mirrored polish. In comparison, I was drab and felt it.

He waved when he saw me and came directly over. We shook hands then he took the seat next to me and ordered a dry sherry. I waited for him to start.

"Peter, I do apologize for the way I have behaved recently. As I am sure, you have correctly assumed I have been testing you. This has not been easy for me, losing my brother, and a specter coming out of the past. Knowing it would happen someday, it's still a shock when it actually does. So, anyway, I have been doing some checking on you."

"And what did you find? Anything of interest?"

"Actually, I did. I do believe you got a raw deal. The evidence against you was not very convincing, especially if you care to take a deeper look at it. Your legal team did a terrible job in your defense—incompetent at best. You should sue them or have them disbarred. However, that is in the past, and perhaps, we can get a modicum of restitution in the future."

"I am listening."

"Not here, Peter. Far too many ears. We have reservations at a nice little restaurant I know just off Bond Street. We can chat as we stroll."

We finished our drinks, which Hans put on his room, and we left for dinner. Hans was right. It was not a long way, a short walk down Bond Street, a quick right onto Bruton Street, and another quick right into Bruton Place. That looked a little dodgy to me.

Separating myself from Hans, I expected the worst. We turned the corner into the main area, and the street opened up. It was well illuminated with multiple other businesses, so I relaxed. The Guinea Grill was about halfway up the street—an old-style pub with a bar in the front, busy with after work socializing. The restaurant was in the back.

Hans declared we had a reservation. The waiter seated us at a small table for two. This early the restaurant was almost empty, only one other couple occupied the dining room. He asked if I would prefer wine or beer.

"Whatever you prefer," I said.

He smiled and told me he preferred beer with steak in England.

"I have no problem with that. The pub has one of my favorite beers on tap. Wells "Bombardier." Good stuff." Looking over the menu, I was glad Hans was picking up the tab. A damned good meal was coming my way.

Our beers arrived, and we placed our order.

Starting with a dozen oysters each, spiked with lemon and pepper sauce, they disappeared in no time, and each tasted better than the previous one. Following the oysters, I had a porterhouse steak, medium rare, roasted potatoes, and seasonal vegetables. Dessert had to be a Crème Brûlée. I really didn't pay any attention to what Hans ordered, concentrating on savoring every mouthful of my dinner.

Our conversation during the meal was as sporadic, as it was generic.

When the waiter cleared our dessert plates, he took our after-dinner drink orders. The waiter returned shortly with our drinks, 1975 Fonseca reserve Port. The waiter left the decanter at Han's insistence.

We were silent until the waiter left. Then Hans started by silently sliding a photograph across the table to me. I picked it up. It was a photograph of a painting I immediately recognized. What caught my attention was the newspaper resting in front of it. A copy of yesterdays' Le Monde newspaper, the date was clearly visible.

Stunned, I was looking at a photograph of Bosch's The Ship of Fools. With proof that Hans had access to the paintings, or at least to one on the list. The question now was, was it copy or an original.

Calmly I addressed Hans, "Very nice. So is that one of one fake, or one of more?"

"Peter, so cynical for one so young." He smiled and continued, "One of more. You know the number, and that is not important for now. I wanted to show some good faith, hence the one painting. I knew you would recognize it. Using the newspaper was a little ostentatious, but it works in kidnap situations."

"Hans, I have also done some research. The information Otto left me regarding his father's, your father's activities, has all proven to be true. The only exception is there are no records of the list of paintings left by Otto being moved or transferred. I have some ideas about that, but I would prefer to hear it from you if you will tell me."

"My brother was right to trust you. You think things through. As far as I know, from the story our father told me, is that it went like this…"

"The war was not going well for the Nazis. My father and his associates decided to change things up. The Nazi party had turned these men into criminals for and by the state. They realized they couldn't do much, and if caught, it would be a death sentence. They selected a number of paintings—the smaller ones because they're easier to work with—switched out the real paintings from their frames, and substituted the copies into the original frame. Putting the real paintings in new frames, they stored them in the work in progress area, away from the main collection point. One of the artists took a huge risk and snuck the paintings out of the Louvre, one by one. It became easier due to the lack of supervision. Troops were drafted back to fight the advancing Allies, so there were fewer soldiers guarding them. They secreted the paintings away. Only three people knew the location. The plan was to either sell them or ransom them back to the French Government.

"The allies liberated Paris, and my father and his

associates surrendered. Sent to different holding places, they lost touch. On his release, he tried to contact the others. Both had died, one in a car accident, the other one caught and died of pneumonia. That left only my father with the secret. He made sure to preserve them. The bank vault was temperature controlled with a stable humidity. They were safe until he could figure out what to do. He collected all the paintings stored in the bank but never figured out what to do with them once he had them.

"He had assumed a French identity by that time and was working for the criminal element that rose up after the war. When I found my parents, they were an established family. I lived with them and took on the role of cousin from Alsace's identity. Without the artistic talent of my father or Otto, my talents relied on a good eye and sales. I did the negotiating and selling. I am sure you know some of this already?"

I ran a hand through my hair and said, "Yes, but it's always better to hear it firsthand."

"Agreed. Anyway, I could sell, so I started dealing for myself. Anything, prints, posters, paintings, and sculpture, whatever I could buy discounted and turn a profit. Some of the pieces I handled, I wanted to keep. I truly loved some of them, but back then I did not have the luxury of keeping them as I do now. I have been successful. I have Galleries in Paris, Berlin and Zurich."

Hans stopped, lost in thought, and I remained silent, trying to wrap my head around the fact I had been right. The painting or paintings in Hans's possession were the originals. This was a major mind-fuck. Each one would be worth a king's ransom.

Together they formed a prized collection that no one museum could afford. Hans came back to the present.

"I have been a curator for these treasures. I can't just give these pieces back without answering too many questions—answers I cannot provide, or answers I am unwilling to give. Otto was closer to the source than I was. I will follow your lead on this, as he chose you to resolve the problem. But I must warn you, I will look after myself first and foremost, whatever happens."

He looked directly at me, warning me, and meant it.

"Why didn't your father complete his plan for the paintings?"

"I am not sure. I think it was because he was reunited with my mother, and they built a new life. He wanted to leave the war behind. That is all supposition. I never asked, and he never said."

"Hans, I don't know what I am going to do...yet. I still need proof that you have all the named items. One with a newspaper in front of it does not make a collection. It makes a start." I paused. "I appreciate your honesty warning me you will be loyal only to yourself. I don't blame you."

"Thank you, Peter. It may be selfish, but I have no wish to experience prison in any country. However, I will help you in any way I can with finance, contacts, information...when you have a plan I can agree to."

"Nothing like tying my hands. I doubt I will need financial assistance, but I will take everything else. One thing I will insist on..."

Leaving that hang, Hans finally asked, "I assume you would like to see all the additional pieces?"

"Correct."

"Well then, you had better come up with a plan on how to return them to the correct owner without mentioning me or getting yourself in trouble."

"Are the items readily available for inspection?"

"Yes. It's easily arranged when the time is ready. They are in Paris and safe."

"At short notice?"

"Yes. That will not be an issue."

Coffee arrived, and the waiter cleared the table and left us in peace to our conversation. "Hans, I will insist that whatever I come up with, the conclusion will be in England. Any issues with that?"

"None whatsoever. It could be to your advantage—working on home soil, as it were, and keeping me out of it. I do hope you create a solid plan regarding how to get the items from Paris to London safely. I would hate for anything to happen to them after all this time."

"Don't worry about that. If I can work it out to my satisfaction, they will be treated like the treasures they are. You are confirming they are the real thing and not copies?"

"Confirmed, Peter. They are all originals. As I said, I am willing to show them to you, and only you…in person."

"Fair enough. This could take some time."

"I am in no rush. Better safe than sorry. There is another item I would like to put to you if you have the time?"

"Sure, what is it?"

"As I said, I have been successful—am successful. I am looking to expand to a fourth location. New York is too expensive and too far. That leaves London which as the financial center of Europe makes more sense. If the current project is brought to a satisfactory conclusion, I would like you to consider working with me. I plan on opening a gallery here in London. Would that be something of interest to you?"

Where the hell did that come from? He didn't really know me from Adam, and Hans did not seem the kind of man to take someone on trust.

"You're kidding, right?"

"No, not kidding you. It all depends on how you perform with our current issue. If as I suspect, you will be successful, we can go forward. If not, I will have lost nothing, and you will probably be in jail somewhere."

"Well thank you for the vote of confidence."

"Please do not mistake me. I expect and want you to succeed. I am looking for proof that you will be a good investment. Shall we?"

Hans stood. This meeting was obviously over. Hans certainly knew how to keep me off balance. That was an offer I could not ignore, but I was loyal to George. He was the only one who had given me a hand, and I was not going to turn and bite it. Another damned dilemma.

Exiting the pub, Hans and I shook hands. I told him I'd be in touch as soon as I formulated plans for going forward. He said he looked forward to hearing from me when appropriate. We parted, and he strode back to Claridge's.

I walked to Berkeley Square, picked up a cab, and watched the London nightlife pass as the cab took me home. The cab was like a cocoon insulating me from the outside world. Almost in a dream, I pondered Hans's confirmation. The paintings were the real thing.

After reaching home, I reviewed the list of

paintings copied from Otto's original papers. They all popped off the page. Raphael, Vermeer, Fragonard... They just could be returned to the Louvre anonymously. I didn't like that idea. Selling them on the black market was a non-starter. I had no idea how to do that.

Knowing I would think better after a good night's sleep, I crashed into bed.

When that didn't work out, tossing and turning all night, I'd slept like crap and gave up. Feeling fuzzy, I dragged myself to the shop to quickly sort out Otto's history. The shop was my comfort zone. I wandered about looking at the items we had in stock, viewing them not as items, but the history they represented. Who had owned the pieces, cherished them, and parted with them—gladly or sadly. They represented the physical history of humanity.

I decided the entire cache had to be returned to the Louvre. Once I made that decision, I felt a sense of relief. It was the right thing to do. Now to figure out the best way to do it without involving Hans or having to answer too many questions. My cell jingled to life. A Paris number. Alistair.

I answered, but before I could say anything, Alistair said, "Peter, hi, it's me. Are we still on for my visit? I will be arriving Friday late. Can we still meet? I will come to you to save you a trip. Would that work?"

"Sure, depending on how late."

"Probably no later than nine, maybe nine-thirty, latest. I will come straight from the airport, and I'm flying into London not Heathrow."

"That's fine."

Perhaps it was my tone of voice or just being tired.

Alistair picked up on it asked, "Peter? You okay? If you don't want to meet, I understand. You're doing me the favor."

"Yes, I'm fine. Bad night of not sleeping, up early, and cranky. It's fine. Call me when you're on your way. You have my home address?"

"No."

"I'll text the address."

"Thanks, Peter. I really do appreciate this."

"Sure, no problem. I'll see you then. Safe travels."

A quick thanks, and he was gone. Why would he want to talk to me about Fentiman? He knew my history with that bastard. Pushing that out of my mind, I continued with my problem of the paintings. Nothing was coming to me.

George yelled out a *hello* and commented on my early arrival, again. I told him what Hans told me the previous night, about the paintings being the originals.

He asked, "Is it possible?"

I shrugged. "I have no reason not to believe him."

"That puts a different complexion on this matter. It takes it completely out of our league."

"How so?"

"How do you think the authorities would react if they discovered that sixteen of the world's greatest paintings hanging in their museum are fake? I think it's not information they want leaking out to the public. It also means the originals are somewhere else, not secure, and perhaps available to steal or buy."

"Good point. Some of these illegal sales make millions. Only Hans knows where the originals are."

"Peter, as soon as you know, that means *we* could be in danger. Tread carefully, okay?"

"Yes, I will. I have already decided they have to be returned to the Louvre. I'm just not sure how to get that done."

"Well, anything I can do, I will. Got it partner?"

"Yes, got it. Thanks, George."

The rest of the day was busy—too busy for me to waste time on something I didn't have an answer for. What George said made sense. Fentiman had a hand in that business, and knowing firsthand how illegal sales made money, I paid the price.

That evening at home, an idea hit me! Could I somehow use his knowledge of the illegal art market to get revenge for what he had done to me? That would be a dangerous ploy, and I was not sure if it would be worth it. That idea did tickle my fancy, though. I chuckled to myself, imagining Fentiman being arrested and going to prison.

Shaking my head, I brought myself back to reality, and I considered what Hans had told me. When no ideas jelled, I went to bed.

Friday came and went just like any other day. George was in and out, customers came and went, and I was busy enough not to think of Alistair until I got home.

Chapter Twenty

Dinner was takeout, again. I didn't feel like cooking. I hadn't felt like doing a lot of my usual things, lately.

Felicity called. We talked for a few minutes before she had to go. She and her co-workers were celebrating something. After saying I missed her and good night, we promised to catch up the next day. I looked over some art books, turned on some music, but nothing hit the spot.

Alistair's visit disturbed me. His mentioning Fentiman, my Achilles heel, caught me off guard. I was anxious and the realization that I couldn't or wouldn't back out now had me on a fine edge. My phone dinged.

Alistair's text said he was on his way.

I paced the floor. Receiving the text made it worse. It was useless to worry, but that didn't stop me. Finally my doorbell rang. I checked the peephole, recognized Alistair, and buzzed him in.

"Thank you for seeing me. I need your advice."

"Come in, drink?"

"Yes, got any English beer? That's the one thing I miss in Paris." He looked nervous, on edge, what the hell was going on?

I fetched a couple of bottles of Wadworth 6X beer, popped off the caps, then handed him the bottle and a glass. We were silent while we poured.

Seated across from each other, I waited for him to start.

"Peter, I didn't know who to talk to. I'm in deep shit, and you are the only person I know who knows Fentiman."

I stayed silent waiting for the story.

Alistair took a long swig of beer, smacking his lips in appreciation, and then he started to speak. "It started after I exhibited in Paris, and I sold quite well. I was getting a reputation, and things were looking good. I had representation in Paris. It was only business, nothing personal, but the agent did a good job even though I wasn't a big earner for him.

"Anyway, after my third exhibition, Fentiman contacted me out of the blue. He said he'd been watching me and liked the direction my work was going. This all happened a while after your arrest. He said he wanted to represent me in the UK and asked if I would be open to that? Well, of course I would. He had a Bond Street gallery. I am an artist not an idiot. I went over the deal. It looked fine. I signed it, and he's done well for me."

He stopped talking, gathering his thoughts.

I went to pick up two more beers, returned, and put one down by his almost empty glass.

"Thanks. After about a year, Fentiman said he wanted me to change the shipping agent who did all the logistics for getting my work to London. I didn't care who took care of that as long as I didn't have to. They have been fine to work with. Then about a year or so after that Fentiman said he thought it would be a good idea to change the company who did my frames. He recommended one for the UK market. I didn't like that idea since I've been very happy with the company I use. They are an old family company and have been around since the impressionists were being laughed at. I dug my heels in on that one and said no. He left it for a while, and I thought that was it. Wrong. Soon he pushed again and said I should try this new company. Just give them a couple of paintings to see how it worked out, and only for the UK market. Fentiman was very specific on that point, saying he didn't want to impinge on my French representation. Only recently did I discover the real reason he wanted me to use this company."

I listened attentively, and urged him to go on.

"The process I follow is simple. I finish a painting and talk to the framers, and we decide which frame will work best with that particular work. I kept the same process with the new framer. Well, a few weeks ago, we had decided which frame would be the right one for a recent work, but I was of two minds. I wasn't happy with my first decision, so I went to the framer. They were at lunch when I arrived, and an assistant let me in. I took the painting back to my studio to review it in my own time. The painting felt odd weight wise, too heavy for the type of frame we had chosen. Taking off the backing, I noticed a thin layer of wood had been attached to the back of the frame. The wood was thin enough not to be obvious, unless you knew what you were looking at. I know my frames. This was not right. The wood layer came off easily.

"Gouged into the frame under the wood ran a channel, and it contained a long thin plastic tube filled with tablets. I never did drugs. I didn't know what they were. I just knew this was something illicit. I covered it up in a panic, knowing if they found out what I'd discovered, I'd be in trouble. I made sure it was exactly as I had found it and just in time. Someone from the framer came by acting very nervous. He said the painting was their responsibility until shipping was complete, and if I wanted to review anything, it had to be at their workshop. He checked it over thoroughly and took it away.

"I called Fentiman. He said not to worry, he would take care of everything. He sure did. A few days later he called me and said unless I kept my mouth shut I would encounter an accident or be arrested for drug trafficking. Then once in jail, I would meet with a fatal accident.

"When you called out of the blue it was fate. I need your advice, Peter." He finished his tale, slumped into the chair, and stared at the remains of his beer.

I sat back in my chair thinking, here is another life at risk due to Fentiman. The bile rose in my throat.

Alistair finished his beer in a gulp and asked, "What the hell am I going to do? I can't keep quiet, but if I don't Fentiman will do what he threatened."

"Hold on, Alistair. Is there any way you can get out of your contract with him?"

"Yes, two ways—a buyout clause, which I can't afford, or a breach of contract. If Fentiman can't or won't meet his contractual obligations to three exhibitions a year, that breaks it. They don't have to be full blown exhibitions. He can do anything from a full gallery showing to a mere five piece showing. Five is the minimum obligation."

"So if he doesn't give you the minimum three shows a year that voids the contract?"

"Yes, unless we come to a prior arrangement and both sides agree. This has never been an issue. Fentiman has always given me the shows and space."

"What happens if you don't come up with enough work for him to show?"

"Then he's out of the three shows a year contract, but I have to live up to my end and supply him with works until I'm caught up."

"A bit one-sided isn't it?"

"I suppose so. I never thought about it being a problem. I'm pretty prolific, and a minimum of fifteen paintings a year for UK was not going to be an issue. I usually had more than enough for both of them to select what they wanted. What do you think I should do? I'm sorry I came to you, but I had to tell someone."

"Yeah, no worries. First thing you do is write it all down, date it, and put it somewhere safe. Second, do not trust Fentiman at all. Third, be very careful about what you say to anyone. In fact, don't say anything to anyone about this. Carry on as if you are complying with Fentiman. By the way, why are you in London?"

"To finalize the arrangements for my new exhibition. My second of the year is coming up soon. In his favor, he has sold me well in the UK."

"Only because it benefits him. He doesn't give a damn about art or artists. Making money is his only concern. You're a product he sells—no more, no less. Same as the dope he's smuggling."

"I hadn't really thought about it that way. Still, what am I going to do?"

"Like I said. Just carry on and comply with whatever he asks. Make sure you document it all, every detail, gotta cover the bum. I know what I said isn't much help. Be patient, something will turn up."

"Peter, thanks for listening. I feel better just having shared it with someone."

"No problem. But you haven't told me anything, about anything, understand?"

"Sure, I get it."

"If anything happens, call me…anytime okay?"

"Yes, I will. Thanks again. I better go."

After we said our goodbyes, I began to wonder if I could help Alistair and benefit myself at the same time—kill two birds with one stone as it were. One thing was certain—if I was going to be the one taking all the risks, I was going to be the one in charge. I placed a call to Hans, not expecting him to pick up at this time of night, but he did.

"Good evening, I hope I am not disturbing you?"

"No, I assume this is urgent?"

"It is to me. I need to visit you as we discussed. If not, then our association is finished. I am going to be the one running this or not involved at all."

"Well that is a change, though not unexpected." He laughed. "I was waiting for you to drop out or take full ownership. I hoped this would be the choice. Please come as soon as you want. I keep my promises."

"Thank you. Am I that easy to read?"

"Not really. Dealt a crappy hand, you paid a heavy price. But you are stronger than you imagine. It did not damage you too badly—not the real you. You picked up a hard shell, that's all. Remember, I sell for a living, and I am very good at reading people. I also had the advantage of knowing our mutual connection trusted you. If he did, I would, to a degree. I look forward to seeing you soon." Hans hung up.

I looked at the phone. *Shit*. I needed to get myself together and sort out a ton of details. Now I knew what I wanted the end result to be, the result would need creative planning and luck to get there. The germ of an idea about how to achieve my intended result had implanted itself in my thoughts. It would include Hans, George, and Alistair. Around Felicity, I would have to be careful with some of the less legal components of what I intended to do.

I needed more information, the sort picked up from another prison connection who I'd put off contacting. Jacob Cohen, a spritely old Jew, an entrepreneur for want of a better description, was my answer. He had done time, taking the place of one of his sons. We met accidentally when a couple of white nationalist thugs harassed him. Three of us stepped in and warned off the two anti-Semitic idiots. Jacob was thankful, and the four of us took to playing chess. That is to say, three of us tried, and Jacob thrashed us every game. We improved immensely, however we always lost to Jacob. Our conversations were always interesting and encompassed a wide range of topics. But just prior to my release, Jacob told me if I ever needed information to contact him. What he meant, I wasn't sure. Now I would find out.

Calling Jacob turned out to be more difficult than I thought. After being on hold, disconnected, on hold, I was put through to a wrong extension. Finally, I was told he was not available, but he would return my call soon. No actual timeline was mentioned, and the line went dead.

Frustrated, I opened the shop and made a flight reservation to Paris. I called Felicity and told her I had a business trip to Paris coming up and would be gone for a couple of days. She had a museum visit up north in the coming days, so the timing worked out well, and we agreed to meet that night. I needed to resolve some questions before I told her anything, even though I wanted to tell her everything. Until I heard back from Jacob, I couldn't. I hoped he was as good as his word.

George was curious about my visit to Paris, and he asked why so soon. I told him what it was about in generalities, not wanting to say too much in case it didn't go the way I planned. He said he understood. If so, then he has more patience than I do.

My new phone buzzed alive, and I answered cautiously.

"Peter, it's been so long. Are you still playing chess or just avoiding another loss. Not so much as a Shalom in how many years?" The same old Jacob, I laughed out loud. He sounded healthier and happier than our last meeting.

"Jacob, you sound well."

"For an old man, not so bad. This is not a social call I assume, and I forgive you. What can I say?"

"You are as perceptive as ever. No this is not a social call. When we last spoke, you mentioned that if I ever needed information, I should call you. Now I am calling you. How does this work?"

"It depends on the situation."

"Urgent."

"Of course it is. It will depend on the difficulties presented. How much and how detailed the requirements, the sourcing and collating of the information, how quickly you need it etcetera. What are you looking for?"

"And the cost?"

"Peter, tell me what you require. Then we will come to an arrangement. You will of course get a discount."

I gave Jacob the details about what I needed on Charles Fentiman, among them were his business holdings, financials, and any offshore accounts. I needed to identify as many of his business partners, contacts, and associates as possible. Jacob offered some suggestions that made sense, so I included them.

Hans was next on my list, but I didn't expect much on him. Alistair Brown too. He was part of getting the big picture, but I wasn't sure how involved he was. I gave to Jacob what I did know. I didn't know his address in Paris, only his cell number, and his French representative's name.

We had almost finished discussing my list, and I had saved one name until last. More out of curiosity than need. I was looking for confirmation.

"This is quite a lot, and some will not be easy. Do you want everything at once, by name or issue?"

"Whatever you think is best. How will you deliver the information?"

"You visit my offices for a face-to-face report. If anything is too important to wait, I will contact you. The final report will also be on a flash drive in the mail, no one messes with the Royal Mail."

"Then please send it to the shop—less chance of it being intercepted."

"As you wish. If you are concerned about security, it can be hand delivered to you personally. Can you tell me what is going on?"

"Probably better if you don't know. Mailing to the

shop will be fine. What will you charge for this service?"

"Don't worry about that now Peter. This is obviously important to you. We can sort financial details out later. I will keep you updated, if necessary, by generic texts. You will get the meaning. It's permissible to use the number you gave my office?"

"Yes, that's the only number to contact me on."

"Very well. I look forward to connecting with you soon."

"I appreciate this, Jacob."

"Think nothing of it, Peter. This is what I do. Shalom"

The last thing I heard was a soft chuckle before we disconnected. Having set the wheels in motion, I wasn't sure what to expect from Jacob, but everything was moving forward. Next step Paris, and I would need Hans to provide the assistance he promised.

The next few days dragged by like a winter week, dull and oppressive. I was packed for Paris since the day I booked the flight. After arriving in Paris, I took the Metro, and reached Yvette's hotel in good time. By chance, my room was the same one where Felicity and I had consummated our relationship. Remembering that night with fondness, I dropped my bag and called Hans who answered on the first ring.

"Welcome back to the City of Light."

"Good to be back, can we meet tonight?"

"Yes, first I will take you to dinner. Then we can discuss what you need, and how I can help. I will text you with the details. Is eight p.m. acceptable?"

"That's fine, see you soon."

Having hours to kill before I met Hans, I decided to

check out some print shops and galleries. I noticed a man I thought I'd seen when I visited the V&A museum. He was across a street from one of the shops I visited. Maybe I was mistaken, maybe not, but this put me in a dilemma. I didn't want anyone to know whom I was meeting in Paris. Time to take a chance and ask a favor.

Alistair answered my call and enthusiastically agreed when I explained what I needed. We arranged a time and place to meet. I did some shopping, buying a wide brimmed hat and a light-colored raincoat. I put my jacket in the shopping bag and continued on to the rendezvous spot. Since I arrived early, I sat at an outside table enjoying a coffee and pastry. Alistair showed up on time going straight inside the café. Finishing my coffee, I sauntered into the café as if to use the toilet. Quickly, Alistair and I switched coats and hats. He put on sunglasses. We are a similar height and build. Unless someone was very close, they would have a hard time telling us apart. Alistair returned to the table where I had been sitting, dressed in my coat and hat.

Not waiting to confirm if the deception had worked, and without looking back, I left the café through a different door. I called Hans while walking to the Metro and told him there had been a change in plans. I would come directly to his gallery and would explain when I saw him.

The metro is an interesting place to hide and people watch, which I did until it was time to meet Hans. Then switching Metro lines randomly, I made certain no one was following me.

Hans looked surprised at how I was dressed. I explained the situation, and he nodded approvingly at my quick and simple solution. Describing my emotions as unsettled was an understatement. I wanted to get down to business and get back to London.

I asked, "Is everything ready?"

"Yes, of course. Please follow me."

Hans led me through the gallery and down into the cellar. The cellar was finished to provide a workspace and storeroom for Hans's inventory. The rooms were nice sized for preparing up-coming exhibitions, or storage for closed exhibitions. They contained adjustable lighting and appeared to be temperature controlled. It was an impressive set up. Having aborted our dinner plans, Hans laid cheese and crusty bread on a platter of cold cuts beside the inevitable bottle of wine, open and ready to drink.

What caught my eye were the opened wall panels. Hanging in the revealed space were paintings which should have been in the Louvre—gems of the artists' genius. My knees trembled, my eyes clouded over, and my breathing turned shallow.

Hans brought me back to earth. "They are beautiful are they not?"

Croaking out a *yes*, I returned to reality. "May I examine them?"

Hans chuckled. "Isn't that why you are here?" He automatically handed me a pair of lint-free gloves.

I put them on and asked another question, hoping he could answer. "Hans, how did your father fool the experts? If the works were examined, it would have been found they were copies."

"You are forgetting German efficiency. They analyzed the colors and pigments and used only what was available at the time. They used the same methods of manufacturing the paint and brushes. You will notice that most of these are on panel, not canvas. Wood from the correct year or close to that of the original is still available in many places in Europe, castles, churches, large family homes, and even on farms. What the Reich wanted the Reich took. Even if today's techniques were used to date the copies, the results would come back as accurate to the time period."

That answered that. Now it was time to ask Hans for assistance. "Hans what I need from you, is the largest and best color photograph you can manage of each individual painting, with a blank or neutral background. The photograph has to be as detailed as possible, showing brushstrokes, everything. Can you do that? And how long will it take?"

Hans pursed his lips and nodded. "Yes, I can provide you with that. They will be digital images of course. Would that be sufficient for your needs?"

"Perfect, but how long?"

"Only a few days, a week at most. I will send the images directly to you, nothing by e-mail. Can you tell me why you need such detailed photographs?"

"Sure, let me examine the paintings. While we eat, I'll fill you in on what I have planned, at least as far as it goes for now."

I worked as quickly as I could. Although I wanted to spend hours with each masterpiece, I suppressed my selfish desire since I was on a timeline and needed to be practical. I handled each one, as if it were the Holy Grail, with reverence and the greatest of care. Examining each of them for any obvious damage, I found none. Hans and the previous caretakers had done an impressive job preserving them. The limited moves and the monitored storage had worked. Now if everything panned out, I would be returning them to their proper home.

Finishing with the last one, I stripped off the gloves, and sat down at the table, joining Hans, who had started nibbling at the refreshments. He started with a question. "So what is your opinion?"

"In awe. First of the works, then the courage it took to salvage them, and you for having the balls to hide them for so long."

"Ha, not so much courage on my part. I could never figure out how to return them without getting caught or involved. Call it self-preservation, but thank you for the compliment. Please help yourself. I am sure you are hungry by now.

Hans was right, I was starving. I hadn't realized how hungry I was until I tucked into the delicious charcuterie and sipped the burgundy he'd poured for me.

Between mouthfuls, I explained what I had in mind. "I need the best images I can get of them because as soon as I can I am going to move the paintings to England, where it will be safer and more efficient for me to work on my home pitch. I plan to use the photographs to make copies by 3D printing the paintings onto wood, since most of the originals are on panel. I'll put the prints in decent frames, *legally* bring them to Paris with paperwork, present them as a new technique in printing. *'Everyone can now own a masterwork.'* When in reality, at the end of my supposed sales trip, we will switch out the 3D prints for the real paintings. I will take the original paintings back to London, legal and above board. The paperwork will prove it. I will store them at a location where they will be secure until we can return them to the proper authorities. You will need to destroy the ones I bring from London. We don't want to leave any trace behind.

"Without what I have seen tonight, everything else would have been moot. There is information I am waiting for. When I have more details, I will let you know, and explain what I hope to achieve."

"Hope to achieve?" Hans sounded uncertain.

"Yes, *hope*. There are a lot of ifs and risks I won't go into until I have a clearer path forward. I promise I will keep you informed."

"That is fair, I suppose."

"Please send over the images as soon as possible. It will take time to produce the copies to the quality I want."

"I assure you they will be with you as quickly as I can do them."

"Thank you. I appreciate the assistance."

Hans walked me to the front door and checked the street before indicating it was safe for me to leave. As soon as I was clear of the door, I heard it shut, and the locks clicked back into place. I went directly back to the hotel, watching for anyone suspicious. Nothing. Alistair was waiting for me, chatting with Yvette in the small bar. His face split into a wide grin and lit up when he saw me.

"You got him. It took him about twenty minutes to realize something was up. He came over to sit next to me and tried starting a conversation. As soon as I answered, he knew I wasn't you. Bit late then. He just cursed, got up, and left. I made my way here and had a nice leisurely dinner with Yvette. Oh, your hat and coat are with the concierge. If I may have my coat back?"

"Of course, and you were a big help. Can't explain now, but I will soon. You'll be interested in a little project I have in mind."

"Good, I could do with something to take my mind off things."

Yvette looked at him with a puzzled frown. He appeared ready to speak until I shook my head. Then he changed the subject. We chatted on for some time before Alistair left, and I begged off, tired.

Once I returned to my room and was safely inside, I called Felicity. She answered sounding tired. When I told her my room number was nineteen, she giggled then said she hoped I was thinking of that night. I said I had a "hard" time not thinking of that night and made her laugh outright. Her laugh always lifted my spirits. We chatted intimately for a few more minutes before she had to go.

"I miss being with you," I confessed. After a moment of silence, she said quietly that she felt the same way. It was an odd ending to a conversation.

I put it down to both of us being apart and tired. Hitting the sheets, my last thoughts focused on how the person tailing me knew I would be in Paris…and where I was staying? Then the blackness of sleep enveloped me.

Waking early the next morning, I breakfasted with Martine before she left for the Louvre. With time remaining before any of the print shops I wanted to visit opened, I took my time having a second café au lait, before leaving the hotel.

Once outside, I casually looked about, not seeing anyone suspicious, and today not caring if they, whoever 'they' were, followed me. The first shop was a bust. Nothing there I liked or could afford and still make a profit. At the second shop, I fared better, making several purchases, all good sellable prints. At the third shop, I hit the jackpot, purchasing a job lot folder of nineteen mixed prints at a good price. One of them had to be a Hogarth. Everything about it was right for a first impression—the ink, the paper, the feel. That one print would pay for everything else, and much more. To celebrate, I had an actual restaurant lunch, rather than the usual café lunch, before returning to the hotel to collect my luggage and head to the airport.

My things were strewn all over the small room. My case was empty, and obviously the person responsible didn't care that I knew. Payback for losing the tail the previous night? Maybe. There was nothing for them to find. Perhaps that frustration was the reason for the mess, or a warning. I gathered my belongings and repacked. At checkout, I asked if there had been any odd happenings. The receptionist said there was an altercation outside earlier. That was the distraction—giving someone time to slip in, get to my room, and do the deed. Someone was still on my case. I wanted—no I needed—the information I'd requested from Jacob. I would call him as soon as I landed in London.

Saying goodbye to Paris is always sad, but as Yvette reminded me, *au revoir* is not forever. "I agree." Then I told her I planned to return soon.

On the way to the airport, I thought about how careful I had to be moving forward, and then I settled in to the airport routine and its usual chaotic mess.

Chapter Twenty-One

The plane was on time, and soon I was in a cab on my way to the shop. I wanted to drop off my purchases and begin checking out the Hogarth print. Jacob had called me while I was in the air. While I enjoyed the cab ride, I returned his call, dialing direct to Jacob.

I began the conversation, circumspect in what I said. "Good to speak with you again."

"Shalom. Would it be possible to call on me? Your choice of this evening or early tomorrow morning."

"Tomorrow would be better. How early?"

"Early as you can make it," Jacob responded. "I do have most of what you requested."

We set a time. "I am looking forward to seeing you."

He responded cryptically, "Be careful what you ask for." Then he closed the call.

His words puzzled me, but that could wait until tomorrow.

Not having a place to store the sixteen masterpieces was becoming frustrating. I had to find a suitable place. The shop was out of the question. Wrong space and way too close to home. Where could I obtain or create a space that would be logistically and sustainable for the paintings? We passed an advertisement for self-storage with twenty-four-hour access, security, and temperature control. Bingo. An anonymous location like that would be all I needed. I could bring in some racks for the paintings, plug in a couple of dehumidifiers, and I was set.

Issue resolved. I stopped briefly at the shop to update George. We were both excited about the Hogarth print. After we closed up, I went directly home.

Closing the door behind me, I dropped my bag and grabbed a beer from the fridge. As the tension melted from my shoulders, I realized how stressful the trip had been. My list for tomorrow included first calling on Jacob. That was my number one priority. The storage unit was number two. Satisfied with where things had settled, I stopped and called Felicity.

She answered on the first ring. "Hi, how was Paris? Profitable, I hope? Missed you."

"That was the best welcome home I've had in a long time."

"Well, if you aren't too tired, I could make it even better!"

"You have no idea how good that sounds. I'll be over in two shakes.'

"Done. I'll have dinner ready for us."

"Don't go to any trouble. I'm beat. I just want to see you."

"Not much. Take out on nice plates."

"Just warning you I have to be up early. There's lots of catching up to do."

"No problem. I am starting a new project, so that works for me."

I hung up and smiled. There hadn't been anyone who cared—well, a female who cared about me in a long time—and I liked it. Before I made my way to

Felicity's apartment, I showered to get rid of the travel dust, and dressed for tomorrow. Parking was the usual bear, and I had a short walk to her apartment. A man came out of her building, I thought he seemed familiar. With the poor light, I could not be sure if it triggered suspicion or paranoia. Either way, I would keep an eye out.

After ringing the bell, the door flew open, and Felicity plastered herself against me. Our lips touched. Breathless she asked, "Dinner, first or after?"

"After."

"Good choice."

We moved like a drunken octopus, undressing each other as we went, staggering and laughing, until, in a tangle of limbs, we finally collapsed on the bed. Catching our breath, we slowed down from the first flush of passion. Our movements became more sensuous and calm. Naked, we hugged, and caressed as if exploring each other for the first time. My cock was erect, and her nipples were hard as buttons. Without preamble, Felicity rolled onto her back, and parted her legs. No written invitation needed. Kneeling up, I moved between her angled legs, and stroked the insides of her thighs. She moaned, and I couldn't hold back. Leaning forward, I moved up into the apex of her triangle, my cock standing out in front of me. She gripped me, slowly rubbing me in her hand, guiding me into her.

When I finally slipped inside her, the sound of us both moaning simultaneously emphasized the appreciation at the feel of being home. I waited as long I could before I moved, savoring the feeling of the warm entrance to her body. Moving slowly, rocking in and out of her, our only connection was my dick inside her. All our senses focused on that joining. Increasing my motion, I began to thrust into her as deeply as I could. Felicity gripped me with the walls of her pussy, making waves along the length of my shaft. She gasped in pleasure.

Wanting to increase those sounds, I listened to her and measured her signals to gauge her pleasure. I kept working her, varying my motion. Usually, I kept my eyes shut during sex, but tonight I could not keep from looking at her, watching the way her body responded.

Her firm tits bounced in rhythm as I plunged inside her, then withdrew. The muscles in her jaw were taught, then relaxed, demonstrating more than basic emotions. Our sexual joining came from somewhere more primal than the usual physical reaction. Her entire body reacted to me, and mine responded in kind.

Felicity's breathing grew more erratic—deep and shallow, long and short—until it eventually shifted to longer and longer intervals. Finally the pressure of her orgasm exploded, and her flesh vice-gripped my cock in its spasms.

Her eyes flew open, and a heart-wrenching moan escaped her lips. She cried out, "Come in me. Come in me now…please."

Her pleading demand pushed me over the edge. Climaxing deep inside her, I kept pumping. We ground harshly against one another, and another orgasm hit her. She bucked her hips, arching under me. Finally spent, we collapsed into each other, our breathing the only sound in our universe. I stayed inside her, recovering while we silently cuddled. There was nothing to say. Eventually we returned to reality.

Felicity broke the spell of silence first. "Peter, that was amazing, the orgasms are getting better, and I didn't think that was possible. Now, I'm hungry! Stay put. I will serve the wanderer returned."

"No argument from me."

Hearing her putter about in the kitchen with the clatter of cutlery, I waited. Soon the aroma of food wafted into the bedroom enticing me to get out of bed. Much to Felicity's delight, I didn't bother dressing. Much to mine she hadn't either. Wearing just an apron looked damned sexy on her. Her breasts slipped out one side or the other, then hid again. Her bum, that firm runner's ass, was framed by the edges of the apron—again, so enticing. I thought we better eat, or I would be more interested in eating her. The food was delicious. The Moussaka and salad tasted like ambrosia. The company, the sex, and my hunger had all been sated at once.

Felicity slipped on a robe. The evening was comfortable and easy. The one subject we avoided was Otto. I didn't want to tell her any more of my plans yet, and she didn't bring up the subject. When I mentioned the mystery man, she looked concerned.

I blew it off. "Actually, you could do me a favor, if you will?"

Suspiciously, she looked at me and said, "That would depend."

"Nothing difficult, I promise. I bought a folder of prints in Paris, and I'm sure one of them is a Hogarth. Would you take it in to the museum and have it authenticated by one of your specialists. I'm willing to pay a fee of course."

"Of course I will. I'd be delighted to." She relaxed

and became excited about my find.

After dinner, we parted reluctantly, promising to speak the next day.

****

As soon as I got home, I went to bed and considered how much I missed the little things about Felicity, like the loose wisps of hair framing her face. Damn, why did I have to meet her now. She complicated things in multiple ways. I was absolutely sure I wanted her in my life, and I believed she wanted me in hers. I would need to deal with that issue eventually.

I woke up before the alarm, anticipating my meeting with Jacob. I grabbed breakfast and coffee, and ordered another coffee for my travel mug. Then, I was off to Jacob's office in Golders Green.

I arrived early, so I scanned both my phones for new emails and texts while I waited. Nothing of import. I checked the time. Still early, but close enough to our appointment time to be acceptable, I approached the building entrance. It was actually a deceptive façade. For all the dilapidation, the CCTC cameras were hi-tech, and the door—a very sturdy one—was set in a steel frame. Pushing the button on the intercom, it came alive immediately.

"Name?"

I gave my name and looked into the camera. After a slight pause, the door clicked open. A very competent looking young man, previously hidden by the opening door, waited for me when I entered. He indicated I should pass him and go up the stairs. Shrugging, I led him up the stairs to another secure door. As we stood side by side on the landing, he passed his ID card over the reader, and the door clicked open. The man opened it, and waved me in.

Jacob was standing waiting to welcome me with open arms. He hugged me. "Shalom, Peter. It is good to see you, and you look so well."

"I think we are both better than the last time we met."

"True my friend, true. It is good to be alive. Come, we will sit in my office, have some tea, and discuss some current affairs."

Following Jacob, he led me through a maze of offices and small rooms. Everything seemed interconnected. We moved through the windowless brightness and passed what looked like vast amounts of technology, packed into each small space. It created the hum of electronics and the glow of computer screens. Every male I saw wore a yarmulke, and the few women all had headscarves covering their hair.

Jacob settled himself into his high-backed chair and called for tea. I sat opposite him, while we made small talk.

"This is an interesting building—very deceptive from the outside."

"It suits my purpose."

"To be anonymous?"

He laughed and said, "In some businesses it doesn't pay to be obvious."

"Exactly what is your business—if you don't mind me being nosey?"

He looked over the top of his glasses, the glint in his eye told me I would not be getting the answer I wanted. "Information Peter, only information."

"I guess that can be sensitive sometimes."

Jacob laughed outright at that comment. "More dangerous than guns, more valuable than gold. Especially to those who want or need it."

The tea arrived, and the person who delivered it carefully looked me over. He poured the hot tea into glasses secured in silver holders. He left and closed the door behind him.

Looking up, Jacob smiled. "Enjoy the tea. You have picked an unpleasant adversary. I assume you would like to start with Charles Fentiman?"

"Yes. Do you mind if I record our conversation?"

"No need. Everything I have I will give you on a flash drive. To begin, Fentiman's businesses are more diverse than you indicated…and are mostly illegal. The gallery is a front, a way to launder money, as are a couple of other cash-heavy businesses. Up until last year, according to his tax records, he was doing very well. He has suffered some setbacks. He speculated on some risky ventures, and they cost him dearly. He was close to going broke. He has been associated with some shady and dangerous persons from Eastern Europe and Central America."

"How shady?"

"Drugs and other nefarious activities. They are listed in the files you will receive. Nothing is proven against him directly, but by association he has to be on the authorities' radar. He is very careful, keeping his hands clean, using cutouts, and intermediaries so nothing can stick to him, as you found out to your detriment. You will find the details listed, including copies of all the records we could access—tax, business and personal, receipts and contracts, contacts Fentiman represents, contacts he has used—some go back a decade or more. He is an intermediary of facilitation and logistics—moving things around but rarely the principal. He is independent and isolated from many aspects of his customers' businesses by choice. It protects him. When you have read the report, you will know as much about him as anyone."

He continued for another fifteen minutes.

"You have been very thorough. I am impressed."

He spread his hands wide and smiled. "This is what I do, and I have a very good team. Now to the other items, first Alistair Brown. He is what he seems, a talented English artist, living in Paris. He is solvent and successful. His work sells well in both Europe and the UK. His prices have been rising steadily. He is consistent and produces interesting work. His Paris representation is an old firm, well founded and reputable. No flags on anything there. However, his UK representation, as I am sure you are aware, is Charles Fentiman."

I nodded in assent.

"Fentiman has represented Alistair well, his contract is a pretty one-sided deal, but he has sold him well. Alistair should probably try to get out of the contract if possible. It seems you met with him in Paris lately."

How the hell did he know about that? If he knew that, what else did he know?

"I assume from that comment you have done some checking up on me?"

"Of course, it's the only prudent thing to do."

He continued with Hans, on whom there was almost nothing, other than him being a successful legitimate businessman. Jacob moved to my last request, and he went quiet for a moment before asking if I really wanted to know.

I nodded, and he provided definitive information, confirming my suspicions and an added surprise. The information would be useful somehow, at some point, I was sure.

Jacob refilled our tea glasses as he completed his verbal report.

"Thank you for all this. What do I owe you?"

"Call this a debt repaid, in part."

"For what? Doing what was right?"

"It is not that simple for people like me. Doing what is right is not always easy to do. You saved me from serious injury when you didn't have to. Many of my people," he paused, "have not been so fortunate. So for me that is a debt I must honor. If you need my services in the future, I will charge you, but you will get the inside rate."

I wasn't going to argue with his logic or his generosity. "Thank you. I appreciate what you have done, and so quickly. I look forward to reading the long version."

"Don't get too excited, it's very dry. But it should give you what you need. Peter, please don't leave it so long between visits. I enjoy your company, and playing chess with you. Shalom."

"You mean, beating me at chess?"

He laughed and rising from his seat, Jacob handed me a flash drive. "This is not the only copy, but do look after it. It would be unhealthy if certain parties discovered you have this information."

He called for his assistant to show me out through the maze of offices. The same security guard opened the door and escorted me down to the street. Whatever Jacob was doing, it was obviously profitable, and it probably blurred the lines of legality. Not my problem.

Dropping my car off at my apartment, I took a cab to the shop. George had opened up and was in full swing with a couple of American tourists, extolling the virtues of English Silver. Smiling, I hid in the office and plugged in the flash drive Jacob supplied to my shop computer.

The information had been compartmentalized by request. Broken down into subsections, and indexed. Wow! This was a thorough investigation. I wondered how Jacob and his team had managed to obtain the information, analyze it, and so quickly produce the result in front of me. Deciding I didn't want to know, I was just thankful he had.

The information on Fentiman detailed his history and his businesses. It also confirmed he was still financially vulnerable. That was good news for my kernel of a plan. The information regarding Alistair was as plain as Jacob said it was—confirming my feeling that Alistair was another innocent, trapped in Fentiman's corrupt sphere. If Alistair were up to it, he would be a crucial part of my plan. Information on Hans, what little there was, was very clean. No surprise there. I was about to get into the last section of the report when George came in and said he needed my assistance with a new customer while he finished up with the Americans.

Closing out the flash drive, I stored it in my pocket before I went to greet the customer.

The customer was a challenge, but an hour later, I closed out the sale to his and my satisfaction. He'd been exhausting, and I decided I needed something to eat. Today was my turn to call in our order and pick up lunch. I soon went out to pick it up and ten minutes later I left the Deli. I looked before crossing the street and saw the man I'd seen in Paris. Too much to be a coincidence, someone still had their eyes on us, or at least me. I wasn't bothered as much as I had been. Until I formulated my plans fully, I really didn't care. We had done nothing illegal.

When I mentioned it to George, he shrugged. "Until we actually do something, they will be very bored. Let's eat, then you can bring me up to speed on everything.

Telling the events as they were, they seemed to compress into a small space. I recalled seeing the same man in Paris, which bothered George the most.

"How did anyone know of your plans on such short notice?" he asked. "Good job, losing him though."

George was impressed by how Hans had preserved the paintings all these years.

I went over my plan to copy the paintings using 3D printing, substitute the copies for the originals, and bring them back to London.

George thought it was brilliant, including my idea of using a storage unit to secure them. He slapped me on the shoulder. His excitement was contagious.

"Peter, you organize that and take all the time you need. I'll hold down the fort here. You have the makings of a great plan. Do you know how it ends?"

"Not sure, yet. Hopefully, it will be a happy ending for everyone except Fentiman."

That comment brought him up sharply. "How so?"

"That's the part I haven't completely worked out."

"Well, you'd better get it sorted out. Fentiman is not someone to take lightly."

"I know that better than most, and it's why I haven't finalized the plan."

"As long as you are sure."

"Yes, and I'll run it by you before I do anything, I promise."

Chapter Twenty-Two

Next stop was the storage facility I had spotted on the way back from the airport. The location was great, not too close to anyone involved, and not too far to be inconvenient. The facility manager showed me several different units, explaining the security set up. He tried to impress on me that my valuables would be safe in his hands.

With a little prompting, he showed me how the temperature control worked to keep an even temperature all year round. I asked about electric outlets in the unit and was shown how each unit had several. Taking his card, I said I was impressed and would get back to him shortly.

The units had everything I needed, and at a reasonable price. Although that was secondary, considering what was going to be stored there would have bought the entire facility many, many times over. Payments could be made in cash. Another plus. I didn't want my name, at least my real name, on anything if I could help it. The 3D printing company was next on my list.

Having called ahead before I arrived, the company's owner greeted me himself. It was a small operation, and when I explained what I wanted, they were intrigued and excited. They were exactly what I needed—small, creative, and flexible. We hashed out the major details, and confirmed I would supply the digital images as soon as possible. They would give me a cost and timeline. The base materials were to be supplied and prepared by me. I knew what was needed for the images to be printed. The day was going very well. I put in a call to Alistair.

He picked up just before it went to voicemail.

"Hello Alistair, it's Peter. I have a question for you. Have you shipped all your work to Fentiman for your next exhibition?"

"Not yet. Why? Is there a problem?"

"No, but we may be able to cause Fentiman one, if you are serious about getting out from under him, and keeping your name clear."

"What do you want me to do?"

"Delay getting your pictures to the framer, for as long as you can without raising suspicion. As soon as you deliver them to the framer, let me know. I will take care of everything on my end. Your involvement ends with your call to me. Fair?"

"Okay, I hope you know what you are doing."

I laughed. "So do I!" I said and hung up. Another piece of the puzzle was in place for when the time was right.

Hans didn't answer my call, so I sent a text *"An updated ETA on the requested copy."* He would get the message. Without those images, I was stuck, and it looked as if timing was going to be critically tight.

Next, I needed something I knew Tel could help with. He answered my call on the first ring. "Ullo mate. Awright, wot can I do ya for?"

"Yes, fine. I need some info. Could you put me in touch with someone who could make me a fake ID, driver license, and something official? I don't need credit cards."

"Yeah, I fink I can andle that. Ow soon? Yestid-d I spose?"

"That would be correct. What do you need from me?"

"Passport fotos, fre uv em, and tu-undred quid as a deposit. U'll need ta get it to me, quick like."

"Today. Tell me where and when."

"Gud man. Drop it orf at the pub, same as the uver time. Jus put Lectric man on it."

"Done. Be there in two hours max, and thanks again for all your assistance."

"Wot me, I ain't dun nuffin gov…honest." He chuckled and ended the call.

Going directly to the post office, I got the passport photographs. Next, I went to the bank for the cash, put it in an old envelope, and sealed it with tape, I headed directly for the pub.

The pub was quiet. I had a beer and slid the envelope to the landlord. He nodded, and put it in with other papers behind the bar. Tel had obviously given him a heads up that I would be dropping off something for him. Finishing my pint, another pleasure I really enjoyed on my release, I felt like nothing could go wrong today. I enjoyed it. This was not a feeling I got very often.

Ding, a text arrived as I drove back to the shop. I glanced at my phone in the holder. Hans. I pulled over for the message. *"Will be with you tomorrow AM."* Oh this was a good day! Progress on all fronts. Calling George, I told him things were going well, and I had a couple more stops to make before I got back. He said to take my time. Business was slow.

I scanned my phone, looking for and finding a wood supplier, who would cut select woods to custom size. Well-seasoned pieces with less chance of splitting would be expensive. Sixteen custom pieces—the weight alone could be a problem. But the internet is a wonderful thing.

Ross's Woods smelled of fresh cut timber. Small specks floating in the air caught the sunlight as it filtered through the skylights. The place was filled with racks of wood, from finished slats to full sized planks, honey colored English Oak to Gabon Ebony, black as a moonless night. The variety and the prices amazed me.

An older man approached and asked if he could help.

"Yes, I am looking for a good wood to print some paintings on."

He looked at me as if I were crazy, which he shortly confirmed by asking, "You mean you want to paint on the wood, not on canvas?"

"Yes, I want something that will take a 3D print of a painting, and not flake or peel."

He shook his head. "Bloody sacrilege. You don't cover up good wood. You use it to its best advantage, follow the grain, polish it up, show nature at its best. Won't plywood do?"

"Not in this instance. I need good wood to replicate the old masters who painted on panel, not canvas."

"Well, I suppose that is a little different, but you won't want the best—just well-seasoned so it don't split. Got the sizes?"

"Yes." I handed him the list.

"Yeah, we can do this for you. I would suggest the

least expensive, stable wood, and if they are all the same type of wood, it'll cut down the cost."

Going with his suggestions, I only needed a good base for the printing. I wasn't trying to fool anyone. He explained that with some of the sizes, there would be joins in the panel. I told him that was fine and thanked him. Paying the deposit in cash, I gave him my number for when the order was complete. He said it would only take a couple days. That would give me time, to prep the wood blanks for the printer.

The art supply store was next for gesso, and I would need a lot of it. Gesso was the base for paintings, since forever. The product I was making had to be good, not great, but it got me thinking that this could be a moneymaker. If I could get really good images of the famous paintings of the world, it could turn into a legitimate business. Why have a poster, when you could have a perfect copy of a masterpiece, not a fake or forgery, a legitimate accurate copy. Thinking I had better not get ahead of myself, I needed to get this project done and complete. There was also Han's offer to consider, running his gallery here in London.

The art store had enough gesso. Done with my list for the day, I returned to the shop where George looked pleased with himself.

"Good day?" I asked.

"Not bad at all. We'll keep our heads above water this month, already."

That was a good day for sure. I told him what I had done with my day, all positive, and he agreed it had been a very good day indeed.

Felicity and I saw each other frequently and she never asked about Otto. I began to wonder why, but I wasn't complaining. To be honest, I didn't want her involved any more than she had to be.

No more visits from the police, no more sightings of Allen Warren, or the mystery man. Tel swept my apartment on a weekly basis with nothing to report. Life was settling into a nice routine for anyone watching us, if anyone was.

As promised, Hans delivered the high-resolution images of the paintings. I copied them to a flash drive, and forwarded the original CD to the 3D printing company. They got back to me later that day with the costs and timeline. The timeline was no problem, and the cost was worth every penny.

The wood supply company called me, as promised, and said my order was complete and ready for pick up anytime they were open. I told them I would be there later that day. I borrowed George's SUV for the pick-up, since my car was too small.

The next issue was, where could I put the gesso on the panels to get them ready for printing. George came to the rescue saying, "You know *I* have a lockup, right?"

"Ah no, I didn't know."

"I had to have somewhere to store inventory before I opened the actual shop. I rented a lockup, and it's cheap. So I kept it. One of my father's old cars is stored there right now. It can be moved, and then you would have plenty of space to do whatever you need to do."

"You sure?"

"Yeah. I should have moved the car back to the family estate ages ago. It's in pretty good condition, needs some TLC, and it would be back in pristine condition. I just never seem to have the time to organize that."

"Well then, offer accepted. How soon can you get the car gone?"

"Bloody hell, Peter, give a man a chance. I'll take care of it today. Ya bloody slave driver."

At least, he'd said it with a smile. Close enough to be convenient to the shop, without being too close. George tossed the keys to me. "Get a couple of keys cut. I'll get the transport organized and let my brother know what's going on. He can make space down there."

"No problem. I'll drop off the stuff and take a look see. Let me know when the transport is likely to be there. I'll meet them and save you a trip."

"Fine. I'll text you."

"Great, going to pick up the panels now and take them directly to the lockup. I'll need to pick up the other stuff from my apartment as well."

"Okay. Just be available to meet the transport."

"Yup, once the panels are dropped off, I can be as flexible as we need."

Leaving George on the phone to organize the transport service, I went to collect the panels. The traffic was horrible and a frustration, taking much longer than I anticipated. When I arrived, the old man greeted me and said he hoped the panels would suit my purpose. Looking them over, I saw they were exactly what I was looking for. I paid the balance in cash which surprised the cashier. They may remember me because of that, but all they had was my new phone number, and that was not a lot. At least this part was not even close to being illegal. I loaded the panels into the SUV. They weren't heavy individually, but together they were a load.

The drive to the lockup was easy. It was on a quiet side street under a road bridge. The opposite side of the road was lined with the backs of windowless industrial buildings. Faded names of extinct businesses were painted on the brick. Narrow pavement, covered in weeds, was littered with discarded beer cans and bottles. The lockup opened easily, and the small door creaked open. The air inside was stale, dry, and musty. The main doors were heavily bolted from the inside. Finding the light switch, I flipped it and the lights buzzed into life. It was a big space, deeper rather than wide with a large, canvas-covered mass in the middle of the front space.

George's car. Curiously, I lifted the front of the canvas. Holy shit! A 1930 supercharged Bentley. The thing must be worth a fortune. Needing to see the rest of the car, I pulled off the canvas cover revealing a beautiful example of British craftsmanship. Smartly, George had put the car on blocks so the tires would not rot and collapse under the weight of the car.

Standing there, I admired the monster. It showed some wear and tear, but overall it was in great shape. The leather seats, worn to a fine polish, were thin in parts. Some parts needed replacing and some refinishing. George was right, just some TLC.

The area was neat and tidy. No surprise there. It belonged to George. A large bench on one wall would allow me to work priming the panels with gesso without bending over too much. It had electrical outlets for my sander which I used to rub down the gesso between coats. There was also ample space for the panels to be laid out to dry.

A text came in. George. The transport for the car would not be here for a couple of hours. Good, enough time to get home, and pick up the rest of the supplies. After switching off the lights, I locked the door and headed home.

On my return, I parked away from the entrance, allowing plenty of space for the transport truck to pull in. I unloaded the supplies, feeling more alive than I had in some while. The multiple purposes of the project, and the activities surrounding it, had certainly kicked me into a positive mode.

The transport truck showed up almost on time. The two men worked quickly and efficiently. They had the old car out, loaded, and away in short shift. The place looked almost lonely. Even bigger without the car, it allowed me plenty of room to work. Setting up two trestle tables, I cleared off the bench. I could prep six or seven panels at a time, but if I had another table, I could split the process evenly, eight and eight. Set to go, I locked everything back up tight and returned to the shop.

****

The next morning, I woke up to a text from Tel. I could pick up my order any time after ten a.m. at the pub and deliver the final payment. He sent a separate text with the amount of the final payment. Tel was very careful about no direct contact. Getting into dirty work mode, I dressed in old clothes. George had arranged for me to pick up a table from the jewelers next to our shop.

George and I caught up. "The transport guys were great and got going pretty quickly."

"Yeah, my brother called to say it arrived safely.

It's being stored in one of the old barns until I can get my act together."

"Okay, next, the space is plenty big enough, and I will only need it for a couple of days, three at most. You won't see much of me until I have dropped off the panels to the printer."

"That's fine. If you need a hand, call me. I have a feeling this is going to get dangerous."

I looked at him. He was deadly serious.

I brushed him off. "We're going to be fine as long as we are careful."

"Huh, famous last words. Things have a way of complicating themselves, without any help from the participants."

"Promise, I will be careful, and I will check in with you, so you don't worry.

"Peter, I'll continue to be concerned and vigilant, only stopping when this is all sorted. Now go do your thing."

Having one good friend to worry about me was reassuring. I returned to the lockup which quickly put me in work mode proper. The panels had been well-finished, good enough for me to apply the first coat of gesso. The extra table worked out perfectly. Working methodically, I had the eight panels coated with gesso and drying. It had taken longer than I planned, but by the time, I returned from paying off Tel, the panels would be dry, and I could prep them for the second coat.

I put the balance of the cash payment in a new envelope and tucked it into my jacket before heading to the pub. The pub was busy with the lunchtime crowd. As soon as the owner saw me, he nodded toward the bathroom hallway. He met me, and we went into his office, where he asked, "Did ya bring the necessary?"

"As requested."

He took the envelope from me and counted the contents. Smiling he handed me a small packet and said, "Nice doin business wiv ya. Cheers mate."

That was it? I was learning a whole business universe existed outside the norm. Sitting in the SUV, I looked at my documents. The face staring back at me was mine, the name and everything else was complete fiction. Yet, the documents themselves looked as real as my own. I had asked for a driver's license and any other official document that could be produced quickly. What I got was the license and a passport, which is a very official document and would be very useful if everything went sideways.

The timing was perfect. On my return to the lockup, the panels were dry. Hanging a large sheet of plastic across the back half of the space, I hoped to keep some dust out of the painting area. The sander was loaded, and I went to work on the first panel. Sanding was tedious because I had to be careful not to remove too much gesso. By the time I finished the eighth one, my back was sore from leaning over, my hands and arms ached, and I was covered head to toe in a fine dust. Thankfully, the dust mask was a good one. Needing a break, I was going to use it profitably by arranging the storage unit. The unit needed to be ready for the real thing.

The self-storage people were easy to deal with. They superficially checked my new ID. I was nervous that somehow they would know it was fake. They didn't bat an eyelid. They had several units in the size I needed. Choosing my unit, I paid for three months up front. My unit was located toward the back of the facility. Perfect for my needs with easy access to the back doors. No one would see what I was doing. I bought a lock from their selection and went to the unit. It was cleaned out and ready for me. Locking up, I returned to work on the panels.

The second coat of gesso went on smoothly, and then I was done for the day. Too dirty to do any good at the shop, I went home and showered. I then called Felicity to see if she was free that evening.

"Maybe" was her coy response.

It was time for me to update her about my plans. Not sure how to broach the subject, I figured easing into it might be the best way. Time passed slowly waiting for her to arrive, and I figured it was the anticipation, often worse than the actual event, making me nervous.

Felicity arrived right on the dot, exactly when she said she would. I loved that about her. She rang the bell, and we greeted with a hug.

"Hi, come in. Good day?"

"Not too bad. Busy—crazy busy. Only time to snack for lunch, so I am starving. We eating in or out?" she asked.

"Out, the Italian place down the street."

"Good. I'm ready for some pasta."

This would give me time to judge her mood and try to figure out a way to introduce suspect activities. At least in England I hadn't actually done anything illegal. Well, not much. But my knowledge of the real paintings in Paris probably broke a dozen French laws. *Oh well, in for a penny in for a pound. Here goes.*

We chatted and romanced over a great dinner, splitting a bottle of Tuscan red. I didn't want to drink too much. I had to keep my wits about me. After returning to the apartment, she sat as I made coffee.

Felicity beat me to the punch. "So, Peter what's up?"

"What do you mean?"

She laughed and said, "Come on. I know you well enough by now to know something's up. Get it off your chest." Suddenly she paused, continuing in a subdued voice, she asked, "It's about Otto, isn't it?"

"Kind of. I couldn't tell you before because I really didn't know, or didn't have proof of what was going on, only bits and pieces. I still don't have everything, but I do have a lot more information, and a potential path forward. Interested?"

"Bloody silly question."

"I do have a request, before I say anything."

"You want me to keep everything to myself."

"Yes. I need your word that what I tell you won't go further than this room. Some of the plans are not quite on the legal side." I looked straight at her searching for some signal that this was not a good idea.

"I give you my word. I'll keep it to myself. One proviso. If I think anyone is going to get hurt, I will not keep quiet. Can you live with that?"

"Yes. If everything works out, no one will get hurt, at least not physically."

She looked at me quizzically and said, "You better tell me everything you can."

I told her about the history I'd received from Otto, and everything I had done while in Paris, only withholding Hans's name. Next, I explained my plans going forward, transferring the paintings to London, and hopefully how I was going to get my revenge on Fentiman. Finishing, I told her about how he was using Alistair's paintings to smuggle drugs into the UK.

"Peter, please be careful. From what you've told me, Fentiman is a dangerous man."

I detected real concern in her voice, and something else I couldn't quite put my finger on.

"If everything pans out, I won't have to meet him more than once, twice max. Besides, I have George. He's with me on this, and his military background is an asset."

"So how are you actually going to "get" Fentiman?"

"I have information that Fentiman is not as solvent as he makes out."

"Where did that come from?"

"A reliable source. Anyway, I figure since Fentiman is the intermediary, he only gets paid on successfully delivered shipments. He is not the source. So if anything goes wrong with a shipment while it's his responsibility, and that event is in the planning stage, Fentiman would be in big trouble with the actual supplier. He'd have to offer restitution because he can't insure it."

"Probably, but how does that help you?"

"Wait. I am coming to that. So he's responsible for the shipment until he delivers it to whomever. He will need to bail himself out of any lost shipment. An offer of proven masterpieces, by me at a deep discount, will take care of his debt. Starting out, I'll ask for a price he won't meet, then settle for less. I'll probably start around thirty-two million for all of them. That should get his attention. He knows he can sell them for much more, and I now know he has the contacts to do it. He may even be able to use one or more of the paintings as payment for the lost drug shipment, etcetera. I really don't care what he does, but when I have confirmation that the payment is in an off-shore bank account, he gets the location of the paintings. There he will be in for a surprise."

"What sort of surprise?"

"Not sure yet, but I will probably use the French authorities. More details to work out before then."

"Why the French authorities, why not the British? Wouldn't it be easier using the British authorities? They are already here."

"Maybe, but Fentiman may have an inside man. I haven't decided about that part. I want Fentiman to end up in prison. Which country gets him is immaterial, as long as he is banged up for a long time."

"You are playing a dangerous game. Thanks for telling me, and I will keep your confidence until I can't."

"What does that mean?"

"If I think you are in danger, I will do whatever I need to protect you."

"I see. I think. Felicity, I need to do this for lots of reasons, and I need you to trust me. I will make this right in the end."

"I do trust you. If I didn't I wouldn't be here. I love you, and that has caught me by surprise." She paused before saying, "Life has a way of tripping you up in the most unexpected ways."

"Will you stay tonight?"

"Not tonight, Peter, I have a lot to think about."

"Well, here is one more thing to think about. I love you, and that is a fact I am now very comfortable with. I wasn't at first, but I am now."

Felicity stood up with tears in her eyes. She shook her head, hugged me. "This is hard, Peter. Goodnight. I love you."

She left, and I felt empty. I had to tell her what I was doing and trust that her feelings for me would override everything else.

Chapter Twenty-Three

The basics were laid out for Felicity. Not everything, but still done and done. I was relieved that I had admitted what I was doing, and anxious because I had placed that much trust in her. Moving ahead, I wasn't looking forward to the chore of putting the second coat of gesso on the panels, but it was unavoidable.

I grabbed a take-out breakfast on the way to the lockup and called Alistair. He answered on the first ring.

"Hi Alistair, Peter here checking in. How are things going?"

"Good so far. I'm delaying sending the latest works to the framers. They have called and asked when they will be ready. I put them off. I expect they will be calling again soon, and more frequently. I can hold them off only for a little while."

"That's all I need. I just need them to be a little off balance and rushed when you do get the works to them. Let me know immediately when they have them, okay?"

"Yes, yes I will. Peter, good luck."

"Thanks." We clicked off. I grinned, thinking I knew what I was doing, hoping I was right."

The lockup was desolate, and it kinda matched my mood. The second coat of gesso went on easily, and in less time than the first. I left the panels to dry. Since seeing the man in Paris, I had not seen anyone who I could identify as following me. That didn't mean they weren't there.

When I secured the lockup, I checked the area and saw an old car parked further down the road. It hadn't been there on my previous visits. Nothing suspicious about that, there were other lockups in a row. Why should I think I was the only person using one? Still, I noted the make, color, and the number plate for reference.

My next stop was the appliance store for the dehumidifiers. Not sure how many would be needed, or the size, I asked the salesperson for advice. Were two medium-sized better than one big one? He really got into it, explaining more things, in more ways, about dehumidifiers than I ever wanted to know.

In the end, I bought one large and one medium capacity. It would be trial and error, on how quickly they filled and how often I would need to visit to empty them.

Next, I headed to a craft store for some racks that would be a safe, temporary sanctuary for the panels. Done, I went back to the storage facility. It was quiet, no sounds other than those I made. I quickly unloaded and carried the machines and racks into the unit. The metal door rolling up rattled, sounding like a herd of wild buffalo on a metal roof. God it was noisy. The sound echoed off and around the other units. Nothing stirred, just someone opening a unit. Switching on the light, I pulled the door down almost to the floor.

Setting up the dehumidifiers was easy. I had them plugged in and running within minutes. As the unit was empty, and the weather warm, I would check on them that night, even though they had an auto off switch when they were full. The racks were also easy to assemble, but more time consuming. All boxes and packing went in the facility's dumpster.

I went back to the lockup and to sanding the panels. This coat required more care working it. I didn't want to have to re-do anything. I frequently changed the sanding pads, and with a light touch, the work went well. As I finished sanding, I wiped down each panel. They felt smooth as polished marble. The surface was probably good enough for a real painting.

Leaving the panels as they were, I went to get packing materials. The panels would need a wipe down again before packing. The packing stuff was easy to find and easy to load. I called George on my way back to the lockup and gave him an update.

"Hey, I need a favor. I'll need your SUV tomorrow to deliver the panels. Can you meet me at the lockup after work? It will be easier only loading up once."

"Sure, not a problem. Is everything going well?"

"No issues so far. I have the duplicate keys for you, including the lock on the storage unit. I will give you the code to get into the facility and directions in case I can't get there to empty the dehumidifiers."

"That's good. Anything else?"

"I don't think so. I'm sure I haven't been followed, but just to be on the safe side, be careful."

"Got it. See you later and ditto on careful."

Getting back to the lockup, I checked the street for the car I'd noticed earlier. It wasn't there. The panels weren't difficult to pack. I covered the fronts with a sheet of heavy smooth paper, next, added a layer of padding, and finally wrapped each in plastic. I wrote the name of the painting on the back of the panel it was to go on, along with a picture—better safe than sorry.

Reaching out to one of the framing company's we used for our clients, I called. "Hello, it's Peter Harper from Estate Antiques. Is Jack in?

"Hold on, I'll see?" The phone went to muzak.

"Hello, Peter. What can we do for you today?"

"Hey Jack, no prints, not today. I have a favor." I let it hang, hoping he would bite. He did but cautiously.

"And what type of favor do you require?"

I laughed outright at his suspicious tone. "Nothing you can't handle."

"Oh yeah, that remains to be seen doesn't it."

"I need sixteen frames done to measurements and done kinda quickly. All the same frame molding for ease and efficiency, how about it?"

"Well, I don't like making a frame to measurements, let alone sixteen, and then on someone else's measurements, not kosher, Peter. Why the rush, and why not let us have the artwork to make it a proper job?"

"I would agree with you in most circumstances. The works in question are in the process of creation. I am copying some paintings, hopefully to promote commercially. The printing will take a few days to complete. When done, I am taking them as examples to the EU on exhibit, and they'll need frames. That's why I called you."

"Peter, you're nuts, no one's gonna buy expensive printed copies. All right, we can do it for you, but it won't be cheap. What size and color molding do you want?"

"When I have given you the dimensions of all the works you pick the size, I trust your judgement on that. For the color, I want all gold, but if the molding doesn't come in gold, would you spray it? The frames are the gilding on the lily and can make or break a picture."

"Flattery will get you everywhere. Send me the sizes. I'll get back to you with the soonest possible date for pick up unless you want us to deliver?"

"No, I'll pick up to make it easier. This is a huge help, Jack. Send a quote ASAP, and I'll give you a deposit. Oh, and send the invoice to the shop. I owe you one for this.

"Well, get off the phone, and as soon as *you* send the dimensions, I'll get to work. Cheers."

Things were coming together nicely, and so far no problems. I assumed problems would arrive at some point, the later the better, and probably when it involved Fentiman. For now, I would take the quiet. Quickly, I emailed Jack a list of the sizes for the frames. I puttered about the lockup, tidying and cleaning up the mess I had made, while I waited for George to arrive.

With time on my hands, I thought about Felicity. The whole thing had surprised me. Falling in love with her wasn't part of the plan. She wasn't even my type, whatever that means. The contradictions were intriguing, a shielded part and a very open caring part. Hoping she would keep her word about what I told her, I felt this leap of faith was worth taking. I missed her shy smile and infectious laugh.

The passport Tel's contact provided would be handy if I had to leave the country quickly and get somewhere without an extradition treaty. It shouldn't come to that, but being prepared, as those canny Romans said *praemonitus preamunitas,* roughly translated "Forewarned is forearmed" and I had a lot of forearming with the information from Jacob.

George honked his horn, and I opened the main door so he could back his SUV inside. As I opened the doors, George popped the SUV's latch as he parked. He got out, and I closed the lockup door. Once our privacy was assured, we carefully loaded the protected panels into the trunk space, and pulled the cover closed to hide the contents from anyone's curious view.

We said nothing while we worked, and when it was time to part, George sighed. "It's kind of getting real with all these parts coming together."

"Yes, it is. I was thinking the same thing earlier."

"Be careful, Peter, I know I keep repeating it. I learned in the Army, repetition makes permanent, not perfect. Keep your eyes about you, and if you need anything just holla. Better safe than sorry."

"I'll be careful, promise. I don't expect anything unpleasant to happen until Fentiman is involved. We're invisible to him right now, and if anyone were onto us, it would be the authorities, and I haven't seen anything. Tel is still sweeping my place every week, just to be on the safe side."

"Good, glad to hear it. Will I see you tomorrow at the shop?"

"Yep. I will come to work directly from dropping off the panels. Oh, they said the images I supplied were "absolutely brilliant" end quote. I am looking forward to seeing what they come up with as a finished product."

"Right then, see you tomorrow."

"Goodnight, and thanks again."

George smiled, shrugging off my words of appreciation. We exchanged keys, and he waved as he drove off. Then when it had been quiet again for a few minutes, I opened the main doors, drove out, and parked. Quickly shutting and locking the doors behind me in under a minute, I went home, parked, and made certain I locked up the SUV before I entered my apartment. By then I was so exhausted, the bed called my name. The hell with a shower. I crashed into an early, dreamless sleep.

****

The morning arrived way too soon, but I was up and out early so I could get the panels to the printing company first thing. Arriving just after opening time, I met the man in charge of the project. He examined the panels and commented on them. "Nice finish on the base. What is it?"

"Gesso—the traditional base for paintings."

"Great. I don't think we'll need to do much prep-wise, just make sure it's grease and dust free, then it'll be ready to print on. We'll get right on it. We are as interested in the result as you are."

I doubted that. I knew what was going on. They didn't.

"Please make sure the right image gets on the right panel, as they are all individually sized. I have referenced which image goes on which panel on the back with a photo. Any questions, please call my cell."

"No problem, we have all the information, and I will personally call you when we are done. Couple of days, maybe three. It depends on if we hit any issues. Is that still good?"

"Yup, excellent. I look forward to your call." Jumping in the SUV, I made a bee line for the shop. On the way, I put in a call to Jack at the framers and luckily he answered.

"Hey, Jack it's me Peter. I'm on the way to the shop. Have you had a chance to look at the list, and did you send the quote?"

"Yes, pretty simple order. Don't see any issues. Of course, I sent the quote, should be waiting for you in your e-mail."

"Well just go ahead and bill the whole thing to the shop. I need them in three days, four at the outside. Can you make that time line?"

"Jesus Peter, where's the fire? I'll check and see what we can do about the shitty timeline you just dropped on me."

"Love you, Jack, and thanks, we really appreciate this. I owe you one."

"Bloody right you do. No promises. I'll call you later to confirm what we can do. Bye."

He hung up, and I laughed. I would bet a pound to a penny, he'd come through. Now I needed to organize a transport rental to get the fake paintings to Paris, and exchange them for the real thing. That meant getting more packing materials and protective boxes to put them in. Updating George on the way, I told him things were starting to move, and probably too quickly. Still, we had no choice.

My next issue was how to notify the police about Charles Fentiman's drug shipment, without implicating Alistair. The call would have to be done in England. Perhaps by George using a burner phone while I was with Felicity for an alibi, just in case. Alternatively, I could do it from a public location. I would work out those details with George when I got to the shop.

George agreed it made sense for him to make the call. He said he would get the burner phone when he went out later to make a bank deposit. When I told him to make sure it was an untraceable one, he gave me a withering look and a rude gesture. I grinned and went to make some calls. The first one was to book a rental van for five days hence. With that taken care of, I could relax for a few days. Great idea, but I was like a cat on a hot tin roof.

George tried to get me to relax, but nothing helped except seeing Felicity. Well…the sex did. She quickly picked up on my excess of energy and asked what was going on. Telling her as little as possible, she seemed satisfied with my explanation. This part of the grand plan was safe for everyone, yet the feeling of energy was still with me.

It would be less suspicious to approach Fentiman, before I compromised his drug shipment, but not before I had the original works safely stashed away, planning to use the same game Hans had with me. Show a current newspaper next to one of the paintings. That should interest him enough to find out if it was the real thing. He could have someone of his choice examine one painting, again of his choice. The puzzle was finally fitting together, and I had to be patient, leading him step by step until the last piece was in place.

The next day, George tried to distract me with all sorts of trivial odd jobs. To a degree it worked. I only called the printing company once for an update, and that was a reassuring call. Everything was on schedule for day three completion. They were all coming out exactly as expected. They even sent me a photo of one of them to prove it. I was impressed, and I knew what I was looking for. Great, now I had to hope Jack came through with the frames.

Speak of the devil...Jack called as soon as I got back to the shop from picking up lunch. My cell went off, and I recognized his number.

"Hey, Jack, all good?"

"Yes and no."

"What does that mean?"

"We can meet your insane deadline, but not with all the same frame molding. We had stock, but when we went to use the second batch it was damaged. So we used two different moldings, and yes, they are all gold. But we have to split your order into eight and eight. If we had used the original only, it would have been thirteen of one and three of the other. I didn't like that split, so we went eight and eight."

"Not ideal, but I like the solution of an even split."

"I figured you could sell it to your customers. Now they have two choices of frames if they don't want their own custom frame."

"I like it. That's great, Jack. The time is the most important thing. Thanks again."

"Yeah, well this is a one-time offer. Don't pull this stunt again, or we will be having some serious words."

I laughed. "If this works out, you won't be sorry, promise."

Mollified, Jack responded, "I will believe it when I see it. I'll buzz you when they're complete. Are you still picking them up?"

"Yes, might be late in the day."

"The later the better. They'll all be wrapped and

ready to go."

"Cheers, Jack."

God, I loved working with competent people. Jack's was a fourth-generation business. Relationships going back decades. Some of Britain's best-known artists were in their records. Even George's family had used them for framing family portraits, which is how George knew Jack. Over time, I'd built my own relationship with Jack, and it was paying off in spades.

The rest of the day was dull, and I was antsy. Felicity was busy that night, so I picked up take-out on the way home and spent the evening going over all the plans and details in my head. I couldn't find any issues. I made notes on the important points, read, and then shredded them.

Chapter Twenty-Four

Morning arrived in a rush. I felt refreshed after having slept better than previous nights, and I was ready. Today was the day I would pick up the panels. I couldn't wait. My breakfast of coffee and a full English would tide me over because I'd need it.

Beating George in to work again, I worked out what packing materials I required to pack the panels for Paris. I would leave on Thursday night, leisurely drive over solo, and rest up on Friday. Then I'd make the exchange with Hans on Saturday, and George would fly to Paris on Saturday evening. We'd meet at the Gare Du Nord train station where we would start the drive back. We agreed that two drivers would work better on the way back, considering the cargo we would be carrying. It was safer.

We planned to pay cash for everything to make it more difficult to track, and we'd use burner phones only if absolutely necessary. We wouldn't frequent places where we'd be recognized, and we'd avoid places where ID would be required. Working the timing this way, kept the shop open on Saturday, and made everything seem as normal as possible. We'd be back in London on Sunday night and deliver the Paris paintings to the storage unit, then drop off the rental the next day. Easy-peasy...in theory only.

George walked in and, as usual, was surprised at

my early arrival. We started the normal routine of opening the shop—just another regular day in the antique trade. As soon as we opened, I left to pick up the packing materials.

Packing the panels as if they actually were old masters was a necessity. Thankfully, the packing store had a variety of options. I ended up using the flat boxes that housed mirrors and pictures, duh. I purchased enough to have spares in case I messed up some of them unpacking, paid in cash, no records, and dropped the materials off at George's lockup.

The printing company called late in the day and said the entire project would be ready and available for pick up the next morning as soon as they opened. Before I could ask why, they said they wanted to make sure the last four printed panels were completely hardened as this project was really cool, and the finished product looked great. Damn it, I was hoping to start packing them up that night, but twelve hours would not make that much difference.

Bitching to George was useless. He just shrugged and said, "Got to expect hiccups. This is nothing. Have you warned Hans you are coming over?"

"No. I was waiting until I actually had the panels. As soon as I have them in the lockup, I will contact him."

"Sounds like a plan. As soon as you have them, let me know so I can book a flight. When do you pick up the van?"

"Thursday afternoon. I figured I would load up as soon as I have the van, and head out to miss some of rush hour."

"Good idea. Will you need any help loading the

van?"

"Nope, all under control. I just need the frames from Jack."

We had a slew of customers who kept us busy off and on until nearly closing time. As I was finishing up with my customer, the phone rang. George answered looking over to me. He drew a square in the air and made a-thumbs up sign. I assumed it was Jack, and the frames were ready for collection.

Good. I finished up with my customer before asking George, "What did Jack have to say?"

He laughed and said, "Not a lot, but he sounded grumpy. He'll wait for you to pick up the frames tonight if you can get there before seven."

"Well?" I looked at the clock.

"Go on, get out of here," George said, "I can lock up. Just bring my car back in one piece and dinner is on you."

"Fair enough," I said, catching the keys he tossed me.

The traffic was horrible, and I was glad I left when I did. When I arrived at Jack's place, I drove around to the back. I got out of the car, walked up to the door, and banged on it. When he answered, he seemed to be in a better mood—probably due to the large glass of red wine in his hand.

"Bout time. Traffic bad?" He laughed at his own bad joke. The traffic was always bad.

"Yup, same as always. I brought you a check for the whole job. Thought it would be better."

Jack smiled at that and thanked me.

"I still think you're nuts with this project. No one will spend money for a 3D print of a painting."

"You want to put money on it?"

"How much?"

"You make a frame for the first one we sell free of charge, in whatever molding the buyer wants."

"That's it?"

"Well, seeing as how you mentioned it, and a case of Chimay Blue label."

"You're on. But if you don't sell any, I win, and you pay me double on three jobs you supply me."

"Jack, I hate taking your money, but I will."

Good naturedly, we shook hands on the deal, cause a bet is a bet, and I hoped I didn't have to pay up. Of course, Jack watched me load the SUV, while he enjoyed his post work refreshment. Sarcastically, I thanked him for his moral support, and left him laughing as he shut the door behind me. The traffic hadn't eased much, so I went back to the shop to pick up George. He was waiting outside the front entrance chatting with the jeweler from next door.

I waved and George hopped in the car. "Any problems?"

"No. Lousy traffic is all. Where do you want to eat?"

"Mario's?"

"Sounds good to me." In agreement, we headed off toward Mario's, a local Italian eatery. Pizza up front and traditional Northern Italian fare in the restaurant at the back. George called to book a table, while I was thinking about what I had to do.

"George, do you mind if I drop you off tonight and keep your car? I need to take the frames to the lockup, so it's empty tomorrow for the panels in the morning."

"You could have waited until I had at least one

drink before bringing that up, but yes that makes sense. When this is all over, you are going to get a decent vehicle, so I can have mine back."

We chuckled at his comment and lapsed into silence until we got to Mario's. Mario greeted us, as always, with a big smile and hugs. Leading us through to the back, he insisted we have a drink on the house and parked himself with us at a table near the kitchen. It was good to see a friendly, happy face. Mario was his usual self, rattling on about everything under the sun, and although it was difficult to follow his conversation, both George and I relaxed in his presence. He came and went as needed. It felt good to laugh. The dinner was excellent, and the Tuscan red, equally so. We hadn't rushed, and by the end of the meal I was surprised we'd been there almost two hours. I really did need to get George home and the frames to the lockup.

The street, even more desolate in the dark, was deserted, and quiet as a graveyard. Nothing stirred. I shivered while unlocking the door, then I backed the SUV in and unloaded the frames. When I locked up and went home, a nagging feeling disturbed me. Something wasn't right, but I couldn't put my finger on anything specific.

****

My night had been unusually restless. Nerves about the trip to Paris left me dragging when the morning crept up on me.

My phone went off and that got me going. It was Hans.

"Bonjour. I hope I am not too early for you, no?"

"No, not too early. We need to talk."

"You have a plan, yes?"

"Yes, I do. I will be arriving in Paris sometime on Friday and plan to leave Saturday night. My partner will fly in on Saturday night to meet me, and we'll drive back to London. You and I need to make the exchange on Saturday afternoon, or early evening at the latest. Will there be any problems with that timing?"

Hans didn't hesitate. "No, none at all. I would like some more details to make sure I can meet your timeline and prepare as much as I can in advance of your arrival."

"Of course. This is a safe line I trust?" I confirmed.

"Yes, very safe."

"Okay, I've had the images you sent turned into full size replicas of the originals and framed. I think you'll be surprised at the quality. It may even become a new business opportunity. But that's for another time. We'll need to switch them out. Like for like. It should take only a few minutes for each, and if you assist me, it will go even faster?"

"Yes, I will be happy to assist." Hans chuckled. "Now you have me intrigued."

"I was hoping it would. We can discuss matters more fully when we meet."

"Agreed, I look forward to hearing from you soon."

"I'll call you when I am close. I have some other details to confirm with you also."

"Very well, *mon amie*, I look forward to seeing you. Please…drive safely."

I laughed at the underlying meaning. "We will drive back even more carefully."

Hans hung up, and I smiled feeling a surge of energy. Travel mug in hand, I took a sip of coffee and began my busy day. First stop…the printers. Of course there was traffic, but there was nothing I could do about it. No point bitching. I forced myself to relax.

When I arrived, the 3D printers were already open, and the crew seemed excited to show me the finished product. They'd left out the final four panels to show me.

Speechless, I understood why the printers were so excited. Maybe 3D printed paintings really could turn into a legitimate business. I'd expected a good job, but to say I was astounded would be an understatement. The colors jumped off the panels. They looked as I imagined they would have when the originals were first painted.

"This is exactly what I wanted," I said. "Even better than I expected. Amazing work."

They went on a bit about the techniques and the technology. Not understanding most of it, I didn't care. They helped me load them in the SUV and waved me off. Even knowing the cargo were only reproductions, I drove as if they were the real thing.

Getting to the lockup took time, but I didn't worry about it. The street looked the same as it had every time I'd been there in daylight. The previous night's dread had passed. I opened up, drove the SUV in, and shut the doors behind me. Even cleaned up, dust still hung heavy in the closed space.

The first four panels I took out were the ones I had seen at the printers. Taking the appropriate frame from the stack, the first frame, I laid it face down on the cloth covered bench and slowly put the panel, "The Ship of Fools" by Bosch into the frame. It was a close fit and nestled in snugly. I affixed the panel in the frame, unsure of what to expect when I saw the whole package put together.

I turned the first painting over and leaned it against the wall. My heart missed a beat. The luminosity and intensity of the image blasted off the panel. Standing there staring at it as if hypnotized, I was captured—held frozen by its beauty.

My cell phone burst to life and broke the spell. In this case it was like pulling off a plaster. I answered abruptly, "Yes."

"Well, aren't we snippy today!" It was Felicity.

"Sorry, I was miles away, in the middle of something."

"Should I call you, later?"

"No, now is fine. Nothing that can't wait, and it seems like ages since I last saw you."

"Not really, but I like the inference. Anyway, two reasons I called, one was to see if you were free this weekend."

"Actually no, and I have a dilemma."

"What's the dilemma? Something to do with Otto?"

"Yes, plans are moving along, and I will be driving to Paris and back this weekend. I was in two minds about asking if you would like to come along for the ride, and the company."

"When are you leaving?"

"Thursday evening, back on Sunday, George is going to fly out Saturday night to share the drive back."

"Tell him not to bother. I'll come with you. Hold on."

The line went to hold. Leaning against the bench, I wondered if I was making a rash decision. Too late now. I made the offer. She came back with a smile in her voice. "Cleared it. I will be available to co-pilot, and we can switch drivers as well. Pick me up at my apartment?"

"Sure, no problem, but this is not a holiday. It is all business, and part of it I have to do alone. The other party insisted. Are you all right with that? If not tell me now.

"As long as you are not dumping me for another woman." She said it with a laugh in her voice.

"Not a chance when I have you with me in Paris. After all, who knows what might happen in our recreational hours. So, what was the other thing?"

"You lucky man, I just got a call from a colleague. Your Hogarth is a Hogarth. Congratulations. It's a winner. My colleague believes it's a first impression, and in pristine condition. Museums can't put a monetary value on items, but she said she would give me the name of an expert for you to contact for a valuation."

"Thank you. I owe you and her dinner for that."

The last thing I heard as she hung up was her light tinkling laugh, and I felt a tingling in my stomach-I wanted her. Smiling, I began to think it would work out.

I immediately called George about the Hogarth. He was as happy as I was, but he questioned my decision regarding Felicity.

"It will look less suspicious, if anyone is tailing me, or us—like a getaway weekend in Paris—business and pleasure."

"If you are sure?" He was appeased with my reasoning.

"Yep, we're good."

After hanging up, I went back to look at the Bosch. The image was still magical, but the spell had been broken. Placing it to one side, I packaged and placed the next panel, the Vermeer, next to the Bosch. Two down and fourteen to go. Marking each one packed with its name would make it easier to switch them out with the real thing.

Methodically working, I watched the packaged pile grow. The only one I had concerns about was Raphael's "Portrait of Baldassare Castiglione." The original was a canvas, mine was on panel, and anyone would catch that. I was up front with these as replicas. The return into the country shouldn't be a problem. Returning with exactly what went out, the same quantity of professional samples, the same everything, and the paperwork would match. Don't borrow trouble.

Finished, the frames were exactly what I wanted. Jack, as usual, had done a great job. A few of the panels were slightly loose in the frame. Using cardboard, I packed them to a tight fit. I hadn't taken much of a look at the panels, knowing I would get side-tracked.

Nothing in the lockup street, deserted. I locked up and made my way to the shop. On the way, I confirmed the van rental and pick-up time. The shop was quiet, one customer negotiating with George over a Victorian tea service. They looked like they would be a while. I placed a call to Hans, and he picked up on the first ring.

"Hello, all is well, yes?"

"Yes, all is well. Only one slight change in plans. I will be bringing someone with me rather than have a flight involved."

"The same person, yes?"

"No. Someone different, she will be a suitable substitute."

"Do you think that wise at this stage?"

"Actually, very wise. We will make the exchange without her, so she will not meet you. Your anonymity will be safe."

"That is much appreciated. Again, please take care."

"See you on Saturday."

"*Au revoir, mon amie.*"

He hung up, and I felt a deeper bond with Hans than I had before. There was something in his voice. Almost regret that his involvement was ending. I hoped he saw what I did in the potential for the replica business. Not wanting anyone to know I was in Paris, which really meant Yvette, Martine, and Alistair, I would use a hotel picked at random.

Chapter Twenty-Five

Thursday afternoon arrived quickly. Understandably, I was anxious about transporting the panels, and for many other reasons. The drive with Felicity, the return cargo, the exchange with Hans, the timing—all had to go well.

The exchange rate was crappy. Using my fake ID to convert Pounds to Euros at a couple of Bureau de Change in London was safer than using my bank. When I picked up the van from the rental lot it had a full tank and plenty of space for my cargo. The trip to George's lockup went well, but loading up the wrapped panels took longer than I had anticipated.

As I finished, Felicity called, and asked, "Where are you? I was getting worried."

I liked hearing the concern in her voice. "Just finished loading up. Be with you A-S-A-P. I'll call as I get closer. Can you be ready, so I won't have to park?"

"I'm ready now."

"Then hang up and let me get over to you."

She hung up.

I shut the van doors, hopped back in, and drove the van out of the lockup. The car I had seen previously was back in the same spot, but it looked empty. Quickly, I locked up and drove off, keeping one eye in the rearview mirror. But there was nothing. Although the traffic grew heavier, edging toward rush hour, I made good time.

I checked in with Felicity. She answered on the first ring. "Where are you? Do I need to leave now?"

"Close and yes. I figure about five minutes max."

When I arrived at the closest corner to her building, Felicity was already waiting. I flashed my lights, and she acknowledged me with a wave.

I hopped out of the van to give her a hand with her bag and we kissed briefly before she jumped into the passenger seat. She glanced at me with a huge smile.

"Why the big smile?"

"This feels like an adventure," she said. "It's exciting, and of course nothing is illegal, well not completely. You are going to get the paintings back to the Louvre, aren't you?"

I laughed at that, but heard an undertone of concern in the comment. "Yes, I am. One way or another they will be returned to their proper place."

Felicity already knew and agreed I would be making the switch alone. I'd promised to keep Hans out of everything, and I would. Taking off carefully, I eased my way into the London traffic and headed for the North circular, then south and east toward the channel tunnel on the M20. The faster we got to our destination, the more time we'd have to rest in Paris and get ready for the critical drive back. With the tunnel, the trip over should take about seven to eight hours, including *Le shuttle*. Our vehicle would be loaded on the rail shuttle. We drive on and off. The system is quick, easy, and very well designed. Since I was going to pay cash, I didn't have a reserved slot on the train. At the time we were traveling, it shouldn't be a problem. The shuttle ran every two hours, night and day. Paying at the terminal cost a little more, but ensuring our anonymity made it worthwhile. I didn't mind at all. We made good time. The traffic increased but moved at a good pace.

"Felicity, have you driven in France or Europe?"

"Yes, not a great deal, but enough to get around safely. A bit late to ask that now, isn't it? We are on our way."

"Just checking. I figure if I drive until we hit the first rest stop in France, then you can take over until we get to the outskirts of Paris. Then I'll take over again unless you want to brave the *peripherique* at rush hour on a Friday morning?"

"No chance. You can take that one on. What route did you plan on taking into Paris?"

"The A16. It's the most direct route to and from. The hotel I want to use as a base is on that side of Paris. Trying to make this as quick and efficient as possible."

"Well, you seem to have thought of everything."

"I hope so."

We lapsed into a comfortable silence with our own thoughts while the radio played a selection of classics, which suited me fine. The conversation was intermittent and intimate.

Felicity checked our location. "I think we should stop in Ashford. Get something to eat and some snacks to get us through until Paris. Good idea?"

"Sounds like a plan."

Ashford came up quickly, and we stopped at the first pub that advertised food. It was good basic food and no alcohol.

Felicity excused herself and went to use the ladies' room, then came back smiling and said, "I am ready for foreign lands."

The last few miles were easy and the directions to the tunnel well marked. I pulled in, paid my money, and had all the paperwork checked. As I expected, there was no trouble getting on the next shuttle. We settled in and started playing a radio game. The first one to come up with the name of the band and song as soon as it started won. One point for the band, one point for the song—one point deducted if you were wrong. I was better at the older stuff, she at the newer. Not surprising really, seeing as I didn't have access in prison.

To make the game more interesting, Felicity suggested, "We need to have prizes for winning this."

Suspiciously, I asked, "What sort of prize?"

"Oh, I don't know—perhaps something intimate and very rude."

"Well, if that isn't an incentive I don't know what is. Do we know what up front, or do we keep it as a surprise?"

"Yes, I think surprise, don't you?"

"A good idea. So when I win, you'll be surprised."

She laughed. "I admire your confidence, however misplaced it is."

We got into concentrating, since we were both very competitive, and we seemed to be evenly matched. I would win one, she would the next, and so on. I thought about letting her win, but she would know and wouldn't like it. Time passed quickly, and the score tied when we moved on to the shuttle. The ride was smoother than I expected, and before we knew it, we were out of the tunnel on the French end. The tunnel blackness turned to night blackness broken by the acid lights of Coquelles. After we disembarked the van from the train, we followed the signposts for the A16 highway.

So far the journey had been easy and stressless. The trip back would be another matter.

The drive went well. We stopped as planned at the first rest stop, for both a bathroom break, and to switch drivers. Felicity took over when we got back in the van.

Too wired to sleep, I tried to organize my thoughts and work through all the bits and pieces of the puzzle. I knew how I wanted it to end. It was just a matter of the pieces coming together. The picture was becoming clearer. Some of my plans required perfect timing, and that would be reliant on fate and other people. I didn't like it but there wasn't any alternative. I put my head back and relaxed, eventually dozing off.

I woke with a start when Felicity, forced her to brake sharply, cursed another driver. We were much closer to Paris.

"Are you okay?" I asked.

"Fine, except for that dumbass driver who cut in front of us. This drive is easier than I expected."

"Why?"

"Less traffic and good company, even when he's asleep."

"I don't talk in my sleep, do I?"

"No, but sometimes you snore."

"Not me. Never heard myself. Can't possibly be me."

"Very funny. So, what's the plan when we get to Paris?"

"Check into the hotel, breakfast, and rest. Take it easy for the day. Then Saturday, we'll chill out, do some sightseeing, and Saturday afternoon we'll do the switch and get back to London sometime Sunday."

"Do you know where you will make the switch?"

"Kinda, but not one hundred percent sure. It's up to the person holding them."

"Can you trust him?"

"You're making an assumption, my dear. How can you be sure it's a 'him'?"

"True. An assumption on my part. So, is it a 'him' or 'her'?"

"I'll contact the person when we arrive and wait for a time and place."

Hans and I had already agreed on the plan. I had to do this on my own, No Felicity. But I was sure she would object. I'd deal with her objection when the time came.

The sun started to creep above the horizon as we approached the City of Light. Felicity pulled over and we switched positions for the drive into Paris itself. I deliberately had not booked a hotel so no credit card would be on file. I planned to pay with cash and use my fake ID. The closer we got to the city, the heavier traffic became. Keeping my wits about me, I still missed the exit for Saint Denis where I saw a sign for a hotel, but too late.

"Damn it." I kept my eyes open for the next one. Got it, Saint Ouen, I pulled off the highway onto the main street and pulled into the hotel parking lot. "Wait here, Felicity, while I check to make sure all is well."

She yawned. "Please don't be long. I'm tired."

Entering the quiet lobby, apart from the tired looking woman in reception, it was deserted. They had a room available, so I checked in using the fake ID with no questions asked, I filled out the registration form, but no other forms were required after I showed my British passport.

Key in hand, I went back to the van.

Felicity asked, "Everything okay?"

"Yup, usual stuff. No problems. We are down a bit and can use the rear entrance to come and go as we please."

"Good, I need coffee and a shower."

"Coming right up, ma'am. I noticed a café just up the road. I say breakfast first, then showers and rest…yes?"

"Agreed." She looked tired, and I felt it.

We drove to the café and had a good breakfast. It was quick, easy, and not expensive.

Before we left, I used the café payphone to call Hans and let him know we had arrived.

After returning to the hotel, I couldn't wait to get to the room and relax. We took our meagre belongings to the room on the ground floor, and I checked the facilities. The shower was really too small for a double, so I let Felicity go first. She was quick and looked refreshed as she towel-dried her hair, but she was oblivious to me drinking in her nudity. I never tired of looking at her.

Next was my turn.

I left my work phone on the desk and took my new phone into the bathroom with me. I left it under my pile of clothes. Not that I didn't trust her, but if Hans called, I didn't want her to see the call.

Showering did the trick, and I felt better, tired but relaxed. Felicity was already in bed, sitting up uncovered, her tits still rouged from the hot water, and her nipples hard from the coolness of the bedroom. I was extremely glad I'd offered her the trip and she had accepted. Slipping in beside her, she slid down beside me. We snuggled, holding each other silently, comfortable just being together. We slept.

Chapter Twenty-Six

I woke not sure where I was, but happy to find Felicity still asleep in my arms. As I came to, the sun lasered a stream of light through a crack in the shades. I untangled myself watching Felicity breathing, slow and even. She sighed and rolled over toward me. The sheets fell back and exposed her bare shoulder. I never tired of looking at her, so peaceful, open, and still so hidden.

Carefully, I climbed from the bed and went into the bathroom. Splashing water on my face, I was fully awake and ready to dress into a change of clothes. A few minutes later, I felt human again. Sitting in the one chair in the room, I checked my phones for texts and email. Then I looked up some tourist sites in the city, planning a day of sightseeing. Maybe we could do Sacre-Coeur in Montmartre. As I scrolled through things to do, Felicity became restless.

"Peter, why didn't you wake me? What's the time?"

"Time you were up. We are going into the city proper to enjoy the day."

"It won't take me long to get ready." She flipped back the covers and strode into the bathroom, calling out as she did. "Have you heard anything, yet?"

I had to be careful with my answer. "Sorry, what?"

"Have you heard from your contact, about the switch?"

"Oh yes, final details will be sent to me tomorrow

morning, late morning."

"Cutting it a bit fine, isn't it?"

"Less chance of anything going awry, I guess. They are being careful and not risking exposure, probably for good reason. I'm going along with whatever they want, no mistakes on our end, either."

"Well, I am all for that. I still think you are playing a dangerous game involving Fentiman."

"I know. He is the only part of this that worries me, but he is also the best way out of it all for everyone, except him."

"Are you sure you're not using this as an excuse to get revenge on him for framing you."

"At first, probably. I've thought about that a lot. It's not an issue now. If I can pull this off, several birds with one stone will go down, including Fentiman."

"As long as you're sure. I meant what I said. If I feel you're in danger, I will go to the authorities."

"Promise me you'll do that only as a very last resort. I do have a plan, and as it matures I will tell you as much as I can to keep you satisfied that we are all safe."

She came out of the bathroom, and it never failed to amaze me, how quickly she could get ready and look so good. Her face was somber, her head down.

"Okay Peter, you know I have fallen in love with you. I don't want anything to happen to you. Promise me you will be careful and keep it as legal as you can."

"That's a promise I can easily make. I'm not a hero, and I certainly don't want to go back to prison."

She brightened at my commitment and said, "All right, I will take you at your word. Let's enjoy Paris, our time together, and worry about tomorrow,

tomorrow.

"Agreed."

We walked to the nearest Metro and made our way to Montmartre. It was the tourist trap I remembered, but it was still fun. We meandered around the Basilica of Sacre-Coeur. Making our way down the steep streets, we wandered and held hands as lovers do. We discussed what it would be like to live in Paris. The romance of the place had seeped into us. We hopped on and off the Metro for the rest of the day.

Lunching at *Les Deux Magots,* we happily paid the premium to sit outside in the early afternoon sun. The comfort of not having to rush somewhere settled over me—the unfamiliar sensation of relaxed bliss—a novelty. I mentioned this to Felicity, and she agreed. She felt the same. We entered our own little world as we strolled through the Luxembourg gardens, arm in arm, in love, and oblivious to the people around us.

The only indoor visit we made was to the Musée d'Orsay. My favorite museum housed many works by two of my favorite artists, Van Gogh and Cezanne. The place always left me awestruck, and today was no exception. Felicity commented that I was like a young boy visiting his heroes. She wasn't wrong.

We meandered around the galleries of the museum, and I then visited the museum shop to purchase postcards I would later send to Felicity. We were among some of the last people ushered out on closing. It had been a good day.

Not wanting the day to end, I suggested a drink and an early dinner.

Felicity agreed, "Yes. Good idea, but dinner is on me. My treat. This has been one of the best days ever.

Thank you."

"It was the company." Leaning down, I kissed her while she held my face and responded, kissing me back with ardor. We melded into one another until she shivered and pulled away. Feeling her body heat, I knew the shiver wasn't from the temperature.

We linked arms and walked slowly until we came to a café-bistro, a local haunt. It was busy, always the sign of good food. Once seated, we perused the menu, lost in our own thoughts. A smile played on Felicity's lips, mirroring how I felt.

The meal was typical bistro fare, good and reasonably priced, reasonable for Paris that is. We killed a bottle of Bordeaux while taking our time savoring the meal and each other. I'd come to realize that just being in her company aroused me. She was a completely sensual being without recognizing how sensual she was. When she relaxed there was no artifice, it was all her.

We finished with a coffee and then ordered Grand Marnier as a digestif.

Later as we walked toward the Metro, she turned and kissed me again. She tasted divine with the orange flavor still on her lips. The Metro was not crowded, so we cuddled all the way to our Metro stop. Our pace slowed as we approached the hotel. Perhaps neither of us wanted the day to end. The hotel would remind us of why we were here.

I opened the door, and Felicity entered our room. I closed the door behind us and stepped up to her. Hugging Felicity from behind, nuzzling her neck, I wanted no space between us. She chuckled, and turned into me, lifting her face for my kiss before I could say anything.

Without haste, we disrobed one another, appreciating each other slowly. Her body never failed to surprise me. I thought I knew her, and yet every time was unique, different. I noticed something I hadn't before, always a surprise, always something more lovely to discover.

Her fingers undid my belt, and her hands pushed my jeans and underwear down. Her face mashed into my chest as she sank down, taking my clothes further down my legs. My dick was hardening as she held it and became fully erect. All I heard was *mmmm* as her mouth took the head of my penis, enveloping it in a moist heaven. She teased me with her tongue. I felt my cock pulse as she slid more of me into her.

Standing still, not daring to breathe, I was being transported, and afraid if she continued I'd come too soon. I hooked my fingers under her bra straps and gently lifted her. Reluctantly, she released my erection and stood close to me. Moving the straps off her shoulders, I unhooked her bra until only our bodies held it in place.

My turn. I knelt in front of her, popped her jeans, and pulled them down with her panties in one smooth motion. I buried my face in her neatly trimmed bush and inhaled her. Using my head for balance, she stepped out of her clothes, naked. I looked up at her, a Venus in the flesh.

Felicity pulled me upright, and we kicked our discarded clothes aside.

We were nude, wrapped up in each other's arms, with our lips fused together. My arms encircled her, and she held me with one arm, her other hand found my cock. She massaged me lightly, touching and teasing the hard length of me. Loosening my hold on her, I felt between her legs. She opened wider on my touch, and she was ready for me. I invaded her with my fingers, entering without resistance. With her head thrown back, sighs and moans of desire escaped her lips. I cupped her face, and one hand touching her lips, I entered her mouth. We took turns kissing, sucking, and licking my fingers, until I couldn't stand any more. I lifted her, and took her to the bed. She was relaxed and pliant in my arms as I lay her in the middle of the bed. Then in a soft demanding voice she said, "I want you. I want you in me now."

How could I refuse? I climbed onto the bed, kneeling between her spread legs. Wanting to be in her, also wanting to make this pleasure last. Kissing the insides of her thighs, I worked my way up alternating legs, with kisses, licks, and nips. The closer to her pussy, the more expressive her breath became, and her hips rose to meet my mouth. Stopping for only a moment I leaned in licking her, which brought a grunt of pleasure, and her hands gripped my head, pulling me into her as deep as she could. My tongue speared her. Releasing my head, she convulsed, her legs and hips, shouting out, "Fuck me now, fuck me."

Rising up on my knees, I leaned forward. Felicity playfully gripped my penis, and pulled me to her. She pulled me down onto her.

Pushing forward, I smoothly entered her, sliding in to the hilt. Once inside I groaned at the ecstasy of being encased in her warm moist heat. Then she clamped her legs around my back as I started to thrust back and forth, and before long, her spasms rippled around my hard length. Back and forth, her tits bounced in rhythm to my thrusts. She appeared fully absorbed in the moment's pleasure, until her breathing became erratic.

Calling out, she chanted, "That's it, just like that. Like that…"

We slid on each other, her legs clamped on my back, Felicity pushing back against my thrusts, and I felt huge inside her. She began to rise to an orgasm, taking in short stuttering breaths.

"Yes, that's it. Do it more, more." The last "more" dissolved into a long low moan as she gripped me and relaxed, repeated, and then convulsed into an orgasm with an explosive, "Yes."

As soon as she said it, I orgasmed inside her. Pushing into her as hard as I could, each ejaculation pumped deeply into her. She went limp, exhausted from her efforts.

Still inside her, I balanced on one elbow and held her hip, rolling us to one side. Even as my dick softened, I didn't want to come out of her, not yet.

Sex had never felt so good. No longer two—we were one, wrapped in each other. Our breathing returned to a relaxed almost meditative state—content, silently two as one.

Later, waking to a chill room, I had slipped out of her, and she had rolled over on her side. Rearranging the covers, I covered both of us, and as I spooned her, she nestled back into me.

Chapter Twenty-Seven

The sun came in through the blinds, confirming the morning had indeed arrived. Awake, Felicity had already slid out of bed.

"Good morning sleepy head," she said.

"Hi, what time is it?"

"I love you, too."

"Sorry. Last night was fantastic. Thank you. What time is it?"

"That's almost better. It was pretty amazing wasn't it? Must be the French air or something."

"Doubt it. I think it's all you."

"You are too kind sir, but I'll take it. I love you, Peter."

"I love you back."

Felicity bounced into the bathroom shouting out she was hungry and needed breakfast. No disagreement. I was starving, and I still didn't know what time it was. We did manage to squeeze into the tiny shower which caused giggling from both of us. One good thing, it was too small to get up to any high jinks, and *ooops* if either of us dropped the soap.

After all vestiges of the previous night's lovemaking had been removed I said, "The hell with the time."

With Felicity, I felt complete—not a feeling I'd had with anyone before. It was strange how it felt right, even with all the events going on around us.

Dried and dressed, we made our way to the same café where we ate the day before and had a delicious breakfast. As we left, my other phone announced a text.

—*Come alone, 8:00 p.m. Will tell you where later*—

I looked at Felicity. "Contact."

"What did they say?"

"Here, take a look." I handed her the phone. I knew she was not going to be pleased.

It showed on her face as a mix of irritation and concern. "I don't like it—I mean you going alone."

She didn't know what I knew.

"Their rules, I guess. They have nothing to gain by setting me up." Smart how Hans got me to agree, insisting I meet *them* alone. Now all I had to do was convince Felicity it would be okay.

"I suppose. I still don't like it. How were you and George going to work it?"

"I was going to make the exchange. George was going to fly in, take the train into Paris, and meet me at the station. Then we were going to drive straight back from there."

"So, you would have made the exchange solo anyway."

"Yes, that was the plan."

"When you called yesterday to say you had arrived, did you say I or we."

"I honestly don't remember. I think I said we, but not one hundred percent sure."

"Did you say where you were staying?"

"No, just we are in Paris. Why all the questions?"

"Being careful, I don't want anything to happen to

you."

"I don't want anything to happen to me, either. I am sure it will be fine. I'm still not used to anyone caring about me. Thank you." It was an odd feeling. "Everything will work out. I am more concerned with what happens when we get back home."

"How do we deal with today?"

"Well, we have a time, 8:00 p.m., just not the place. I figure it has to be somewhere in Paris proper, since the whole operation is here. The plan was to come back out this way to get on the highway. So, I make the pick-up and meet you somewhere near here…unless it would be easier to meet you at another location. Let's play that one by ear."

"That kind of makes sense as long as you are sure. How about I come with you and you drop me off near the meeting place?"

"I thought of that, but if someone is watching I don't want to take the chance of you being spotted. The best plan is I go alone and trust them. If I think there's something off, I'll cancel and let you know, and we high tail it back to the UK."

"Deal. As long as you promise…anything suspicious and you call it off."

I smiled and said, "Promise."

Felicity didn't look happy but seemed to be content with the plan. The rest of the day we were both anxious to receive the location. I expected Hans's choice to be a decoy to satisfy Felicity, and that I'd meet Hans at his gallery. Everything was in place, and unless something unexpected came up, it should be smooth sailing.

We had hours to kill. Felicity suggested we go back to the flea market and do some more exploring.

The idea would keep our minds off the evening's exchange. The route by metro was a crazy one with too many changes, so we took a taxi. The driver dropped us off at the market entrance—much quicker and easier.

We meandered through the lanes and stalls. Whatever took our fancy, we stopped and browsed. The place had such an eclectic mix of stuff, I could have spent days just looking. While Felicity was looking in a stall, I noticed an art deco enameled broach in another across the way. It was beautiful. I wanted to surprise her when we got back to London. Asking the price, I didn't think it unfair, and I wasn't going to bargain to get it lower, risking Felicity seeing me. Paying up I pocketed the find.

She appeared satisfied with her negotiations of whatever she was after, and when she looked at me, she narrowed her eyes. "You look like the cat who got the cream. What did you do?"

"*Moi*? Nothing, just happy you got what you were after. What is it by the way?"

"That's called changing the subject. Another Hermes scarf. The prices are really good but still expensive. The scarves are classic and never go out of style, so I can use them forever."

Enjoying her enthusiasm, I put my arm around her, and we wandered on, stopping frequently just because we could. It was an easy day. Lunch was at a local bar—fresh baguette sandwiches and Kronenberg 1661 beer. That would be the last alcohol until we got home. By then I would need a beer. After lunch, we perused some of the antique shops near the market, looking at a lot of very nice items but not buying.

Mid-afternoon, my non-work cell beeped a text—

an address and a new exchange time. The time was brought forward an hour to 7:00 p.m. Nothing else. I showed it to Felicity. "Would you pull the address up on your phone?"

"Sure."

It turned out to be a parking garage near the St. Lazare railway station. Shrugging, I grinned at Felicity. "At least it's fairly public."

She nodded, and the tense set to her shoulders relaxed a bit. "True. Maybe they are worried about you as well, and wanted a public place."

The text brought us back to earth with a bump. We made our way to a taxi stand and took a cab back to the hotel. Packing took no time, and while Felicity took our stuff to the van, I paid the bill in cash. The receipts would be destroyed leaving no evidence of our stay.

"Any problems?" Felicity asked.

"Nope, none. Ready to get this over with?"

"Yes. Where are you going to drop me?"

"Check and see if there's a Printemps store nearby. They usually close at 8:00 p.m." I concentrated on driving while she checked out the store.

"It is close by and they do lock up at 8:00. Will that be enough time to make the exchange?" she asked.

"I hope so."

We lapsed into silence as I maneuvered through the Saturday traffic and made our way to the store. I stopped illegally to drop her off, and she leaned over and kissed me. "I'll be right here in one hour."

Nodding in agreement, I pulled into the traffic and made my way to the parking garage. Pulling into the first empty spot, I called Hans.

He answered on the first ring. "Are you alone?"

"Yes, and thank you for making it easier for me to separate from Felicity. Are we still on to do the exchange at your gallery?"

"Yes. All is ready. They are packed for the exchange."

"Good. I'll be there as soon as possible."

Hanging up, I dialed Felicity to tell her all was well and that I should be done within the hour. I wanted her to be ready to be picked up as agreed. A ringing sound came from the passenger door pocket. I hung up and redialed, but the ringing started again. Felicity had left her phone in the van. Accidently? Or on purpose?

I called Hans back and said, "We have a slight problem."

I explained the situation, and he agreed it was only a slight problem. "Stay where you are, I will come to you."

"Hans, are you sure? Do you need any help?"

"Good idea, Peter. Get a taxi to the gallery, it will be quicker if you are here to help me load the items. I will drive us back to make the exchange. After that, I can manage unloading the samples myself, and I am curious to see what you have done."

He ended the call, and I locked the van, then flagged down the first cab available.

The driver nodded when I gave him the gallery address. The traffic flowed, but I was still on edge about the time it was taking. Once over the Seine, the traffic became lighter, and I arrived at the gallery in good time. Hans was waiting for me, and the door opened as soon as I pressed the intercom.

"Welcome Peter. Quickly come through to the back, everything is ready."

I followed Hans, who moved quickly and easily for a man of his age, as he led me through the gallery to the back door.

I stopped short. All the packages were leaning against the wall. I broke out into a sweat just thinking about what they contained.

Hans opened the door. An old Mercedes station wagon waited. The rear seat lay flat, making plenty of room for what we required. Hans lifted the tailgate and opened the back doors. It made carefully and efficiently loading the paintings easier. Carrying out the packages in twos, we moved them, making sure they were secure. It only took ten minutes to load the car—millions of euros, dollars, pounds, or whatever currency you chose, moved in such a short time.

Hans closed the gallery while I sat in the passenger seat, and then he drove as a typical French driver, deftly missing other traffic by centimeters. Within minutes, I was more anxious about his driving than I was about the cargo we were carrying. The drive back to the van was quicker, and as we approached the garage, I told Hans the van was too close to the exit for a clandestine exchange. I suggested that I follow him to a lower floor.

He agreed and drove down several levels, parked in a remote corner, as I parked with the side door of the van next to him. I opened it from the inside, and we pulled out the copies from the van and leaned them against the wall. Once he got in the van, I quickly handed him the real works. Hans carefully secured them against the van sides with bungee cords.

I could hear other cars and pedestrians at a distance, but nothing close to us. Everything went smoothly. We loaded Hans's car with the copies, taking practically no time, since we needn't be quite as careful loading them as we had with the originals.

I was ready to pick up Felicity with a few minutes to spare.

Hans shook my hand and said, "Thank you, Peter. I didn't realize how much relief this would be. If you need anything from me to bring this matter to a successful conclusion, do not hesitate to contact me. Please be careful, yes?"

"Yes, I will. I would value your opinion on the merchandise in your car."

"I will look it over and give you an honest opinion."

Laughing at that, I said, "I would expect nothing less. You'll be hearing from me, and hopefully the originals will soon be back where they belong. *Au revoir, mon amie*."

"*Au revoir* indeed, my friend."

Hans got in his car and took off. I double-checked the cargo, satisfying myself it was good for the trip home.

Now to pick up Felicity. She was close by so the drive only took a few minutes, and as promised, she was waiting in the same spot where I'd dropped her off. She climbed in and before I could say anything, she said, "Peter, I am such an idiot. I think I left my phone in here or in my bag. I went to call you and couldn't find it."

"I know. I tried calling you to say everything was okay and your phone rang in here. At first, I thought I was hearing things, so I called you back. Your phone is in the door pocket."

"Thank goodness for that. Everything went well?

No problems?"

"None to speak of. They were late. I think they were checking me out. When they did arrive, we went down a couple of levels so there was less chance of someone seeing us doing the exchange. All tucked safely away. Now let's get the hell out of here and go home."

"Good idea." Felicity seemed to relax, picked up her phone, and started checking it.

My calls would be there as I said, and she could check the GPS to confirm my story of the exchange if it registered that many levels underground. At least it would show the van never left the garage until I came to collect her.

Retracing our way to the channel tunnel, we headed north on the A16 and stopped only for fuel and refreshments to go. Felicity drove the van and made great time, so we were able to take the earlier shuttle back to England. She was surprised how easy it was to load the van onto the shuttle.

The ride was smooth, and with nothing to do, Felicity probed me about the paintings. Who, where, what? I told her whatever I could and kept information about Hans out of the equation.

Several times she asked, "Are you sure these are the real thing, just not very good forgeries?"

"No, I can't be one hundred percent sure. Though I can't think of a reason it would be in anyone's best interest for these not to be the real thing. Everything Otto told me, and from what I've found out from the items he left me, has been confirmed, and so far it's all been accurate. Besides, he asked me to look after his daughter, and I intend to do so."

Quietly Felicity said, "That's very noble of you."

"A promise is a promise."

She was quiet for some time after that before continuing with more questions. "Where are you going to keep the 'merchandise'?"

"Safely. Better you don't know. You said to be careful, so I am being very careful."

"Good, I just want to help, that's all."

"You are and have been extremely helpful. You are much better company than George, and you're more attractive too."

That brought a laugh, and we both eased back into a more relaxed feeling.

Customs was a breeze after a cursory look at the paperwork and the contents of the van. They waved us through, and in no time, we were on our way to London.

Stopping again in Ashford, we needed a bathroom break, fuel, and more coffee. We switched drivers and continued on. By this time, it was getting late, and Felicity seemed worse for the wear. She leaned into the side of the van, using her jacket as a pillow.

I kept to the speed limit, and the miles went by quickly. I was happy to see the signs for the North circular and soon cut down to Finchley. Felicity was still asleep when I pulled into a spot close to her building.

She stirred when the van stopped. "Where are we?"

"Home."

"What! Why didn't you wake me?"

"No point. Would you like me to walk you to your door?"

"No, no I am fine—just out of it a bit. You should

have awakened me."

"Hey, thank you for the company, and for *caring*. I picked this up for you as a small token of my appreciation and as a reminder of our weekend." I gave her the art deco broach wrapped only in a paper napkin from the bar where we had lunch.

She looked at me in amazement. Tears welled in the corners of her eyes, but she brushed them away quickly, smiled, and kissed me. "The trip was my pleasure, but this is…this is a nice surprise. I will treasure it, Peter. Thank you."

"Caring is always something. You sure you don't want me to see you up?"

"No. I'll be fine. Will you call me tomorrow?"

"Of course."

She climbed out of the van while I opened the side door and pulled out her bag. I handed it to her, then we kissed again, long and deep. I watched her walk slowly up to the front doors of her building, turning she waved, and when she disappeared inside, I drove off. Suddenly I felt very tired and still had one chore to finish—drop off the paintings in the storage unit. The drive was easy without much traffic at that time of day, and there was no one in the facility.

Parking the van close to the entrance and using a trolley, I was able to transfer the packages in no time. I moved eight at a time, as they were awkward rather than heavy, and stacked them around the walls. Tomorrow I would unpack them for storage.

After locking up the unit, I took the most direct route to my apartment and parked as close as I could…half way down the street. I went straight to the fridge for a beer. It went down easily, and then exhausted, I collapsed on the bed not bothering to undress.

Chapter Twenty-Eight

My phone ringing sounded like a drum beating in my head. I came awake and answered slowly. Before I could say anything, Hans's voice greeted me, "Good morning, *mon amie*. You are a very clever person. I am impressed with the merchandise you left with me. If this is what you achieved from the photographs I provided, think how much better it could be with a laser scan. This is a great idea, and I believe a very sound investment opportunity. I will be sending you a bank draft for twenty-thousand euros to show my interest is real. Please send me your bank details today. Speak to you soon. *Au revoir*, Peter."

To say I was stunned was an understatement. I wasn't sure what had just happened, but when it sank in, it was good. I focused on what to do next—shower, coffee, and call George in that order. I set up the coffee maker and headed to the bathroom.

My shower felt so good I stood under the hot water longer than I planned, soaking the weariness from my bones. I dried off quickly once the smell of coffee called my name from the kitchen, and by the time I called George I almost felt human again. Giving him a quick update, I told him I would fill in the blanks when I made it into the shop.

"Take your time," he said, "I'm looking forward to hearing about your weekend with a beautiful woman."

"Get your mind out of the gutter. See you later."

****

Unpacking the new merchandise was the priority of my day.

I grabbed breakfast and inhaled it on the drive to the storage unit, then used the time in Monday morning traffic to think through my next steps. One of which was to buy a copy of the Times newspaper. If that idea worked for Hans, to indicate he had the paintings, it would be a good way for me to tempt Fentiman. My section of the storage unit was deserted.

As I opened up the unit, my heart beat faster, knowing what was waiting for me. I still couldn't quite believe this was real.

I started unpacking and picked the piece closest to me. It was one of the smaller packages. My hands trembled slightly as I took a blade to the tape on the first package. I nicked the edge of the tape and pulled it back, repeated the process, and carefully removed it, strip by strip, until the stiff packing came away. I finally freed the interior materials. I pulled it and the paper covering the painting out, then I tentatively peeled back the paper.

Revealed was *Portrait of a Man* by Antonello da Messina.

Star struck, I held it in front of me, staring at the history in my hands. The sound of someone opening another locker brought me back to reality. It reminded me I had work to do. The panel slipped easily into the rack that I'd prepared. I worked slowly and methodically. I couldn't risk rushing any of the unpacking. Slowly the racks filled. One by one. Bigger pieces on the lower part, smaller panels on the upper.

I didn't allow myself the luxury of studying any of the paintings. This was pure labor, and I was on a time line. The *Lacemaker* by Jan Vermeer was a small work, and it would be one that Fentiman would, or should recognize instantly. Leaning it up against the wall on the folded Times newspaper with today's date showing, I used my non-work phone to take the picture. Not great, but it was clear enough.

Cleaning up the packing materials took little time. I saved some of the packing materials and put them aside just in case I needed them for future use. The remainder I tied up and put in the dumpster. I stood and inspected my work. The dehumidifiers had been emptied and were running. Everything looked to be in order.

I closed up the unit, and as soon as I got in the van, I called Fentiman's office. The number was one I'd never forget. The assistant had to be new, so my name didn't mean anything to her.

She put me through, and Fentiman answered, "Peter my boy, how are you? What a pleasant surprise."

"I am not your boy, and if I had any alternative I would not be calling you. Can I meet you this morning at your office? I need your expertise."

"Quite sharp. Well, I am not sure I want to meet if you have such an attitude."

"You will once you see why I need you."

"Well. You have peaked, my curiosity. Come on in. I will be able to manage a few minutes for an ex-felon."

I laughed at that. He was not going to get under my skin, not now, not with what I had planned for him, and had to offer. "Be available and sitting down."

My response seemed to take him aback. It wasn't

the response he expected. Good!

Hanging up, I found I was suddenly shaking. God, I hated that man. Returning the van to the rental depot, I picked up a black cab and gave the driver the Bond Street address. The cab ride gave me time to review what I was going to say to Fentiman in order to hook him.

Keep it simple. Tell him as much of the truth as need be. *Remember he isn't going to trust you.* He didn't trust anyone, and I certainly wasn't going to trust him.

The cab dropped me right outside the front entrance to the gallery. I pressed the intercom, the door immediately buzzed, and I entered. Everything was as I remembered…very polished and smooth. A young assistant approached me, asking if he could help. I gave my name. Someone I remembered from my days in the gallery interrupted him.

"Daniel, still dashing I see, grayer hair though—perhaps from the stress of working for Lucifer?"

"Very funny, Harper. Follow me."

Following Daniel, we stopped at the office door, and he patted me down. After a cursory knock, we entered Fentiman's office. Charles Fentiman hadn't changed at all. He was still dapper, well dressed, and perfectly at ease. Sharp Saville Row suit, a Jermyn Street shirt and tie, and I was sure he would be wearing shoes from Lobbs—classic English gentlemen's clothing. But the way he wore them looked less authentic than it did on someone else who had the correct pedigree.

"Please be seated, Peter. Coffee?"

"Yes, expresso please."

He smiled. "Good coffee is one of life's little pleasures. So what brings you to my door, cap in hand as it were."

"You mistake need for want."

"Well, you must *need* something from me. I am sure you don't want to be here anymore than I want or need you here."

To change the subject, I said, "I'm surprised you didn't have me frisked for a wire before allowing me in here."

"It makes no never mind in here. We are safe from prying ears. After all, my clients deserve and demand privacy. So whatever you have to say…say it."

I nodded to Daniel and asked him to leave. Fentiman nodded and Daniel left. Taking out my phone, I showed Fentiman the photo of the old master with today's paper.

"What am I to say? It means nothing to me. Copy of a nice painting?"

"Actually, it's the real thing."

"Rubbish, the real one is in the Louvre. Are you really stupid enough to try and scam me?"

"No, I'm not. Let me tell you a story."

I told him about Otto and his history, how we met in jail, what had happened to him, and what he had asked of me. The only time I stopped was when the coffee arrived. He nodded in the appropriate places.

At the end of my tale, I said, "I have in my possession sixteen old masters."

I gave him a list of the artists and the paintings. "As you can see, they are all fine examples of the artists' works. I want to unload them, all of them in one shot, and I want a decent price. I know you can sell them and make a good profit. What you make, I could care less. I want mine so I can retire and never work again.

"Hypothetically speaking, these are stolen items if they are genuine. I would, if I were interested of course, be taking a substantial risk in moving them."

"Cut the crap, Charlie. I know you have the contacts to move these paintings and make money on them. I want thirty-two million pounds for the lot."

He laughed outright at my number. "For fakes? Grow up, Peter. Nice try, but I wasn't born yesterday. You tell a good story, but I am not interested."

"You know people who would drop that on one old master, never mind sixteen."

"On real ones, yes…with a provenance, something you can't give me. Can you?"

"I thought you would say that. Not the usual provenance no, but one that will satisfy you, yes. Pick an expert, and I will make any work on the list available for their inspection. Privately, only them, the painting, and me. Any one of them. You pick. Don't wait too long. I am sure you will check out Otto's story. I have documentation from Germany validating the whole project. These sixteen were switched out and never left Paris."

Charles Fentiman was pensive. He steepled his hands and closed his eyes. When he opened them, he looked at me like a reptile, cold and expressionless. "I will take you up on your offer of an examination, and when the painting is proven to be a fake, I will make sure you regret it."

Got him. I knew the paintings were real. "Just make sure your expert is a real one because I have sixteen old masters, and he or she will need to be very careful in their examination. I have a direct line to the people who acquired them, and they have already been authenticated. So, if your report doesn't match mine, you will be the one regretting it." I wrote my phone number on his desk pad. "Don't leave it too long."

As I left, Fentiman said, "Always good to see you, Peter."

Daniel gave me a look of contempt, as he escorted me out of the gallery with a warning, "Don't contact us again, unless you are expressly requested to do so."

"We will be seeing a lot of each other, I am sure. Now go and be a good dog, stick your nose up your boss's ass."

He looked like he was going to respond, but I didn't give him a chance as I slammed the door behind me. The fresh air, if you can call London air fresh, felt good on my face, cooling and energizing.

Meeting Fentiman again had been stressful. I finally relaxed, at least enough to be aware of my surroundings and considered how Fentiman was on the hook. Now came the most dangerous part.

Actually reeling him in would only happen with patience. I wondered which painting he would pick for his expert to examine, sure that it wouldn't be the Jan Vermeer because it was the one I'd shown him. No, he would pick one of the others. Playing different scenarios, I ended up without a particular pick, and to be honest, I didn't care. They were all authentic.

I would just have to wait and see. I figured Fentiman would delay and take his time to put pressure on me or try to, anyway. The only problem I had was timing. Fentiman had to have his expert confirm the work was genuine. Then I could rat out Fentiman about the drugs stashed in the frames of Alistair's paintings.

When I arrived back to the shop we had some customers, so I got straight to work. When we had a minute, George said he was pleased to see me, and I briefly told him about my visit to Fentiman's.

He became serious. "Careful, Peter. He's a dangerous man."

"I know, and when the time is right, I will call in reinforcements."

"From where."

"You don't want to know."

"Just be careful…yes?"

"Yes, now let's make some sales."

The rest of the day flew by. We made some sales, which all in all made it a good day. Felicity called and offered to make dinner, which made it a better day, and after we'd closed up, I made my way over to Felicity's apartment. Now I was even more aware of my surroundings since I'd stirred the Fentiman hornets' nest. Mutual distrust meant he wasn't going to trust me an inch further than I would him. But I had some high cards up my sleeve…if it all worked out.

Felicity welcomed me with a smile and a long kiss.

"Paris obviously agrees with someone," I said.

"It was an adventure, even though you are still keeping secrets from me." She laughed. It wasn't an accusation, more a statement of fact.

"True, and believe me, it's for your own safety. What you don't know can't hurt you."

"Maybe, but perhaps I'm willing to take that risk. Why should you take all the risk for Otto and me?"

"Because Otto asked me to, and I agreed. You have

been patient, and I've told you what I can so far. I can update you now."

That got her attention, as expected. "Really, what's new?"

"Well, now we have the real thing here in London."

She interrupted. "You mean all the paintings on Otto's list are actually the real thing, not forgeries or copies?"

"Yup, authentic, each of them is an old master."

"Oh hell, this is getting very real." The concern in her voice was genuine, which made me feel good.

"Yes, it is, and I have contacted Fentiman."

She glanced at me with a suspicious look. It was only there a second, but I saw it.

"Why? Are you going to sell them to him?"

I decided to push her a little more. "And if I do?"

"I don't think that's a good idea. He is dangerous, and with your previous history he won't trust you."

"Exactly why I went to him. There are plans in motion which will nail Fentiman and get the paintings back where they belong."

A look of relief passed across her face. Good, another confirmation of sorts. "We can go over some details while we eat," I said. "What's for dinner?"

Felicity looked more relaxed and said, "Home-made lasagna."

We ate and drank an intimate dinner for two. As promised, I told her what I wanted her to know about my plans, and that I'd let her know more when everything was coming to a final resolution. She seemed satisfied with that, at least for now.

After dinner, we went to bed and the intimacy

between us seemed closer. We enjoyed each other's bodies without rush. Although lingering and contented, with our bodies entangled, I knew it was time for me to go home.

Chapter Twenty-Nine

Fentiman was predictable, and as expected, I heard nothing from him for a week. Then he called out of the blue. "Peter my boy, how are you? Well, I hope. Apologies for the delay in getting back to you—had a little difficulty getting hold of the right person, don't you know? It's not always easy getting these academic types to function in the real world. Anyway, long story short, I got the expert. The paintings he will examine are the two you claim to be by Hans Holbein the Younger."

"Are you hard of hearing? I said *a* painting, as in the singular, that means one not two."

"Well, dear boy, it's those two, or I am not interested in going further."

"Let me think about it."

"Don't think about it too long, my interest in your fakes won't last."

"Then you will be the one missing out. I'll be in touch, and don't put me off. Only you answer the call."

"That I can agree to. Don't wait too long."

"If I decide to go along with your request, be prepared to move at short notice."

That call confirmed Fentiman was deeper on the hook. By him choosing the only two paintings done by the same artist in the collection reinforced the fact that he had found a mercenary Holbein expert. Excellent.

Wanting some idea with whom I'd be dealing, my first move was to ask Felicity to get a list of all the Holbein experts.

She answered on the first ring. "Hello, Peter. This is a nice surprise."

"I need a favor."

"Well hello to you too, how are you? Sorry, couldn't resist, what do you need?"

"A list of all the Hans Holbein the Younger experts in the UK, and if possible, in Europe as well, with photographs. Head shots are fine or whatever you can get."

"That's all?"

"For now, thanks. Fentiman wants his expert to examine the two Holbein paintings. He suspects I am trying to scam him. It's better if I know who they are."

"That makes sense. I will see what I can do through our contacts here at the museum. Get back to you as quickly as I can."

Smiling at that, I thanked her, and cut the call. It was a risk to move the two Holbein paintings to George's lockup, but one worth taking. There was no way I was taking anyone to the storage unit.

Of course, I was in a hurry, and the traffic wasn't. I forced myself to calm down…think, and use the time to process what Fentiman could, or would do, to screw me over. How I could pick up the expert, so whoever it is won't be able to give any information to Fentiman? I needed back up, and I didn't want to use either George or Felicity, for different, but good reasons. Tel would know someone who could run some interference, and Harry could follow me and watch for anyone tailing me. After making the call to Tel, I felt better.

Once I reached the storage unit, I checked for other visitors. There were some but none in my area. The first thing I did once I opened up the unit was to check the dehumidifiers. I emptied and reset them, not knowing when I would be able to get back again.

The Holbein's were on different shelves. I was tempted to look at them. Instead, I resisted and packed them carefully. The sound of someone coming along my corridor reminded me to pull down the door. After the footsteps passed and faded, I checked that no one was in sight before letting myself out. I locked up and put the paintings in the back of my car. My heart beat faster. I was growing paranoid. Hopefully, I wouldn't have a stroke or heart attack before I completed this project.

I had time to calm down before reaching George's lock-up. Fortunately, the drive was uneventful. I opened the main door and closed it behind me, then unloaded my precious cargo. I left the paintings, packed for added protection, on the workbench.

Laughing quietly, I opened the lock-up door and backed out. With no one in sight, I closed up, and made my way to the shop. My relief was palpable. A calm settled over me. I wasn't sure why, but the feeling that I could take on the world and win sure felt good.

I parked at the back of the shop just as Tel returned my call. "Ullo mate, wotsup?"

"Tel, thanks for getting back to me so quickly. Can we meet? I need to bend your ear for some advice? Drinks are on me."

"Well tha's different init. Sounds good. Can't make it ta nite, ow bout tomorra?"

"Done…where to meet?"

"The pub you dropped orf the necessary. It's me local. I gets orf abat foive, see ya at foive firty?"

"It's a date."

"Ear that's not gonna happen. I gotta wife. Jus kidding wiv ya. Tomorra it is then. Cheers, mate."

As he hung up, I smiled to myself. *What a character!*

I slipped my phone in my pocket and opened the door to the shop and immediately noticed how quiet it was. It seemed as good a time as any to bring George up to date about what was happening.

"Hey, since we've got a few minutes, I want to run a few details past you."

"Sure, of course. Go ahead."

He kept silent for the most part, paying attention, but he did occasionally nod while he made a few notes on a pad. I told him my plans to meet a contact for advice regarding how to get the "expert" and the paintings together without compromising the location of either the lock-up or the storage unit.

"Good idea. I'm certain your contact will have some good suggestions about using technology. Don't forget, I'm here for you as well."

"How can I forget? You keep reminding me!"

"Peter, I am serious."

"I know you are, and I appreciate it. Trust me, I will call on you if I need anything. Promise. How's business?"

"Pretty good. Not much yesterday, but a goodish week all told. Oh, I almost forgot, Jack from the framers called and said you owed him something. What's that about?"

I laughed. I'd forgotten our bet about selling the

replicas in Paris. Jack was in for a surprise. The twenty-thousand euros from Hans would convince him I was right. If he expected to hear from me, he'd have to wait until later in the day for my call.

By the time I got around to calling Jack, it was almost closing time.

He answered with a smug, "Peter, thank you for the three double priced framing jobs."

Keeping my voice flat, as if I had lost, I said, "Well done, Jack only you are wrong. An investor in Paris put up twenty-thousand Euros to prove his interest in the concept, and said more would be available."

"You're shitting me."

"Nope, he is very serious when it comes to money, especially his."

"Well, I called that one wrong, didn't I."

"Should have had faith in me, but you don't need to settle up.'

"Yes, I do. A bet is a bet. If I had been right, I would've collected, trust me."

"Fair enough. I'll let you know when our frame is needed."

"In any case, you will need frames for all of them won't you?"

"Yes, Jack, we will need frames. Now, cheers."

"Cheers, Peter."

After closing, I left for home, picked up my usual take-out dinner, and called Felicity to finish the day. I explained to Felicity some of what I was planning. She thought I was being smart and careful.

"I'm collating the Holbein expert info, and you should have it tomorrow or the next day, at the latest." As we said goodnight, she said she loved me. What more could a man want?

The next day was business as usual—customers came and went. George seemed on edge about something, but when I asked he blew me off. Knowing better than to push him, I let it go. He would talk when he was ready. As I left before closing to meet Tel, George reminded me again to be careful. I assured him, I would, then made my way to the tube station.

Once I arrived at the pub, when I didn't see Tel, I ordered myself a pint and settled in a corner where I could see most of the Pub. Tel arrived half way down the pint, shook hands, and gave me a pat on the shoulder. We went to the bar for his drink and another for me, then we settled in, with his back to the wall he faced the whole interior of the pub. As he raised his glass, saying, "Cheers mate, wot's up?"

"First thanks for meeting me, and listening, I am a bit out of my depth."

"Anyfin ta do wiv the bugs in yor place?"

"Kinda sorta, but not really."

"Wow, that don't make sense."

"Okay, then here goes. This is just between you and me, right?"

"Roit, ya got me word."

Not sure how to begin, I dove in. "What I really need is to make this safe for me and everyone involved."

"It's a situation, where I have some merchandise, which needs to be examined by an expert. However, I don t want them, or their principal to know where the merchandise is. I am not sure how to go about it, I don't trust the principal, at all, he's dangerous to me."

" 'Oo is it."

"Fentiman, Charles Fentiman."

"Weern't 'e the geezer wot framed you?"

"Yes."

"Wot the hell you playing wiv im for."

"Tel, if this works out, its pay back in spades, and some money as a side benefit."

"Awright, lemme fink. You needs to get this bloke to a location, wiv at 'im knowin, or anybody else where 'e's at, then return 'im to wherevaa, all in one piece I s'pose?"

"That's it pretty much."

"Well, not so big a deal, gotta 'ave the right crew tha's all. I fink I can 'elp ya out. 'Arry would be me furst choice as chaser, then we needs one other to do the pick-up, me bruver-in-law, Jimmy is a good bloke. So we're set."

"It's that easy?"

"Well, not quite. We'll need some readies in compensation for our time like."

"How much?"

"We'll come to a moochoolly satisfactree arrangement when we gets more details abaat the job, and the time like. Won't be stooped money tho."

"How will you make it work?"

"You gives me as much details as possbl. I choose the pick-up place and drop 'im where you is waitin. I assume it'll be in Landan?" I nodded. "Roit. Will I get to drive into the locashun so the geezer won't see anyfin?" Again, I nodded. "Good. Pick 'im up, then we delivers 'im to you. Let 'im do is fing, and then reverse it, and drop 'im off, wiv out telling 'im. Keeps 'im all off kilter like."

"Sounds simple when you explain it like that."

"Ya don't want to make it too complicated. Keep it simple stooped. Less to go pear shaped. 'Ow long will ee need to do 'is thing."

"A couple of hours, maybe a little longer. How will you know if you are being followed, Harry?"

"I'll sweep the geezer for a wire, GPS locators, and basically anyfin electronic wot could track us. The best day would be a Sunday in daylight, less traffic so easier to spot a tail, but wotever day you chooses, it's gotta be in day light. Awright?"

"All right, you are the expert on this stuff."

"Put it this way, not me first time at the circus."

"Then let's drink to that. Another?"

"Yep, same agen then. Ta."

We had a couple more drinks while going over details, and then generally conversed. Tel said he had access to a windowless van for the job. We parted, with him happy for the extra cash, and me with a problem resolved. All I needed to do before calling Fentiman was get the expert info from Felicity.

Making it home without incident, and not used to drinking that much, I crashed into bed, prepared to regret it in the morning. I was right.

An air raid siren was going off in my head, and when I opened my eyes, I shut them again quickly. Today was not going to be a good one. This time I slowly opened my eyes, allowing myself to adjust to the morning brightness. Food and coffee would help me feel human again, so I dragged myself to the local greasy spoon, had a bacon sandwich, coffee, and several painkillers. After the second cup of coffee, I started to feel more like I'd survive, not great, but better.

George looked up. "You look like shit," he said, as I entered the shop.

"Thanks, I love you, too."

"I hope it was worth it."

"Oh yeah, no question about that. Tel had it sorted in minutes." George was impressed when I told him the plan.

He agreed it was sound. "I can't pick any holes in your plans." So to say I was reassured was an understatement.

Mid-morning my cell went off. It was Felicity texting me with a reminder for me to check my e-mail. Immediately I went to my e-mail, and then located and opened the file from Felicity. She said there were more Holbein experts, but these nine were the cream of the crop.

The list started with one each of American, Italian, and Danish experts, followed by two English, and as expected, four were Dutch. Each name had a picture of varying quality with a short biography. Quickly scanning the bio's, I discarded the American for distance. Too far to come on short notice, and why choose him when there were eight in Europe.

Fentiman would probably go for one of the Dutch or English experts. The choices were down to six. They all seemed to be well-qualified and above reproach. I would just have to see who turned up.

I'd put off calling Fentiman long enough. Dialing his number made the hate rise up in me. I had to calm down to make this work, and then he would get what he had coming to him. Fentiman answered on the first ring.

"Fentiman?"

"Yes, Peter. Ready to accept my terms?"

"On the items, yes. But everything else is on my terms."

"That will depend on what they are. Please continue."

"The name of your expert."

"Jurgen van der Valk."

"Interesting choice." He was one of the Dutch experts on Felicity's list.

"Next, Peter."

"He is the only one who gets to see and examine the items. He can have as long as he wants, he can take samples of the panel and the paint…very small samples. You will receive directions for him to follow. If you and he don't comply, it's over, cancelled. The meeting will be on a Sunday, you can pick which one."

"Sorry Peter, that is not acceptable. It has to be a weekday, and I have a list of six days over the next three weeks that work for Jurgen. This week only Friday, the following week Wednesday and Thursday are available. The final week is mostly open on Monday, Tuesday, or Friday. Any issue with that?"

"No. I will get back to you on which day. It will only be the day before, so you and he better be flexible."

"Acceptable. Next."

"I will choose the pick-up place and drop off. Please do not try to tail him. The two items have been separated from the others, and I will have taken other precautions."

"Well, you almost sound like a professional." His laugh was unpleasant.

"No, I just don't trust you."

"Excellent perspective, which I also follow. It seems you are serious about this. Perhaps I misjudged you on this matter."

"What makes you say that?"

"You allowed me to choose the items for examination at random. Besides, if you knew they were fakes, you would not allow Jurgen to take samples. Interesting, if they are the real thing, we will both make out on this transaction. Of course, that doesn't mean they are all the real deal does it? A warning Peter, paintings aren't the only things that can be faked."

"Do you really think I am stupid enough to try conning you? I have priceless items and am offering them to the only person I know who can move them. And at a price that makes it more sensible and profitable for you to deal with me than to kill me. You will make your money, and I don't care what you make over and above my price. In fact, I expect you to screw me, but as long as I make what I need, I really don't care."

"Perhaps Peter, perhaps not. We will see the results of the examination. I do look forward to hearing from you soon."

"Just be ready."

"I always am." With that, he ended the call.

Totally focused on getting Fentiman's expert sorted out, I almost missed his comment about paintings not being the only thing to be faked. His comment set me thinking.

Then George poked his head around the door and broke my train of thought. "We've got customers."

Rejoining the real world, I took care of the customers, and when we were quiet again. I called Tel, giving him the dates that Jurgen was available.

He immediately picked Friday of this week. "Git it over and done wiv. Don't give the uver side any time ta do any noughties. Oil tak care of evrefing moy end. Gimme all the detells when you get 'em."

"You'll have them as soon as I do, promise. Don't forget to let me know what I need in the cash department."

"No worries mate, I know where you lives." With his easy laugh ringing in my ear, he cut the call. I called back Fentiman, and again he picked-up on the first ring.

"Peter my boy, you are quick off the mark."

"This Friday. Is he flying into Heathrow or London airport?"

"Is that relevant?"

"Yes, which one will depend on where he will be picked-up."

"I will get back to you ASAP." He hung up.

All I could do was wait, but I didn't mind, because whichever one it was, we had it covered.

Fentiman called back within an hour, which surprised me. "London Airport, on KLM scheduled to land at 7:25 a.m. What else do you need?"

"Tell Jurgen to take the tube into central London. He will be met at the bottom of Regent Street, Piccadilly Circus, and taken directly to the items."

"I will let him know."

"Don't contact me until you get confirmation that the items are genuine. Then we can go from there."

"You are very confident, Peter, but I agree. However, I will be contacting you, real or fake, just different outcomes."

"Just line up your buyers, I want my get out

money." My turn to laugh, as I cut the call. It was all now in play.

The rest of the week, I concentrated on the shop during the day and going over the 'Jurgen' plan as we called it, at night with Tel until we had it down.

Chapter Thirty

Friday arrived in a hurry. I laid out the final plan with George so he knew that I would be out of the shop all day. He agreed the plan sounded like a good one and wished me luck.

Tel and Jimmy were going directly to London Airport to pick up Jurgen, as we planned. That way, anyone tailing me, would be SOL, cutting out at least one possible tail situation. If all went well, I arranged to meet them at George's lock-up. If not, Tel would dump Jurgen, and I would call Fentiman.

The lock-up street was deserted as usual. I opened up and drove deep into the space, leaving room for Tel's van behind me, and then I locked up. The anticipation was driving me nuts, but no news from Tel was good news. It meant no problems. We all knew the timeline.

—The plane lands. Van der Valk walks off without going through customs. He goes to the exit where Tel awaits him with a sign that reads: Mr. Van Der Valk. Tel escorts him to the windowless van, then if there are no tails, directly on to the lock-up. If Fentiman had someone at the meeting place I'd stated they would be out of luck.—

Easy enough if nothing went wrong. So far it all looked good.

My cell went off like a fire alarm, unusually loud

in the empty space. When I answered, Tel said, "We're abat ten mins aat, be ready."

"Got it." Ready to open the doors. The doors were unlocked, and there was plenty of space for the van to pull in. Waiting by the small door until I heard a vehicle coming down the street. I hazarded a look see. It was Tel. The lights flashed. Doors opened, the van drove straight in, the doors closed. All took mere seconds. I locked the doors and breathed a sigh of relief. Tel hopped out from the passenger side and introduced the driver Jimmy, who nodded and remained silent.

I asked, "Any problems."

"Nah, Arry says ullo an no tails. This one in here, is a smart one, lots of tech. Bin disabled, no one could find 'im in a munff of Sundis. We'll op it, give us a bell when yer dun, and we'll tak 'im back ta tha airpout."

"Thanks, I appreciate it."

"Twernt nuffin mate, we'll bill ya later, awright?"

"Perfect."

Tel and Jimmy left through the small door. I assumed it was Harry who picked them up.

Slowly, I opened the side door of the van. I saw a slight middle-aged man, well dressed, sitting uncomfortably on a make-shift seat in the darkness of the van. He stared at me before asking, in accented English, "You have two items for inspection?"

"Yes, I do. I apologize for the subterfuge."

"I am used to it. Many collectors are eccentric. Some completely paranoid, but we are not here to discuss them. You have good light, yes?"

"Yes, follow me."

I led him to the bench, where the wrapped items were stored. Turning on the brighter lights, I left Jurgen to put his two bags on the bench. He proceeded to lay out his equipment. He started by examining the wrapping before carefully and with a slow exactness that indicated to me that he was who he said he was. He removed the first item, and I heard him inhale sharply as he looked at the painting. I thought it was a good sign.

He worked methodically, examining every inch of the work, front, back, and sides. He asked, "Is it true? You will permit me to take samples?"

"Yes, as few and small as possible, please. I want a positive result, so whatever you need."

"Thank you."

Sitting closely, but not intrusively, I watched Jurgen work. There was too much at stake for me to take my eyes off him for even one second. Jurgen put the first painting aside, opened the second, and I heard the same intake of breath. He spent time going over it. When he was done, he took off his glasses and squeezed his nose.

He thanked me when I offered him a bottle of water, then took a long swig. A moment later, he went back to work. He put the two paintings side by side, moving from one to the other and back again.

Seeing him pick up a scalpel, I said, "Please be careful."

He looked at me over his glasses and said, "If they are fakes it doesn't matter, if they are not it will prove it. I know what I am doing."

He bent over them, took samples of wood panel, and tiny scrapes of paint from different areas, meticulously labeling everything as he went.

Another hour went by before he said, "I am almost

done. Just some photographs, and I will have completed my examination. Then I would like to be taken back to the airport, please."

"Of course, but I have a question."

"You want to know if they genuine Holbein's?"

"Yes." I wanted his opinion.

"Until I have completed my tests back in Amsterdam, I can only say for sure that whoever painted them, did both." He waited with a frown creasing his forehead before continuing. "I do believe they are the original works of Hans Holbein the Younger, which should be in the Louvre. I will not insult you by asking how you came by them. Only that they have been very well cared for. Now, please let me continue."

Jurgen bent down again to his task, cleaning up as he went. He took multiple photographs of each, including all the edges, and back of the panels, then finally photographs of the two next to each other. As he finished up, I called Tel.

"Ya done?"

"Just finishing up now."

"Be there in ten ta fifteen."

"We'll be ready."

Good as his word, Tel arrived in ten minutes, honking the horn once. I told Jurgen to face the back of the lock-up. Assisting Jurgen, I loaded his bags into the van and thanked him for being so diligent.

He smiled. "That is my job. You have been more courteous than most, and I thank you for the privilege of seeing what I do believe are original Holbein's. Don't quote me. The principal who hired me will receive my report in due course. Goodbye."

"Goodbye and safe travels."

He nodded and entered the van. I shut the van door and opened the main doors. Tel shot off into the afternoon sunlight. On my own again, I felt a sadness come over me. I suppose it was a normal response after the tension of the examination. Re-wrapping the paintings, I returned them to the storage unit, feeling better on the return to the shop. My mood improved even more when I saw Felicity waiting for me and chatting with George. Before I could say anything, they both jumped in. "How did it go?"

"As well as could be expected. Jurgen on his preliminary examination believes they are the real thing and will confirm that after he has done the tests on the panel and paint."

Watching Felicity rather than George, I saw an expression flash across her face, and then it was gone. Satisfaction? Maybe.

"Let's celebrate," I said.

They agreed, and we puttered about the shop until closing. The celebration was a quiet one at our local pub. After we left, Felicity and I went back to my place. She stayed over, making the perfect ending to an almost perfect day.

The next day, all I could think about was Jurgen's report. I forced myself to concentrate or try to concentrate on the shop which provided a good distraction. I drove George crazy with ideas for changing the shop around. At the end of the week, I was talking with a potential customer when my "other" phone rang.

Fentiman.

I excused myself and went into the office before I

answered, "Well?"

"Well, indeed Peter. It does seem you have the real thing. Jurgen was very impressed. He would not give them a hundred percent pass but would go with ninety-nine. That satisfies me to a degree. I do have some contacts who could be useful. However, I am giving you fair warning." His voice turned icy. "If you are foolish enough to try and pass any fakes through me, my clients will take a dim view and settle that error permanently. I do hope we understand each other."

"That was never a question. If you want to waste time, get all the appropriate experts to examine all the others. If you can find, shall we say, flexible experts, we can go that route. Like I said, I want to move them as a job lot, which is why I priced them to sell."

"Peter, dear boy, thirty-two million pounds is not priced to sell. Not in this day and age."

Barking out a laugh, I said, "Cut the crap. You know you can sell each one for a good deal more than two mill. Even you will be able to retire on the Raphael alone."

"Which is why I wondered why you priced them the way you did?"

"You really don't listen, do you? I don't trust you. I only want to deal with you once, not sixteen times. Even with the splits, I can retire on my share. I'd never have to work again. Selling one at a time, I could get more, but it increases the risk, and I would have to deal with you. Not worth it."

"Peter, you must let go of the past. It was purely business, nothing personal."

"It was personal to me. So are you willing to meet my price?"

"No, not yet. I want to know who your partners are. Also about your Felicity."

"Otto's daughter will get a share. She knows nothing about this transaction, or about the previous custodian of the paintings. The paintings are not in England, and I will not reveal their location."

Fentiman laughed, "I didn't really expect you to tell me, but I had to ask."

"So what happens now?"

"Have to do some thinking and make some calls. I will call you shortly."

"Don't leave it too long." I hung up on him. My next call was to Jacob, who of course was not available. I left my number for a call back. Jacob called back within the hour.

"Peter, shalom. How may I assist you."

"Thank you for calling back so promptly. How would I go about opening a secure no questions asked offshore bank account?"

Silence, I could hear him breathing. He answered, "Peter? This is regarding the matter we spoke of recently?"

"Yes, it is."

"You are being careful?"

"That is why I need an account no one knows about, and one that is very secure. Can you help me?"

"Yes, of course, Peter. I will assist. Can you obtain twenty-five thousand pounds on short notice?"

"Yes."

"The holding account cannot be opened with anything less, with the expectation of higher balances following. Can you add more to that account?"

"Yes, and if everything works out, a lot more, and

soon."

"Then I will send you directions on where to send the amount. It will not be the final account, but you will be notified as soon as that is set up. The bank sends you your account information directly. Do not lose it. They only send one set of numbers. I hope you know what you are doing, Peter."

"So do I."

"Please do not hesitate to call me. I have resources available if you require them."

"Thank you, Jacob. Hopefully, I won't need anything except a holiday. Shalom."

"Shalom."

Hearing the worry in his voice, I wondered what he wasn't telling me. I had enough to worry about so now back to waiting for Fentiman to contact me. He wouldn't accept my initial asking price, not without some push back and negotiation. My drop-dead number was twenty-one million. That number ensured Otto's daughter, Hans, and I would be financially secure for life. With that taken care of, I went back to working the shop. The bank information from Jacob was waiting for me on my computer along with the direct communication from the bank itself. Memorizing the numbers, I hid the hard copy safely…just in case.

Fentiman called two days after I had the bank information. "Peter, dear boy, it seems that you were actually telling it true. I did have Jurgens results looked over by another expert, and he confirmed the results of the physical tests on the samples. There are some folks who I happen to know who would be interested in the items, but your asking price is too high, fifteen is the most I can do."

"Perhaps I should just offer them to the French Government and ask a finders-fee. Goodbye, Fentiman"

"No wait. Peter, I am sure we can come to some arrangement that benefits us both, can't we?"

"Not at fifteen."

"Well, thirty-two is out of the question. Suggest a number."

"Twenty-seven."

"Still a bit steep old boy, how about twenty?"

"Twenty-five."

"I could go as high as twenty-three, best and final offer you will get from me." Before answering, I paused, silent as if I were assessing the pros and cons of his offer.

"Agreed, but it has to be done in one transaction, and I want a good faith deposit, of fifty percent. I will supply bank details. You get to hold the Holbein's as my good faith gesture."

"Oh, my dear boy, that's not the way it works."

"It does this time."

"Not a chance of fifty percent. I will put up four and half million, the Holbein's will be mine to keep if everything falls through, take it or leave it."

"How long do you need to raise the balance?"

"Couple of weeks, maybe three at the outside. It is a large sum."

"We meet in a public space for the simultaneous exchange of your deposit and the two paintings."

"That will be satisfactory. All the remaining items are in one location?"

"Yes, you will get the location once I have confirmed the correct balance is deposited and can't be reversed."

"Peter, I am hurt."

"No you aren't, and I still expect you to try and cheat me somehow."

"What about my trust, I only get the location when you have my money. That's trust."

"No, it's not. If I cheat you, you will find me and kill me. I have no illusions about that. For all your veneer, you are really just a thug."

"We do seem to understand each other. I'll let you know when I have everything arranged. In the meantime, be very careful with whom you associate. Not everyone is who they seem to be, and I may have to take some action."

"Is that a threat?"

"Not at all, dear boy, just a friendly warning."

With business concluded, I hung up, pondering Fentiman's last comment, that was the second time he had dropped that comment. It reminded me that Otto had said the same thing. I wondered what he knew. That brought me back to thinking about how to set up Fentiman regarding the drug shipment in Alistair's frames. I had to put Fentiman in dire need of cash, but not in jail, yet. I would need to be very careful.

With information and pieces falling into place, I called Alistair, saying to go ahead with releasing his work to the framers. As soon as they were ready for shipping, he had to let me know. He promised he would.

My next call was to Hans. After leaving a message, I went back to work, reality, and the shop while waiting impatiently for Hans's call. When he hadn't called by the time we closed the shop, I went home and puttered about aimlessly. My cell went off, and feeling unsettled, I grabbed it.

"I apologize for not returning your call. I was travelling back from Berlin. How are things progressing?" Hans asked.

"Very well, however I need your assistance. Can you supply an appropriate contact name in the Paris police department, in antiques or fine art? Someone with clout and the ability to send a team to London at short notice? Is that do-able?"

"Yes, of course. In my business, one has to be careful. So yes, I have contacts. You will have all the information you need. It will be with you tomorrow. My name will not be mentioned, correct?"

"Correct. I also wish to remain anonymous on this one," I said with a chuckle.

"Please be careful. Do not relax your guard. That could be fatal."

"Trust me, I am being very careful."

As promised, I received a text the next morning with the name, rank, telephone numbers for office and cell, and an e-mail address of a contact. Hans's German heritage showed in his thoroughness and efficiency. He had provided all I needed, and I had the plan and the information. Now it was waiting and timing.

****

Felicity seemed to be more available to me than she had been. The evening after Hans's text, she stopped by the shop on her way back from an appointment. It was near closing time, so we all decided to have dinner early. George was meeting a date later, so he wasn't going home first.

We were walking to the restaurant together when George shouted, "Watch out!"

I felt a violent shove that knocked me into Felicity, then the both of us tumbled and landed hard. As we fell, I heard several loud bangs, and then George cried out. Behind us, were more very loud bangs sounded as a car screeched down and around the corner. What just happened? My knee hurt like hell where I'd landed on it, and Felicity held her head where she'd hit it on the wall when we fell.

I glanced around looking for George, then I saw him a few feet from us, lying on his back. A dark patch formed on his left shoulder and a larger one spread on his right chest. There was a gun in his right hand, laying by his side. I went to him and shouted, "George, George are you all right?"

He croaked, "I-I think I need an ambulance."

"Yes, yes you do," I said. "Felicity is calling emergency services, now." I took off my scarf, I pressed one end at George's shoulder and the other end on his chest to control the bleeding. He winced and stifled a cry.

Felicity appeared shaken but spoke clearly into her phone maintaining her composure as blood dripped from the cut on her forehead and rolled down the side of her face. I wanted to go to her and help, but she was still on her phone, and George was in serious condition.

Within minutes, a crowd gathered, some asking if they could do anything. But soon the air was shattered by police and ambulance sirens, accompanied by the flashing lights.

My concern for George kept me with him until the EMT's pushed me out of the way. I saw George's gun, partially hidden by his open jacket, and moved it away, scooping it up with my scarf, and stowing it in my pocket. The EMT's started cutting off George's clothes to access the wounds.

A police officer moved me to one side, and asked if I was all right. Dazed, I answered, "Yes."

The police cordoned off the area, detectives showed up, and I was separated me from Felicity.

The detective questioned me and took my statement. Eventually he said, "I am sure you are in shock, but we will need to talk to all of you tomorrow. The EMTs advised us that your friend's wounds are serious. Once we are done here, we'll take you to the hospital, all right?"

Nodding, my agreement, I joined Felicity who stood talking to another detective. There was quite a crowd forming, and other police officers were busy canvassing for witnesses.

Needing to get to the hospital, I asked Felicity, "Ready?"

She nodded. I put my arm around her and went as directed to the police car. The detective told the driver which hospital.

We were both quiet on the ride, probably at the realization of the dangerous game I played. This was way out of my realm. Did someone want to harm or kill me? It didn't make sense. If it weren't me, it could be Felicity or George. But why? They were peripheral to my involvement. This was crazy.

By the time we arrived at the hospital, George was already in surgery, and it would be some while before they would know anything. The nurse did say the surgeon had done tours in the Middle East and was an expert with puncture wounds. Not sure what else I heard after that comment. What seemed like hours passed with me in a daze. Felicity seemed to be handling the situation much better than I was. Eventually the surgeon came out to meet us, asking if we were family.

"No, I am his business partner."

"He's a fighter. He has lost a lot of blood, and we have given him a transfusion. The shoulder wound looked worse than it actually is, a through and through without much damage, just muscle, no broken bones. The chest wound contained significant damage and was difficult to repair. It is serious, but the bleeding is controlled for now. He is in critical but stable condition. If he makes it through the next twenty-four to forty-eight hours, it will give us a good indication of his chance of recovery. Expect a long recovery, and he will need physical therapy for his shoulder and probably respiratory therapy for his chest wound as well."

"Thank you, we appreciate it."

"His are the worst wounds I have encountered in the UK. We don't get many shootings in London, thankfully. But as I said, he is a fighter. I would not bet against him," he said, and gave us a thumbs up.

Well, neither would I, but I suddenly realized how exhausted I felt. Sitting back down, I just wanted to sleep.

Felicity shook my shoulder and brought me around to face her. "Let's go, my place is closer, and we need to get some sleep. I'm sure the police will want to talk with us tomorrow, or technically, later today. Come on." Letting her lead me, we headed for the exit. She hailed a passing cab.

Our dinner had turned into a crisis. Thoughts buzzed in my head, and none would stay still long enough for me to fix on them. But something was there, bothering me, and I just had to pin it down. Getting to Felicity's place didn't take long, and we'd been lost in our own thoughts along the way. We were quiet until we entered her apartment, then she faced me and gripped me by my shirt. "I am so sorry about what happened to George. Why do you think they were after you?"

"I don't know. This doesn't make any sense. If I go, everything goes, and no one wins."

"If you need anything, Peter, I'm here for you."

"I'm just so tired," I said. "I can't think."

We undressed, and climbed into bed holding each other, then I went out like a light, but I didn't remain asleep for long. I woke in the early hours, finally facing the realization that my best friend was critically injured. He'd saved me when I got out of prison and again now. He sacrificed his own safety in the process. My tears started slowly, and then turned into choked sobs. Felicity woke and just held me, saying nothing.

Being next to Felicity always felt good. I needed someone, and I wanted it to be her.

Chapter Thirty-One

The new day arrived, whether I wanted it to or not. Without waking Felicity, I got up and sat in a chair watching her sleep, peacefully in repose. I played the events of the previous evening over and over in my mind. Everything happened so quickly, I had to stop and start and replay everything over and over again. Slowing it down helped clarify things each time I replayed it. Finally after breaking it into sections, the truth suddenly hit me. Felicity had been the target, not me. George was trying to save Felicity. He used me to save her and put himself in the line of fire. This was a revelation, and a disturbing one. Felicity was going to be out of the picture from now on, at least until I finished my current business. I made a promise to Otto and I was going to keep it.

While making breakfast, my shock turned to anger. I didn't know how, but I was going to get whoever almost killed George. Making the call to George's brother was not something I looked forward to doing. They were close, and this would affect him greatly.

I picked up my phone and made the call. He responded as I expected, very stoic and stiff upper lip. Why do we British keep our emotions buried so deeply? Wanting to rant, rave, and explode, I followed Stephen's lead instead and kept everything inside. Then repeating a promise to myself, I vowed I'd deal with the culprit.

Stephen said he would be coming up to town, and thanked me for the call. I told him, I would let him l know if there were any changes and hung up.

When I turned around, Felicity was standing in the doorway, crying. She opened her arms and walked into me. We clasped and silently held each other until the boiling kettle broke the spell and reminded me of things I needed to do.

Breaking away from her, I kissed her lightly on the head and said, "This is not over, and I added George to the tab. You keep your promise. Do not go to the authorities on this one, please."

"Peter, it's too dangerous. You have to go to them now."

"No, not a chance. This will be finished on my terms, and if Fentiman has something to do with this, I will prove it. Then the bastard is going down."

"Peter, I mean it. You have to go. If you won't, I will. I don't want to lose you. This is just too dangerous now."

"Promise me you won't do anything until I tell you."

"What does that mean?"

"It means when the time is right, you can tell whoever you want, but not until I tell you. Promise me?" Looking at her face fixed with determination, I saw how badly Felicity was torn between what she wanted, and what I wanted.

I won this round.

"Okay for now, Peter, but you must promise me, you'll take care and make the right decision at the right time."

I smiled a determined smile. "Promise said and kept. I don't want to lose you, either. Before you, I didn't have much to live for. I went through the motions. Now I have many reasons to live."

What Felicity didn't know was that she may have been the primary reason, but revenge was up there, and the combination of love and hate was going to get me through to the end of this shit-storm. As we finished up breakfast, the doorbell rang. I checked the peephole. It was the police.

On entering, they offered their good wishes for George before setting in with a raft of questions. Felicity seemed at ease and answered quickly and succinctly. On the other hand, I took my time with every question, making sure my answers were truthful, but gave away as little information as possible without raising suspicions.

Once they left, Felicity asked, "Why were you so reticent, about answering their questions?"

"You forget. I have had some unpleasant dealings with the boys in blue."

"This is different. This is George we are talking about."

"You think I don't know that. You are going to have to trust me. I have resources the police don't have and can't use. I have them, and I am going to use them."

"Legal or otherwise."

"Yes."

We argued for the first time, no shouting, or ranting, just deeply held convictions, point and counter point. Neither of us backed down. Leaving everything unresolved with her, I went home, still wearing clothes covered in George's blood. I needed to change.

On the way, I left a message for Tel to give me a buzz, then I called Hans. There was no answer, so I left him a message to return my call. Anger is energy if it is controlled and focused in a positive way. My next call was to Alistair. Again no answer. Again I left another message.

Frustration reinforced my anger. Showering and putting on fresh clothes helped me get myself under control. By the time I made it to the shop and opened up, late, I'd calmed down to cold anger. Was it Shakespeare or someone else who said...*revenge is a dish, best served cold*? Ice cold would be a good description of how I felt.

The phone was quite busy. Everyone seemed to already know what had happened to George, and many called to offer help and good wishes. The offers of support were genuine and gave me a feeling of warmth, but the hurt inside was as painful as a car crash. Nothing would take this pain away. Losing Otto was bad enough, but the concept of losing George was so intense it bordered on unbearable. If he died, I wasn't sure what I would do.

Shaking off my maudlin thoughts, I responded to the sound of my phone. It was Tel.

"Sorry, Pete, we 'erd abat yor mate. Wot jue need?"

"You heard already?"

"Yeah, shootins ain't so common. Lots a cracked 'ed's and stabbins, but shootins? Not so much."

"Tel, ear to the ground. I want to know anything and everything. Whatever you can pick up about the shooting, anything at all. Who? Why? You know better than I do. Don't worry about the cost. I am good for it."

"Yeah, no worries on the fees like. But I would sagest leavin this wun to the filth, theys gonna be all over it, an'aas resources to."

"I know, but I want the real information. Besides, the police won't tell me what I want to know. Will you do it?"

"Yeah, we can keep an ear out for ya. Sorry again, mate."

Hanging up with Tel, he was probably right. I should leave it to the police. Hell. I put the closed sign on the front door and went into the back area office. I just didn't feel like dealing with customers.

Sitting pondering things, I ran my mind back over everything that had happened since that day I had seen Otto. There were no straight lines. As I thought through everything, it was clear Fentiman was involved from the start. He knew Otto and had dealings with him in the past.

Was I right about Felicity being the target? Why her and not me? Going back to the time when she visited to examine the Durer and Schiele, and the thoughts I'd had about her then. Plus the information from Jacob…that was the answer to something but not everything. And now I was certain Fentiman was responsible.

Hans called, and we had a short conversation. He passed on his best wishes when I told him what had happened, asking if I still wanted to continue. "More than ever," I responded. Nothing and no one was going to stop me now.

I locked up the shop, feeling exhausted, and drove around aimlessly in my own cocoon.

There was nothing I could do right now. Things had to play out in their own time. Fentiman would call when he called, and I would be ready to deal for the paintings. It was late in the day, and I had been home for a while when Alistair rang.

He was shocked to hear what had happened. "Anything I can do?"

"Just keep with the plan. Are all the paintings with the frame company?"

"Yes, they gave me an approximate date for shipping to Fentiman's. Monday next week. Takes a few days to get to London. The shipment will go directly to his East End warehouse to get prepped for adding to the gallery."

"Good to know. Now forget about it and me."

"Are you going to be okay?"

"Don't know. We'll see when all this crap is finished. Talk later. Bye." I hung up abruptly, suddenly wanting to wallow in my own company. Stress and worry are weird things.

Missing George…and I hadn't heard from Felicity. I guess our argument *had* done some damage. I didn't feel like eating, so I had a beer and went to bed.

Chapter Thirty-Two

The alarm hammered me awake. Rolling over, I hit snooze, not really wanting to get up and face it all, thinking there wasn't much point until I had something to get up for. No news on George's condition. Oh, woe is me and all.

Fuck it. George wouldn't appreciate me being pathetic. I checked my phone for messages. Nothing. I wasn't hungry. I took my time getting to the shop and was still on time to open on our regular schedule. Puttering about, looking busy, I found stupid things to occupy me, like losing myself in the history of the items we had for sale.

Customers came and went. Some bought. Some didn't, and neither really got the juices going, marking time. George's brother, Stephen called and told me where he was staying. I told him I would call in on him later, but it would probably be the next day. He said that worked for him as there were some items to go over. What they could be, I didn't know or care. Actually, not much bothered me, and that, in fact, bothered me.

Felicity called me on my way home. I told her I was driving and would call her when I got home. After I dropped my bag, I popped a beer and called her back.

She answered on the first ring, "Peter, I am sorry we argued. I was...am upset, and I am concerned about you. You know that, right?"

"Yes, I know. I'm sorry too, but I have to do this my way. I owe it to both Otto and George. Believe me, everything will work out. Trust me. I am not going to risk prison again."

"I know I should trust you. I love you and am scared for you. Promise you will be careful."

"Promise made and promise kept. I love you, too."

"Do you want me to come over tonight?"

"No, not tonight. I am not good company, but I would like you to come with me to visit George, if and when he is allowed visitors."

"Of course, anytime. Just let me know when. Are you sure about tonight?"

"Yeah, thanks. Can I call you tomorrow?"

"Of course. Take care. Peter, remember whatever happens, I love you."

"Love you too…talk tomorrow."

Ending the call, I felt maudlin. Moping about the apartment didn't help. I realized I hadn'tchecked the dehumidifiers in two days. I finished my beer and took a drive to the storage unit, checking my rear-view mirror to make sure no one followed me. Thankfully, the large machine was not full, but the medium one was. I emptied them, replaced the buckets, and tidied up. This time, I couldn't resist looking at least one of the treasures. At random, I picked out one, the Bosch *Ship of Fools*…an appropriate title for my current undertaking, and it fit my mood. The painting's subject is a comment on the moral corruption of all members of society. Well, I was definitely dealing with corruption.

That concept hadn't changed much over the centuries which tickled my sense of humor, and I laughed for the first time since…I wasn't sure. But with my mood lightened, I started to think about how I could anonymously drop the dime on Fentiman's drug shipment. The call would have to be local, and with George out of the picture I would have to make it. A hotel lobby phone made sense for anonymity. Who to call was another issue. Not knowing anyone appropriate, I called Jacob for advice. Calling this late, I did not expect anyone to answer. Well, I got that one wrong. My call was picked up on the first ring. I gave my name and asked for Jacob, and while on hold with Hebrew muzak I decided it was no better than ours.

"Shalom Peter, you have my sincere best wishes for your partner. How is he doing?"

Not surprised he knew, I apologized for calling so late. "He is holding on and improving, but not out of the woods yet. Thanks for asking."

"That is good news. Your call is a business call, perhaps?"

"Yes, business."

"I assumed so. How can we assist you?"

"Who would you contact, if you wanted the correct authorities to know about a drug shipment you knew was coming into London?"

"That could be a dangerous thing to do, Peter."

"That is why I'm calling you. The information needs to get to the right people, at the right time."

"If you are sure?"

"I am certain, in fact."

"You will get a text tomorrow, name and number, would that be satisfactory?"

"Perfect and thank you. Shalom."

"Shalom. Peter, please be careful. I still need

friends to beat at chess." He chuckled and ended the call.

I planned to brush up on my chess. There would be a next time I vowed, and after all this, I'd likely be a more formidable challenge. My recent experiences were a lesson of life and death. Much like chess, wasn't it?

About to call it a night, a phone went off, not the shop phone, my second one. Few people had that number, and I didn't recognize the number calling.

"Yes," I answered.

"Good evening Peter."

I recognized the voice. Fentiman. "Do you have the full amount as agreed?"

"Just calling to pass along my best wishes for your partner. Of course, I am working on the financial arrangements. It's taking some time but getting there. You do have an appropriate bank to receive the transaction?"

"Yes, I do. Goodnight."

"Be seeing you soon, dear boy."

"Hopefully not often."

His laugh was the last thing I heard as I hung up. Knowing he would try to screw me, I had to be very careful. Plan meticulously. I had to be suspicious of everything to do with him.

Sleep did not come easily.

Chapter Thirty-Three

Meeting Sir Stephen under these circumstances wasn't something I wanted to do, but I couldn't avoid it. I hoped he wouldn't blame me for his brother's actions—I blamed myself enough for his injuries. We joined up at Brown's Hotel, Stephen's usual haunt in town, where it is required to dress up with at least a tie and jacket. Curious, I eagerly wondered what he wanted to discuss when we met in his suite.

He greeted me solemnly and offered me a seat. We moved to the formal seating. "Welcome, Peter. Sorry it's under these circumstances. Can I offer you anything?"

"No, nothing, thank you. I'm just so sorry, Sir Stephen. George was a hero, a life saver."

"Any idea why it happened?"

"Yes and no. I got involved with a project, doing a good deed...and it seems to have turned dangerous for no reason that I understand. Perhaps because of his military training, or whatever, George apparently saw something and put himself in jeopardy to save Felicity and me. When he shoved us out of the way, we went down, and he took the bullets meant for one of us. I'm still not sure which of us—maybe both."

"I see. George did mention something about your project when he came back from Germany. He was excited about it."

"How much did he tell you?"

"Enough to get me interested from the outside. He actually asked for my opinion on a couple of aspects. As an observer, I told him to trust you and his gut."

"You don't blame me for his present state?"

"Oh God no, Peter. Don't ever think that. George is an adult. Makes his own decisions and choices. He didn't need me or anyone else to approve. Anyway, I need to let you know a few things before the circus starts."

Here it comes, I thought.

"In the event of his passing, George, not being married, and with no issue that we know of…" He laughed at his own joke. "George left the shop to you, lock, stock, and barrel. Oh, and also that wreck of a car he shipped down to the family place."

Stunned, I didn't know what to say. I stared at Stephen and stuttered, "Are you sure?"

"Perfectly. All been discussed and settled. It is what he wanted. He does have to die first of course." Another joke in bad taste. "Had to get this out in the open, be prepared, and all that. The quacks at the hospital think he will make it, but you never know. If and when George is fit to travel, he will convalesce at the family home. You are, as always, welcome to visit and don't think you need to call ahead. Just show up. We have plenty of room to accommodate."

"Stephen, I hope…I don't get any of this." My inside flipped with concern. I didn't want anything at my friend's expense.

"Neither do I, and I don't suppose George does, either." He laughed again at his own dark humor. "I meant it about the visit, though. When it's okayed by the docs. Until then, I don't need to tell you to be careful, do I?"

"No, I will be careful." Damn right. Suddenly facing deadly force, I'd be evaluating this caper from a different perspective.

"Make sure you are. If he makes it, George will need you during his recovery."

"I sincerely hope he makes it, for so many reasons. I'll be there for him." And I'd be approaching the consequences with a new attitude. No more nice guy.

"Hope to see you soon at the house and under better circumstances."

With that we shook hands, and I left Stephen to close the door. I realized how worried he was, using those bad jokes to cover his concern.

God, I hope I didn't end up with that inheritance. George was full of surprises.

****

Two days later I finally had permission to visit George, but when I arrived he was still out and, though no longer critical, he was still listed as serious. That was the good news I needed to hear.

In the shop, I was on autopilot, focusing only on the final deal with Fentiman, and planning how I could walk away unscathed.

I needed to get this sorted and finished. Running back and forth to the storage unit to empty the dehumidifiers was becoming a liability. The chance of being followed, increased with every trip. Tel hadn't contacted me, and that was bothering me, so I called him. "Leave a message."

Damn it.

Tel called back within the hour, and I let out a

breath I didn't know I'd been holding.

"Ullo mate. Nuffin, got nuffin, no wun nose anyfin, a complete zero. Which is info in itself. Them in the kno, says it means it wus contained wivin a small team like. If it 'ad bin sourced owt, somebuddy wud 'ave 'eard sumfin. Best I can do fur ya.

"No worries, Tel. It's still useful. Gives me ideas about who could have organized it, and executed it."

"You ain't gonna do anyfin stooped ar ya?"

"I hope not. Thanks again." The fact that no one knew anything about the shooting confirmed that it was isolated and insulated. Fentiman. But he wouldn't pull the trigger himself. Someone else would handle that.

Jacob came through with a name and number to contact in the Drugs squad.

Time to use it.

My plan required me to go to a crowded hotel in the West End. I picked a busy time of day, listened for a room number—the number didn't matter.

Got it. 817. Then I went to the house phone, asked for an outside line, and gave the room number I poached.

The line rang, and when it was answered I asked for the name Jacob supplied. There was a sound of a click, and then the hold—

The call was being traced. I was sure.

A new male voice answered, then I muffled my voice and gave him the information regarding the drug shipment from Paris—who was shipping it, where it was going, the type of product, and the hiding place.

Before hanging up, I told them where I was calling from, the room number, and explained what I'd done. All I heard on the other end was…*Shit*…emphasizing the urgency. I clicked the line dead.

Done.

Looking down at my hands, I noted they visibly shook. Well…that had been stressful. Surreptitiously, I wiped the phone down. Anyone watching would think me a germaphobe. Knowing there was no backing out now, my body relaxed as I walked out of the hotel with a smile taking over my face. I was now committed to whatever happened next.

Once out on the street, as I walked back home I put a call into Hans, and I thanked him for the contact information about the French Antiquities department.

Waiting for the hammer to fall and push Fentiman to make the deal for the paintings, I considered his options. If preparation were a key component of my plan, why wouldn't it be for others? It would be. Now patience was essential.

Part of my plan involved the French authorities, not the British, just in case Fentiman had a bent Copper in his pocket. I needed to warn the French what was going on and prepare them. I also required a new burner phone. The authorities probably wouldn't believe me right off. No one would seriously believe a claim that so many paintings were fakes. First they'd need to confirm the truth, and that would take some time even if it was a priority.

All that was for tomorrow. As soon as I reached home I went straight to bed. My swirling mind slowed down, and I crashed into a deep sleep.

****

The next morning, my blood-stained clothes were right where I'd dumped them in the bathroom. The disturbing reminder of what had happened, sparked me into cleaning up. They were just all going out to the trash, anyway. But when I picked them up, the weight surprised me.

Oh shit. George's gun. With all the craziness, I forgot I'd put it in my jacket pocket. It slipped my mind.

I pulled it out and sat at the kitchen table examining a semi-automatic CZ75. I grabbed my laptop, and within minutes, an Internet search brought up a multitude of answers. *European made, a reliable weapon used by many military units.* Not a surprise choice for George.

Looking at the instructions—safety, magazine release, how to load, and cock it—and reading everything I could find, I decided it didn't sound too complicated. I released the magazine and cleared the chamber as instructed. I clicked the safety on, and now the gun was safe. The magazine was full, and with the extra round from the chamber, I counted twenty-one rounds. I wondered where George had kept this. After thinking it through, he didn't need it at home. The shop!

I put everything in my bag and left for work. Getting caught up with the gun ended up making me run late—which had become a regular occurrence, lately. The first thing I did after opening for the day was consider where George would have kept the gun. We each had our own desks and file drawers. His bottom drawer contained a gun case with lock and no more ammunition. The filing cabinet. The bottom drawer individually locked. George's spare key was in his desk, neatly labelled. The lock popped, and I found what I was looking for—several boxes of ammunition, two spare magazines and a gun cleaning kit. One box was open and half-empty.

Loading my bag with the cleaning kit, the two spare magazines, and a box of bullets, I got back to my day. I ordered lunch to be delivered and ate quickly. Then I slipped out to pick up a new burner phone and paid cash.

Busy with customers—on a day like today, the shop was definitely a two-man job, but I took advantage of a customer lull in the early afternoon and used it to call the French contact Hans had supplied. Speaking only French, they must have realized I was not a native speaker, but I don't think they cared—not with the information I gave them—and by closing, I was exhausted.

Felicity called just as I was closing and invited me out to dinner. I countered with take out at my place and she accepted.

****

Because Felicity was visiting, I tidied up a little, but I was too tired to do a great job. The knock announced she'd arrived—on time as usual. I smiled. I loved her punctuality.

We decided on Indian take out, and called in our order while she poured the wine.

When she seemed a little subdued, I asked, "Everything all right?"

"Not really. I'm worried about you." She sounded exasperated. "When I'm with you it's okay, but when we're apart...I keep thinking about all the bad things that could happen. Uh...Peter, I love you."

"I love you, too. And I want to be with you, but I have to finish this. I couldn't stop now even if I wanted to. Let's not argue. Can we just have a nice evening?"

"Yes, we can." She leaned forward and kissed me, deeply. I stroked her face, and as she reached for my hardening cock, she slid off the sofa and knelt between my legs, deftly undoing my jeans. She slid the zipper down. Her warm hands released me, and her lips moved teasing over the tip, and as I watched, mesmerized, it disappeared into her mouth.

Closing my eyes, I felt the warm pleasurable movement, up and down on my shaft. Then trying to adjust my position, for a better angle, my cock came out of her mouth with a loud pop.

"No moving," she said and descended again. As I spread my legs and lay back, I became lost in the glorious feeling. One hand massaged me, as her mouth concentrated on the head of my penis. The sensations pulsed through my body, tensing, and relaxing at the same time.

The pressure built as I looked down at her on her knees, her breasts moving as she bobbed over me. She used her tongue to gently probe the head of my penis. I had never felt anything like it. I bucked, my balls tightening in anticipation, oblivious to everything except the feeling of her on me. I groaned in torment, then came in a shot, deep into her mouth.

Rather than coming off me, she went down on me. My hips rose as I squirted into her again.

To my ever-grateful satisfaction, she continued to suck and lick, and when she was finished, she said, "That was nice. You have a very nice cock, Peter, and you taste wonderful."

"You're amazing. I needed that." I hadn't realized how stressed I'd been. "You should be a prescription." I winked at her.

"My pleasure," she replied kissing me lightly. We were brought back to earth when the doorbell chimed. Looking at each other with surprise, the realization struck us at the same moment. "Dinner…"

Adjusting myself back into my jeans and I composed myself to answer the door. I took the food and paid the delivery man. We sat together in the kitchen, holding one hand while eating with the other.

I asked, "Would you stay over tonight?"

"Yes, I want to be near you."

Early as it was, we undressed each other, slowly luxuriating in each other's body. Time seemed to stand still. Falling in love with her was the best thing that had happened to me. It wasn't just the sex, it was everything about her—the way she played with her hair, her shy smile, or a smart comment.

I was suddenly overcome with memories of the attack and the sense that I could lose her. Pushing that thought to the back of my mind, I stroked her neck, ran my hand through her hair, and we made it to the bed without falling over. But once there, we slowed down. Gently, ever so deliberately, we aroused each other…no urgency on either of our parts. We knew each other. I knew what pleased her, and she knew me. Making love was a mutual gift. Her nipples tightened as I hardened. We each selflessly concentrated on the other.

Her long, silky-smooth legs enticed me just looking at them and when I stroked them it made her squirm with anticipation. I enjoyed making a game of kissing them, licking them—exploring every nook and cranny. Even though I had done this time and time again, I never tired of it. There was always something new to discover about her reaction to the effect my touch had on her. She moaned as I worked my way up her thighs—her muscles flexing, rippling beneath her skin in response. As I reached her apex, the neatly trimmed curls invited me on. I nuzzled her mound, and my tongue teased her entrance. I continued licking her, and she mewled like a cat purring.

When Felicity pushed my head down into her, I enthusiastically complied. All I wanted was to enjoy the vision of her orgasm with her legs spread wide. I lifted them over my shoulders, and they came down on my back. She was open and beautiful, making access easier for me. Plunging into her with my tongue, she bucked as I devoured her. Following her lead, I continued to lap at her, but she was ready, writhing, and moaning.

This was different. We usually spent more time in the arousal stage. Tonight, she wanted me fast and hard, and I wasn't going to argue or complain. Hearing her intakes of breath grow more and more ragged, I slowed down and became more deliberate in my actions. Her arousal rose rapidly as I heard her say, "No, no more. I want you inside me."

Pulling back and rising up, then leaning forward, straddling me, Felicity took my cock, and slid me inside her. Once sliding in to the hilt, I began to move, and we both sighed. As her tight heat surrounded me, I groaned aloud. Slowly pumping back and forth with short strokes that became longer and faster. I watched as she massaged her own breasts, pulling on her nipples.

Having come so short a time ago, I wasn't sure I could manage another orgasm…better if I just brought her to orgasm. Me coming or not wasn't a concern. This one was for her.

The combination of me being inside her, her using

one hand on her tits and the other jammed between us was arousing both of us. She was groaning loudly.

Suddenly with her arms and legs wrapped around me in a death grip, she called out, "Fuck me, harder, Peter. Make me come."

I thrust deeper and harder and as if pre ordered, she came in a shuddering rush, going rigid as her orgasm hit her. I could not believe it. She let out an explosive breath, and my balls tightened, and that tingling sensation hit my spine. I shot my load inside her, plunging into her as deep as I could go, and my release was cathartic. We were just one being at that moment. Nothing else existed.

Silence. The only sound was our breathing—rapid breathing, slowing to a somnambulant rhythm. Tangled up in each, we made a sweaty union, but neither of us moved to uncoil. We must have slept, because sometime later, chilled, I moved and stretched, then Felicity murmured, "That was terrific. I may have to keep you around forever."

"I may just have to comply with that request." Shortly, we slowly made our way to the shower. Something between us had shifted again, and I was glad of it.

After we cleaned up, we returned to the bed, huddled together, and slept.

****

I awoke with a start. Felicity was still beside me asleep, but my mind wandered to the previous night. It had felt so right that I didn't want it to end. Her deep, even breathing was soothing, and I soon relaxed.

Later I carefully escaping our tangled limbs and got up to make breakfast.

Coffee on, toast in, I tried to decide how to do the eggs. That was all I had. Too busy to shop, I'd been living on take out for too long. Never mind, I smelled the coffee, and while I poured, Felicity came up behind me. As I went to turn, she hugged me tighter from behind. Her bare breasts and the length of her warm body felt too good on my naked back—skin to skin.

God it was tempting to make love all day, but we both had things to do. She had to get to work, and I had *stuff* to do. We kissed, got dressed, and then we sat in the kitchen and had breakfast together. It felt so natural, like we had done this forever. But while we got ourselves ready to leave, the conversation stalled, and things between us became strained. Awkward really.

I turned Felicity toward me and held her with my hands at her waist. "Thank you for staying over. I really needed that…and you." I wanted to rephrase everything I just said—make it sound more like the way I felt, but I just didn't have the words.

"My pleasure," she said and cupped my face between her hands. "I meant what I said last night. We never know what is around the corner waiting for us, do we? Peter, please take care."

"Promise. I'll see you later." I kissed her, hoping I was putting into the kiss the feelings I hadn't been able to verbalize.

Downstairs we parted ways, Felicity to Kensington, and me to the shop. But a chill ran up my spine when I looked over my shoulder to check on her and she was already out of sight.

Chapter Thirty-Four

On the drive to the hospital, I called asking about George. Good news. He was awake and making progress. If everything went well, by week's end George would go to his brother's house by private ambulance for his recovery with an attending nurse. Great. I would see him before he went and then make sure I visited him again in the country.

Feeling good, I called Fentiman, assuming he wouldn't be in yet. Wrong. He answered on the first ring. "Good morning, dear boy, I assume you are wanting your deposit?"

"Got it in one. Do you have it?"

"Of course. Now about the exchange. Care to come to the gallery?"

"Not a fucking chance." That caused him to chuckle. "Somewhere public and busy."

"How about tea at the Ritz?"

"No. Harrods' food hall. We can do the money transfer there. I will have the paintings with me, but not on me. Any problem with that."

"None. Today is convenient for me. Shall we say around four this afternoon?"

"That's fine. Good job that it's convenient for me as well." That brought another chuckle from his end as he hung up.

Returning to the shop, I switched out George's

SUV for my car and drove to the storage unit. No one followed me that I could discern. Even if they tailed me, they would have no way of knowing which unit was mine. I'd used fake ID, so if they enquired after me, my real name would mean nothing to the people at the storage unit.

Packing up the Holbein's was easy—I used the packing materials I left in the unit. Then when no one was about, I loaded them into the trunk of my car. This was insane. Still, better safe than sorry. I was driving around in an old car worth almost nothing, carrying millions of pounds worth of old masters in my trunk. I had to laugh at the irony.

****

It was a quiet day, shop wise at least. A busy one would have at least kept me occupied, because I was itching to get on with it. I put the paintings in a large canvas bag I often used for taking large prints to the framers. Nothing suspicious about using that bag, and it was easy to carry. Then with time to spare, I ended up leaving in a taxi.

London passed by as the ride took me one-step closer to closure. As I intended, I arrived early and left my *parcel* with Harrods' coat and bag check. Pocketing my ticket, I began to wander the glorious food hall, enjoying the various scents of the cuisines. Fentiman found me by the cheese display.

"Hello, dear boy. All is well I hope?"

"Yes, as long as you have the transfer."

"And the merchandise?"

"Here."

"Ah, I do not see them."

Pulling out the reclaim ticket, I showed Fentiman

saying, "As soon as I have the money you get the ticket."

"Sorry, Peter, same time exchange." He signaled, and Daniel appeared at his side. He continued, "As I transfer the agreed amount into your account, Daniel receives the parcel."

I could live with that. I handed Fentiman the card with my bank details. He started plugging in the numbers. He nodded to Daniel. I handed him the ticket and he left. Minutes later, a second phone rang in Fentiman's pocket. He looked at it and pressed send on the original phone. He said, "Peter you may want to check your balance."

Taking the bank information card back, not wanting him to have any more of my information than necessary. I opened my phone, and pulled up my account. It was there—a new deposit—four and half million pounds.

Smiling, I said, "Part one, now all you need to do is get the balance to me. When I'm sure you can't screw me over, you will be happy with the result. There are plenty of packing materials at the location for you to use. Don't leave it too long."

"My dear boy, hope to have it all sorted by the weekend. A pleasure doing business with you Peter, so far."

Daniel came up behind Fentiman and whispered something to him. Fentiman smiled, and they both turned and left. Dazed I stood in the middle of the food hall not really there. Brought back to earth by Felicity's voice asking me, "Peter, are you all right? What are you doing here?"

"Oh what, I could ask you the same thing."

She laughed, a light and easy laugh that I liked hearing. "Remember, I work down the road. I left early today to pick up a few bits and pieces. This is a nice surprise. Want to get a cup of coffee?"

"Sure."

We left Harrods and found a café around the corner. Sitting at a cozy table for two, we drank our coffee. I was still coming down from the fact, I now had four plus million pounds, and it wasn't about the money, it was the revenge. The money just made it sweeter. I updated Felicity with more details about Fentiman and my progress.

"Sorry I was miles away. Fentiman had just left when you arrived," I explained more about what I was doing there.

She turned quite serious, listening intently. Holding my hand, she again asked, "Peter you are sure about all this?"

"Certain." I was remembering the previous night, and the promises we made each other.

****

We parted ways, me with a more relaxed outlook about everything. Felicity had that effect. Unable to sit still after returning to the shop, I drove down to the storage unit and emptied the dehumidifiers to stay busy. No problems.

The next two days dragged by with nothing to do except sit in the shop pretending to work. The visit to George was a good one. He was sitting up in bed complaining about the food when I got there, so I was convinced he would be fine. It took me about thirty minutes of chatting to bring him up to date on the project.

"I'm impressed with the progress," George said, with a wince.

"You're still in pain, eh? How are the wounds? Which hurts the most?"

"Both wounds hurt the most. They alternate. Each trying to be the most annoying. I'm not looking forward to the physical therapy."

"Sorry, George. I promise to visit at your country estate." That made him laugh and caused a spasm of pain in his chest.

"I'll let you be." I felt better now that he was out of danger. "There's plenty to keep me busy."

That evening while I was half listening to the late news about a big drug bust in London, my interest perked up. Hoping it was Fentiman's shipment, I heard pills mentioned not opiates. *Yes*. Now the pressure would be on Fentiman to do a deal.

Now that he had lost his drug shipment, it was going to be interesting to discover how he would get the balance. He would need the profit from the drug shipment and a lot more to raise the balance owed for the paintings. He'd also need the profit from the paintings to cover his losses on the drug shipment.

I called the French authorities again to reiterate that they needed to be ready to move at short notice if they wanted to recover the original works. This time, I added that they were located in England, and that I would give them as much advance notice as possible. Then I hung up and quickly shut down the phone. No way the call could traced in such a short time.

Now to wait.

****

Screw that I wanted to put pressure on Fentiman.

The next morning he beat me to it. My phone buzzed to life as soon as I woke up, and he started without preamble, "Peter, dear boy, we need to restructure our agreement."

"What? No way. I knew you would try to screw me."

"I have had a slight reversal of fortune, and I need the deposit back for a very short time—a few days at most."

"You are kidding, right? You keep the Holbein's, and I give you back the deposit? Do you really think I was born yesterday? Not a chance. Get me my money."

"This is not going well. You really should reconsider. Eventually it will be to our mutual benefit."

"Fentiman, I have been screwed by you once. It's not going to happen twice."

"An incentive perhaps? We agreed twenty-three million. How about we up it to twenty-seven?"

"Nice try, but no. You will leave me with nothing. Not falling for it."

"A great shame, Peter. Now I will have to make other arrangements. I hope you won't regret your decision. Goodbye."

After he hung up, I hadn't missed the underlying threat. What *other arrangements*? That comment bothered me. From now on, I would need to be even more diligent and, legal or not, I would start carrying George's pistol.

The next morning, before getting in my car, I looked around for anyone suspicious. Fentiman had warned me, and I was taking the warning seriously. Opening the shop, I secured the back door behind me. Even knowing there was probably little or no danger during the day with the shop open, I looked every customer who entered my domain over carefully, for anything out of order.

Nothing.

Since I was running the place alone, having lunch delivered made sense. Everything else, I handled by phone or e-mail. Another quiet day, but I had the feeling the worst was yet to come.

Home, dinner delivered, and me safely locked in, Tel had done his weekly scan of the apartment, and nothing was there that shouldn't be there. Something was not right. It prickled the back of my mind, while sleep eluded me.

The morning came slowly through the curtains, and feeling like crap, I dragged myself to the shower. Better, but not much.

Coffee worked its magic, and I started to feel more alive. Not having spoken to Felicity the previous day, I waited until I knew she would be on the way to work and called her cell.

Answering on the last ring before voicemail, she clicked on and said, "Hi, I have a crazy couple of days, and it'll probably run into a third day. When I have a better idea of the time, I'll call you. Then dinner?"

"Of course, be delighted, your place, mine, or out?"

"Let's decide when I am clear."

"Sounds like a plan."

"Be careful, Peter. I love you."

"Love you, too. Miss you and please be careful yourself." Something to look forward to, I smiled. The thoughts warmed me.

Back to cold, current issues. I wondered what

Fentiman had planned for me. Following every precaution I could, I opened the shop on time, and sat around thinking—only dealing with customers when they wandered in. I had a few phone calls, nothing much to bother with. But not hearing from Fentiman was worrying me. Maybe my plan wasn't as good as I thought after all. He needed an out. The paintings would give him that, but not cash. They would, however, be good as collateral against whatever he needed. Being sure no one other than me knew where the paintings were hidden was reassuring. Having the timing down to a science, I only needed to empty the dehumidifiers every other day. That was a relief.

That tickle still bothered me. Needing to scratch it, I called Tel.

He answered, "Ullo mate wos up?"

"Do you know anyone who wants a really boring job?"

"Pends on wot it entails like."

"I need eyes on two locations. Fentiman's Bond Street gallery and his East End warehouse."

" 'Ow long an 'ow many eyes?"

"Few days at most, but probably around the clock."

"Wos going on, Pete. Sands like yor in truble?"

"No trouble. At least I don't think so. Covering my ass, more like. Can you help?"

"Yeah, no worries mate. Oi'l fix yu up. Money an issue?"

"Nope. This is important to me."

"Gotcha. Tell us wot yor looking for, text me addresses, an oi'l get back to ya. Report anyfin directly to ya?"

"Yes, on this number. Thanks, Tel."

"Pleasure doin' bisness wiv ya."

Satisfied with the call, I quickly texted him what I needed, including the two addresses. That put in place, I made my way to the shop, opened, and prepared for what the day would bring. The morning was quiet, and I was glad of it. I needed time to recharge my batteries. Following the procedures of the previous days, I ordered lunch delivered. Quiet day and a quieter evening, I missed Felicity, but had a good night's sleep for a change.

Taking nothing for granted, I was careful in everything I did.

When opening up the shop the next day, my phone went off and interrupted me. "Hello?"

"Tel said ta call, this numba, an' report anyfin."

"Yes. Anything going on?"

"Only fin goin' on is lots of po-lice activity at the ware'ouse.

"Thanks, if anything changes call me, otherwise once a day check in is fine."

"Gorrit…cheers."

Five minutes later the phone went off again.

"Hello."

"Ullo, Tel said ta call this numba, reportin' in like."

"Yes? Anything?"

"Na, nuffin goin on at Bond Street. Quiet as a grave."

"Thanks, if anything changes, call me, ASAP. Otherwise, once a day check in is fine. Thanks."

"No problem, mate."

Good, it looked like the police were in Fentiman's face, and he still had a financial problem.

Expecting him to have contacted me again, I was beginning to worry that he had found other financing, and my deal would be delayed. All the information about Fentiman proved beyond doubt that he was financially stretched. He should be jumping at my offer.

Using the quiet time, I called the French authorities again. They were more interested this time and tried to keep me on the line. Reminding them to be ready, I added that London was the location. They responded that they were ready to move as soon as I gave them the exact location.

Again, I hung up and shut down the phone, giving them no chance of tracing the call.

Doing nothing was driving me insane, but there was nothing to do. Following the instructions about how to clean George's pistol, I cleaned it twice out of boredom.

I went online and browsed nothing in particular. The day drew to a close, and I went home and locked myself in. Felicity already told me she would not be calling until she was done with whatever she was doing. No point calling her, and missing her was almost painful. I wasn't sure yet how we would make it going forward.

After a disturbed night's sleep, I got up early and left with that tickle of concern still gnawing at me, unresolved. At least my schedule was predictable, and my location.

The day started with a bang. A car backfired and made me jump. Sir Stephen called to let me know George had been transferred and was settling in nicely. Everything looked good. I said I would visit soon and thanked him for the call.

Late in the day, Jack from the picture framers came by with a completed order, and my case of beer. That brought a smile to my face. He still insisted he couldn't believe someone would cough up twenty-thousand euros to invest in fake paintings. Explaining to him again that they were copies not fakes, and insisted when he saw the quality he would be impressed. He left unconvinced.

Another day done, and as I was shutting up shop, my second phone rang. Number unknown I answered anyway. "Hello."

"Tel said to report anyfin to this numba."

"Yes, correct."

"Well, there is a boat load of po-lice aktiv-ity at the ware'oss. Looks loik, they is closing for the night. Won't call agin unless sumfin 'appens, aw-rite?"

"Yes, perfect, and thank you."

"Nuffin to it, mate."

After hanging up, I sat down as a feeling of foreboding came over me. Fentiman should have contacted me by now. He needed the cash from selling the paintings, or at least as collateral. The drug bust would only increase pressure on him—as planned.

I was missing something.

Had I thought of everything?

Fentiman's deposit money was safely stashed, and I was the only one who knew where the paintings were stored. He had to come through me.

Sitting in the encroaching darkness, I knew I should be doing something. The silence became oppressive. Nevertheless, I decided to stay at the shop because it had easier access to the warehouse, Fentiman's gallery, and the storage unit if anything happened.

Felicity was supposed to have called. *Shit.* We were going to have dinner. My stomach flipped with concern. Now I was beginning to worry. She hadn't called, and she was punctual to a fault. I immediately called her cell, but it went straight to voice mail.

Directly to voice mail? Something was wrong. Panic set in. Felicity usually answered or called back. Something wasn't right.

My phone rang. "Hello." One of the numbers from the watchers.

"A van jus' showed up, backside of the gallery. Passenger 'ussled inta the back door. Didn't look if they was goin' voluntary like. Couldn't see who. It was too dark. Faught you shud know."

"Yeah, thanks. Please keep watching, and let me know if anything else happens."

"Ya betcha."

Something was definitely happening, and I was not in control. Decision? Do I stay here waiting or take a chance and go to Felicity's apartment. If she wasn't there, then what? The phone went off. This time Fentiman's number showed.

"Do you have my money?"

"Ah, not quite, dear boy."

"Then why are you bothering me?"

"Well, as I explained, I am having a cash flow issue. I required the deposit cash back only for a short time, which you sadly declined to oblige. Had to make other arrangements."

"That's not my problem."

"Not quite true, Peter. Of course, the paintings would suffice as collateral for a short-term loan."

"Not a chance in hell. Fuck off."

"Oh, I am not asking. I have something of yours that it appears you value greatly."

"I don't have anything of value, other than the paintings."

"Peter, dear boy, don't sell yourself short."

"Spit it out, or I hang up."

"I have your Felicity." He let the statement stand in silence.

"Prove it."

"Well, if she could have answered your call a little while ago, wouldn't she have done so?"

"Harm her, and I promise I'll go to jail this time for something I will be guilty of—killing you."

"My dear boy, this is just a business negotiation. I want the location of the paintings in return for your Felicity. She was adamant that she didn't know the location. Very smart on your part not to tell anyone, and Daniel can be very persuasive."

"You bastard, if you have harmed her, I promise I'll nail you—"

"She is alive, perhaps a little worse for wear, but she is strong."

"How do I know she's alive?"

"You're being tiresome, Peter. All I want are the paintings. Neither of you are important to me. Someone will contact you shortly, and you will have proof of life. Then I expect you to give me the exact location of the paintings, understood?"

"Understood. Use the phone number I give you. This one is dying, and I don't have a charger." I gave him the number for my original cell. He hung up.

Fuck him. I was mad angry. He did the one thing I

hadn't thought of, and he was going to pay for it.

Rushing back to my apartment, I rummaged through an old box and grabbed a set of keys I hadn't used in years. and then I headed to Fentiman's gallery.

Dialing French authorities, I left as the line answered on the first ring. I asked, "Are you ready to move?"

"Yes."

"Are you in London."

"Yes."

Giving them only the general area of where they should be waiting, but not the exact location, I told them more information would follow very soon and reminded them to be ready.

While driving, I called the number of the guy watching the gallery.

"Anything new?"

"One guy jus' left, nuffin else."

"So only the passenger and…?"

"They wus two of 'em, takin' the fird person in. One left, so there's one an' the ovher person."

Betting it was Felicity and Daniel at the gallery, I was trusting a lot, everything, on being able to get Felicity released before I had to give Fentiman the location of the paintings.

"Thanks." Hanging up, I was careful to obey all traffic signs on the way. I could not chance being pulled over. The timing would be close. God, I hoped the French team was as competent as their reputation.

Traffic for once was in my favor. I parked legally and waited for Fentiman's call. *Come on you bastard.*

My original phone went off like a fire alarm. "Yes."

It was Fentiman. "You just received a photo.

I checked. The background was the basement of the Bond Street gallery behind a tired, bruised, and disheveled Felicity.

"Got it."

"She is alive, if somewhat tired. She is a very stubborn woman. However, that's not the point. Location, Peter, is the point. If you please."

Needing to sell this hard, I said, "As soon as I give you the location you'll kill her…and then me."

"Why would I do that? I will have what I want. What are you going to do, run to the police? It would be the word of an ex-con with a grudge against me, a pillar of the community. No need. You aren't that important. Sorry, Peter. It's just business."

He hadn't said anything about Felicity. He was going to kill her, and I knew why. He would do nothing until he had the painting in his hands, then she would be dead. I gave him the exact location, then Fentiman clicked the call off.

Ready with my other phone, and the number ready to go, I pressed send. The French police answered on the first ring. "Get to the following location."

I gave them the exact location of the locker including the entrance code, with a warning. "It's important you get there first and wait. The people you want are collecting the items tonight—soon. Be careful. They are likely armed."

I needed to get to Felicity. Whoever was watching for me had done their job. Calling the number in my recent calls, he answered quickly.

Thanking him for his services, I told him he could leave, saying I would settle-up with Tel.

I was betting that Fentiman, in his arrogance, hadn't changed the gallery locks. After I'd been arrested, foolishly, no one had asked for my set of keys. Now because someone was in the building, I assumed the alarm wasn't set. From the picture they sent to me, Felicity was being held in one of the old workrooms in the basement. Knowing the building well, and certain they hadn't changed much after I'd last been there, I pulled on thin leather gloves and got out of the car.

The shadows in the dark alley leading to the rear entrance of the gallery covered my movements. Feeling my way carefully until I was under the light at the back door, I inserted the key. The key turned easily, and the lock slid open. Quietly, I opened the door. The safety lights were on, giving enough light for me to see my way without a problem. I locked the door behind me. Pulling out the pistol, I made sure the safety was off and that there was a round in the chamber. The cocking of the gun sounded loud. I stopped and listened…nothing.

Moving easily through the gallery, I reached the basement door and silently opened it. I descended the well-carpeted stairs, and heard faint sounds coming from the far end. I cautiously made my way through the basement and stopped at the far door. I heard Daniel's voice and a woman's cry of pain. I ground my teeth and resisted losing control. I had to remain calm no matter how I felt.

When I threw the door open and burst in holding the gun out in front of me, I took everything in at once. The room was bright. Daniel stood behind Felicity with a look of surprise on his face. He held jumper cables in each hand, but he stopped mid move when he recognized me and the weapon I had pointed at him. Smiling, he raised his hands.

I stared straight into his eyes and warned him, "Daniel move back very carefully."

I glanced at Felicity and took it all in quickly because I didn't have time to dwell on what I saw. She had been bound to the heavy chair at wrists and elbows, using zip-ties. Her feet had been lifted off the floor, and her legs zip-tied at ankle and knee. Her clothes had been ripped open, all the way down the front, leaving her exposed and vulnerable. She was wet from sweat and the water Daniel must have splashed on her. She was covered in bruises and burn marks all over her breasts, arms, and thighs. Anger greater than anything I'd imagined, rose in me, but I had to maintain control. I couldn't afford to lose it now.

Keeping my attention on Daniel, I asked Felicity, "Are you okay?"

She groaned out something unintelligible, through swollen lips.

"What now, Harper?" Daniel asked, meeting me, eye to eye.

"You go to jail if you're lucky."

He laughed. "Probably not."

Felicity let out a groan, and in spite of how tempted I was to look at her, I stayed transfixed on Daniel.

"You really don't have a clue about your Felicity, do you?"

"Actually, I do, but the name doesn't matter," I said. He looked surprised. "I also know you were going to kill her and me."

"Well, not 'til after I'd had my fun with her, of course. Doin' a proper job this time."

Suddenly it dawned on me. "You were the one who shot George."

"Well, that was not the intended outcome, but oh well. Just tidying up loose ends, now. God, you are clueless. Same with the old man in the clink."

That proved to me Fentiman was responsible for Otto's death, too. With each realization, the gun in my hand was feeling heavier by the moment.

"Back up and put the cables down," I ordered. Figuring he would try something, I had to end it quickly. Neutralize him. Stop the threat. I had no idea how to do that.

With a big grin, he said, "As you wish."

He dropped the cables onto Felicity, the metal clamps hit her shoulders sparking. She screamed as they fell, and Daniel leapt around her, catching his foot in the coiled jumper cable around the chair, and tripped.

That gave me time to react. I squeezed the trigger. The explosion of the gun going off was deafening in the enclosed space, but I automatically squeezed again and again, until Daniel was face down in a pool of blood.

Shaking with the adrenaline rush, the noise, the smell of gunpowder, and the fact I had just killed someone, I put the gun in my pocket and went to Felicity. She'd passed out with her chin dropped to her chest.

Anger rose like bile. I could taste it.

I glanced around, looking for something to cut the zip-ties and release Felicity. Picking a large chisel, I easily cut the plastic ties that had cut into her wrists. The fingertips on her right hand were raw from the missing nails.

My anger boiled over. I stomped Daniel as I passed

his body. Nothing would be enough.

I carefully and gently cut Felicity's remaining bonds, and lifted her limp body. I carried her up to the gallery and laid her gently on one of the desks, I ripped down a bright wall hanging to cover her and dialed emergency services. I gave the name and location, and details of the victim and injuries.

Unlocking the front door from inside, I waited with her until I heard the sirens. Then I left by way of the backdoor and walked out into the night.

Leaving her was the hardest thing I'd ever done, but necessary. This was not quite over. There were loose ends I had to tie up. I hoped Felicity would understand. If she did, there was a chance that we'd have a chance together.

As I got in my car, the EMT's entered the gallery.

I went home.

Chapter Thirty-Five

First things first. I cleaned the gun thoroughly and put it in its case. All my clothes, hat to shoes, went in a big plastic bag that I would dump later tonight. Showering, scrubbing, I wanted to feel clean again. Packing quickly, I dressed for travel, taking only what I could carry in one travel bag, and the other, what I needed to dispose of.

Next, I called Tel.

"Wot the hell you got into mate. The filth wus all ova the Bond Street place. Ain't seen that menny filth in one place at one time in fur evva. Wot jue need."

"Thanks for everything you've done for me. I need you to hold something for me. Can we meet now?"

"Name it."

"Paddington Station."

"Christ, be there in abat un 'our. Unda the deparchures board."

"Thanks. I owe you, and I'll settle up with you and the watchers as soon as I can…okay?"

"No worries. I'll settle wiv them, and then we cun catch up layta. I no's you's gud fer it. See ya be safe."

Driving to the shop, I parked my car and transferred everything to George's SUV and moved to the next part of my plan. The supermarket close to us had big dumpsters at the back. In went every stitch of clothing I'd worn while rescuing Felicity. Next was the meet with Tel. Parking wasn't easy at Paddington Station. I finally managed to squeeze into a tight spot.

Tel was right where he said. I nodded to him, and he followed me into the restroom. Luckily, it was empty. I handed him the bag with the pistol case and said, "Appreciate no questions. Just hold this for me. I am not going to be available for a while. Not sure how long. Text me what I owe as a total, and I'll get the money to you?"

"Pete, no rush, mate. Send it care of the pub, same wiv anyfin else you need, awe-rite? Take care and see ya soon—I ope." He took the bag and melted into the crowded station.

Returning to the SUV, I made my way to the hospital closest to Bond Street, parked, and looked up the phone number. I called for an emergency patient. It had been a few hours since the Bond Street events. Processed as an emergency and treated, by now Felicity should be in a room. The hospital information confirmed she was there. I walked into the hospital, and looked for her room. Easy to find. It was the only room with a police officer outside. Walking directly up to him I asked, "When can I see her?"

"And who are you?"

"Her fiancé." A stretch, but better than friend.

"No visitors until tomorrow at the earliest. The doc's orders. Then, not until she has made an official statement."

Leaving with a sense of relief, I understood if her condition had been serious, it would be no visitors at all. Good, I would be back early. Back in the SUV, I called France. Again, my call was answered on the first ring.

"A successful mission. *Merci monsieur*."

"Did you get everyone? Was Fentiman there?"

"*Oui* we ave heveryone,. Fentiman was captured along with two uzzers. All ze paintings, hexcept two were recovered."

"You will find those two, either at his gallery in Bond Street or his home." I asked if the thieves were in England or France. That brought a laugh.

"Zey are secure. Zis is a serious crime, and zey will answer for it. Would you identify yourself? We would like to zank you in person."

"Maybe later. I am not sure of my plans in the near future."

"We are working on a reward for you. A quiet reward if that helps?"

"Not really, but thank you. I will be in touch." It was late, and I was tired. The drive home was easy. But I didn't bother with the bed. I crashed on the sofa. I set my phone alarm for six and was out like a light in no time.

****

The alarm made me panic, and everything was fuzzy. Felicity! Jumping up—that was a big mistake. My head felt like the lead balloon of a bad hangover. Steadying myself until the lightheadedness passed, I readied for my trip to the hospital. The ride was as easy as the previous night. A different police officer at her door told me I had at least an hour to wait before any visitors. He checked my identification. Obviously, he'd been informed of who I was, and that I'd been there the previous night.

Breakfast in the closest greasy spoon was good, but I wasn't hungry. I left it half finished. The coffee? That went down well. I needed to see Felicity. On the dot of an hour, I was back at her room. This time I was allowed entry, and she was awake.

"Hi, how are you?"

Through thick lips, she answered, "Hello, Peter."

"Are you okay?"

"I'm going to be fine. May take a while though. Everything will heal. But it's very painful right now. You saved my life. Thank you."

"Me?

"Yes, you. I was aware enough to know it was you who rescued me. Nice shot by the way. Right through his left eye."

If she was that aware, there was no point denying it.

"Not really, I was aiming at his chest."

She laughed, which ended in a spasm of pain.

"How long have you been a police officer?"

"What? How did you know?"

"A lot of little things. The kind of sneaky way you asked questions. You always called Otto by name, never dad or father. And you didn't know about his brother. You should have. A big ooops was when you handled the Durer print and Schiele drawing. I left lint free gloves in plain sight. You just went right ahead and picked them up with your bare fingers. No one with any experience of handling rare documents, as you claimed, would dream of doing that. Knowing you weren't who you said you were, I had someone dig into you. They confirmed you weren't Otto's daughter, and surprise, you were a police officer. The real Felicity seems to have disappeared a while back. You don't have the same physical characteristics as her, either. Hair color can be changed, not height. I am sorry I had to leave you."

Silence, then she spoke again. "It's a long story, and yes I am a police officer. Antiques squad."

"But no experience at all with rare documents?"

"No, I was the female officer closest to her age with art crime experience, and that was more with the crimes themselves, not the actual items. You know you are safe, there will be no charges against you for killing Daniel. It was self-defense, and you saved a police officer's life."

"No proof I was ever there. You were delirious and imagined it was me, that's all."

"No, Peter. I know the man I love was the one who got me. Daniel used your name."

"Again delirious. Any forensics?" The only things I'd left behind were the three shell casings. When I first cleaned the pistol, I'd wiped everything down wearing gloves, no prints, no gun, no GSR…nothing.

"I will be putting it in a full report. I will stand with you. Self-defense. You will need to be interviewed."

"Really? As Felicity or the real you."

"Not the name, but everything else was the real me. I love you, Peter."

"I don't even know what to call you."

"Chloe, Chloe Anderson."

"I need to think this through. Now I know you are going to be fine, I'm going away for a while. Loving you is hard."

Tears welled up in her eyes. "I am sorry I deceived you. I had no choice. Especially when you started getting involved and Fentiman showed up.

"Why were you at Otto's place?"

"I was looking for anything to help find Felicity. The museum folks reported her disappearance, unsure if it was work related. There were rumors about Otto and Fentiman, regarding fake and stolen paintings. When the drug squad got involved, there were rumors of Fentiman smuggling drugs. No one could prove Fentiman was involved with anything. You came along and seemed to drop right in the middle of it. The only thing unplanned was falling in love with you. Can you forgive me?"

"Forgiven. Falling in love with you wasn't part of my plan, either, but I don't regret it. I'll call."

"Promise?"

"Promise."

"I do love you, Peter." Tears were rolling down her cheeks.

I had to get out of there in a hurry before I changed my mind.

My next move was to visit George at his brothers' estate in the country on the way to the Chunnel. I needed to get away for a while, and Paris seemed like a good idea.

Plugging in the address, I was in no rush. The drive to Sir Stephen's was a pleasant one, especially since I beat the rush hour traffic out of London and entered the Kent countryside. Turning onto the long drive, fond memories of the few times I had visited here with George returned. George said his family had always played it smart and managed to keep everything intact for at least three hundred and fifty years.

Parking where I usually did, I went up to the main door and rang the bell. Nicholas, one of Stephen's children, answered and greeted me warmly. He remembered me and took me directly to his father's office. When I stepped inside, Stephen looked up and smiled rounding the impressive desk to greet me.

"Glad you could make it. George is not the best patient. He's chomping at the bit to know what is going on. I'll show you up."

We made our way up the heavily carved staircase to the bedroom George had as a child. With the door closed, I could still hear raised voices. Sir Stephen opened the door, and the voices stopped dead. George's nurse was admonishing him for something. He was sitting up in bed, but he looked thinner, with one arm in a sling and the beginnings of a good beard on his chin.

"The beard makes you look older."

He shot back, "No, working with you is what's aged me." He laughed and that still caused him discomfort.

Sir Stephen said, "On that note, I will leave you two to fight amongst yourselves." He ushered the nurse out and left us alone.

George started, "What's been going on? No one will tell me anything."

"It's over. Well, for the most part. I called in to see how you were, feeling guilty about your injuries. Just wanted to make sure you were okay before I left. I am going away for a while."

"Wait a minute. My injuries are on me not you. My choice. You figured out that they were after Felicity and not you...right?"

"I did, and her name is not Felicity, it's Chloe, and she is a police officer." The look on George's face was classic surprise.

"What?"

Sitting in the chair near his bed, I explained everything up to and including the previous night, finally. George just lay back and listened, taking in everything. When I finished, his first question was, "Is my gun in a safe place?" Forensics will match the bullets to my gun if it's found."

"It's safe. I will return it as soon as I get back. What will you do with it."

"Ream out the barrel, then the rifling marks won't match those you fired from it. No one will be able to prove what weapon was used to kill Daniel."

"I am still in shock about all the events. No regrets, but it's a strange feeling. Anyway, it's over. I am really glad you are going to be all right."

"Me, too."

That comment lightened the mood. We chatted on for a little while, and I said my goodbyes to him, promising to stay in touch. I found Sir Stephen in his office, and he followed me out the front door.

"If you need anything legal wise, please let me know. I do have some useful contacts in the city." With suspicion I looked at him. He smiled and continued, "George did tell me something of your project. All in favor, by the way. Just a friendly offer if required."

"I am not sure what you mean."

"The docs said if you hadn't been so quick to put pressure on both his wounds, he would not have made it. Thanks for saving my brother's life."

He shook my hand, smiled, and reiterated his offer of assistance. Shaking my head, I got back in George's SUV and drove to the Chunnel. While driving to the Cross Channel train station, my mind was in turmoil. I wanted to get on the next train, and luck was with me. I just made the cut off, paid cash, and used my alternate ID. If anyone was looking for me, I was not going to make it easy.

The journey reminded me of the trips with Felicity, I missed her presence, her fragrance, and most of all, her. I hated myself for leaving her alone back at the scene waiting for the Emergency Services, and again now. It had to be this way. Too many questions I didn't want to answer—at least, not yet. The dust had to settle. Most of the journey, I slept. The nightmare of rescuing Felicity kept playing in my mind. It bothered me that shooting Daniel didn't affect me more. Otto was dead, George was seriously injured, and the woman I loved was battered and tortured. It hurt. God it hurt. Even knowing she was safe and recovering didn't help much. Escaping to France was creating physical distance from my problems, but I needed some clarity.

Making good time to Paris, I arrived at Alistair's apartment studio. He was in and surprised to see me. "I need a place to crash for a while. No one can know I am here. No one. Is that okay?"

"Sure. Why? Does this have something to do with Fentiman?"

"Yes. Can I get some coffee, please? Then I'll explain."

Dropping my bag in his spare bedroom, I returned and flopped onto his deep sofa. A wave of emotional exhaustion swept over me. I felt my eyes closing. Jerked awake, for a moment I didn't recognize where I was. Then it started slowly coming back to me. Alistair had lifted my feet onto the sofa, and covered me in a blanket. I got up stiff and tired, but feeling better. I wandered into his studio.

"'Bout time sleeping beauty. You were out like a light. How are you feeling?"

"Better. How long was I out?"

"Ten hours-ish."

"Sorry about showing up unannounced. There is a lot to tell."

"Coffee is already waiting...or would you rather have wine?"

"Coffee, then wine please."

Sitting and recounting most of what had happened, I only left out what he didn't need to know. When he realized he was free of Fentiman, he shouted, hugged me, and danced around like there was no tomorrow.

"You look like you have something on your mind," he said.

My mood was hard to miss. I told him I needed to go for a walk to blow away the cobwebs. "Don't worry, I'm just tired." I excused my mood as exhaustion.

"Do you want company?" he asked.

"No, not necessary." I declined, and he gave me a spare key.

Walking aimlessly around the block, I thought I'd take care of a few calls I had to make. When Hans didn't answer, I left him a cryptic message I hoped he would understand.

****

Alistair was a gracious host and treated me like royalty. At loose ends, I wandered Paris for the next few days, trying to make choices and decisions. I would probably take up Stephen's offer of legal advice regarding the killing of Daniel.

With Fentiman's deposit money stashed away safely, I intended to keep quiet about that. He couldn't say anything without incriminating himself further.

Felicity-Chloe was my biggest concern. I loved her for her, whatever her name, but the situation itself could be problematic. Not calling was hard. I missed her and wanted to know how she was healing.

I had missed Hans's returned call, so I called him back. We spoke briefly and I asked him if we could meet up. I was ready to talk to him about the future, assuming there was one I wanted, but I neglected to tell him I was already in Paris. We set a date to visit his gallery for dinner and conversation…as he put it.

When the evening arrived for Hans's dinner, I arrived early and strolled up and down the street. A taxi stopped at Hans's address, and a woman exited. Hans's door opened, and she entered, gone in seconds. Interesting. Giving them a few minutes, I pressed the intercom and the door opened. Hans gestured a welcome. "Good to see you, Peter. All is well, I hope."

"Good to see you, Hans and for the most part, yes. Well. There is a lot to tell."

"I thought as much, and we need to discuss what you intend to do going forward."

"Been giving that a lot of thought."

"Have you reached any conclusions?"

"Some, but not about everything. Only one for sure. I have not made any final decisions."

He tried to conceal a smile. "I understand. Well, here's hoping we can work something out to our mutual benefit. Dinner will not be long."

A dining table, centered in the middle of the gallery, was set for three diners. The mystery woman? I said nothing.

Hans continued, "A glass of something to whet the

appetite?"

"Please. I see you are expecting another guest. Anyone I know?" If I were right, I would know her without ever meeting her.

"I don't believe so. Magda manages my Berlin gallery. She is just freshening up, after her journey. She will join us shortly."

We made small talk. Hans had heard about the adventures in London through the news feeds, but he wanted to wait to hear all the details from me first hand. Magda entered the gallery, slim, pale complexion, blonde, and athletic looking. A runner. At least she had that in common with Chloe. She carried herself with an air of confidence. Her hair stylishly cut, dressed in fashionable business attire, she looked picture book Anglo-Saxon. She approached me and held out her hand.

As she was about to introduce herself, I said, "Pleased to meet you Felicity." You could have heard a pin drop. The look of surprise on both faces was complete.

Hans said, "What!"

"Come on, Hans. I am not a fool. Felicity disappears, just as Otto's problems become serious. Otto must have provided at least one set of documents for Felicity to disappear. You are her only living relative. Why wouldn't you be involved. I'm right, aren't I?"

Felicity looked at Hans and shrugged. Hans replied, "Yes, Peter you are correct, except it was three sets of papers. No one would be able to track the paper trail. We thought it wise to move her for her safety, and for Otto's peace of mind."

Felicity chimed in, "I have Uncle Hans's talents, not my father's regarding the art world."

"Did you ever work at the V&A museum?"

"Yes, my expertise is in antique and rare documents, why?"

"The person, who impersonated you, had the back story, but not the knowledge to back it up."

"Impersonated me? Hans?"

"We will let Peter tell this. Now dinner."

They sat, one on either side of me. The food was excellent, and the wine flowed. Conversation was sporadic while we ate. When we settled in with coffee and Hans's fine cognac, he insisted I start from the beginning. How I'd been framed and jailed and continue up to date. There were periods, where all I heard was the sound of my own voice. Other times, one or the other asked questions, or interjected a comment. The time passed quickly, and we were soon talking about the future.

Hans said, "Peter, I am serious about manufacturing the copies of masterworks using 3D printing, I am really impressed, and I must admit I did not destroy the samples we switched out, they are too good."

"Shit, Hans, that could have been a disaster for both of us. If anyone had seen them, I could have been in deep trouble, and so could you."

"I hid the real things for decades without a problem—trust me, they were as safe. Anyway, now we can move forward with plans for starting that project. Magda is also very enthusiastic about it."

She added, "I love the idea of using technology to promote and preserve the world's heritage. It means I will be able to visit England again if I want to."

Looking at them both, they seemed genuine. How do I trust anyone, again? Everyone had kept secrets from me. Yes, I worked it out, but it was exhausting. The thinking I'd been doing over the last few days had crystalized many things.

"The shop is non-negotiable. George was there for me when no one else was. If you are serious about opening a gallery in London I know a prime location that will be coming on the market very soon."

They both knew what I meant and laughed.

"The old master idea is also one I am very interested in. I believe I can get us access to the Louvre. Probably any painting we want to copy."

Hans scoffed. "How will you achieve that?"

"The French authorities want to meet me to honor me for assisting in the return of their paintings. Access would be a good reward, and they would of course get a royalty on the sales."

The look of surprise on their faces made me burst out laughing. I enjoyed having surprised them. We continued talking late into the night, discussing everything. Plans were made, and further contact arranged. Hans would visit London to start the process of acquiring Fentiman's gallery, of which he would be the principal until it was established.

Felicity, now Magda, would manage the continental galleries until Hans was satisfied with the London gallery and the 3D project got off the ground.

A proposal I considered, as we discussed the future, was to set up a corporation as an umbrella to include Estate Antiques, the 3D project, and Hans's London gallery. Hans was skeptical at first, but he realized I would not leave George out of my future.

More discussion was needed on that proposal.

Me, I would return to London, sort out any legal issues for killing Daniel. During all this churn, I wondered how Chloe would fit into the picture. Why would she give up her career? If we were a couple, how would that look? Her and a convicted felon? I hoped Stephen and his legal contacts could provide some answers to that question. That would be the call for tomorrow.

We said our good byes with promises of a bright future. Magda thanked me for attending her father's funeral, and then I remembered the couple in the cemetery. Hans and Magda.

Returning to Alistair's apartment, I tried to be quiet. Apparently, not quiet enough, because he was waiting up for me.

"I was getting worried."

"Sorry. It was a great night, and I'll fill you in, in the morning."

****

What a way to wake up…to the wafting aroma of fresh croissants and coffee. For the first time in quite a while, it felt good waking up. Stretching for a minute, I joined Alistair and told him most of what I had discussed with Hans. I omitted the part about Otto's daughter. Then it struck me, Alistair would need new representation in the UK. With Fentiman's arrest, he would not be able to fulfill his part of the contract, and I knew just the person to step in. Me.

After Alistair went to work in his studio, I put a call through to Stephen, but he was out. Patti, his wife promised he would call back. Good as her word, he called back.

The story took some time to tell, but he was a good listener. At the end of the story, he assured me he didn't think anything would happen to me. He would consult with a couple of associates, and if there was an issue, they would provide the best representation for me. I thanked him for his trouble.

"I should be thanking you," he said. "I hope you know how much what you did means to our family. We will take care of you. See you right. Cheers."

Chapter Thirty-Six

The only thing left to do now was get back to England and wait for Stephen's call. Alistair was enthusiastic about my suggestion that I represent him in the UK. Artist representation? I would mention that to Hans too, as something else we could work with. Alistair and I said our goodbyes with promises of follow up. He claimed to be charged up, and told me I should expect an awesome selection for his first exhibition.

Driving back through the beautiful and relaxing French countryside was what I needed. This recharge to my batteries was good, but the only thing missing was Felicity, meaning Chloe. The name change would take some getting used to. The drive also gave me time to reflect on the loss of Otto. I would never forget him. Financially secure for the first time in my life, I now had options.

Arriving back in England and driving through the Kent countryside, as beautiful as the French countryside was, it wasn't England. This was my home, whatever happened.

I found police tape on my door. Shrugging, I called Stephen, who immediately insisted that I stay with his family. We had dinner as a family. George looked better and claimed he felt better, too. As soon as the children left, Stephen, George, and I went into his study. Out came the port which I accepted...and cigars which both George and I declined.

Once comfortable, Stephen started and, in between cigar puffs, said, "Peter, it's only been a day or so, but the right words have been dropped into the right ears. From what one can gather, the person who shot this Daniel fellow left almost no forensics. Crime scene techs have no leads on the shooter, and to be honest, they are not looking very hard for him or her. Apparently, the rescued police officer was a little delirious from her abuse and thought it was you. That couldn't have been correct, your phone's GPS places you at the shop at approximately the time of the shooting. The police found a pistol in the gallery basement with Daniels fingerprints on it. The bullets matched the one recovered from George's chest. Seems like whoever it was that killed Daniel, did us a favor. Whoever it was rescued a police officer in distress, solved an attempted murder, and all with no expensive trial. A win, win situation all around, wouldn't you say? Cheers."

We all raised our glasses in salute, and he mouthed, "Thank you."

Stunned at the speed at which things could move when you had the network and connections, I felt relieved to be free of that issue. Now for another issue that was bothering me. The three of us sat and chatted for a while. Stephen admitted he was not the legal expert I needed for that one, but knew someone who could help, and would put me in touch.

Thanking him, I made my way to a guest room. Sleeping deep and easy, I woke to the cacophony of a busy family morning. George and I joined them for a boisterous chaotic breakfast, and George remarked on why he was still single. The normality of it brought me back to reality. I needed to get my life back on track.

George and I had a good chat, and looked forward to the future. I told him the real Felicity was alive and well, and I explained my plan for creating an umbrella corporation to include Estate Antiques.

"Peter, you owe me nothing."

"Yes, I do. You were a lifeline to me when no one else was. Like it or not, I will always be grateful. This has the potential to be good for all of us. When I was running the shop on my own after you were shot, I realized it's too much for one person. We need help, an apprentice or whatever. The 3D project is going to be a lot of work."

"I will think about it. I am not holding you to stay with me. And if it's a good deal, I will be putting my money into it as partners. No free rides."

"Did I mention the French authorities want to honor me for my part in the return of the paintings. Oh, before I forget, I am now representing Alistair Brown in the UK."

"You're kidding?"

"Nope. With Fentiman unable to fulfil his side of the contract, Alistair is a free agent."

"We do have a lot to discuss, and I am going to be out of action for a while, but I will be back in town shortly for PT. Good luck with everything and see you soon."

As I made my way back to London, I called Chloe and asked her the name of the officer in charge of her case. Surprised that I'd asked, she told me. "Why? What's going on?"

I told her I would see her later and hung up.

After contacting the officer, he told me I didn't need to come in or make a statement about anything. My apartment was clear to enter. End of story. Surprised and pleased, I went home. Stephen and his contacts definitely had pull. It also made it easier for the police to close the case.

Alistair came to London to reclaim his paintings. Fentiman had rolled on the French end of the drug ring. The French authorities had most of them in custody. Alistair stayed with me, and we talked about the future, a promising one. Hans visited and, of course, stayed at Claridges Hotel. He hired a firm of lawyers to represent him in the purchase of Fentiman's gallery, which since his arrest had ceased operation. Fentiman needed the money for his legal defense.

Hans said Fentiman would be facing English justice as well as charges in France. Bottom line? He was going to jail for a long time, probably in both countries, even if he made a deal, which doubtless he would.

We officially created a partnership for the umbrella corporation. Hans was shocked when I told him I had squeezed four and a half million pounds out of Fentiman, which I had safely stashed. He and Magda were both in for a third each. We would sort that out later. Surprising Hans was fun. I wanted to make sure he knew I was no fool.

Feeling positive about the future had taken a long time to sink in. I visited Chloe at home. She was recovering physically, but mentally was a different matter. I explained what was going on in my world, and what I intended to do. How I was working with George, who was still recovering, and Hans, and all my projects. There was a lot on my plate.

She was excited for me, but something had changed between us. Nothing said, but it was there, and it had to go.

"What is it?" I asked. "Something isn't right between us, and I want it to be. I love you."

"Peter, I lied to you, deceived you. You knew who I was, am, and still came for me. I could have gotten your friend killed. Daniel, when he was questioning me, told me that they knew I was a police officer. That's why Fentiman tried to have me killed. Fentiman needed your deal to go through. He was desperate. They tortured me to find out where you had hidden the paintings. They didn't believe you hadn't told me, at least not at first, so they used me against you as leverage."

"Chloe, I fell in love with the person you are, not the name. By the time I found out you weren't who you said you were, it was too late. I'd fallen for you. Now I miss your smile, the whisps of hair that escape, and most of all your kind eyes. I just don't feel complete without you. Knowing didn't make any difference. I'm very sorry for what happened to you. It never occurred to me they would go after you. What happened to you was my fault."

"No, Peter. That was on me and my job. Sorry, I feel guilty about a lot of things. Physically I am well on the mend. I just need time."

"I am not going anywhere. When you're ready, you know where I'll be."

She looked despondent.

"Oh, one more thing, Stephen and his legal

contacts think I may be able to get my criminal record expunged because my legal representation was so incompetent, and because of what has happened with Fentiman. That means you wouldn't be partners with a felon... Just a thought."

She looked surprised. I kissed the top of her head and left. Now it was up to her. Being busy with my new life, I hoped, hoped beyond hope, that she would share it with me. Only time would tell.

A word about the author…

Richard Albion lives in San Mateo California with his wife (Who is the pillar which supports him) two grown children out of the nest, and multiple rescued animals making the nest better.

He is a European melting pot, exceptional cook, clothing designer, artist and writer of erotic Fem-Dom fiction. Graduate of both UK and US colleges. Retired sales professional now engaged in working on the artistic side of life. Enjoys travel, volunteering, martial arts, San Francisco and NorCal weather. Cannot live too far from the ocean-its genetic.

Richards novels are contemporary, erotic BDSM, Fem Dom, love stories. The first series, Maid to Serve, Maid for Service, and Maid in Service track one man's journey into submission and finding physical and psychological satisfaction but most of all love. "Bodies in the Bay" is a mystery/thriller with erotic BDSM overtones. The latest a gender flip of the "Mistress of O".

Thank you for purchasing
this publication of The Wild Rose Press, Inc.

For questions or more information
contact us at
info@thewildrosepress.com.

The Wild Rose Press, Inc.
www.thewildrosepress.com

www.ingramcontent.com/pod-product-compliance
Lightning Source LLC
Chambersburg PA
CBHW051127030726
47504CB00004B/753